BLOOD AND POTIONS

THE DARK CROWN TRIALS

MAYA MORRISON ~ S.L. KINGSGATE

First published in 2022
Morrison, Maya
Kingsgate, S.L.
Blood and Potions

Cover: JOY Author Design Studio
Editing: Roxana C
Proofreading: Lamb Delphi, Helenreads
Formatting: Maya Morrison

To the book boyfriends who are jealous, possessive, and can dick you down. And the 'good girl', who begs each time. This one is for you.

AUTHOR NOTE: CONTENT WARNING

This book and its series contain dark elements and deal with the following themes: stalking, kidnapping, blood play, voyeurism, murder, violence, torture, and sexually explicit content. Reader discretion is advised.

The characters within this series are morally questionable and are not meant to be heroes, heroines, or redemptive. Please proceed with this in mind, and do not hold them to *any morally* righteous standards.

BLURB

An assassin who lives for the hunt. A vampire who loves the chase. A job that went wrong and a bite that changes everything.

It was supposed to be a simple job. Steal an artifact from a top-secret location, and gain intel about my sister's killer. Instead, one false move lands me in the hands of the renowned vampire overlord, Quillian Kingsley.

Quillian is cold, callous, and notoriously ruthless. I was prepared for my death...until he tasted my blood.

After days of interrogation, we come to a mutual understanding, and I agree to his terms by swearing a Blood Oath. I stay in Esneoh to help hunt down his enemies and play the role of his doting wife. In kind, he will help me find my sister's killer.

The job should have been easy; however, with every new kill and pursuit, I find myself drawn to the dangerous and sinfully gorgeous overlord.

There is just one problem - all roads point to him as one of the main suspects. And in this game of power, secrets, and lust, neither of us might come out alive when the truth unveils itself.

PROLOGUE: BLOOD IN, BLOOD OUT

The forest moved and breathed around me. Trees swayed, leaves ruffled, and branches creaked, moving harmoniously with the wind. With each step further from its heart, the trees danced in rhythm, birds chirping in accompanying synergy.

The woodland sat against an inky blue overcast night sky with thin streaks of aqua, teal, and magenta. As I drew close to the edge of the river, the moon illuminated the river's surface with a fluorescent glow.

This was it. The quarter mark, a reminder to hold on a little longer.

I was almost there. Soon, very soon, I would leave the confines of the forest, be initiated into the Alokari, and make Alessia proud.

I peered down at the river, taking in my reflection yet unable to recognize the image that stared back.

This person looked older. Older than I was two months ago when I stood in my room and cleared out the queen-sized bunk beds that overlooked the never-ending forest near the orphanage.

That day, the remnants of my childhood were taken with the boyband and girl group photos that I had hidden under my bed.

The princess-themed dolls, toys, and memorabilia went soon after. My heart was in pieces.

I scanned the outline of the forest, straining my ears for any irregular sounds and movements. Satisfied, I briefly placed down the sheath of my dagger and cross bag. I rolled back my red sleeves, cupped my hands, scooped water into my mouth, and drank. My throat bobbed with each swallow, and I gasped, grateful that this nightmare would soon come to an end.

My body ached and my stomach grumbled, a harsh reminder that I had barely tasted water or eaten anything beyond the occasional elderberries and blueberries I had stumbled upon during the last two months.

I was hungry, and my weakened state served as a cold reminder.

I repeated the act several times, water running over my hands and wrists, in between my fingers, and down my chin, soaking my clothes. Once I had my fill, I stepped back, settling my body against a bristlecone pine tree, and closed my eyes briefly.

I needed rest.

Bloodshot eyes, darkened pupils, and a face covered with dark facial hair stared back at me when I opened my eyes again.

Vampire.

I clasped the dagger tightly and struggled to my feet. The bearded vampire followed my movements, and I lunged for his throat with the dagger's tip. He bypassed my movement, taking a steady step back, as he observed me with hooded interest.

"You smell divine. I don't usually go for..." - his nose flared, scenting me like a hunter cornering its prey - "...children." His eyes dilated, and rounded red orbs appeared in his vision. "But I'm hungry. And hunger is a poor teacher of morality," he added, his eyes darkening.

In the two months I had fended for myself in the forest, I had stayed hidden by covering my tracks, minimizing the sound of my footsteps, and covering my scent with rockrose bush. I took deliberate steps to implement all the training advice my sister Alessia had given me about survival.

Except killing.

The most important rule of all - kill or be killed.

I arched my feet into a fighting stance and angled my dagger directly toward his chest. "Stay back," I replied, trying to hide the tremor in my voice.

It was one thing to be taught how to kill and hunt using the anatomy of animals. It was another to do so to a sentient being.

The vampire smirked, a devious glint passing through his eyes. His wide jaw tensed, his pupils dilating, and under the light of the moon, the noticeable sight of dried blood covered his lips and his now extended fangs.

His white shirt held splatters and streaks of blood. And as I peered closer, I noted over ten similar marks across his dark-colored pants. The marks on his pants were fresh, though, and trickled down the lower half of his body, creating a crimson overcast.

He had killed, and some of those kills were recent.

Training had taught me that I had to be one step ahead of the game to survive. Vampires were tricky creatures who would resort to manipulative techniques or illusions to get what they wanted.

To continue eating at the orphanage, I had to slaughter him. This was my calling now, my new life.

He blurred effortlessly toward me, and within the blink of an eye, had his hand wrapped around my throat. I gasped for air, trying to fight his hold, yet my fighting only seemed to spur him on.

His laughter echoed all around as the smell of copper filled my nose, overpowering my senses. His eyes dilated until nothing but empty, distant black orbs stared back at me. The air charged with currents of electricity, and the inevitable truth became clear. I was now his kill.

Rule number two: always remember you are the predator. They are the prey.

My hands reached for the stake inside my cross bag as his hold on my neck tightened. I kept my body afloat, nuzzling the weapon behind my back. My hands clasped around the head of the stake, waiting for the right time – the right moment to launch.

He raised his head, arched his neck, and closed his eyes. I lunged the stake directly into his chest and watched, his hold on me loosening as he staggered back. His gaze burned into my skin, and a look of astonishment and bewilderment flashed over his features.

"That has..." His words came out as shallow breaths. "Silver? And...you're human," he mumbled under his breath as he peered down at the weapon stuck in his chest.

His gaze returned to me, filled with the haunting truth of what had just transpired. A human child had stabbed him with a silver dagger.

There were three ways to kill a vampire: remove their heads from their bodies, carve their hearts out, or allow the poisonous effect of silver to destroy their body until they become empty bones and shells of themselves.

I stepped forward, my heart ferociously beating in my chest like the burning rage of a thousand suns. Blood spluttered from his mouth, and he gasped for air while keeping his eyes locked on me.

The silver had rendered him immobile. This was my moment.

"I'm going to...k-i-l-l...you," he sputtered. Rage radiated from him in waves, and before I could allow myself to think about the image before me, I stepped closer, towering over him. I placed my hand over the edge of the dagger and pressed it down deeper. He groaned in pain. I kept my eyes trained on him as warmth and adrenaline spurred my movements.

I kept pressing until his body grew limp and the dagger passed through to the other side. He fell headfirst to the ground.

The forest and everything around me grew eerily still. It was as if time had stopped as I recounted this victorious moment.

This was my first kill.

Currents of electricity shot through me, and instead of fear, or regret, something else lay there. A pang of hunger and craving that Alessia had mentioned but I could never fully comprehend. Until now.

Without thought, I reached for his body and turned it around. I pulled out the dagger and got on my knees, hovering over where his heart would be. With quick movements, I cut through his breastbone and spread open his ribcage. Raising the dagger, I carved his heart with the blade, blood splattering over my face, hair, and clothes.

Sweat beaded my forehead and my breathing heightened. Nervous jitters made my stomach churn and my palms sweat, filling me with so much adrenaline that I didn't know what to do with myself. The coppery scent of his blood floated around me as my hands held to his once beating heart.

"What happened here?" An unfamiliar male voice startled me, and I jumped to my feet, the creature's heart in one hand, the stake in the other. He moved toward me with speed, and from a distance, I could make out the outline of another body.

His height, the warm red tint on the edges of his pupils, and the predatory sway of his movements told me he was a vampire.

"You're a child?" he uttered, and my gaze briefly fell on the vampire on the ground, then back to him, noting the clear similarities between them. The figure in the shadows grew closer, but I kept my gaze on the vampire before me, never wavering.

His eyes fell on the body of his brother, turned to the heart clasped around my hand, then back to my face. The weight of his rage pressed in the air like a furnace.

"Who are you?" he asked, and the glint in his eyes told me it wasn't from curiosity but something else. He wanted a piece of me to hold on to as he avenged his sibling's death.

My eyes scoured the forest and my blood-soaked hands as trails of crimson droplets covered the floor around me.

I killed someone. I actually killed someone.

"Red," I replied tentatively, my voice unrecognizable to my

own ears. Each assassin in training was made to choose an alias after completing The Initiation, one that would conceal the agent's identity and reflect some element of who they were.

The vampire stepped closer to me. I dropped the heart in my hand and threw the dagger at his chest, turning my sights to the presence of a horned succubus a few feet away. The dagger landed in his chest, and he fell, shock clouding his features.

As he did so, the succubus slammed into me, and I tumbled to the ground, groaning as I struggled to get back on my feet. She reached for me and, before I could reach for another weapon in my bag, gripped my hair and flung me to the far right of where the first vampire's body lay.

Pain coursed through me, and I groaned, slowly rising to my feet. She ran toward me with blood-raged speed and urgency. I reached for my bag and pulled out another dagger. Clasping them both behind my back, I waited for her to draw closer to me.

Use your body's weakness as a weapon.

Alessia's words echoed in my head as blood trickled down my nose. My hold on the weapons tightened, and as the succubus drew a few feet from me, her steps slowed, a victorious smirk tugging the corners of her lips.

If only she knew.

Three.

"You're going to die a painful death, little human," she spoke, her long blonde hair blowing against the subtle wind. Her pace quickened, her words fueling every movement.

Two.

"I'm going to leave your charred body in midtown Jersey Hill as retribution for what you did," she added, her voice rising with each step. I stood immobilized on the spot, allowing currents of fear to trickle through me in waves.

Like vampires, demons feasted on emotions, and I knew that those same emotions were their inevitable downfall.

I closed my eyes briefly and pressed into memories of Gael, one of the boys I had obsessed over at the orphanage. I recalled the late summer evening he had pulled me to the back of the dining hall and kissed me. I focused on that memory, allowing the wave of lust that trickled through me to permeate the space between us. As I did so, her nostrils flared, and her steps began to quicken even more.

One.

She took her final steps toward me, but instead of initiating an attack, she stood still, taking in the outline of my body with piqued interest. "What a fascinating thing you are," she smiled, the atmosphere thick with waves of her unmissable scent - eucalyptus burned with wild herbs.

She took another step, and I jumped back and threw two daggers at her simultaneously. The first bypassed her collar by a few inches. The other landed on her abdomen. She staggered back, turning her attention to the weapon. I lunged toward the dagger that fell, and she followed me, screaming a slew of curses, with the weapon still stuck in her body.

I hit the ground, and she jumped atop of me, scratching and clawing at my skin. I rolled to the side, grabbed the daggers, and pushed her with all my strength as I jumped up. She rolled to the right.

The succubus sneered and made a feeble attempt to rise to her feet. I flung one of the daggers at her head, and it found its mark. Her head fell from her body and rolled away.

I scanned the space again, straining my eyes and ears for anything out of place. I knew that demons always traveled in pairs or small groups, and it was only a matter of time before the other showed up.

I turned to the beaten path ahead and began to run until the trees of the forest grew more distant and the willow trees and the landscape of the training center came into view.

Finally.

The subtle scent of lavender, thyme, and the undertones of hawthorns and magnolias filled the air. As I drew closer to the center, a slew of voices grew into loud chatter.

Three of Darya's henchmen stood in line on opposing ends, their gazes locked on me as I neared. Joy and a sense of accomplishment pulsed through me, and my eyes immediately scanned the open field for traces of Alessia.

"Where's Alessia?" I asked. Two of the guards stepped forward. A deep sinking feeling weighed against my chest, and I turned my attention to Darya. "I passed, didn't I?" my voice rose, afraid that I may have failed and let my sister down.

Darya shook her head, her expression solemn. "Yes, you did, Meraki," she answered. The other guard walked behind me.

"Did I do something wrong?" I asked, turning to face the guards behind me, then back to her. My head tilted to the entryway of the center a few feet away, waiting for Alessia to show up.

Before I departed, Alessia had promised that she would be the first face I saw when I returned. Alessia always kept her word.

"Congratulations. You're now the newest agent in training in the Alokari," Darya spoke, without addressing my question. "Now, more than ever, you're needed," she added, her words strained and clipped.

"My sister?" I repeated the question again, the discomfort I had felt earlier spreading through my chest, bile threatening to overcome me.

"She's dead," Darya spoke, and the words floated around me until the ground beneath me began to give way.

Dead.

She's dead.

She's gone.

Black spots appeared in my vision. A sharp pain pierced my chest. I staggered back as breathing became impossible. My back landed on one of the guard's chests and darkness clouded my vision. Something within me broke loose. I screamed out.

"Hold her down," Darya's voice continued to echo, growing fainter and more distant by the second.

I screamed, clawed, and fought my way through their hold, unable to seize control of my own body or voice.

A needle punctured my throat, and reality dawned on me.

Alessia was gone. I was alone.

Tears streaked down my face, and the warmth of the needle flowed through my body until I had no more strength to fight.

Alone.

"Blood in, blood out," the wind whispered as everything around me ceased to exist.

PART I

"...gray eyes with the heart-stopping power of storm clouds and thunder stared down at me, and I knew I was screwed. This vampire was going to be the death of me."

1

SILENCE

Q*uillian*

SILENCE.

The aching void of emptiness had been my companion for the last millennium.

Darkness filled my vision and the space all around me. In my weakened state, I could only make out the cement cracks on the walls and the warmth and heat that trickled in as the sun set each day.

Dusk consumed my waking thoughts and senses, and the only sounds that I could hear from beyond these walls were the constant movements of distant footsteps and the never-ending *drip* of running water. Occasionally, the murmurings, chants, and the clicks of incoming footsteps would make their way to me.

Someone had placed me here, cursed me to a never-ending limbo of loneliness, agony, and despair. Every inch of my body ached and thrummed with unshed anger.

My mouth had become a sealed vault of nothingness, haunted by the last words I had uttered to my siblings. My family.

I don't need any of you.

I was a fool.

I was a fool to believe I could become the living embodiment of pride and reverence without the support of my community. And in my rage, I had dismissed their warnings.

My life, once filled with music, lustful escapades, blood delicacies, and the influence of affluence, now paled in comparison. The memories that once brought pleasure now haunted me in this empty vacuum. And each day as the sun set and darkness grew, so too did my hunger and thirst for vengeance, bloodshed, and chaos.

Sleep and rest had become a distant memory as the ideal of pleasures haunted me. My body was now a fortress I sought to conquer. The weight of its stillness and its inability to move reminded me daily that I was *weak.*

The antithesis of everything the Kingsley name had been built upon.

Drip. Drip. Drip.

Day in, night out, I waited, mulling over my imprisonment and the carnage I would release. I waited, using the distant magic still hidden within the depths of my being. I clung to the blood that kept me trapped, feeding on its essence like a coat of armor.

I waited. Soon my freedom would arrive.

Click. Click. Click.

My body was dead. Still. Motionless. Yet my spirit breathed with life and thrummed with the possibility of revenge and taking back the time stolen from me.

Soon.

My freedom was close.

They were close.

She was close.

2

THE ASSASSIN'S CODE

M*eraki*

BE SWIFT WITH YOUR KILL, AND NEVER SHOW MERCY.

I replayed the words in my head as my hands pressed against my abdomen where the vampire had shot me with my *own* gun. I gritted my teeth and exhaled a frustrated breath. How much longer did I need to keep up this ruse and pretend to be a helpless damsel in distress?

"Data has almost loaded," Skye's voice echoed in the discreet headpiece in my left ear. I grunted in response, waiting for the perfect moment to finish the stratagem.

I struggled on the carpeted floor, reminding myself to make disgruntled and pained noises. Normal people who were shot felt pain, screamed for help, or pleaded for their lives. I fit into none of those categories, but Jennifer Rose did.

"One more minute," Skye added, the sound of her keyboard clicking in the background, followed by silent mutterings. She and I had worked on enough assignments that we had become attuned to each other's gibberish.

Hold on a little longer.

"Little human." Elias, my latest target, bent with his face inches from mine. His elongated chin and bearded face came into focus, and a shiver of disgust ran through my body.

I whimpered, and my body shivered in turn, maintaining my ruse of fear. If there was one thing assholes like him got off on, it was fear.

"I have no idea what you're talking about, baby," I began as a floodgate of tears opened. "Why are you hurting me?" I whimpered, allowing snot to trickle down my nose.

This was a top-class performance. I deserved some sort of award for it.

Skye laughed into the comms device, obviously finding this shit funny.

This situation right here served as a reminder for why I preferred doing *sneps*. They were simple assassination jobs. You chose an assigned target and had a set amount of days to eliminate them. Done, finished, no questions asked. The money was immediately put into your account before you could even say ABC. *Sners,* on the other hand, were not so straightforward. They involved a lot of intermingling with the target, honey traps, and the occasional interrogation to get their tongues wagging and collect the information needed to complete the assignment. They also paid the most.

"I am over a thousand years old, little human," he sneered. Flashes of red colored his irises. "And I have fucked myself out of some questionable situations. I am a pretty good judge of character, and the timid, naive student with an insurmountable amount of debt trick isn't going to work this time." He raised the gun to my head and slowly trailed it around the outline of my face. "Why were you looking through my things?" He lurched closer, his morbid breath dancing across my skin reminding me of the cheese and onion chips he ate before we got to the motel.

The goal was to feign a staycation and tolerate his presence for a few hours until Skye hacked into his computer and collected the data needed. Everything was going to plan. I had signed into his computer and linked it to hers. All I had to do was sit back and wait.

Unfortunately, when my eyes landed on a phone, he had hidden deep in one of the drawers, curiosity got the best of me.

"A thousand years old?" I shook, lowering my voice to a barely audible whisper. "What are you saying, baby?" I continued, my face drenched with tears.

"Thirty seconds... It's a lot of data..." Skye stated, the amusement in her tone more evident now than it was before.

"Oh, little human, you're lying. Do you know who I am?" He pressed the barrel of the gun harder against my head.

"Please. I have no idea what you're on about," I continued crying. Elias's pupils dilated, and waves of anger flowed from him. He bared his teeth, raised his left hand, and slapped me across the face. Blood oozed from my nose, and his eyes glistened. His fangs elongated at the sight.

I shook my head and cried out in pain, intent on keeping the ruse going for a little longer. This was going to be a sweet kill.

"Got it," Skye announced, her tone filled with pride.

Why couldn't I have opted to be a tech nerd instead?

"Do you need backup?" she asked. The clicking sound of her keyboard had now come to a halt. I grunted irritably at the question. She and I both knew that even if I needed help, there was nothing she could do. The Alokari would never send backup, nor would she be able to get here on time, especially not since she was assigned over two hours away for another job.

This was my job, my mess, and the rules were clear. Only I could clean it up.

"How much for his head?" I spoke out loud, and Elias's eyes widened.

"What did you say?" he queried, and when I made no move to answer, he flung the gun away and wrapped his hand around the end of my ponytail. He was lucky this was a wig. Otherwise, I would have made him eat his own intestines.

"Who are you talking to?" he asked, slowly rising to his feet and probing my body with the heels of his feet.

"The data, as you know, is worth five hundred thousand," Skye replied, followed by a beeping sound. "But there's a hit on him. He is worth just over thirty-five thousand." I could sense the twinge of disappointment in her voice. It was a small amount, especially compared to similar jobs. However, this was a kill I was willing to do for free, as long as it rid the world of this vile imbecile.

I grunted in response to let her know I had it from there. The connection ended, and I found myself being dragged through the motel room. Prickles of currents stretched from my arms, legs, and side with each pull. I made no attempt to fight, keeping my focus on the outline of his big-ass head while anticipating the warmth of his blood splattered across my face.

He stopped at the center of the room and pulled me flat against the darkened carpet. "Do you know who I am?" he asked, kneeling down to face level. I released my hold on the gunshot wound and reached for the lipstick container in my pocket.

The one he had seen and not thought much of when he had frisked me before. That was the problem with men. They always underestimated women.

"A vampire?" I answered, gazing into his eyes without flinching. His nose flared, knowing he could no longer scent the prevalent fear that was there before.

"You little bitch-" The lipstick case cover fell, and an elongated silver stake stretched from its depth. My hands curved through the air, and I directed the stake directly into his shoulder blade.

His face contorted, his breathing hitched, and his body fell on top of me.

"Fuck my life," I grunted, pushing the weight of his body off me. Our eyes connected, and that familiar haunted look stared back at me. It filled me with energy I didn't know I still had. No one expected a short, innocent-faced, woman to stab them. Especially not vampires with egos that could fill whole continents.

I rose to my feet, the wound from the gunshot now a distant throbbing ache. I scanned the room, and my eyes fell on the large clock that towered over the bed.

10:45 p.m.

Blood rushed through my head, and irritation skirted my skin. I groaned aloud. I had allowed this imbecile to hold me down for over an hour, and all I could give him now was a swift death.

"Oh no, you don't, asshole." I stepped toward him, using the heel of my foot to press the stake deeper as he attempted to roll over. Now, he was at my mercy. There was nothing he could do and nowhere he could go, and the thought exhilarated me.

"How does it feel to meet the same death as the women you usually fucked and killed?" I snarled, circling his limp body. The mission was for intel, but I had made up my mind a week ago after checking his file that I was going to kill him. The fool had a spreadsheet of mounting assault cases tied to him, and since he technically didn't exist in the human realm, the police could never give the victims justice. I was no Robin Hood. My focus was and always will be money. But I occasionally got my fix from inflicting pain on men whose existences brought women nothing but agony.

He released a series of disgruntled snarls, and his fangs elongated even more. "Who. Are. You?" he asked, his red-rimmed eyes darkened, and blood oozed from his nose.

His nostrils flared, and he inhaled and exhaled in a desperate bid to make sense of my scent. Because the idea of a woman overpowering him was downright impossible. "You're not a shifter, vampire, or demon...You're just a *measly* human." He emphasized the last part, intending it as an insult.

"A measly human who is about to kill you?" I laughed, and the subtle tingle in my abdomen reminded me I was losing blood.

"Measly. I've never been called that before." I smiled as I turned my back to him.

I walked to the bed where I had placed the suitcase I brought with me. I pulled out a cotton shirt and took off my black top. I ripped the cloth in half and tied it around my waist to stop the excessive flow of blood.

Then I unzipped the small compartment in the bag and took out my angular comms device and a mid-sized hunga munga concealed under a pile of clothes.

Elias's voice echoed around the room as he screamed a slew of curses. My eyes locked on to his, and I couldn't help the small smirk that stretched the corners of my lips. I slowly walked to the wardrobe he had caught me snooping around an hour prior.

I pulled out the phone again, turned it on, and went through the series of images that had caught my attention. "Who sent you? The shifters? The witches?" he continued shouting as I made my way over to him.

"When I get....my hands on you...you're going to pay," he mumbled, struggling to catch his breath. "What did you do to me?" The question was followed by a series of weird clicking sounds, caused by his tongue slapping against his teeth and his slackened jaw.

"I think you already know." I smiled, lowering myself to his face to see the moment when realization dawned upon him. I needed to see whether it was fear or disdain that stared back when he realized a *measly* human woman had outwitted him.

He glared at me for a long while, then frantically scanned the room as if looking for a means of escape. No one ever said vampires were the smartest creatures.

"Found what you're looking for?" I mocked. His eyes fell back on me. Fear streaked his vision, and I laughed in turn.

"Who am I?" I spoke slowly, ensuring my words were clear.

"Red," he whispered the name like a plea for mercy. It echoed around the room like a prayer call, one that was whispered in the dead of night. I cloaked myself in the terror reflected in his eyes, trying desperately not to imagine Alessia experiencing the same things before she was killed.

I nodded, acknowledging the alias. It had been a long while since it was whispered with such fear. "This is my favorite type of torture," I said, tapping my French-manicured nails around the phone screen.

"There's a way to make this all go away, you know." I stood and began to circle him, stopping at his head. I reached for one of the gray accent chairs near him and propped the top half of his body against it.

"Who does this belong to?" I asked, pressing the phone close to his face. His brows furrowed and his mouth twitched, yet he gave nothing away. I slowly began to slide through the images, stopping at the most important one.

The ring.

The image of that ring had haunted my every waking moment. Over the years, I had stared at a similar picture and taken it with me on every job, hoping that one of my kills would know something or give me a clue as to who the ring belonged to.

Each job proved more useless than the previous ones, and I was becoming desperate. The tenth anniversary of her death was fast approaching, and Alessia deserved better. Her death needed to be avenged. The life she never got to live and the future she never got to see had to be accounted for, even if it meant killing every supernatural being I came into contact with.

The last ten years my life had been lived in a limbo. There was nothing I could do because the truth was her killer wasn't someone that could be found here in the human realm. He was in Esneoh, the City of Darkness – the home of supernatural beings. Humans could not access it unless one of the leaders of the four houses allowed it. Access I had been trying to gain for a decade.

Elias stared at the image for a long while. Again, nothing shifted within his pupils. He knew nothing, and that irritated me even more. I rose to my feet, staring at the image of the gold ring encrusted with the outline of a lion with a crown. These feminine hands, unlike the ones that I had found on Alessia's phone, were bronze in complexion.

Did several people have this ring? Had my intel been wrong that there was only one of its kind?

"I don't know...but I can find... someone who does," he grunted under his breath, his eyes moving around erratically.

"The image is on your phone." I lowered myself again. He may not have known whose hands these were, but he at least knew of the sea of bodies in the picture. "There are no faces," I added, raising the phone closer to his face again and sliding through the images.

"Because the images were an accident. I had my hand on the phone without realizing it," he coughed, his voice growing distant with each passing second.

"Where was this?" I pressed, using my comms device to take a picture of the images. I raised my head and noticed the devious smile that washed through his features. I knew then that talking to him any longer was a waste of time.

I do not negotiate with assholes.

"I'll tell you if-"

"Now knowing what you do, do you think I'm a stupid, *measly* human?" I laughed, placing the sharp edge of the hunga munga across his neck.

"I.... erm, no. I spoke out of turn." He stumbled through his words, and the sight alone irked me.

"You know the rules. If you're of no use, then you are useless," I spat, gauging his reaction, needing any excuse to prolong his death.

His lack of intel was the confirmation I needed.

"Where were these images taken?"

"Esneoh," he answered without even taking a breath.

I zoomed into one of the images, noting a set of champagne bottles inside an ice bucket placed on the table of a large, rounded booth. And from the blurred lines of the image, I could make out the name of the location from the ice bucket – The Den.

"I'll only share if-" His words died as the sharp edge of my weapon cut his head clean off. His blood splattered against my face, chest, and exposed arms. I groaned inwardly, relishing its taste and cringing at the thought of having to clean this shit off my body. Dry cleaning in Jersey Hill wasn't cheap.

"That was messier than anticipated," I mumbled to myself. I rose to my feet and followed his rolling head to the other end of the room. Standing over it, I took a series of images on my comms device, then immediately signed into the Alokari's encrypted server. I uploaded the images and left a note stating the two jobs were now *closed*.

I immediately sent a message to Skye, asking her to request a cleaning team. The last thing we needed was a human maid to walk in here and find the lower half of a decapitated body. It was one thing to alert supernatural beings of the Alokari's presence. It was another to make humans aware of their existence altogether.

Walking back to the bed, I picked up my suitcase and made my way to the emergency stairs of the motel. The room was located on the second floor, which worked well for exiting the building without drawing any unwanted attention.

The long, carpeted passageway was empty, and the lingering scent of cigarettes, alcohol, and marijuana clung to the walls.

Walking down the stairway, I picked up my pace, feeling the fabric of my shirt and pants dampened by the blood from my wound. With each step and passing moment, my body grew more and more faint. Finally, I rushed through the emergency exit door and briskly walked to the nearby parking area.

When I reached my car, I opened the trunk and placed the suitcase inside, pulling out the small emergency aid kit I had stashed deep within it. I closed the back and stepped into the car as I grew lightheaded with each strained movement.

This was part of the job requirements. As agents, we were trained to anticipate the worst. Death. I had long made peace with the fact my body wasn't my own. It belonged to the Alokari as an instrument to create pain, pleasure, and vengeance.

I placed the key into the ignition, and the car roared to life. With one hand on the wheel and the other frantically trying to open the emergency aid kit, I swerved through several traffic lights until I reached an empty highway. Confident that I was at a safe distance from the motel, I pulled over at the nearest rest stop and looked through the rear-view and side mirrors, wanting to ensure I wasn't being followed. There was no such thing as being overly cautious.

Satisfied, I pushed back my chair, lifted my shirt, and began the painful process of extracting the bullet from my abdomen. There was no way I could drive back home to the Upper East Side without losing a lot of blood and consciousness along the way.

"Vampires are the bane of my existence," I mumbled, biting my lip. This was not how I imagined this evening would end.

A notification on my comms device drew my attention to its screen.

Payment has been made

I released my hold on the emergency kit, signed into my Alokari account, and transferred the money into a private offshore account in the Caymans.

"Another job, another dollar," I muttered, releasing the device, and reaching for a small bottle of vodka inside the kit. I poured the contents of the drink over my wound.

This was going to hurt.

3

NEW JOB, NEW INTEL

M*eraki*

"Iris," I answered my phone, connecting it to the Bluetooth headphones on the nightstand.

"Hold on, Raki," she said, followed by the clicking sound of her heels against marble flooring and teenagers screaming and shouting.

I could deal with near-death experiences, assassinations, stealing intel from a hit, and even handsy human men, but I drew the line at kids, especially teenagers. How Iris had kept her wits about her these last few months while working at the orphanage was a testament to her character.

I begrudgingly rose from my queen-sized bed, wrapped my body in a silk robe, and dragged myself to the large open-plan kitchen area. Pulling back the blacked-out curtains by the living area, I stood still, taking in the panoramic view of Jersey Hill.

The night sky loomed over the city's expanse, illuminating its skyscrapers, office buildings, and mountains in shades of magenta and hues of blue and aqua.

I pushed open the large French windows and walked onto the balcony, inhaling the fresh air, feeling a sense of ease at the never-ending sounds of traffic.

"Hello, my babies," I muttered, dropping to my knees to feel the soil on the ZZ, corn, sago and ponytail palm plants. "Mommy has missed you guys," I continued, paying particular attention to Nelly, the ponytail palm plant that had been a gift from Alessia.

"I've had the worst couple of days. Shot by a vampire, and still no intel on Alessia. I'm feeling a little frustrated," I grumbled, picking up the watering can Iris had filled during her last visit.

"Now look at you showing off. Fresh, dewy skin? These other basic bitches in the streets ain't got nothing on you," I continued, sprinkling the leaves with light speckles of water.

"Are you talking to those plants again?" Iris whispered, her steps still echoing in the background. "Skye is cat obsessed and has more cats going in and out of her house than mosquitos on a hot summer day," she stated, followed by her sending out a slew of instructions to whomever was in the background. "And you spend the majority of your time talking to plants or painting them. Is this what adulting is about? Because if it is, I hate it here."

"Nelly is a constant friend, Iris. You don't need to worry about her taking a more important role in my life than you. There's enough love to go around," I teased, running my hands affectionately through her leaves, placing the water can down.

"Help me, Lord. I need new friends," she said, and I could imagine her rolling her eyes. "Hold on, girl. These people won't let me rest for five minutes," she said, continuing with the conversation in the background.

I walked further down into the greenhouse I had built as an extension of the balcony. Plants curled around the edges of the glass as if they had become one with the space. The black and white furnishings contrasted with the green plants. The brightly colored canvas made my heart beat with glee.

This was home, my escape from the world.

I ran my hands over the two large portraits I recently started but had given up on. Once upon a time, they were all I painted. Now...

I staggered back to the kitchen, placed my phone on the marble counter, and fumbled through the first aid kit. I unwrapped my robe and slowly removed my bandage. After last night's job, I had rushed back to my apartment and passed out before I had time to take care of the wound.

Taking deep breaths, I cleansed the skin, took some painkillers, sterilized a needle and scissors in hot water, and mentally prepared myself for the inevitable.

I was going to have to stitch myself up. There was no way around it.

The Alokari had its own private medic team of agents that I could call upon in emergencies like these, but I was twenty-six years old and had been an assassin since the age of nine. I knew better than to put my life into anyone's hands. A weakened agent was an easy target, and advertising my weakness was the surest way to mark myself.

Iris breathed against the phone, and I could hear rustling sound of fabric and a series of closing doors. "Where have you been? I've been trying to reach you for a week," she spoke after a moment of silence.

"I was on a job." I gritted my teeth as I pushed the needle through my flesh.

"A job? Where?" she whispered, her voice hitching. I exhaled, pushing the needle deeper into my skin, ensuring I stayed above the fat.

"Iris...shit...Fuck." I bit my lip. A fresh flow of blood coated my fingers.

"Are you okay?" she asked, the worry in her voice evident.

"I'm okay...just tired," I lied, continuing to stitch the open wound.

"You're lying."

"Yes, I am, but I'll be okay. Just a little worn down," I replied, speeding up the process so she could have my full attention. With quick, steady movements, I maneuvered through the final stitch, creating an overhand knot with two loops. I repeated it, this time creating three circles in a row. Once satisfied with the knot, I cut off the excess thread and breathed a sigh of relief.

"Did something happen on the job?" she pushed, and though a small part of me wanted to confide in her, I knew better.

"I'm fine," I answered. I slowly began to clear the counter and the trail of blood on the laminated floor.

Iris and I both knew the rules. Agents were to never share the intricate details of their jobs to another. It didn't stop her from asking, though, and I had become accustomed to not answering.

"Where are you now?" I asked, trying to steer the conversation in another direction. She exhaled, picking up on the social cue.

"Sent to the orphanage again," she mumbled, and I could practically feel the irritation trickling off her. "I'm convinced I've been flagged because I keep getting these babysitting jobs. Like what the actual fuck?"

Being flagged on the Alokari systems was the equivalent of social suicide. Though agents could leave their portal open and choose whom they worked with, they could also do the latter. And too many declined jobs from one of the IT nerds did not bode well.

"How long has this been going on?" I opened one of the drawers, searching for some caffeine because I knew there was no going back to sleep. And since I couldn't sleep, I might as well use my time to go through the intel I had on Alessia's suspected killer again, to see if there was anything I could have missed.

"Since the shit with Ezra ended," she muttered, and I rolled my eyes, biting back the need to say *I told you so*. Ezra was the tech genius that had worked with her on most of her jobs. A few months back, after years of flirting and skirting around gray lines, they finally did the dirty. Iris thought he was a one-woman man. Turned out he was for the streets. It ended badly.

"You think you've been flagged?" I echoed the question she seemed to be avoiding.

"Without a doubt. That asshole snitched on me, and now I'm getting the jobs that no one wants to do," she stated with certainty. Though every agent had access to the same system, jobs were allocated electronically to whom the head, Darya, thought best. And depending on how she felt that month, you could be on the paying jobs or tending to the orphanage the organization had in Midtown, the same one it drew most of its recruits from. It was the same orphanage Iris and I had met at.

"Last thing I need is Darya on my ass. I kill vampires, demons, and shifters monthly, but none scare me as much as she does. What does that say about me?" A subtle thrumming laughter followed her words. "And I know you told me to never ever get involved with anyone I work with, but the asshole was a silver-tongued devil. How the hell was I supposed to resist? You know I have a thing for tech nerds," she added, and I couldn't help but laugh out loud.

"I'm telling you! I'm more pissed that after all his bravado, his dick was beyond lackluster, Raki."

"But-"

"Yes, you would think someone shaped like Johnny-fucking-Bravo, could dick a sister down. Instead, I got Squidward, not even close to SpongeBob."

"First of all, leave SpongeBob and Squidward out of this shit," I laughed, feeling the tear on my stomach. "Second, nothing good comes from sleeping with a guy shaped like Johnny Bravo. Did we both watch the same show growing up?" I added. "The ladies loved Johnny. His words, not theirs."

"I fucked up, didn't I?" Iris asked, making soft mewling sounds, something she did when she was lost in thought.

"I'll speak to Skye about accepting an assignment or two and choosing you as the lead agent she would like to work with," I offered, thinking about what I would need in order to bribe Skye. Like me, she was a creature of habit, and we generally stuck to offering each other's names when it came to assignments.

"You know that if I asked, I would be in for some serious lecturing, and right now I'm not in the mental space to deal with Skye's *logical reasonings*," she muttered. "But you're the best," she squealed.

"That's what they all say."

"How long are you back?" she asked as the sound of children and a window opening in the background trickled through.

"Disappearing today. I'll be home again next week. I'm taking a break from assignments for a while," I lied, knowing if I said otherwise, she would insist on showing up at my apartment. And the last thing I needed was for her to see me in this state. "At least two weeks of not taking on any jobs," I added, knowing she would be pleased to hear this. Iris was forever complaining that I spent far too much time chasing jobs and not enough time living in the present and enjoying the spoils of the kill.

"I can continue watering the plants and checking on the glasshouse," she offered.

"No need. I'll take care of it when I get back," I said softly, making my way around the kitchen in a bid to find something to eat. The pantry, fridge, and drawers all came up empty for groceries, except for a few perishable items.

"I cleared out your fridge," Iris sighed heavily. My best friend had long given up on stocking my fridge with homemade food, especially after several attempts at doing so had ended with moldy food and strained arguments.

It was no secret that I barely ever slept in my apartment. Most of my time was spent in hotels, trailing targets, and chasing kills. The only things that grounded me here were my plants and artwork.

"Anyways, the plants were better behaved this time, especially our BFF Nelly," Iris laughed.

"That's my baby," I snickered. "She is the most easy-going person," I chimed, scrolling through a series of grocery delivery apps. I needed to recover quickly within the next week, and the only way around that was to ensure I was well rested and kept my body nourished.

"I also looked through some of your work. I know you told me not to but a few days ago it was so hot I was convinced everything in there would melt."

"Iris..." My movements halted, and I wasn't sure if I was irritated or surprised she had gone this long without snooping.

"I know, I know, and I felt shitty about it. But Raki, they are good, really good. Art studio in the heart of the city good-"

"I don't want that," I replied, keeping the irritation from my voice. I knew she meant well and that I should register what she was saying as a compliment, but I was never going to be okay with sharing my art with people.

Sharing my art with the world was like exposing my heart, soul, and being to people who were oftentimes cruel and critical. They would reduce the beauty of my labor and journey through their myopic lens. And my art was simply that: mine. An extension of everything that grounded me. A celebration of love, loss, joy, and friendship. Sharing my art was like allowing those pieces to be publicly placed under a microscope. I was never going to be ready for it.

"I know, girlie, I know. But-" She hesitated, and though I couldn't see her, I could imagine the exasperated look on her face. "You're right," she resigned, but I sensed this wasn't the end of the conversation. Iris wasn't one to give up easily.

"Since you didn't answer my question, I assume you are not back in Jersey Hill?"

"Something like that...." I evaded the question and headed for the living area.

"Okay, let's meet up. How can we live in the same city and

yet I barely get to see you? Honestly, Raki, I see those friggin plants more than I see you, and that's saying something," she screamed into the phone. "Say yes. A girls' night out. You, me, and Skye."

"I don't know." I hesitated, knowing that nights out with all three of us always ended with one of us being too intoxicated to recount anything. And it was usually me.

"Raki!"

"Okay, let's do one night since I've canceled so many times," I replied, taking a seat on the cream-colored velvet sofa facing the wall-mounted fireplace.

"I've missed you, you crazy bitch."

"I've missed you more!" I bellowed, unable to hold back my laughter.

"Any update?" she asked, softening the tone of her voice.

"Hmmm," I replied. A strained moment of silence passed between us. Alessia's death had been a sore spot for both of us. And although she had been *my* sister, Iris had long claimed her as her own too.

"No new leads, but I came across something that may be of some help. I haven't chased the lead fully yet, as I've only just got back." I reclined on the sofa, recalling the images in my head.

Ending the call, I dragged myself into the shower, got dressed, and sank back into bed. I reached into my bedside table and pulled out the growing file of intel I had been keeping on Esneoh and Alessia's killer.

Esneoh was a magical city hidden within the heart of Jersey Hill. It was believed to have come about eons ago when Nephilim's governed the earth and were relentlessly pursued by humans. The strongest supernatural beings at the time formed an alliance to stretch their longevity and power in an ever-changing world.

The city was divided by those four groups. The north, Kinavari, was governed by vampires. My intel on that area was limited, as the previous reigning leaders had simply disappeared from the face of Esneoh society, not having been seen or heard from in decades.

The east, Aldrata, was controlled by a coven of witches, while the west, the Fleelens, was ruled by shifter clans. Oloh in the west was governed by the current ruling party - demons. However, there was another location I recently obtained information about. Aarin. It was believed to be a metropolis in the heart of Esneoh, a hub that connected the supernatural regions and ensured the treaty between the beings remained in place.

I looked through the pages and sketches of the various leaders I had obtained. I frequently questioned the accuracy of a large chunk of the information. In my line of work, I knew people generally lied. However, those desperate to stay alive were likely to say anything to survive, and since most of my intel was ill-gotten through interrogations, I found myself questioning its validity.

After a few minutes, the comms device in my bedside drawer began to beep. The sound was immediately followed by the alarm system in my apartment being set off. I pulled out my gun from under my pillow as the door to my bedroom flew open. I jumped out of bed, pulled back the slide, and aimed the gun at the outline of a female figure by the door.

"You look like shit, Red," Darya spat, pressed against the wall of the door in her usual trench coat.

"Darya? Why are you here?" I lowered my gun.

Privacy wasn't something the leader of the Alokari was well versed in.

"Why else, darling?" She reached into her pocket and pulled out a cigar and set it alight. "I wanted to visit my favorite mentee," she spoke after inhaling the smoke. "Don't tell anyone I said that, though. I'm not supposed to have favorites, remember?" She smiled, her attention landing on the papers on my bed. I gathered them quickly and placed them on my bedside table.

I reached for the security panel on the left side of the bed and entered my security details. The ringing sound in the background stopped.

"You've been busy." She cocked her head toward the papers, stepped back from the door, and made her way to the living area. I grunted in response and followed the trail of smoke behind her.

Darya was the mentor I never asked for and the mother figure any assassin would dream of having. She had taken a liking to Alessia during our time in the orphanage and had helped her grow within the Alokari in a short number of years. And after Alessia's death, she had taken me under her wing, offering me support, guidance, and the best work opportunities.

Darya stood by the sofa, removed her coat, and sat down, motioning for me to do the same. She removed another cigar from her pocket and passed it to me. It wasn't a question of whether I wanted to join her. It was a demand. And what Darya wanted, she got with no discussions or arguments.

I held the cigar to my mouth and drew in the smoke, then released it, savoring its sweet, earthy, and nutty taste.

After some time, I rose to my feet, walked to the kitchen, and pulled out an unopened bottle of cognac and two tulip glasses.

"How did you find me?" I asked, recounting the fact I had only recently moved into this complex a few months back.

I placed the tulip glasses on the glass center table and poured small portions of the drink into each glass.

"I know where all my agents are," she answered, raising the glass, and taking a sip. She reclined on the sofa, closed her eyes, and continued with her cigar.

I sat back down, enjoying the silence as I waited for her to fill me in on the purpose of her visit. Though I was one of her favorites, I was smart enough to know that nothing good came from unexpected visits. There were enough rumors circulating around the organization about missing agents after such visits, and I wasn't planning to join them soon.

"I'm guessing these are my final moments. Though I would like to live longer. There is still some shit I would like to do...like travel, eat, and have sex. You know, the usual," I said, keeping my eyes trained on her.

"I see the rumor mill has been on full speed," she laughed, a subtle knowingness to it.

"You started it?" I asked, taking a sip of my drink.

"You know the answer to that. Fear is a powerful tool, Red," she replied, releasing more smoke into the air. "Do you think I built this organization on gentle words and kind rapport? Especially as a woman?" She snickered, the light from the fireplace dancing across her warm mahogany skin and long gray locs. "History has taught us that the world doesn't take too kindly to powerful women. I decided long ago that I didn't want to be liked. I simply required submission and obedience." The warmth of her brown eyes blazed with an emotion I couldn't name.

"How long does that take to heal?" She pointed at my loosened robe.

"A week or two max," I replied curtly.

"Have you checked your comms?" She arched a brow, turning her full attention to me.

I shook my head. "I was trying to deal with an intruder before getting to it." I stood and made an attempt to retrieve it. She motioned for me to sit back down.

"I announced that you've been promoted," she stated, placing the cigar on the ashtray before her.

"A promotion?"

She nodded. "You will be supervising the tech team and ensuring they follow the rulebook," she added, and I couldn't help but smile.

"Why the tech team?"

Darya chuckled lightly and took another sip of her drink. "Always were too smart for your own good." The tech team was the cornerstone of the organization and the glue that held agents together. Outside of Darya's role, looking after the tech team was the equivalent of filling her shoes.

"You've been with the organization a long time." She took another sip. "You have the highest kill record and have shown nothing but loyalty and dedication throughout the years I've known you."

"Okay?" I pressed. Those reasons called for a team leadership role, not an entire department.

"I have no kids, by choice. And unlike these supernaturals, I can't live forever," she smirked. "I don't want to leave my baby, my blood, sweat, and tears in the hands of a man or someone who hasn't labored in the trenches for it," she added, placing her glass down and tapping her manicured nails on the edge of the sofa.

"Thank you," I said once the truth of her words hit me.

The Alokari wasn't just a job. It was my life. It was the reason I was still alive and able to live well above the average citizen in the city. Darya's public acknowledgment was gospel and a political play regarding the future of the organization. It was the acknowledgment I needed and the engine that would propel me forward.

"You will be paid...obviously." She smiled mischievously.

"You know my love language is money," I said coyly.

"You can say that again." She raised her glass and motioned for me to do the same. "To money," she toasted, drinking the remainder of her liquor. I filled up our glasses again, bobbing my head to the side.

"I find it hard to believe you came all the way here just to tell me that though." I reclined back in my seat, knowing that there was something else outside of the news she just delivered.

"I made the correct judgment for this job," she laughed. "You're right."

"A job?" I offered. She exhaled, shifting her focus to the fireplace ahead.

"My biggest regret and failure was Alessia...." She trailed off, biting the inside of her lip. "Have you been able to find any new leads?" I shook my head, my grip on the glass tightening as I recounted the images on Elias's phone.

"You?" She lowered her head, unable to meet me eyes.

"No."

Usually, I would have disclosed any information I had and sent her images of what I had found on Elias' phone, but years of failed leads, blood-raged kills, and arguments about the case's lack of progress had worn me out. Over time, I had noticed it had become the same for her. I wanted to pursue this lead myself, without the added burden of sharing the failure if all roads led nowhere. Again.

"I may have something." Her long nails continued to tap the edge of the sofa. I sat forward, wanting to be optimistic yet cautious. "Someone recognized the image of the ring," she announced. My ears grew hot, and my heart beat frantically against my chest.

"We've been here before, Darya..." I leaned forward in my chair, running my hands through my hair.

"The others were through word of mouth or info acquired through some...*persuasion*," she interjected before I could gather my words.

"And this intel is different how?"

"This is neither. This intel comes from an old acquaintance. Someone who is well versed in the supernatural," she answered, reaching for her coat, and pulling out a long envelope from the inside pocket.

"Come." She waved her hand, rising to her feet and walking to the kitchen counter with her drink in tow. She opened the envelope and placed its contents on the counter, spreading them out evenly.

Sprawled before us were fifteen images. The first five images were of a large gallery space I was familiar with on the Upper East Side. They were shot at varying angles of the gallery and gave some insight into its security setup. The next consisted of the building's internal outline and entry and exit points. The final set had pictures of a round pendant with intricate gold markings. The pendant's heart seemed to change color in each picture, and what started out as a translucent crystal became a deep shade of burgundy.

I lifted the final image closer for inspection, mesmerized by how beautiful the pendent was. "What is this?"

"Your next case and the clue to finding out who your sister's killer is," she answered, peering down at me.

"What does this necklace have to do with Alessia?" I asked, sifting through the photos again.

"My acquaintance asked for this to be retrieved." She pointed at the image of the pendant. "If we can get it, they will share the details," she stated, shifting her weight against the bar stool.

"And what's my role in all this?" I pointed at the series of images on the counter. "Last I checked, I killed and retrieved data. I don't collect relics for the Alokari. Isn't there a department for that?" I turned toward her.

"This pendant has been missing for decades. My acquaintance believes it's a chalice that holds power. And it might be the reason for the veil that separates us from *them*," she replied, her attention focused on me. "And he is paying a lot of money. You know how I feel about my money."

"So, the acquittance is a *he*?" I pressed, knowing Darya wasn't going to reveal any more. Privacy was the cornerstone of the Alokari. Right now, she was going beyond the remit of her job by disclosing this much.

"I need someone on the job that has extensive experience in assassinations and heists." She smiled and pointed at me. "Someone I can trust to complete this job because they also have something huge to gain from it," she added, and there was nothing I could say to argue with that logic.

"This acquaintance...Why now? We sent out the images of the ring years ago to all the Alokari's contacts. We heard nothing back. Why are they coming forward now?"

"You know there's only so much I can disclose," she exhaled, piling the images together. Then she stopped. "They've been undercover on a mission..." She hesitated.

"Another assassin," I mumbled, leaning my weight against the desk. "Interesting," I whispered, the earlier doubts I had about the intel dwindling.

"I like you," she said. "You remind me a lot of myself when I was younger. Driven, focused, and unstoppable once you set your mind on something. Those are qualities that you can't instill in someone. They are inherently built here." She raised her hand, placing it against her chest where her heart lay.

"We can trust their word?" I pressed, warmth flooding my chest.

"Yes," she stated simply, and for Darya, that spoke a thousand words. A long bout of silence stretched between us. My skin tingled with discomfort, and my chest tightened at the possibility of what this meant.

I ran my hands through my hair, exhaling the breath I didn't know I was holding. "There is also a financial benefit for this job... Over half a million." She drank the rest of her drink.

"That's a lot of money," I noted, reaching for the image of the pendant. That was the largest sum of money ever accounted for in any of my kills.

Darya made her way back to her coat and pulled out another envelope. This one was smaller than the first. "When can I retrieve it?" I finally spoke. She smiled, walked over to me, and placed the envelope in my palm.

"Two weeks," she stated, motioning for me to open the envelope. "The security rotation and all the intel we've gathered on the gallery space," she said as I opened it and flipped through the paperwork.

"Two weeks," I mumbled, wanting to be sure this was happening. "I'll be off-grid until then," I announced, collecting the images on the table, and placing them all into the large envelope.

When I turned to face her, Darya had wrapped herself in her coat and was making a beeline for the door. "And, Red?" she called just before reaching the long corridor.

"Yes?"

"This is one of the most important jobs of your life. I trust you will do it well?" It was a demand, not a question

"I've never failed a job. I won't start now," I answered calmly.

"Good." She smiled and walked out of the apartment. Warmth filled my chest as I stared down at both envelopes.

Finally.

4

A NIGHT TO REMEMBER

M*eraki*

"Yes! Yes! Yes! I'm so happy you came out," Iris screamed in my ear for the hundredth time since we had arrived in the club. She pushed another shot into my hand as she moved from the bar and motioned for me to drink with her.

We drank our shots successively, and the warmth and burn of the drink slipped from my throat to my stomach. I had drunk enough to get me buzzed, loosen my inhibitions, and make me forget about the fact that today marked the tenth year of my sister's death. It also marked one week before my next case. The one I was hoping would change everything.

Iris had insisted that tonight was the best night for our long-overdue girls' night out, and I didn't bother fighting her about it. I needed it. We all needed it.

"This club is fire!" she giggled as she swayed her hips to the rhythm of the music. Her yellow off-shoulder midi ruched dress moved in tandem with the fullness of her hips. The neon lights that filled the room glistened against her golden-brown skin, and her eyes sparked, morphing her dark eyes to a light shade of brown. Her blunt bob accentuated the asymmetry of her heart-shaped face.

"This place is new?" I asked as she edged toward me. She reached for my face, readjusting the intricate, red-laced mask over my nose, cheeks, and temple.

"It's a few weeks old, the latest buzz in Jersey Hill." She motioned to the sizeable retro club now bustling with a sea of bodies. Large oakwood covered its walls, and massive chandeliers hung strategically at various spots within the interior, creating a relaxed but exclusive atmosphere.

"The masks, though?" I pouted, pulling on the string that kept it in place behind my head. Iris had suggested we each carry one, but the bouncers at the door had insisted we kept them on.

"Carnival season," she whispered in my ear, swaying to the music. "There's been an endless list of celebrations in the city. Plus, this works out for the new job I have." She readjusted her black mask.

"A new job?" I pulled her close. She nodded hesitantly.

"Undercover..." She trailed off, her mouth twisting and eyes scrunching in a contemplative manner.

"Didn't you do one last year and a few months before?" Agents were not usually assigned so many in a short period of time.

"It's the same one. I've been in and out of it for a while..." She interlocked our fingers in the way we would as kids when we wanted to forget whatever interrogation training the Alokari had us endure. The list was usually endless.

"Is it safe for you to be here right now?" I tightened our interlocked fingers and pulled her into a tight hug. She melted into my hold, exhaling loudly.

"It's in another location. I should be fine for one evening. There was no way I was saying no to this outing, or the opportunity to celebrate your crazy ass. And where the hell is Skye?" she laughed, pulling back.

"Speak of the devil." I motioned to the entryway of the club. I stood on the bar chair, waving my hand frantically to draw Skye's attention.

"The dress code was '*slutty*', Iris, not headmaster. Didn't you see my message?" Skye laughed, pulling us both in for a hug.

"I thought that was for Raki? Isn't she the one that's supposed to get laid?" Iris pointed out as we all pulled from the embrace. "And I didn't have time to get home. I've been traveling between a job and that damn school." She frowned.

"Raki is right here," I laughed.

"And Raki needs to get dicked tonight," Skye noted, turning her attention fully to me.

"Raki is capable of finding dick herself," I retorted.

"Raki should probably stop referring to herself in the third person," Iris added, making us burst out in peals of laughter. Skye had become a recent addition to our friendship group within the last five years. Though we had both worked with her professionally on and off, it was always at a steady distance, as building relationships with other agents was sometimes a hit or miss. Trusting people was hard, especially when everybody was out solely for themselves. Skye had passed the test of time and remained consistently true to herself. It was also easy to bond with her, as we had both lost our sisters in the line of duty.

"No, seriously. When was the last time? And I'm not talking about that guy you entertained one year ago for like a month," Skye stated playfully, and motioned for the bartender to bring us more shots.

"Put some respect on her name, Skye. Two months was a very long time for her," Iris added with a wink. "Wait, what did she say was wrong with that one?"

"He snored too loudly." Skye rolled her eyes.

"He snored like a pig," I stated dismissively. There was

nothing worse than a man with the drive of a turtle and the blocked airways of a dog.

"What did she say about the others before that?"

"Too stingy, spoke too much, his house was too sterile, the list goes on. Should I continue?" Iris tugged on my hand playfully.

"I hate you both." I raised my hand to dismiss them, realizing why I hadn't gone out with either of them in a long while. I didn't need a constant reminder of my growing forest landscape below.

"It's been so long I'm sure she's become a virgin again," Skye mouthed, motioning to the rows of shots the attendant had placed on the counter.

"Don't be absurd. Just because I haven't had anyone underneath me doesn't mean I haven't been using Mr. Purple." I rolled my eyes, taking one of the shots without waiting for an invitation.

"Mr. Purple?" they shouted as they turned to glare at me.

"The fucking dildo, bitch?" Skye whisper shouted.

"Don't judge me-"

"Okay, this is worse than we thought, she named the damn thing. Who the hell names their dildo?" Iris shook her head. "And Mr. Purple for that matter?"

"It's long, purple, and does the job. What else was I supposed to call it?" I chuckled, almost choking on the next shot I took. Iris and Skye burst into laughter, and I couldn't help but join in.

Maybe I do need to get laid by an *actual* man.

"Okay. I have to get back to the longest job of my life and those demonic children. Skye has to go back to...Her house? Desk?" Iris handed us each a shot glass.

"Look at you learning to be funny," Skye poked at her.

Iris smiled. "It's now or never. Let's not forget that Raki is about to go incognito for a while. We need this." She pointed at the drinks.

"To your promotion. You're technically my boss now?" Skye stated, her face beaming with pride. "To the latest boss ass bitch in town." Skye raised her shot glass, and Iris and I followed.

"To money, bloodshed, and vengeance," I added, our glasses making contact.

"And sex, plenty of sex," Skye screamed, not caring who heard her.

"Do you think about anything else but dick?" Iris laughed playfully.

"Yes. Money." She took her shot, and I motioned for the bartender to bring more.

"Okay. That I can agree with." Iris and I smiled and nodded.

Three new shots arrived, and we huddled together, taking them together in a timed manner. Iris and Skye pulled up the barstools beside me as we caught up on everything that had been going on with us since our last outing over six months before.

After an hour, the club had begun to fill up, and the music pounded. We moved to the middle of the dancefloor and lost ourselves to the beat of the music and the sway of the endless sea of bodies.

"Another set of shots?" I motioned to the bartender after dancing away most of the liquor from earlier. From the distance, I could make out Iris and Skye's bodies locked in the arms of two men.

The female bartender came back after a short time and placed four shots before me. "The gentleman there paid for it," she announced before I could pull out my credit card.

My eyes followed the direction of her hand to where a man sat, his form towering over the rows of bodies between us.

A gold metal steampunk mask covered the top part of his face. The lights briefly illuminated his face, calling attention to his bronze skin and raven black hair that fell around his neck. As if sensing my gaze, his eyes locked with mine, and a sinfully gorgeous smile stretched across his lips. The outline of two subtle dimples dotted on his cheeks.

The room grew still, and my lower female region danced in celebration. He was large, stout, his presence demanding the attention of the men and women in the room. He oozed charisma and promised danger, excitement, and a tandem of mayhem. Just how I like my men.

He raised his scotch glass, and the glimmer of something dark and mysterious danced in his vision. He motioned to the shot in my hand and took a sip of his liquor. His Adam's apple bobbed, and my hold on the glass tightened. It was official. I needed to get laid.

Something caught his attention from across the bar, and he stood quickly, motioning with his hand. There was something about the movement that was graceful yet domineering.

"More drinks?" Skye tugged my elbow, jolting my attention to her.

"It seems like it," I answered, unable to keep the gleam from my expression. Her gaze shifted to where Mr. Tall Dark and Handsome sat, and a mischievous look glimmered in her eyes.

"Well, well, look what we have here," she teased, making no attempt to hide the fact she was staring at him. "You better fuck the living daylights out of him. He is fine as hell," she said, licking her lips.

"Skye!"

"Okay! Okay!" She raised her hand in mock surrender. I turned my attention back to where he sat and found the seat empty. My eyes briefly darted around the room but could not make out his form in the sea of bodies. Disappointment coursed through me, but I squashed it down, refusing to focus on it for too long. I was a strong, independent woman, more than capable of picking up a man if I wanted to. Tonight, I just wanted to have fun with my friends. Nothing else.

Drinks flowed. The club grew more jam-packed, the dancing more erotic, and the air thick with lust. I closed my eyes, my hands in the air as I moved my hips to the backdrop of Zouk and kizomba music. Warm, thick, coarse hands trailed the low-cut opening of the back of my dress. The hands slowly moved to my hips, holding me in place, my ass resting against their growing bulge. My eyes shot open, and I tilted my head back, finding myself face to face with Mr. Tall Dark and Handsome.

From a distance, he was gorgeous. Up close, he was a work of bronzed and chiseled art. His clothes gripped his body, accentuating every dip and curve. And the evidently erect mandigo stick behind me told me he was more than well endowed.

Very well endowed, indeed.

His hands clasped around my neck, turned my body back around, and pressed my back against his. Under normal circumstances, I would have told him to *fuck off* and shoved him away, but the force of his presence and the silent, deep, intense lust radiating from his pores made me arch into his hold and dance.

His woody aromatic scent coiled around my chest, making me heady with lust. His body moved in tempo with mine, and each sway and thrust was met with slow, sensual, smooth, grounded movements.

His hold on my waist tightened, and I bit down on my lip, stopping myself from moaning out loud. This was sweet, delicious torture, and I didn't want it to end. Any man who could move so smoothly was bound to know how to please a woman.

We continued like this, our bodies melting until we became indistinguishable, our lust the engine that kept us grounded, moving as one.

Slowly, his hold loosened, and I turned back, expecting him to make a move, but he stood morbidly still, trailing his eyes from the crown of my head to the soles of my feet. His scrutiny made my body shiver with desire and need. Who was this man? And what the hell was wrong with me?

His attention immediately turned to someone behind me and remained there. I followed his line of sight, and my vision landed on another man at the far end of the room with a similar mask and a scowl on his face.

Mr. Tall Dark and handsome walked forward, his hands resting against my waist. His fingers tapped the dent there, and after a few strained moments, he let go and walked off without uttering a single word.

A weaker woman would have been offended, but I was used to dealing with assholes in my line of duty, and I was not easily swayed by men's lack of chivalry.

I turned my back to him, not wishing to give him any more attention. It was bad enough that I had gotten myself hot and bothered on the dancefloor. I refused to throw away the ounce of pride I still had left.

"I'll be back." I motioned to Iris and Skye who were lost in the deep haze of the music. They nodded in acknowledgement, and I stumbled through the club, following the pathway to the restroom.

As I reached the long empty passageway, the outline of Mr. Tall Dark and Handsome caught my attention from a distance. He was deep in conversation on the phone, and the man he had been staring at stood beside him. After a moment, the call ended, and he and the other man seemed to argue. He then motioned to the emergency door, and they walked out.

Watching the whole interaction play out made me feel a sense of unease. Life had taught me to always trust my gut. And right now, mine was screaming danger. It was also screaming for me to mind my business, but I had never been one to follow instructions without questioning them.

I slowly made my way to the exit door, wanting to see if I could keep up with them. If caught, I could simply pretend I was out to get fresh air, as the club was packed.

"Hey, why don't you show me a good time?" Wet, clammy hands ran over the back of my exposed neck.

I sneered and jerked back. "What do you think you're doing?" My gaze landed on a blonde-haired man with bloodshot eyes, doused in the scent liquor and cigarettes.

"Come on." He stepped toward me, and his hand reached for mine. I swatted it mid-descent and stepped back again. "Don't play hard to get. I saw how you danced with that dude earlier. I know what you're looking for, and I can give it to you." He licked his lips, and I shuddered with disgust. The audacity of some men.

"Listen, I'm only going to say this once. If I have to repeat myself, your family will be mourning over the remains of your scarred body." I stepped in front of him boldly, rage coiling all around me.

My anger only seemed to spur him on. He chuckled, his eyes overcast with lust. "I like when they play hard to get," he replied, towering over me.

Being one hundred and sixty-five centimeters tall meant that men usually underestimated my strength and capability. They never saw me as a foe, threat, or opponent, usually to their detriment. Whenever I retaliated, it was with the cunningness of a wolf and the bite of a cobra. Short, swift, and deadly.

"I would rather fuck a ten-foot pole than allow you to ever touch any part of me." I spoke slowly, wanting to ensure he got the full weight of what I was trying to convey. "You're not my type, and clearly, you lack any tact whatsoever," I added, turned my back to him, and headed for the emergency door. As I took a few steps forward, his hand tugged at my ponytail, pulling me back forcefully. My back landed against his chest.

Raising my right arm, I elbowed him in the side, pressing my elbows deep into the dip in his waist. He groaned, releasing his hold on my hair, and cursed out loud. His hand immediately reached out for me, and I swatted it away in response. His face morphed through a series of emotions from shock to irritation to anger.

It was one thing to deal with supernatural beings like vampires, werewolves, and shifters. It was another thing to deal with regular men who had a false sense of ego. They were equally as vile.

"You think you're all that? Women like you are easy and throw themselves at me all the time," he hissed. I took steady steps back, wanting to keep distance between us for his sake. The last thing I wanted to do was pull out a weapon or retaliate in a way that would cause him severe harm. The Alokari was usually forgiving when it came to dealing with the supernatural, not so much when it came to humans.

I rested my hands on my waist, then checked the long passageway behind him when I realized he wasn't going to relent.

I would have no choice but to defend myself. Why were men such despicable beings? Why were they unable to grasp that *no* simply meant *no*, there were no ifs, buts, or in-betweens?

"Is that so?" I mocked, goading him further. I knew doing so would push him to retaliate. I was just hoping he was stupid enough to go through with it.

"So, why don't you stop playing hard to get and wrap your mouth around this cock?" He motioned downward, his hand drawing emphasis to his enlarged bulge.

He reached forward, making a drunken attempt to pull me into his embrace. With the heel of my foot, I kicked him in the groin, and he curled into himself, holding onto his crotch as he muttered a slew of curses.

When he raised his head again, a flash of anger radiated through his features. I smirked in response, my hands and body aching to knock down his false sense of masculinity.

He bolted toward me headfirst. A thunderous voice echoed behind me as thick, muscular hands lifted him up from the ground and threw him against the wall, holding him in place by his shoulders.

"Touch her again, and I will have you eating your intestines for dinner." The deep baritone voice set against broad shoulders and thickly muscled body gave away my intervenor.

Mr. Tall Dark and Handsome kept him in the air, and the spark of defiance that was behind his eyes when he attacked me a few seconds ago had disappeared. In its wake lied fear, raw and repentant in its anguish.

"Apologize to the lady," Mr. Tall Dark and Handsome demanded, his voice filled with disgust.

"I-I-I," he stuttered, and I snickered in response, watching the man who a few seconds prior had sworn to make an example of me. "I'm...sorry," he uttered the words as his body shook.

Mr. Tall Dark and Handsome forcefully released his hold on him, and he fell to the floor. He scrambled to his feet, briefly turning to first look at me and then back to the giant before me. He then jumped to his feet and ran off, not uttering a single word.

The man before me turned, his mask now slightly tilted. Everything else about him, from his attire to his stiff expression, remained in place, his gaze fixed intently on me.

If it was a thank you, he was looking for, he was sorely mistaken because he would never receive one. I was more than able to defend myself, and any man who sought to intervene in any of my battles did so to boost their ego. I didn't need saving. I was no damsel in distress.

"Why were you following me?" he asked, his words slow and calculated.

"Following you?" I snickered. The first rule in stalking is to ensure you don't get caught, and if you do, pretend you're oblivious of what you're being accused of.

I brushed the comment off and began to head back in the direction I had come from, feeling stupid that the only thing that was remotely suspicious about him was his penchant for breaking the law by using the emergency exit instead of the main exit. He was a bonified criminal, no doubt about it.

As I turned, a subtle wind blew against my neck, startling me. In my peripheral vision, I saw him reaching out to pull me into his hold, and I immediately arched back, his hand floating in the space between us.

"What the fuck do you think you're doing?" I glowered at him.

"Testing a theory," he replied, his eyes bleeding with an emotion I couldn't name. My hands immediately reached for the pepper spray laced with wolfsbane I had hidden in my clutch.

Though vampires and other supernatural beings lived in Esneoh, many crossed over from the City of Darkness, masking themselves in Jersey Hill. And unless you were familiar with their general disposition or mannerisms, they could easily pass as humans.

"What the hell is that?" he coughed as I aimed the bottle at him and pressed down on the nozzle.

I waited for him to choke and begin to convulse as it made contact with his skin. Nothing.

He stood perfectly still, with a glimmer of irritation in his eyes. Before I could register what had just happened, he reached forward, wrapping his hand around my throat.

When I asked for some fun in the bedroom, this was not what I had in mind.

He slammed my body against the wall and lifted me into the air until our faces were level.

He wasn't a vampire or shifter, which left the possibility that he could be a demon, but from my previous view of his back, I didn't see the four-pointed triangular mark behind his ears. Demons could conceal themselves in human form, but they could never hide that symbol.

That left one option. He was most likely human and a member of a local or regional clan, and not minding my business had gotten me into business I had no business being in.

I fought to free myself from his hold. Each punch and kick were met with a deep-throated laugh. When nothing seemed successful, I aimed my feet for his groin. As if anticipating the move, he flipped me over, my back against his chest, my feet locked between his thighs. My breathing hitched, my pulse spiked, and every nerve in my body sparked to life.

Here I was in a near-death situation, and my body's instinct was to give in to the growing throb in my lower region. Smooth.

His breath fanned my skin, and his erect dick pressed against my back. Either I was imagining it, or Mr. Tall Dark and Handsome was equally turned on by this shit.

"I wasn't." I gritted my teeth. He tilted my head toward him, and his gray eyes bled into mine. One part of my brain told me to fight back. Another relished in the feel of his hands wrapped around my neck.

This was a new level of fucked up even for me. I was the girl that killed vampires, werewolves, demons, and witches for gain, not the one that got fucked in the hallway of a club.

"Why do I feel you're lying? Too much of a coincidence, no?" he whispered against my ear, gently nibbling at it. My body shivered in response without my consent.

"They say once is chance, twice coincidence, but what do you think will happen after the third time?" he continued, and like earlier, that blaring alarm kept ringing in my ears that something was off. Something was not quite right with this man. Or it could be the fact that he and I were bred from the same cloth of fuckery. We thrived in chaos and bloodshed, and like an invisible cloak, it drew us to each other.

A fresh wave of adrenaline coursed through me, and as much as this shit turned me on, there was another part of my brain that screamed self-preservation. Getting dicked down was not going to be at the expense of my life.

"I'm not going to entertain that with a response," I murmured, gasping for air while trying to free myself from his hold. But all I managed to do was grind harder into his dick print.

Meraki, get your shit together.

I wrapped one leg tighter around him, practically straddling his waist, and used the other to knee his lower half. He dropped me, and I stepped back, calculating the odds that, if I shot him here, the Alokari would cover for me and clean it up, but it would be at the expense of possibly never breathing again. An agent who acted outside of their usual protocol kills was seen as a potential hazard. It was the equal sum of trying to leave the organization. Blood in, blood out.

I had no doubt that my brain matter would be splattered on the streets of Jersey Hill not too long after. I was Darya's favorite, but even favorites had an expiration date, and I was no exception.

The whole situation would be a lot easier if I wasn't enjoying this back-and-forth dance, we were participating in. It had been a long time since I met a man who was able to go toe to toe with me and keep me on my feet.

He stepped toward me again, his hands outstretched as he made another attempt to pull me into his hold. This time, I countered each move with a swat of my hands.

He growled loudly, but the deep pools of his eyes told me it wasn't from irritation. It was something else. An emotion as clear as the moon on a midsummer night. Lust, raw and unfiltered. Yet behind its depth was something else, something I was unable to name.

He stepped forward, making another attempt to reach for me. He stopped halfway when the sound of laughter drew near. My head tilted right in the direction of the incoming group of three women and two men.

His gaze turned from me to them, examining my movements as if I was the answer to his prayer. I stepped back, entranced by his heady scent, the pull of his presence, and the ticking time bomb called my vagina.

I needed to get away. Now.

Without uttering a single word, he let me know that if we had not been interrupted, our encounter would have taken a different turn. And instead of finding out whether that turn would have led to mind-blowing sex, I made a beeline and ran past the approaching group.

This was a first, even for me.

I slipped into one of the marked disabled toilets to the left, my heart pounding against my chest, my underwear soaked.

"You are seriously fucked up, Meraki," I mumbled to myself, placing my clutch on the counter while giving myself some breathing room to recover.

After fifteen minutes had passed, I slowly opened the door, checking both directions to ensure there was nothing out of the ordinary. Once satisfied, I pulled it completely back and found myself slammed back into the room by a piquant force.

"Explain," he ordered, raising the pepper spray he had taken from me, his mouth set in a frown.

"Explain what pepper spray is? You can't be that out of touch with reality," I replied, my brows arched.

He stared at me long and hard, dropped the bottle, and took two bold steps toward me. I stepped back, assessing that there was only one way out of this room, and it was either through the door or under him. And I wasn't sure which was more appealing.

"I love a good chase." He smiled, towering over me. He lunged forward, clasping his hands around my waist. I elbowed him, releasing myself, and took another step back. "I love a good hunt even more." With an unexpected swiftness to his movement, his hand wrapped around my neck, and his hold tightened with enough force to choke me while allowing me a few small breaths.

"Fuck you-" He slammed me down on the large marble counter and used his thighs to spread my legs.

"Well, Little Hellion, what's this?" his eyes landed on my leg holster as my Glock 19 peeked out. My body stilled with unease. "What does an everyday woman need with this?" My hands instinctively reached for the weapon, and we both fought to gain hold of it.

"Interesting," he muttered, slowly pulling it from the strap, watching me writhe in his hold. Warmth flooded my body, and goosebumps erupted on my skin.

"Protection from predators like you," I replied through gritted teeth. He tightened his hold on my neck by another fraction. Black spots danced in my vision, and I released a series of gurgling noises as I struggled to inhale. His hold remained tight on the gun. His eyes swam with emotions.

"You seem to enjoy being the prey, though?" He smiled, this time releasing his hold a little, and I moaned out loud, no longer caring how lewd and deprived this was.

"Why do I feel that you're enjoying this just as much as I am?" The words sounded like a deep rumbling in his chest.

"Maybe I am," I replied boldly, my body thrumming with

anticipation. A smile tugged at the corners of his lips. Using the head of the gun, he slowly nuzzled it against the outline of my pussy, moving it in round circular strokes. His eyes remained locked on mine as the outline of his manhood grew larger, pressing against my leg. My legs shook, and my body spasmed with excitement.

"No underwear," he mumbled, and his eyes rolled back. "What would happen if I pulled this?" he whispered in a low animalistic way, then proceeded to slowly rub the gun against my clit.

The euphoric adrenaline shook me to my core, and I found myself moving to the sway of his movements.

"Fuck," I moaned, my skin growing more heated by the minute.

"Ride it," he instructed, edging it into me. "Or I'll pull this trigger," he added, a crazed look in the depths of his eyes. I followed his command, not needing to be told twice. If I was going through with this, I needed to see it through to its full depravity.

"Good girl," he murmured. He hitched up my dress and pushed the weapon deeper inside me, his finger pressed against the trigger. He arched my neck. Fear and adrenaline spiked my blood with a clawing need to flee.

I didn't.

I enthusiastically rode the gun, moaning, whimpering, and sighing at the knowledge of the heightened sense of danger. My legs shook, and stars danced in my vision. Before long, I found myself mumbling a series of incoherent words as I came all over the barrel.

"Lick it." He edged the weapon from in between my legs and placed it on my lips. "Open. Now." He growled the words, demanding I submit to him. If this were any other situation, I would have fought back and perhaps even killed him without blinking an eye. There was nothing I hated more than being told what to do by men. Unless it was in the bedroom. And though this wasn't in an apartment or the confines of a bed, it was close enough.

I stared down at the weapon soaked and coated with the remnants of my orgasm. He watched me, closely assessing my every move. Slowly, he pushed the weapon into my mouth until the thought of whether this was hygienic had gone out of the window.

I obeyed, wrapping my lips around it and moaning with each lick. I kept my eyes trained on him, imagining that this was his dick. Saliva pooled around my mouth and chin, and I made no attempt to stop it. He released his grip on my neck and reached for my ponytail instead, twisting the length around his fingers while forcing the weapon deeper into my mouth.

"You're such a dirty whore." He muttered the words with such reverence that I almost came.

I wrapped my legs fully around his waist while continuing to clean all traces of my cum from the weapon. It wasn't enough. I needed more.

Reaching for his pants, I unbuckled his belt and pulled down his zipper. His dick sprang free. The sight of it, like him, was magnificent.

He stepped back, removing the gun from my mouth. "On your knees," he ordered, this time placing the gun against my temple.

I wrapped one hand around his dick, the other on his balls, as I pumped it with steady strokes. His head fell back, and his hold on the gun tightened.

Fuck. This shit was hot.

His dick pulsed in my hand, and he grunted so loudly that the music in the background became a distant sound. "Be a good girl, and suck this cock," he growled, his fingers pressing against the barrel in that vaguely threatening manner.

At this point, I was no longer sure where the game ended, and reality began. Perhaps that was what was so alluring about this whole experience.

He shoved his dick into my mouth, using his hold on my hair to force me to take all of him. Which was practically impossible. I pulled my head back, slowly working my way down his length with subtle licks and strokes while keeping my hand on his balls.

"This mouth is pure filth," he groaned to no one in particular, and I smiled, picking up my pace with ferocity, desperate to not only please him but to find some release from the ache between my thighs.

My left hand slipped under my dress, and I began to touch my pussy with fast strokes, moaning around his dick.

I placed my other hand against his thigh to keep me balanced. I took in the full length of his throbbing dick, gagging and bobbing, trying to take as much as I could. Tears streaked my face. Saliva dripped down my jaw, chin, lips. All that could be heard in the enclosed space were the sounds of his groans of pleasure and my overly enthusiastic moans.

Have you truly given good head if tears haven't trailed down your face and mascara stained your cheeks?

My eyes fell on his, and I kept my gaze on him as I pulled back, lightly grazing the outline of the thick swell of his dick. His legs buckled around me. I knew he was close, and the idea alone made me almost come.

He pulled my ponytail tighter, and my scalp prickled, sending me into a more depraved frenzy. He forced my mouth fully down his length, and at first, I choked, gasping and coughing as I tried to catch my breath. This seemed to only spur him on, and he released a series of groans, his eyes locked on my lips with nothing but intrigue marring his features.

I couldn't believe I was doing this.

I continued to rub my clit, feeling myself getting closer to my release while humming and gagging on his dick. Tears continued to trail down my cheeks. His movements started becoming more erratic, his dick pulsing in my mouth. He tugged tighter on my hair until dark spots covered my vision and my legs shook. I leaned forward, taking more of him.

He released a low howl as thick spurts of his cum filled my mouth. He made an effort to pull back, but with my hand around his waist, I held him in place, swallowing each drop.

The scent of his release and the look of amazement on his face drove me over the edge. My eyes rolled back, my legs buckled, and I groaned as I finally reached my own release. I pulled back, and drops of his cum fell against my lips, cheeks, and chest. Yet the gun remained in place, his hold on it unrelenting.

"Who are you?" he asked, smudging the remnants of his release against my cheeks and swollen lips.

"No one," I replied, trying to catch my breath. There was no need to share names or exchange details. This was simply one of those nights to remember and nothing else.

"Turn," he commanded, tilting the gun against the crook of my neck. I hesitantly turned, wondering where this was going next and how far we were willing to take this game. "This was not part of my plan," he mumbled as he shuffled behind me.

After a few seconds, his hold on my hair loosened, and the weight of the gun against my head disappeared. A cold chill ran through my back, making the hairs on my neck rise.

I turned back, finding myself alone in the space. The gun lay atop the counter, and the slightly ajar door reminded me that I had not just imagined this whole encounter.

I wasn't expecting a goodbye, but a *thank you for giving the best head of my life* would have sufficed.

Instinct told me to follow him, to track his every movement and find out who the hell he was. When was I going to have such a mind-blowing sexual encounter again? Happenings like these were rare.

I knew better, though. This meant nothing. It was simply sex and could never go anywhere else. Our worlds and paths were too far off to ever cross again. It was best to hold on to the memory than try to recreate it again.

I rose to my feet, struggling to get my knees to cooperate with the rest of my body. My gaze fell on my reflection in the mirror.

Mascara streaked down my cheeks, my red lipstick had smeared down my jaw, and my perfectly laid ponytail had now grown frizzy on my head.

I wiped the streaked makeup with tissues and opened my purse, reapplying it again, refusing to feel an ounce of regret or shame. At least now I knew why over the years sex had always felt it was missing something. A spark, drive, depravity. Nothing ever seemed to tick. Until now.

I reapplied my lipstick, wiped my chest, and readjusted my dress. It was time to go home and prepare for my next job in seven days.

Getting dicked down was always a bonus, though.

5

STORM CLOUDS AND THUNDER

M*eraki*

THE NIGHT AIR WAS COOLER THAN USUAL TODAY. THE lights of the city glimmered in a kaleidoscope of colors, pulling my attention from all directions. Brief images of my encounter with the stranger flashed through my vision. I pushed the pictures down, deep down in the recess of my mind, refusing even to entertain the idea.

Tracking him or finding out who the hell he was wasn't the problem. Stalking was part of the job description in the Alokari.

My life and job required me to be a beast of prey, but when it came to the bedroom, I preferred relinquishing that role and the burden of the responsibility. I wanted to be chased, the one pursued and hunted. Whether that was with a gun over my pussy was another story altogether.

"Why are your missions always at the butt crack of the evening?" Skye yawned, followed by a series of clicking sounds on her keyboard.

"I call this hunting hour," I replied, placing the contents of my travel bag on the rooftop.

"Hunting hours?" she asked. "Normal people are sleeping at this time."

"Normal is so boring and mundane," I added sarcastically, turning my focus to the gallery building ahead of me. I opened the black rifle bag. It contained the weapons I would need for the job.

"Right now, I wish I had normal," she mumbled, followed by a series of yawns.

"I'm sorry. Did you say something? My earpiece is malfunctioning," I teased, breathing loudly to distract her.

"You owe me, bitch," she snickered. "I'm not getting paid enough for this shit. This was supposed to be my vacation week," she continued to grumble.

"There's no other IT whizz I trust working with. Thanks for picking up the job," I replied. My hands wrapped tightly around the binoculars as I watched an unbending sea of bodies walk out of the gallery.

"A bit late for gallery visitors, no?" Skye mentioned.

"The space is usually rented for private events. That's why the job took so long. After this, there's a two-day break before another series of events picks up. Tonight was the best night to strike," I said, switching on the infrared night thermal setting on the binoculars.

"Are you able to hack into the system?" I asked after five minutes of silence. The gallery space was now empty apart from the single night guard that covered the main floor of the building every night.

"Don't insult me, Raki," she hissed into the device, reminding me that a not well-rested Skye wasn't the best company.

"Late night?" I reached for my comms device, signed into the Alokari systems, and updated the status of my mission to *in transit*. This was a simple way to notify Darya the heist was underway. After tonight, she might not hear from me for at least a week.

No heist was ever clear or straightforward. And training had taught us that it was always best to disappear immediately after completing a job in order to give time for the steam to blow over.

Stay low. Keep your head down. Once the heat cools, reappear with the items.

"Hmm, I was doing a job..." She grew silent, and the typing stalled. "A personal one," she added hesitantly, and I took that as code for she wasn't yet ready to discuss it. "Plus, you know what I'm like without sleep and coffee," she chuckled, continuing with her job. "So close. Almost in. Fuck yes." Her voice hitched, laced with excitement.

"Shit. I'm in. I've accessed the security system." Her breathing increased.

I peered down at my watch, noting I still had five minutes before the guard would make himself scarce in the security room. Luckily, the night guard was a lazy, potbellied man who spent most of his shift sleeping and relied on the laser security system to do his job.

Their loss. My benefit.

"How many?" I tightened my hold on the binoculars, twisting the focus wheel for a better glimpse of any thermal activity on the other floors.

"Twelve cameras. Eight on the first floor. Eight on the basement floor outside the vault where the pendant is locked up," she answered.

"Can you disable the cameras? Or at least keep me from sight?" I asked, placing the binoculars back in the bag once I was satisfied everything was going exactly according to plan.

"On it now!"

I pulled the black hoodie over my head and pulled out a dagger and two guns, each loaded with at least four rounds of silver bullets.

"Thanks." I closed the bag, placing it in the small compartment in the wall.

"Turning it off will draw suspicion. However, I can place it on a one-minute loop. It will just keep replaying the same video for one minute, then repeat, until you're out. These suckers won't suspect anything," she added smugly, her excitement palpable.

"Time frame? How long do I have to go in and out?" I strapped one of the guns and the dagger around my waist. The other gun went into a garter around my thigh.

"Ten minutes tops. If you go above that, you have an additional two minutes to get out before security shows up," she responded, mumbling under her breath as the sound of the keyboard clicking intensified. "Interesting."

"What's wrong?" I pulled out a wired rope and pulley, throwing the rope to the gated hook on the roof of the gallery. It landed, and I repeated the action to hook the pulley on the metal poles at the center of the roof. Once both had been fastened, I tugged and pulled, ensuring everything was in place and safe for flight.

"I've never seen the security system registered here as backup security." she noted, typing.

"I'm crossing over," I relayed, hooking the pulley on a shorter rope to propel me forward to the other building. "I'm on the gallery roof," I announced, leaving the hook attached for a swifter escape. "What security system is it?"

"The data is encrypted..." She trailed off. "I think I've seen it before. A.V.R.L....It's similar to the ones I've tried to hack into from Esneoh..." Silence fell, and she whistled under a low breath. "Some big players want to keep this pendant hidden."

"Why would they place it here outside of the City of Darkness? In plain sight?"

"That could be the point. Having it in Esneoh could be risky, especially if they were trying to hide. But having it in Jersey Hill, the human realm, is... smart," she whispered. The words rolled off her tongue, like a silent lament. "Supernatural beings won't think to search for it here. It's like stealing from someone and hiding the stolen item in the same place you stole it from. They'd be none the wiser," she snickered. "Do you know what the fascination with the pendant is about?"

"Do we ever know anything?" I replied sarcastically. Our job was to kill and collect items. Occasionally we would get a glimpse into the reasons for kills and the purpose of certain relics. But agents knew that too much knowledge came with a hit on your head. The less you knew, the better, and that was the reason the Alokari had gone undetected for so long. If agents were limited in their knowledge, there was nothing that could be traced back or used against the organization.

"I've opened the security door on the far right," she instructed. I followed the curved pathway, allowing the white walls and bright artificial lights to direct my trail. "Go left and climb up the pipes. This will lead you all the way down to the main floor."

I stopped at the end of the long passageway, halting at the door of a room containing only a ladder. Angling the ladder vertically, I placed it directly under the large opening above me.

I inhaled and exhaled steady breaths while struggling to maneuver myself through the tight vent system.

"Turn left. Once you reach the end of the line, just keep going straight down," Skye spoke after a few minutes of silence.

"When I said I liked being on all fours, this wasn't what I had in mind," I whispered. Skye laughed heartily, the clicking of her keyboard becoming more erratic.

"Well-"

"Don't respond to that," I interrupted, anticipating some sort of lewd remark.

"My lips are sealed, Raki," she replied mockingly. "Thirty seconds more. When you reach the edge, there should be a huge gap below you. That vent will take you directly down to the janitors' room on the first floor."

I placed my hands on the walls of the enclosure, angling the lower part of my body downward. "Fuck," I muttered, losing my footing and slipping down the tightened space.

"That does not sound good," Skye commented, a sarcastic undertone in her voice.

"You better not save this audio sooooouuuuunnnnddd," I whisper shouted, landing in the janitor room, my ass sprawled across the floor atop a series of mops.

"You're lucky I missed it by a few seconds," she replied, followed by the faint sound of a phone being locked. "The guard is seated in his usual spot still."

"I'm scrubbing my body nonstop after this," I muttered, rolling onto my hands and struggling to get to my feet. I slowly edged my way to the door, ignoring the dull throb of discomfort from my waist down.

"Turn left and take the stairs. You'll end up by the basement floor," Skye stated, this time a serious edge to her tone.

I pulled open the janitors' room and ran across to the other end of the marbled open space, ensuring my footsteps did not echo or create any squeaking sounds.

Once I reached the spiral staircase leading to the basement floor, I pressed my body against the walls, keeping my eyes and ears alert for any sounds or unexpected movements.

I followed the staircase down six flights until the final blockade to the pendent came into view – a gigantic metal wall that acted as a security safe. I quickened my steps and lowered myself to the ground, my knees keeping me upright. Opening one of my holsters, I removed a pen-sized digital stethoscope, pressed its diaphragm flat on the door, and wrapped its binaural spring against the dial spring of the safe.

"Six minutes to go," Skye spoke, reminding me she was still present. "You have three minutes to crack this, or else the timing for you to escape will be too tight."

I grunted in response. My hands reached for the holster on my left leg, and I pulled out a small circular code cracker. The hybrid technology that was a cross between a calculator and a smartphone turned on. I pressed launch on its irregular pads, tightened my hands around the binaural springs, and connected the diaphragm to the device through a small opening on its side. The code-cracker spun, and through the earpiece of the stethoscope, a series of clicking sounds ensued. Each sound displayed a number on the code cracker until it halted altogether.

I hurried to my feet and turned the dial until each number was spun. "Almost there," I mumbled as a fresh wave of excitement bubbled in the pits of my stomach. A series of five clicks followed once the final number was in. After a few moments, a loud thump echoed in the basement, and the door opened.

"One minute and thirty seconds. That's a new record," Skye praised, seemingly impressed. "Be careful of the laser security lights."

Placing the equipment back in my holster, I pulled the metal door further back to get a clear glimpse of the large space. At the center of the safe, fixed above a stand, was a transparent glass. The glass held the pendent upwards as light shades of burgundy illuminated the room.

I pulled out my small digital glasses, placed them over my eyes, and watched as the laser lights came into focus, allowing me to get a clear view of how the lights intersected each other.

"Wish me luck," I mumbled as tiny beads of sweat fell from my forehead. It had been a while since I had cracked a safe or been on a heist, and I was worried I might be a little rusty.

"One minute and thirty seconds to collect the pendant," Skye breathed into the earpiece. "The coast is still clear," she added, her mouse the only thing that could be heard in the background.

I stretched my body and cracked my neck, anticipating the restrained poses I would have to get into. I took a series of steps forward, leaning the weight of the top half of my body forward. I arched my body down into a handstand as I veered forward over a series of laser lights until I reached the center of the room. I slowly curled my body down to the floor and crawled my way to the space closest to the pendant.

"Shit. That was close," I moaned. I leaned my head back, strands of my ponytail almost making contact with one of the lasers.

"Be careful," Skye ordered.

"Always," I whispered, rising fully to my feet, and scanning the remainder of the distance. Raising both of my hands into the air, I held one forward over the light, then proceeded with my leg. Sweat beaded my body, and my black pants and crop top clung to my skin. I repeated the series of steps again, edging closer to the stand.

"Forty seconds," Skye spoke slowly, inhaling and exhaling restrained breaths.

"One more series of lights," I grunted, lowering myself to the floor and using the curve of my back to edge between the gaps.

Finally, I lifted myself from the floor and found myself staring directly into the heart of the pendant.

"Don't lift it," Skye warned. "I think there's another security system embedded under the stand," she noted, and I retracted my hands that had surrounded the case.

I pressed the buttons on the side of my digital glasses, scanning through a series of functions. I settled for the optic blast option, angled my head above the glass, and clicked *initiate.* Red beams of light shot from the glasses, creating an opening at the top. I pressed down on it, and a *plop* sound followed. I deactivated the device and stared down at the pendent through the now opened clearing.

"Come to mommy, you sexy beast," I mumbled with glee and excitement. I reached down to the holster around my hips and pulled out the silver jewelry case. Warmth and electricity trickled through my fingers as I picked up the pendant.

"Oh shit. The security guard has moved. He's heading your way now. Hurry," Skye said. I placed the pendant in the jewelry case and then locked it in the holster around my hips.

"Too late," I noted as a loud blaring sound rang through the space.

"How the hell did that even happen?" she mumbled. "Fuck, the pendant...It seems the case keeping it upright was the third security mechanism in place. Damn it. The security company has been called. You have two minutes to get the hell out before they arrive," she added, her panic palpable.

"What will happen if I run through the laser system now?" I asked, looking through the room, noting there was no quick way out without running directly through the lights.

"The alarm is already off, so it makes no-"

I ran across the space, not waiting for Skye to finish her sentence.

"What if I were going to say something else?" Skye gasped. I removed the glasses, locking them back into place.

"Whatever it is would be better than being caught or locked down there," I replied, continuing ahead. I ran past the safe lock and up the long staircase.

"Be careful. For some reason the guard wants to act as Captain Save-a-Hoe today."

"I hope he knows he's not getting a promotion for getting his ass handed to him," I responded.

"Or getting killed. Some people take their jobs so seriously," Skye exhaled, and I couldn't help but chuckle at the irony.

I pulled out my gun and continued to rush up the stairs, keeping my eyes fixed on the top of the staircase. A few steps later, the guard and I locked eyes, and we both stopped in place.

"Don't do anything stupid." I rolled my eyes, aiming the gun higher. He intuitively reached for the walkie-talkie on his side. I aimed a shot at the device, and it fell to the ground.

"No, you don't, asshole," I ran forward, shooting his left shoulder before he could lunge at me. He fell to the floor with a pained sound as blood soaked his white shirt.

"Doors on the lower floor are now locked. You have to get to the top quickly," Skye said, her keyboard back on overdrive. I ran a few feet ahead and stared up into the center of the building. "Staircase leads to the roof. Quick!"

"You don't have to tell me twice," I answered, pulling an electrical wire rope and aiming it for the railing at the end of the building. The rope landed, securing itself around the railing. I centered my body and pulled on it, letting it hoist me all the way up. Once I reached the top, I released my hold on it and headed for the stairs that would lead me onto the roof.

"Ten seconds," Skye's voice echoed as I continued running up. "Five," she continued as my hands clasped around the door to the roof. I twisted the lock and ran out into the open air. I halted, taking in steady breaths to get my body back in check.

"Stop," a voice called from behind as I edged forward.

"Who the hell is that? They did not appear on the security system." Skye's voice hitched with confusion.

A tall man with an army-cut hairstyle stepped forward from the shadows. His hands were clasped around a small angular device I had never seen before. Reaching for my rifle, I quickly shot him with a silver pistol in the juncture of his thighs. He grunted a slew of curses in response, yet his hand clasped tighter around the device on his hand.

"I don't think he's human," Skye spoke, her voice sounding more distant. "The security team just arrived," she added.

"Just die, asshole," I shouted, shooting him directly in the chest this time.

"Ughh, I really didn't want to spill blood today," I grumbled as his body fell to the floor with a huge thud. "Who the fuck was that?" I asked, scanning the space around me for any other unexpected surprises.

"Someone else knew about the pendant and was out for it tonight," Skye stated as if thinking aloud. "It must be a-"

"Either a vampire, shifter, demon, or a witch," I finished. "Well, this shit just took a turn. I will definitely have to stay low." I ran forward and tugged at the wired rope and pulley. I lunged forward as the rope propelled me forward, back to the initial building on which I stood watch. My body landed on the edge of the roof, and I struggled to propel myself up top.

"Security is almost on the roof. You got less than a minute to disappear," Skye said, the sounds in the background halting.

With renewed strength, I lifted my weight up and propelled my body forward as I jumped to the roof. I ran forward and pulled out the rifle bag I had concealed, strapped it over my back, and ran ahead, jumping onto the other sets of roofs.

"I'm further down. They can't see me from here," I said through hurried breaths. Reaching into my bag, I pulled out an electrical rope wire and scanned the distance between the adjourning buildings.

"I'm clocking out. Catch up in a week?" I asked once a few seconds had passed. This was the final threshold of the job, and there wasn't much Skye could do from here on out.

"Okay. Keep me updated," Skye replied. I removed the device from my ears, turned off the system, and locked them inside the bag.

The night sky towered over me, and the moon bathed my skin in its glow. The air carried a poignant sweetness, filled with the scent of flowers and freshly mowed grass from manicured lawns. The lights of the city gleamed through a kaleidoscope of colors, from the brightest blue to the deepest shade of lavender. I continued my ascent from building to building until the gap between me and the gallery became indistinguishable from the distance. Yet I couldn't shake the eerie and haunting feeling that something was off.

"You're a hard one to follow," a familiar masculine voice said behind me, making the hairs on the back of my neck stand on end. I halted in my next descent, and my hands instinctively reached for the holster around my waist. "You have something I need, Little Hellion." His sultry voice melted on my skin like raw shea butter on a warm summer day.

I slowly and anxiously turned around, finding myself face to face with familiar broad shoulders, regal bone structure, and gray eyes that glimmered under the moonlit sky. The same eyes that had watched me climax and had given me pleasure a week ago.

Our eyes locked, and his demeanor grew rigid. My heart pounded, and my vision narrowed as a sickly coldness spread through my veins.

What the actual fuck?

My eyes immediately scanned the open space around me, trying to make sense of who the hell he was and how he had managed to track me all the way up here.

"Don't come closer," I snarled, taking careful steps back. His eyes darkened, and those familiar gray tints were now covered by red orbs.

This wasn't the leader of some gang. The man before me was a vampire.

Shit. How had I missed that?

"Little Hellion, I won't ask again," he growled, with the same familiarity he had when he held the gun over my body.

I opened my mouth and closed it again as words failed me. Mr. Tall Dark and Handsome's eyes lingered on me, his deep-set gaze piercing like an ice dagger. My skin tingled with unease as time seemed to still, allowing me a better glimpse of the black pristine tailored suit that clung to his body and the hard crease on his forehead that highlighted his evident distaste and distrust of my presence.

"You're a vampire," I whispered, not quite sure whether to be repulsed that the best orgasm of my life had come from one. I removed the gun from my holster, keeping my eyes fixed on the subtlety of his movements.

There was no guidebook about dealing with vampires after blowing them. This was new territory.

"Quick and perceptive," he mocked. His eyes blazed with disgust, his voice filled with mirth.

He stepped forward, and I raised my gun high, my fingers clasped around the trigger. "I said, don't come closer, vampire," I warned, prepared to spill blood.

He took another series of steps, and the warning bells in my head rang, reminding me that regardless of how well I orgasmed over that gun, he was a threat, and his kind would kill me without mercy. He disregarded my warning and took a few more steps toward me. This time, two bullets were the only cautionary words I uttered.

"You shot me?" He blinked twice, his steps faltering. He looked down at the trickle of blood spilling from his shoulder where the bullet had entered. "With silver," he added, with a calm, curious disposition.

"Perceptive," I mocked in the same tone he had used. I took steady steps back, scanning the space for the easiest means of escape.

"You will fucking pay for that, human." He raised his head, his fangs now elongated. He stepped closer, and again I turned my attention to his other shoulder with two rounds of bullets.

"I won't repeat myself, vampire," I sneered, unable to keep the disgust from my voice.

"You-" He faltered, his breathing growing more strained and his steps halting altogether. My eyes turned to the low-rise building to my right, and without waiting for what came next, I jumped, training my attention forward.

I landed on the adjacent roof, almost tripping over my ankle. I kept running forward, reached for my holster, and removed the wolfsbane spray bottle I had hidden within one of its compartments.

Jumping to the next building, I pressed on the nozzle, coating myself in its scent. As I landed on the following roof, his feet made contact with my back, and my body propelled forward.

"Enough," he shouted, his voice echoing the command around me, tugging at the hidden depths of my soul. My steps faltered, and the need to submit to his control pulsed through me. Some sick, depraved part of me wanted to give into it.

This was just lust, raw fucking lust and nothing else.

Before I could comprehend it all, he blurred before me,

knocking the gun out of my hand, and his hand coiled around my throat. "I'm going to have fun, human," he snickered, his rage palpable.

Using the heel of my foot, I kicked his leg, slipped from his hold, and rolled toward the gun. I took hold of the weapon, jumped to my feet, and aimed the gun at his chest.

My eyes fell on the two spots I had shot him, trying to make sense of how he was still standing. I had shot him four times with the highest quality silver. He should have been paralyzed for at least an hour. How was he still moving and breathing with such efficiency?

In all my time as an assassin, no one - vampire, werewolf, or demon - has ever been left unscathed after being shot with silver. Except him...

"I can taste your fear. It tastes delicious," he murmured. He probed my eyes with his and grunted with amusement. "I'm going to enjoy breaking you, Little Hellion."

"Not if I kill you first," I shouted, straining my free hand to reach for a stake in my bag. There was something different about this vampire, and I needed as much ammunition as possible.

The vampire lunged for me, and I stepped back, tilting my hand to stake his heart. His hand gripped mine, twisting my wrist so that the smooth underside was facing upwards. My hold on the dagger tightened and using my other hand, I aimed the gun at his thighs and released two shots.

His hold relented, and I jumped back. "Who are you?" My breath came out in uneven gasps.

He smirked deviously. "Your worst nightmare," he replied. His feet made contact with my chest. I fell back, struggling to keep my balance. Agony and anger pulsed through my body, demanding his head as reckoning.

No man touches me without my consent.

I stepped back, tightening my hold on the dagger and gun. He strode forward, grinning from ear to ear. I aimed the dagger at his heart and hurled it forward. He angled his body away from the weapon with the swiftness of lightning and the sharp calculated moves of a predator.

My assault seemed to annoy him further, and a string of deep animalistic groans erupted from his chest. He blurred before me, his hands wrapped around my neck, and he lifted me up into the air like a sack of flour.

I aimed the gun at his temple with my right hand and held the dagger against his neck with the other. "Who the fuck are you?" His hold on my neck tightened, and I pressed the silver dagger harder into the crook of his neck.

"I could...ask the same...question, asshole," I choked, spurred on by adrenaline.

"The wrong fucking vampire to fuck with, little human," he snarled the words. "Quillian," he added, his gaze probing into mine, almost as if expecting some sort of recognition.

I should have known any man who could give such a mind-blowing orgasm was a devil incarnate.

I shifted the dagger closer to his neck and pressed the gun higher while taking steady breaths through my nose and mouth. His fangs lengthened, and I knew if I didn't break free, I was bound to be vampire dinner.

I raised my knees and kicked him in the groin. He stepped back, laughing and cursing at the same time. I ran to my right and leaped for the adjacent roof, landing on my knees. I grunted, irritation building up inside me to explosive levels.

This is what you get when you sleep with the enemy.

Without looking back, I continued to jump ahead, lunging from one roof to the next. When some time had passed, and no incoming sounds or footsteps could be heard, I stopped, analyzing the space around me.

Sweat trickled down my forehead, and I wiped it with the back of my hand as I struggled to catch my breath. I knew vampires. They were unrelenting when it came to a chase.

I stepped forward to leap for the next building, and an unexpected kick to my right side knocked me hard across the floor.

"Enough, brother," a female voice rang out beside me. I rolled across the floor and jumped to my feet. My eyes fell on a gray-haired female with finger-curled waves, golden brown skin, and light brown eyes that glimmered in the soft moonlight. Quillian blurred beside her, and as I took them in, I could see their evident resemblance.

"The pendant." Her hands reached out like a child waiting to be given candy. I laughed mockingly, stepping back, and aimed the gun at him and the dagger at her.

Fighting one vampire alone was problematic, but two smelled like dead corpses and animal carcasses.

"I told you to wait for me!" Quillian shouted at his sister, and she rolled her eyes with an exaggerated sigh.

"You were taking too long," she huffed in response. I scanned the clearing, knowing that I had to be swift with my next steps in order to get away with the necklace.

"You're human," Quillian's sister noted. Her nose flared, and eyes filled with intrigue.

"You and your brother aren't the smartest, are you?" I replied, and she laughed heartily.

"The humans of this time have changed. How morbidly intriguing," she replied, edging toward me. She lurched forward with a series of kicks and blows. Keeping my eyes trained on her brother, I responded to her every move, blocking and dodging while keeping my hands tightened around my weapons.

Quillian moved behind me, following his sister's assaults. Dodging another blow, I released the final two bullets, aiming one at him, the other at her, and jumped toward the next rooftop.

My mind recalled the pendant in my holster, and Alessia's face flashed in my vision, reminding me of all that was at stake. I could not allow myself to be taken by these monsters. I had too much to lose.

A current of electricity shot through my body, startling me mid-jump, as thick, masculine hands reeled me back. My body shook uncontrollably, and I struggled to regain control.

This was not going to be how I died. Not when I was this close...

The sharp prick of a needle pierced my neck immediately after, and any fight I still had left began to disseminate.

When I looked up, gray eyes with the heart-stopping power of storm clouds and thunder stared down at me, and I knew I was screwed. This vampire was going to be the death of me.

PART II

"Survival first. Revenge later."

6

UNCOMPROMISING SITUATIONS

Meraki

Pain coursed through my body, and my mind spun like a whirlwind, unable to make sense of anything. My throat ached, and my mouth felt as if it was stuffed with some dry substance.

"Fuck my life," I muttered. Stars flashed in my vision as I struggled to open my eyes. After a moment, my eyes adjusted to take in the dimly lit room with cemented floors and walls. The room held no furniture apart from a plastic folding chair and a single bed with the springs from the mattress visible.

An image of the vampire's gray eyes and regal bone structure flashed in my mind, and the remnants of his woody aromatic fragrance that had clung to my skin a week ago now filled my nose again.

His name was Quillian, and he was a vampire.

My mind ran through the series of events that had played out in the club that day. I had listened to my gut. I sprayed him with wolfbane, the one thing that had constantly worked on the others. Yet it had no effect on him.

I stared down at my body sprawled on the cemented floor, noting that I had been stripped bare, left in nothing but my bra and underwear.

What a gentleman.

I shuffled, taking inventory of the fact that my hands were also bound with cuffs, and each attempt I made at tearing myself from their hold was rewarded with an electric shock.

I dragged my body from the floor and rested my head against the bed. Laughter bubbled inside my chest at the absurdity of the predicament I had found myself in. Not only had I managed to get myself kidnapped, I had also lost the most important thing I needed to gain intel about Alessia's killer. Now I was fucked. I needed to find my way out of here and collect the pendant, and something told me it wasn't going to be easy.

I grunted, scanning every crook and corner of the room. There were no windows and, judging by the warmth that filled the space, no cold draft coming from the small ventilation system at top right of the bed. There were no echoing sounds of cars, trees, or the subtle blowing of wind. This was a basement, and the only way out was through the main door. Shit.

A flicker of light at the top right part of the ceiling caught my attention, and the cold realization that I was being watched dawned on me.

This was bad, pretty fucking bad.

In my decade-long career as an assassin, I had encountered countless near-death experiences and had shot, bitten, and even sold my body to the highest bidder to complete a job. Getting kidnapped was not part of any of those experiences. Agents were well versed on what the potential dangers were if you were ever caught on a *sneps* or *sners* job. A slow painful death was the inevitable promise.

That wasn't going to be. I was a cat, one who had lived past her nine lives and still continued to thrive. Dying in the hands of the man who made me orgasm with a gun pointed at my head wasn't how I was going out.

I was left with one option: find a way to escape, recoup, gain intel on my kidnappers, and return to retrieve the pendant. I knew it wasn't going to be easy, but if I played my cards right, it was possible. I just had to analyze whom I was dealing with before fully formulating my plan.

My eyes locked on the camera overhead. Someone was watching this feed and needed me alive. Vampires were not known to take hostages and keeping me locked down here meant only one thing: they were desperate for some type of intel. Or this was a power play, a warning to the Alokari and a statement of force to the supernatural community. Both options would inevitably end in my death, and dying wasn't something I planned to do, especially when there was still money to be made and my sister's killer to hunt.

"You're awake," Quillian announced as the door flung open. He strolled in with the presence of a battalion and the confidence of an impenetrable empire. The lights in the room grew brighter, and my eyes trailed down his body, looking for a weak spot or anything that would give me a clue as to who he was.

His gray sweatpants and white shirt accentuated the refined curves and arches of his muscled body. The top part of his hair was pulled back into a loose bun while the bottom lied loose, resting against his shoulder, water trickling from it.

"I can tell you don't know who I am." He stepped further into the room with a glass of water in hand. His predatory eyes followed the hungry trail of my treacherous eyes, and I scolded myself for ogling.

"Like what you see, Little Hellion?" His deep voice rumbled through the walls of the room in a mocking manner.

"Nothing I haven't seen before," I replied flatly, training my focus on his eyes. I remained seated on the floor, assessing his every move from the tick in his jaw to the subtle flex of his arms and chest when he moved. He was strong, restrained, and calculating. I had to be careful.

"You weren't saying that when you had my cock in your mouth and gagged as you made yourself cum." He arched his brow, letting me know he remembered who I was.

"I'm flattered. Clearly my head game was so good, I permanently etched myself into your psyche," I retorted, spreading my legs wide open for his amusement. His eyes followed the movement, and he made no attempt to deny the statement.

Interesting. I can work with that.

Slowly, he lowered himself into a squatting position and pressed the tip of the plastic cup against my lips. "What are you doing?" I muttered through my teeth. What was his angle here? To poison me or feed me some sort of narcotics that would get me talking?

"If I was going to kill you, you would be dead already," he stated, his eyes locked with mine in a battle of wills. He cocked his head to the side, watching me like I was a safe he was trying to crack. He pressed the cup harder against my lips, and I stared back, refusing to drink it.

He smirked, seemingly entertained by my response. I pulled the cup from my lips, raised it above my head, and poured the full extent of the liquid over me.

Degradation was his kink, his first show of power. If only he knew who he was dealing with.

I fastened my eyes on the trail of water that now beaded on my chest, stomach, thighs, and the gap between my legs. I looked up at him, allowing the water to fall over my mouth. Slowly, I stretched out my tongue, lapping it up in my mouth.

"Hmmm," I murmured. "Who knew water tasted so good?" I continued, moaning while dragging my tongue across my lips. Quillian's gaze followed my mouth, making no attempt to cover his evident pleasure at the wet sounds I was making.

If he thought he was going to intimidate me with that, he had a lot of work to do.

"Like what you see?" I retorted, using the same ammo he had used when he walked in. He leaned back, amusement flashing in his expression, yet there was something else there, something he wanted to keep hidden. "I'm sure you didn't keep me alive to become your permanent cumslut?" I pressed, enjoying his silence and the intensity of the staring match we were engaging in.

"A perceptive cumslut," he answered, derision and jest in his tone. He slowly rose from his vantage point and placed the empty cup beside me.

"As entertained as I was by our little escapade-"

"Escapade?" I arched a brow. "Funny way to refer to someone whose fluids you had smeared all over you, no?"

His eyes fell to my lips. "Keep testing me, mortal, and the next thing you'll experience is me cutting off that tongue of yours. Don't fucking test my patience." His gaze fell on the cuffs. "Now, let's start again. This time, remember your place."

"And what exactly is my place, vampire?" I cocked my head. He reached for the cuffs, and they sparked to life, electricity passing through my spine. My body convulsed.

"That you and your despicable kind are nothing but lying, thieving swines who all deserve to be burned alive. Everything about your existence repulses me," he bit back through gritted teeth. "Why did you steal the pendant?" he asked, composing himself and taking a seat on the chair at the center of the room. He turned it around, ensuring he was directly facing me.

So, this wasn't because he knew about the Alokari or who I was. Now this I can work with.

"It was pretty, and I like pretty things," I answered, lifting my legs to my chest, ensuring they were still widespread and that he could see everything.

He rested his hands against his thighs, and his nostrils flared. "You're not afraid, Little Hellion?" he asked, leaning forward.

"What is it I'm supposed to be afraid of?"

"Me," he stated simply, his voice filled with warning. "Your people have written countless stories about me, and I've feasted on their rotten corpses and partaken in their executions. Oh, Little Hellion, you have a lot to be fearful of. By the time I'm done with you, you'll be a broken image of your former self. You want to keep testing me? You want to feel the wrath of what I'm capable of?" He leaned back, his hands folded into fists.

"I'll repeat my question again. Why did you steal the necklace? And who sent you?" he asked, his right foot lightly tapping the floor as if he was holding himself back.

If he was also chasing the pendant that evening, then it meant his intent was to steal it, and I had got there just before him. This interrogation and my kidnapping were his way of cleaning up any loose ends, his way of finding out who else knew about it.

"Now I'm starting to think our encounter wasn't a coincidence?" His right foot continued with the subtle tapping.

I laughed out loud. "That ego of yours is huge. In case you don't remember, you're the one who sought me out on the dance floor. You locked yourself in my restroom after I had gotten away from you. You're also the one who chased me over several roofs. Some could say I'm the unfortunate victim here."

"So let me get this straight. You're just an innocent human at the wrong place, wrong time?" He moved his chair forward, the force behind it threatening. "An innocent human who was able to break into a state-of-the-art, security-protected gallery and steal an important object. The existence of which many are not even aware." He scooted closer. "The same human who's aware of the existence of my kind? Should I continue?" he stated, a low rumbling emitting from his chest as he crossed him arms.

"This was my attempt at reasoning with you. I should have known better. Your kind only responds well to pain." He rose from the chair and stood to his full glory. "You're evidently hiding something, little human, and I'm more than willing to break your bones, gouge out your eyes, and leave the remains of your carcass spread out on the streets of Jersey Hill as a warning to your kind and whoever the fuck sent you." His fangs elongated, and he blurred before me, that predatory gleam in his eyes.

"I need a name. Now!" he snarled.

"Is that supposed to scare me?" I asked, closing my legs, realizing appealing to his baser instincts wasn't going to be my way out of here. "Names should only be exchanged between friends or mutual acquaintances. Right now, we are neither," I answered, my eyes following the curve of his fangs.

He sneered with disdain and edged toward me, lifting my body into the air as he slammed it against the wall. The full force of the impact shook the walls, and the cement behind me chafed against my skin.

I kicked and kneed the lower half of his body, but he blocked the movement by lifting me higher and placing his thighs as a barrier against my knees. With one hand, he pinned me against the wall with my hands above my head. He used his other hand to raise my chin, blocking my view of everything around me until his face became my sole focus.

Wrong move.

His pupils dilated. His hold tightened and the air in the room became stifling. "That compulsion shit isn't going to work on me," I replied, making no attempt to keep the smugness out of my voice.

"Oh?" he answered coyly, and after a few moments of tense silence, the weight of my words played against his features.

"Not so smug now, are we?" I fought against his hold.

"There's more than one way to get what I want, Little Hellion," he chuckled lightly. My body stilled, anticipating his next move.

He slowly released his hold on my chin and moved his hand down my neck, throat, finally resting it on my chest. His nails elongated, and he smiled, dragging his index finger from my chest to my neck.

His nail dug into the flesh of my skin, and blood trickled down my chest. I flinched at the feeling, and he saw this as an invitation to dig deeper, scraping the nail of his forefinger over the spot again, drawing out more blood.

I felt nothing.

Pain was something I had become accustomed to. It was now the fabric of my being. Our training within the Alokari included a series of interrogation methods to ensure we became resistant to them. But I knew that in order to survive and break free from here, I would have to pretend.

"This side of your neck and throat" - he slowly dragged his fingernail further down - "just above where your Adam's apple would be. This contains your carotid artery and jugular vein." He slowly massaged that spot with his thumb. "If I were to cut or press just deep enough, you would bleed to death." His eyes glimmered at the prospect. "You will first become unconscious and inevitably die within five to fifteen seconds," he added casually. "Isn't the human body such an interesting vessel?" he said, the threat evident in his voice. His fingers rose again, following the initial cut.

He pressed his palm against the trickle of blood that now trailed down my neck and soaked his shirt. His eyes glistened a deep shade of amber as he trailed the movement of the blood. Raising his blood-soaked finger, he lifted it close to his mouth, then smeared it over my face.

"Perhaps I should keep you as more than my cumslut? Bloodslut would be more promising, don't you think?" he laughed, his face inches from mine.

"Fuck yo-" My words were cut short as he tilted my head, dug his head into my neck, and bit down.

My body stilled, and laughter bubbled in my chest. He pulled back, his lips covered with my blood. His expression morphed through a series of emotions from intrigue to shock, then irritation.

"My blood isn't to your satisfaction, vampire?" I questioned, knowing that he would now be feeling the full extent of the wolfsbane coursing through his body.

His jaw tightened, and his hold on me relented slightly. "You were found with a series of weapons made from silver. Now your blood..." He slowly licked the blood on his lips. "...tastes like wolfsbane," he added, his eyes widening.

"Who the fuck are you?" he asked, his hand moving to my neck. His attention briefly turned to the camera as he waited for a response. "Only a few people know of my people's weakness and would possess such weapons. Assassins or artifact thieves, for example," he continued, his hold tightening. "Which one are you?"

My gaze flickered over his body, wondering why and how he was still standing. Wolfbane was guaranteed kryptonite for his kind.

"It will take more than wolfsbane to get me, human," he growled, his hold on my throat now unbearable. "Still not talking?" he arched his brow and squeezed tighter. Tears streaked down my cheeks as I struggled to breathe.

"Still...no...response...to...why...I'm...still...alive." I gasped, struggling to formulate the words. I wasn't dealing with a regular vampire and showing any form of weakness right now would be my ultimate undoing.

His gaze went to the camera again, and he pulled me from the wall and slammed me back into it with extreme force. Warmth tingled through my body, and the room slowed. Blood trickled from my head and down my shoulders, encapsulating everything around me.

"I was hoping you would take the hand I gave you, little human. I see you're not one to be reasoned with," he laughed, his gaze following the trail of blood. He slowly loosened his hold on my neck and took several steps back. I fell on my ass, gasping and panting for breath.

"If you thought the wolfsbane would have affected me, then it's fair for me to conclude you don't know who I am." He raised his hand in a dismissive manner, a subtle smirk forming on the corners of his lips. "But then again, you're what? Eighteen years old?" He lowered himself to the floor.

"Are you complementing me? Or is that your way of letting

me know you're into age play?" I raised my head, and my gaze locked with his in a questioning manner.

"I like my women more seasoned," he laughed, the words echoing across the space. He rose and leisurely began to remove his shirt. As it fell to the floor, two large midnight wings unfolded from his back, covering the expanse of the room. My breath hitched as my eyes fell on the phoenix tattoo that covered his right arm and chest.

The door to the room flung open. There stood his sister, her arms crossed against her chest.

"Q, we have a family meeting," she spoke, her eyes falling from her brother to me. "And what did we say about the mess? We just got back and the last thing we need..." She released a frustrated breath. "Honestly, why do the men in this family not listen to simple instructions? Enzo and Silas are waiting," she added, hesitantly stepping back from the door. She stopped and turned to face me, her eyes following the trail of blood that covered my body.

"Don't kill her. I think I like this one," she spoke softly, the deep brown of her eyes softening. She walked away, the echo of her heels following behind her. My attention turned back to Quillian, who was using his shirt to clean the blood that now covered his arms. My eyes continued to follow the tattoo as a memory surfaced in my mind.

"Kingsley," I uttered the family name that was well known within the Alokari and spoken of with fright by other supernaturals. Quillian stilled, and subtle laughter followed in its wake.

"Perceptive, Little Hellion," he replied as he walked out, and the door closed behind him.

The Kingsleys were the head of Kinavari in Esneoh. They were infamous for being cold, callous, and ruthless to those who crossed their path. And I had just declared myself their enemy by stealing from them.

Getting out of here wasn't going to be as easy as I anticipated.

7

A NEW DAY, A NEW DAWN

Quillian

"Quillian," Enzo called, his face beaming with that usual smile that reached his eyes. I parked my motorcycle by a weeping willow a few feet from the entryway of the laboratory. The space was covered with large sprouts of shrubs, trees, and plants. The place was so hidden that unless someone was actively looking for it, they would miss it altogether.

"Enzo!" I announced as I removed my helmet, and the scent of wildflowers, herbs, and fruits filled my nose.

"You don't know how strange it feels to say your name again after so long, brother." He took a few steps toward me. "Come here," he said teasingly, pulling me into a hug.

"I see time has softened you," I laughed, tapping his back with my hand. He smiled, yet there was something within its depth that spoke of untold stories and darkness I was too familiar with.

"Something like that," he answered, his body growing rigid.

"I see there's a lot you and I still need to catch up on." I arched a brow, and he nodded. Enzo and I had grown acquainted millennia ago. He had initially been my older brother Alaric's acquaintance. However, as time passed, he soon became an integral part of our family. The same family that had saved Brielle, Silas, and me from our imprisonment.

"Where's Silas?" he asked, his attention turning to the expanse around us.

I shook my head, tightening my hold on my helmet.

"My baby brother is up to his old womanizing ways again. It seems a millennium without pussy has turned him into a bigger fool than before." Enzo laughed, clutching his stomach in the process.

"I wonder where he picked that up from?" He muttered under his breath once he was able to conduct himself again.

"Enzo..." I warned.

"What?" He stretched out his hands innocently. "I never said any names. Why would you think it's you?"

"Well, it's certainly not Alaric-"

"I think we were all convinced he was either asexual or gay for a long time. He barely looked at or entertained any woman. He was more focused on his scientific studies..." He trailed off, a warm smile filling his face. The familiar smile that usually adorned the face of those who had encountered him and grew to respect him. Alaric was everything I wasn't.

"And it's certainly not Brielle. For all I know she could be married or having wild illustrious affairs. She's a vault of impenetrable secrets."

"Nothing has changed then. I see you waste no time." He turned his attention on my motorcycle. He lowered himself to study the chassis and cockpit.

"It's been a long while since I've ridden. Cars still don't give me the same thrill," I answered, lightly tapping the bike's fender. "Too long," I added as images of the cave I had been trapped in flashed in my vision.

It had been a millennium since I had ridden on the streets of

Kinavari, even longer since I felt the warmth of the sun against my skin or the wind blowing through my hair. Everything around me now was familiar yet foreign and new all at once.

"She's beautiful," Enzo added, running his hands over the matte black exterior.

"*He,* brother. *She* implies trouble, and I've had enough in my lifetime," I replied, the words bitter on my tongue. Enzo laughed heartily and stood back up, our shoulders at an equal height.

"I heard you captured such a *she*?" He motioned for me to follow him through the entryway of the laboratory. "Perhaps I'm not the only one time has softened?" He raised a brow.

"Contrary." I followed beside him.

"Is that so?" he pressed, leading me through the long clinical passageway that had now been stripped of the blood that painted its walls the last time we had all been here.

"Everything else remained the same," he pointed out when he caught my attention fixed on the walls for too long. "You kept her alive," he noted, and I stepped ahead of him, not wanting to entertain the conversation for too long. How was I to explain that, as much as I hated their kind, the little hellion intrigued me the night my ears caught wind of her high-pitched laughter over the bass of the music? My eyes conspired against me when they caught sight of the curve of her body and the swell of her breast. Worse, after watching her respond to my depravity that evening, my dick has not been at peace.

She was a depraved itch I needed to scratch, and the idea of breaking and mastering her like a wild mare was one that both spurred me on and kept her alive. For now. A millennium of imprisonment meant I could at least feed into my desires, choke her, and drain her of her blood without repercussions.

This was my condemnation. The humans had taken a lot from my family and removing one more from their world wouldn't make much of a difference.

Enzo released a frustrated breath, and I ignored it, continuing ahead. This wasn't a new conversation. Brielle and Silas, who had been there with me that night, had argued relentlessly when I had picked up her frail body and carried it into our car.

We had one simple rule we abided by. Kill first, ask questions later. And on that one night during our first week back, I had already broken it.

"She could be useful," I stated, not sure if I even believed it myself.

"You brought her through the walls, Quillian." He stopped, not picking up on my cues that this wasn't a negotiable topic. Or maybe it had been too long, and I had lost the ability to make myself clear.

"And?"

"You've exposed her to this world. She is now bound here... For life. You know the rules and laws that govern this land-"

"And what is it you think I should have done? I thought you of all people would have appreciated that I didn't just kill her and splatter her blood on the roof of that building?" I stopped, turning to face him, unable to keep my irritation at bay.

"I said to lay low, not bring a human into Esneoh, especially not to Kinavari. What happens if-"

"Nothing will happen. She is my prisoner and will remain so." I raised my hand dismissively, motioning for us to continue.

"I will call you out if I think you're making a stupid decision," he responded, his voice rising in pitch.

"Enzo-"

"We agreed to stay low. This isn't low. I didn't expect you to kill her. You were supposed to retrieve the pendant. You could have simply sedated her. Left her on the roof but-"

"But she knew too much. She entered that building, and I watched as she bypassed every security system and stole the pendant. She knows something, and I couldn't just let her go like that," I replied, running my hands through my hair, frustration gnawing through my skin.

"And that's all?" His brows arched in an accusatory manner.

"What does that mean, brother?" I whisper-shouted, seeing movement in the main room ahead.

"It means that I saw you that evening. I was there with you, remember? She looks like the same girl from that club!" he shouted, stepping toward me.

"And?" I replied, no longer caring how loud I was.

"And you can honestly say it has nothing to do with-"

I laughed mockingly. "She's human," I snarled.

"Q..." He trailed off, pacing the space between us.

"Don't insult my intelligence. I still hate their kind, especially after what happened to Alaric." I crossed my arms over my chest. "We underestimated the last human female in our midst and look what happened. I won't do that again. If my suspicions about her are wrong, I'll simply wring her neck and bring an end to her mundane life." I continued walking ahead, not waiting for him to catch up.

"And in the worst-case scenario, I have you to help clean up the mess. Nothing to worry about then," I concluded, wanting to diffuse the mounting tension between us. I hated arguing with family, especially with Enzo.

"That's what I'm afraid of," he mumbled and shook his head as he followed me ahead.

"How's the house? To your satisfaction?" he asked after silence had lingered between us.

"You maintained it all this time?" I had been surprised when I returned and had found the estate still in its former glory.

"I knew I would find you all inevitably," he muttered, raising his hand to the glass security bar at the front of the door. He entered a series of numbers, then motioned for me to place my thumb on the bar. "Access has been reinstated. I've done the same for Brielle and Silas," he added. The door opened, followed by a low ticking sound. When the door closed, the sound stopped.

"No one else has access to this place or even knows where it is. I've also had the witch Hera spell it so that only those with access can see it," he noted, pointing to another glass room to the far right where the outline of a woman with a head of thick, curly hair could be seen.

My gaze turned to the office space beside that room as flashes of Alaric's lifeless body replayed in my mind. "Hera is already here," Enzo announced, pulling me from the dark path my mind was heading down.

The witch turned toward us, her face twisted into the scowl that awaited me after she had freed me from the cave. "How do we know she can be trusted?" I spoke, making no effort to lower my voice.

"I can hear you," she called out, turning and rolling her eyes.

"Then you should know I don't trust you or your kind," I pointed out, drawing closer to the room.

"I don't need you to trust or like me. I just need you to stick to the bargain we agreed on," she answered, her hands resting against her hips.

"And what exactly is it that you require from me? Because last I checked, there was no clear answer regarding it." I walked through the door and stepped closer to the center of the room where she had moved to. Enzo closed the door behind us and silently trailed behind.

"I'm still working on that. But a time will come when I might need your support or service. When I call, I expect that you'll answer...All of you," she said as our attention turned to the pendant before her, sitting on top of a high table. "And you're welcome by the way. I saved your ass from centuries of damnation. Most people say thanks," she muttered under her breath.

"Thanks would imply that you did me a service or a favor from the kindness of your heart. We know witches are incapable of that."

"Look at the pot calling the kettle black," she laughed mockingly, and the sound of it irked my skin. I turned to face her, took hold of her hand, and twisted her wrist.

"I don't like disrespect, witch," I bit back, pressing hard enough on her wrist to remind her who had the upper hand. "Do not for one minute overestimate your importance. You're dispensable, and don't you dare forget it."

She raised her hand in retaliation, murmuring incantations under her breath. "Let's all calm down," Enzo jumped in, separating us with haste. Her magic strummed against my skin as a reminder of her power.

"Let's all remember this is a mutually beneficial relationship. We need each other," he shot, training his attention on me.

"If I remember correctly, Enzo bargained with me. He sought me. I didn't go looking for you or your kind." Hera raised her voice, the surge of power growing like a gust of wind. "You and your siblings' bodies lied immobile in caves across the human realm. I brought you back with the same witch magic you so despise," she shouted, pounding her hand against her chest. "I did! And you will respect me," she continued, her palm raised, with currents of her magic flowing through it.

"Fascinating," I grunted, disregarding her presence.

"She is correct, Q. This is a mutually beneficial relationship, and we are indebted to her for her help," Enzo added, his frown deepening.

"We may need her, but trust isn't just given. It is earned. And I don't trust her," I say, stepping back to properly analyze the witch before me.

She had balls, I would give her that. Others of her kind who had previously faced me were not so vocal. They also didn't meet promising ends. And if the circumstances now were different, I would have bled her dry for even having the gall to raise her hand at me.

"Continue, witch." I motioned to the pendant, ignoring all the other theatrics that had just occurred. My only focus right now was uncovering its secrets, nothing else.

Enzo's attention strained between me and her, his prolonged silence an indication of his growing frustration.

"Relax. I know what's at stake," Hera stated as she raised her hand and started chanting a series of spells. The pendant shook and illuminated the room with specks of gold and burgundy. "Interesting," she mumbled, reaching forward and running her hands over the intricacies of the flower that decorated it.

"What is it?" I probed when she had not uttered a word for a while.

"Blood," she called, motioning for me to give her my hand.

I laughed, my face a carefully masked warning. "Do you think I'm stupid enough to just give you my blood? Especially knowing what your kind can do with it?"

It was no secret that access to our blood allowed witches to perform dark spells that were beyond the remit of their white magic.

The witches from Aldrata had long been a thorn in my side, and each encounter we had with them for decades had always led to some sort of betrayal. They could not be trusted, and I refused to start doing so now.

"Do you need help figuring out what this is, or do you want to keep fighting by yourself? Because I have places to be and disappearing for this long will only draw suspicion from my coven," she answered, her voice tinged with irritation. She turned her attention to Enzo as if beckoning him to interfere.

"Q-"

"Are you not tired of fighting? And this?" She motioned to the space around us. "I'm extending an olive branch. I went against my coven and used most of my magic to free you. I'm also sneaking around doing this shit." She pointed at the table.

"For a benefit..." I trailed off, my arms over my chest, assessing her.

"And?" She stepped toward me, unwavering.

"And?" I snarled, reflecting her movements.

"Why is it different when you do it?" she asked, the venom in her words unable to disguise the evident hurt.

"Excuse me?"

"Why is it that when women adhere to the same standards that men follow, it suddenly becomes a problem? When a man does it, it's seen as a symbol of strength and power. Heavens forbid a woman think for herself or try and build allegiances and ties that better her standing. She is then called untrustworthy, a traitor, a conniving bitch! Everything but the name given to her at birth."

"You and I both know that's not what I'm talking about! Your people and I have had a long history of betrayals-"

"Is it not? Because since you've been here you've called me everything but my name," she interrupted, her voice rising in pitch. "Hera. Hera is my name, and you will respect it," she added boldly.

I smiled, stepping back and taking her in fully for the first time since we had arrived. If anything, the witch was spirited, a quality she would need later when I was wringing her neck. She was bound to cross the pact we had made. This time, unlike in the past, I would ensure that I threw the first blow.

"Carry on, witch." I raised my hand toward her. "Betray me, and I will feast on your corpse myself," I warned, stepping forward and laying my hand in her palm.

"Yeah, you'll burn it and hang my head for all to see. What else is new?" She took hold of my hand, lifted a small knife beside the table, and with its blade, sliced through my wrist. A small smirk formed on her lips when I winced, and something told me she enjoyed delivering that small bit of pain.

Fucking witches.

"On the pendant." She motioned for me to step closer and drip my blood over. As I did so, a light glimmered from its core, grew in intensity, then dwindled after a short while.

"Well?" Enzo asked, finally stepping forward.

"It is the necklace that held you and your siblings bound," she announced, wiping my blood from the knife on a cloth beside her.

"What is it?" I asked, knowing its existence was going to be a problem. A big fucking problem.

"It's imbued with some type of magic," she answered,

running her hands over the pendant. "I've never seen anything like it before," she added. "Your blood or some type of blood maintains it," she added.

"So, something created by one of your kind then?" I spoke, unable to help myself.

"Maybe, but I'm not sure. I can't trace the cords of the magic," she answered, sincerity in her tone. She turned toward me, her face a mask of indifference. "Were you fed blood during your imprisonment?"

"Why the sudden questions, Hera?" The skin of my hand healed itself, and I pulled it back.

"Because when I freed you and your siblings, you were still conscious. If you hadn't fed in millennia, your bodies should have been corpses, and it would have taken a lot of blood and feeding to get you back to this state." She pointed at my face and body.

Enzo edged closer to her, watching, and waiting for my response. He had tried prying my experience out of me in the week and a half since I had been back, but I refused to divulge more than I needed to. The silence wasn't a place I wanted to revisit.

"Yes," I spoke after a moment of hesitation.

"Did you see them?" Enzo blurred before me, his rage tangible. I shook my head hesitantly and turned my attention back to Hera.

"I never saw anyone. But I concluded the magic was imbued with blood. I occasionally would suddenly feel energized, and remnants of a distinct taste of blood would flow through me," I replied, recounting the sweet and peculiarly aromatic aftertaste that lingered afterward.

"You think that blood had a role in it?" Enzo asked, moving to stand beside me.

"Yes...." she replied, her gaze darting back and forth between me and Enzo. My eyes and ears trained on the subtle beat of her heart to the restraint of her movements, confirming she had no direct role in my family's imprisonment. "It's that blood that empowers the magic in this pendant."

"What blood would that be?" Enzo asked, the question running laps in my mind.

"I'm not sure, but there are still remnants of it in your system, Quillian." She stepped to her right, taking out a small vial. "Your brother Silas has agreed to help me study it further. Under his watchful eye of course," she said through an exasperated sigh.

I bite down on my wrist and drain the blood into the container. "Thank you," she mumbled, sealing it once it had filled to the brim. "If anything comes up, I know where to find you," she added, turning her back to us in a dismissive manner.

Enzo motioned for me to follow him to the next room, the same one I had intended to avoid today. Hesitantly, I stepped into it, and Alaric's woody scent clung to me.

"I didn't move anything. Apart from cleaning up the mess from that day..." Enzo said hesitantly. I stepped forward, flooded with images of our family and a few of Alaric at the various institutions he had studied at over his lifetime.

Alaric had always been the most studious of us all. He was always fascinated with life science, from raising questions about how the universe around us was organized to studying insects, plants, and animals. That same curiosity and thirst for knowledge turned him manic and blind to everything else around him.

While my edges were rugged and steeped in rage and bloodshed, Alaric was the very essence of life itself. Calm, patient, collected. People gravitated toward him and drew strength from his words.

I strolled to the center of the room, halting by a centerpiece image of Alaric with his arms wrapped into Vera's deep red hair. Their eyes were interlocked, their faces a few inches from one another. If I didn't know she was a fraud, a trickster sent to assassinate him, the image would have fooled me into believing that she was in love with him. Vera had fooled us all.

"Any update on her and her family?" I took hold of the picture, gripping it tightly as rage boiled inside me.

"Records show she was an orphan," Enzo answered.

"No friends? Living relatives?" I turned to him, desperately trying to hold back my rage. I had sworn on the day of his death that I would destroy the existence of everything and everyone she loved. Friends, family, lovers. I was going to wipe out the entirety of her bloodline. I needed to make them all bleed as my brother did when he took his final breath.

"I had a few leads, but that came to a halt," he stated. I released my hold on the picture.

"Let's get back on it. I also need intel on the human I brought back," I added, walking out of the room, and heading for the door. I had seen enough for one day. It was time to go back to the hellion under my basement and release some of my pent-up anger.

It was unfortunate the only woman whose cunt I wanted to sink myself into after a millennium was human, the same beings that I had grown to hate. Just my fucking luck.

8

MY ENEMY'S APPROVAL

M*eraki*

"Vampires are the bane of my existence," I cursed under my breath as heavy metal music shook the walls of the basement. Again.

Since my last introduction to Quillian and his sister, it had played nonstop. Every ten minutes or so, the music would halt, allowing me a small moment of respite.

The message was clear. Quillian wanted me exhausted, hungry, and docile, unable to tell the difference between day, night, or reality. It was the oldest torture technique in the book. Fortunately for me, I was used to running on two to three hours of sleep on a good day. My dreams were usually plagued by nightmares. You didn't kill like I did on a weekly basis and not feel its toll on your body and mind. The money made up for it, though.

I stood from the bed, stretching out my legs, and raised my cuffed hands in a meek attempt to release the tension on my shoulders. From the brief exchanges I had overheard between brother and sister outside of my cell, I had deduced this was my third day here.

Three days without showering and being left in nothing but my bra and underwear. Not even a piece of fabric to cover myself with. My only saving grace was that the small basement room had terrible ventilation, which allowed it to carry enough heat to keep me warm.

It also meant three days of no upkeep or care for the red shoulder-length wig on my head. My body itched with discomfort, and I was somewhat grateful there were no mirrors in this room. The last thing I needed to see was the state of my skin, especially as I was someone big on a clean and healthy skincare routine.

I began pacing the room, closing my mind to the blaring sound of metal music. Instead, I focused on my breathing, allowing my thoughts to drift off to the little information I knew about the Kingsleys' disappearance from the face of the earth. It had first started with the rumors of their eldest sibling Alaric's death. Within a short number of weeks, the whole family disappeared. The Alokari's intel regarding the matter was limited, as they had come into existence decades after them.

The Kingsleys were known to be guarded and secretive, keeping themselves. They were notorious for having a kill-first ask-questions-later approach. The fact I was still alive was a miracle in itself. It also meant I was at an advantage, one I could utilize if I played my cards right.

There had been no update about the re-emergence in the Alokari systems, which meant that their re-emergence was recent. Perhaps as recent as the first night I had bumped into him at the club. If that was the case, then did their arrival have something to do with the pendant?

Since there had been no mention of the Alokari, I knew I wasn't being kept alive to extract information about them. This gap in their knowledge was one that could work in my best interest. It was easier to survive and get out of here alive under the guise of an art thief than that of an assassin.

I needed a good and convincing story about who I was and why I stole the necklace. The story needed to be believable enough to sow a seed of doubt about whether I was more valuable dead or alive.

The music stopped, and approaching footsteps caught my attention. The door flung open and Quillian strolled in, this time decked out in similar attire to what I had seen him in when we first met. A glimmer of a smile tugged at the corners of his lips, and unease settled down my spine.

"Human," he said, the word like a slur. He took several steps toward me, watching my reaction with evident disdain. It was one thing to hate me for stealing that necklace, but something told me Quillian's loathing ran deeper than that.

"Vampire." I turned to fully face him, now more aware of my nakedness.

"Still not talking?" he queried, his brows arching. I made no effort to respond, letting my emotions slip through me like a wave. "I'm going to enjoy breaking you, watching you plead as the life is choked out of your lying, scheming mouth. Maybe if you're lucky, you might get the privilege of having my cock buried in your mouth as I do so," he snickered, taking another series of steps forward.

"I'd rather fuck a ten-foot pole than get that thing anywhere near me again," I snickered, taking a few steps back to get a better view of the brightly lit cemented hallway.

"Is that so? Then I'm just going to have to ensure I fuck you with such said pole to remind you of this exact moment." He continued with slow, steady steps. "I'll give you one more chance to confess, and maybe - just maybe - I won't rip your body to shreds and drain you of that shit that runs through your blood."

"I have nothing to tell-"

"Who sent you to retrieve that necklace? And what did they want with it?" he pressed, blurring in front of me. His scent clouded my senses, sending my mind into a tailspin. "Fuck yo-" My body grew limp, and the room began to spin. The asshole had injected me with something.

"There, there, Little Hellion. Since I can't bend you to my will, I had to get creative. I've injected you with something that will loosen you up a bit, and hopefully with enough persuasion your tongue will start wagging." His voice echoed all around me as the strength in my legs wavered and my body limped to the side. He reached for me before I could fall, lifting me to his chest and wrapping his hands around my body. The room moved and everything turned into a blur of images and sounds until his slow beating heart became the loudest sound in the room. "We are going to play a game, and the game won't stop until I've washed all the lies and deceit from your tongue."

"You...are...scum..." I slurred, unable to jerk myself out of his hold and take control of my body.

"Bring it in, Silas," he said, turning to face the door. The outline of a man with a similar build appeared. Silas stepped inside with a blue tarp in his hand.

"You were...on the...roof," I struggled as his face slowly came into focus. He nodded solemnly, his movements slow and tinged with a sense of apology.

"Are you sure this is necessary, brother?" He exhaled a frustrated breath. "We should have never brought her here."

"Don't fucking question me, Silas. She shot you with a silver bullet on that roof, meaning she knew about our kind. She also saw mine and Brielle's faces. The last thing we need is word out about us before we get the chance to do so ourselves," he replied with evident condescension in his voice.

Silas spread the blue tarp out. Quillian strode forward, slightly loosening his hold on me. He threw me into the air, and I found myself atop the tarp, which had now been fixed to the wall facing the bed.

I closed my eyes and focused on memories of Alessia as probing hands bound my feet. The rough hairs of the rope made my skin itch with discomfort. When I opened my eyes, Quillian stood over me and poured ice cold water over my body. Fire danced through my skin, and I bit down on my lip, gasping from the initial shock.

"Q-" Silas spoke, his voice almost pleading.

"Leave!" Quillian replied, a carefully concealed warning in his voice. Silas flinched at his reproach and stepped back, his movements filled with unspoken anger.

"This is my problem with you! You always take it too far," Silas shouted. "Alaric-"

"Is dead, and I'm here, still cleaning up his mess!" Quillian responded, stepping toward his brother as they began their argument.

I watched with fascination, the room and everything around me spinning. Laughter bubbled up inside me as I realized getting out of here would take some work, but the answer lay in the hands of the other Kingsley siblings. Brielle had already reproached her brother about keeping me alive, and Silas was evidently the guilt-ridden sibling with a conscience. That conscience was a weakness I could prey on.

After some screaming back and forth, Silas left the room, slamming the door behind him. Quillian and I were left alone, and a deafening silence followed.

"Your brother, Silas, seems...nice," I mocked, struggling to keep my gaze focused.

"Don't ever have my family's name in your mouth," he warned, looming over my head, a gentle reminder that my estimations about my escape were accurate. The only way to tame him and find my way out of here would be through said family.

"Who sent you, Little Hellion?" he growled as more ice-cold water fell over me. My teeth grinded against each other as the cold slowly began to numb my fingers.

"No one sent me," I lied, the rest of my body slowly becoming numb. Another bucket fell over me, a a mixture between ice and water. Quillian didn't stop there. He continued filling the tarp until goosebumps covered my body and my breathing began to slow.

"Now, be a good girl, and tell me what I want to hear," he spoke as he strolled across the room and stood over my feet. "This can all go away very easily," he continued, his hands playfully running through the ice that now covered my body.

"Are you an assassin?" he finally asked, and when I gave no response, he laughed and sauntered toward my head.

"Are you an assassin?" he asked again. His elongated fingernails dug into my neck, reminding me of his threat a few days before.

I shook my head.

"Good girl," he cooed as if this information had greatly impressed him. My body quivered at the sound of those words, and I held back my reaction to it. "Not an assassin. The plot thickens," he murmured. More ice fell over me until the tarp began to make quiet creaking sounds.

My heart pulsed erratically, and I could no longer feel the lower part of my body. "Are you an assassin?" he asked again, his breath looming close to my face.

"No," I snarled the response, needing it to be as believable as possible.

"Even now you still carry that fire," he laughed.

"I'm not...who you think...I am," I continued, more impressed by my own performance. The cold had now rendered me immobile, and I felt myself slipping out of consciousness.

"Then who sent you? The Invisible Suns? The Grim Hold?" he pushed, and I waited, anticipating his mention of the Alokari. But nothing came.

Just where I wanted him.

The Grim Hold was a hunter's guild infamous outside of Jersey Hill for maintaining order and killing vampires and demons alike. The Invisible Sun, on the other hand, was a guild infamous for stealing rare artifacts from the supernatural community to sell on the black market.

Now was my time.

"All you have to do is tell me who and this can all go away, Little Hellion," he whispered, scraping his hand against the lace of my wig. My mouth remained closed, which seemed to irritate him even more. He reached forward, adding more ice to the mix, this time using it to cover my neck until all that remained was my face.

Where was all this ice coming from?

"Speak human, or your death is impending," he murmured as my eyes twitched and my muscles began to contract on their own.

"I steal," I mumbled, taking large gulps of air.

"And?" His hold on my hair tightened.

"And that's all you'll ever get. Loyalty is everything...in what I do...I'd rather die...than sell out-" I hissed as the echoing sound of something creaking caught my attention. "If you're going...to kill me, do so," I replied, my breathing coming out heavy and faint. Quillian continued to tower over me, his expression blurring between rage, irritation, and what could be misinterpreted as admiration.

I was losing it.

The creaking sound intensified, and the hooks that kept the tarp situated gave in. My body hit the floor, and I blacked out.

"Up," an unfamiliar voice commanded, jolting my body upright from the bed. My eyes scanned the room and fell on a slim, white-haired vampire pulling in thick twisted ropes, a hose, and an iron.

"Who are you?" I croaked, unable to utter the words. My throat burned as if I had been awake and screaming throughout the night.

"Call me Ryder," he announced, halting at the center of the room and placing the chair there. I peered down at myself on the bed, finding a large blanket had been placed over me. Right now, I was unsure if it was Quillian's or Silas' doing. Instinct told me it was more likely to be the younger brother.

I pulled back the cover, realizing I was now clothed. A large white shirt that reached my thighs covered me. It smelled distinctively like Quillian. The wounds on my body from before had also disappeared.

Perhaps the vampire asshole had a conscience, or he was keeping me alive on the merit of obtaining more information.

My plan worked.

I needed to offer him something that would quench his thirst until I found a way to get into Brielle and Silas' ears. I smiled down at the shirt, realizing that while I was knocked out, he had removed my cuffs, clothed me, and covered me with a blanket when he could have simply left me for dead. There was still hope. Ryder's presence, however, told me the piece of information I gave him wasn't enough.

"And you are?" I replied, trying to shift from the bed. The rope around my feet had not been removed.

"Your worst nightmare," he replied as darkness danced in his eyes. I shifted back, bile burning at the back of my throat. Though it had been days since I had eaten, I couldn't shake the nausea that came with Ryder's presence or the lingering scent of copper that followed in its wake.

Was water the latest craze in the vampire torture manual?

Ryder pulled the hose and placed it beside the chair, turning his focus on me.

Quillian was sending someone else to do his dirty work. I should have known pretty boys didn't get their hands dirty. They paid others to do it for them. How disappointing.

His attention turned to where the camera lay, and with a quick nod, he proceeded further into the room. Quillian was watching, that much was blatantly obvious.

Ryder edged toward me, and the lingering scent of liquor and rotten meat made my nose burn. He reached into his pocket and released a blade, brandishing the weapon over me like it was some sort of prized possession.

"It's been a while since I've had some fun. I'm going to take my time with you." He smiled, his face a blur of indifference. "Maybe I should start by marking this pretty face of yours. Women will usually beg for mercy and surrender when their greatest asset comes into play," he snickered, his foul breath too close to my face.

"Can you do that over there?" I motioned to the far end of the room. "I can't breathe with you beside me," I added, knowing that comment would come with some sort of consequence, but I was past caring. I had gone days without food, water, or sunlight, and my mind was reeling.

"That you will regret, I'll ensure you do," he stated angrily, brandishing the knife over my chest. He laughed heartily and stepped back, dragging me off the bed by tugging at my feet.

His hands clasped around my body, and I made no effort to fight him. I needed to preserve my strength and have my wits about me. Fighting the inevitable wasn't part of that.

Ryder dragged me to the center of the room and dropped me onto the chair with ferocious force. A dull ache reverberated from my back to my waist. He placed the dagger at my feet and picked up the rope he had brought. He wrapped it around my chest and stomach, immobilizing me on the seat. I desperately wanted to tell him that all the theatrics weren't necessary. I would have moved willingly because I was intrigued by whatever he had planned for me.

He picked up the dagger, and with a single move, he tore through the hem of the shirt, leaving me exposed before him. He repeated the act again, this time pressing the dagger into my skin and leaving visible cuts. I groaned, watching as blood splattered from my neck to my chest.

"You could have just asked me to take it off." I gritted my

teeth, forcing tears to streak my cheeks. "Why don't you remove the handcuffs and I'll show you what I can also do with a dagger?" I struggled against the restraint.

He snarled, watching the blood trickle from my chest. Suddenly, my vision began to blur as the ability to breathe became more and more difficult.

"You feel that?" His eyes bore into mine, and a devilish grin spread across his face. "Quillian told me the serum yesterday didn't work. So, I upped the dose." He began walking around the chair, the speed of his movements making me woozier.

"I should have...known you...were a coward," I laughed as my body slowly shook with tremors.

"Coward?" he snickered, halting behind me. His hands roughly dug into my shoulders while the blade of the dagger pressed against my neck.

"All this for a... simple human... like me?" The words came out slow and slurred.

"Perhaps I simply get off on the thrill of seeing you suffer. There's just something about the futility of your body. Look at you." He pressed the blade deeper into my neck, and more blood began to fall against my chest, staining what remained of the white shirt. He laughed aloud, then released the dagger. Slowly, he walked back around until he stood before me, lowering himself to my level.

"You haven't eaten in a few days, and your body has started degenerating already. If I bleed you a little bit more and leave you starving for a little bit longer, the wolfsbane will no longer be in your bloodstream. That is when the fun will really begin," he noted, his excitement palpable.

"Impressive," I retorted, keeping my face stoic. At least now I knew why Quillian insisted on not doing the dirty work. He was buying time. Unfortunately for them, I was well versed in the art of seduction and persuasion. Being bled was not going to be the end case here.

Ryder reached for the hose, his eyes never wavering from

mine. "Much better," he muttered as he angled it directly on my face. He slowly rose to his feet and stood directly above me. He turned on the hose to its full capacity, spraying the water directly against my face. I closed my eyes and attempted to breathe through it, yet with each passing second, my body grew more lucid.

"Now, let's begin again." He halted as my throat burned. "Your name," he demanded, lowering the hose.

"Meraki," I replied boldly because I knew if they tried digging up records on me, they would come back empty. He stepped closer, tilting my chin toward him. "Human, you wouldn't be lying to me, would you?" He tightened his hold on me. He raised the hose again, holding my head in place as the water drenched me. He laughed as I struggled to move and breathe through the onslaught.

I was definitely going to have fun when I skinned this asshole alive.

Ryder grew more incessant, repeatedly asking me my name as if waiting for me to confess to the fact it was some sort of lie.

"Why did you steal the pendant?" he continued, allowing me no moment of respite. "Answer now," he commanded, lowering the hose and angling it to my body. The water was stained with my blood, and with each passing moment, my strength waned.

"I'm a thief. I steal art, artifacts, anything that can be sold..." I halted, straining my voice into a whisper. A look of triumph flashed through his eyes, and I knew I had him where I wanted. He believed that his technique had broken me and that giving into his questions now would be somewhat believable.

"Sold?" He arched a brow, raising the hose.

"On the black market," I whispered, waiting for him to read between the lines and assume that I somewhat worked for the Invisible Suns.

He raised the hose again, and somewhere in the midst of my interrogation, I blacked out.

Everything was going according to plan, I was close to

attaining the sympathy of two of the Kingsley siblings, and they would inevitably fall for the lie that I was a thief. It was only a matter of time before Quillian came around.

9

GOOD COP, BAD COP

M*eraki*

I awoke fully naked, sprawled on the hard springs of the bed. I shifted around, noting that it was unexpectedly dry, but water was still prevalent on the floor. I had been clothed with another large shirt, but this one, unlike the first one, did not smell like Quillian. The mix of sugary cocktails with a hint of citrus smelled like what I could only assume was Silas.

The door swung open, and Brielle strolled in with a first aid kit in tow. “Don’t make this hard for me. The last thing I need to do is get into a fight with my brother,” she grumbled, taking a seat beside me and placing the kit on her lap.

“So, you’re playing good cop?” I arched a brow, recalling her voice but unable to piece anything else together after that.

“That would require me to be good,” she laughed and motioned for me to raise my hands. I hesitantly did so, finding my chest and abdomen marked with an array of cuts and bruises that were shallow yet still deep enough to cause bumps and dents on my skin.

Ryder was going to pay, one way or another. Survival first. Revenge later.

"So how does this work? I've never had to clean up a human before." She fumbled with the bag, a confused look on her face. "We have to use this until another healing potion arrives from the witch."

"Hmm," I replied, watching her cautiously while trying to get a better angle on her. Silas was an open book. Brielle not so much.

"And why aren't you in pain, screaming and crying?" Her attention trained on my chest.

"It changes nothing," I replied blandly. "And I know vampires feed on it, so maybe-"

She shook her head. "This is your middle finger," she laughed under her breath, her focus locked on my face. She pulled out an antiseptic wipe and cautiously wiped the wound.

"Why are you helping me?" I asked as she pulled back after cleaning the wound.

"So, your name is Meraki?" she asked, her eyes falling to the kit as if waiting for me to direct her on what came next.

I nodded. "You're a thief." She stated it as a fact rather than a question. I leaned back against the wall, trying to keep the smug grin from forming on my lips.

"What if I can guarantee you'll leave this place alive?" she whispered for our ears only. Her movements halted, and she briefly turned to face the camera.

Finally.

"I'll ask what the cost of that freedom is." I motioned to the ointment, and she reached for it, taking it out with a steady grip.

"A promise to fulfil two requests," she replied, her expression giving nothing away. I allowed a moment of silence to linger between us, not wanting to raise any alarm bells if I seem too eager.

"What are these two requests?" I asked, watching her open the ointment and rub it against my wounds.

"You're a thief, right?" she pressed with an undertone of suspicion in her voice.

"You want me to steal something," I spoke quietly, following her lead. "How do you know I can be trusted? If I leave here, what guarantee do you have I'll come back?"

She slowly rose and smiled, a knowingness in her movements. "I have my ways," she replied tentatively. "We have a deal?" she spoke, this time without whispering the words. I nodded slowly, questioning whether I was in over my head.

"I also have a request," I offered as she closed the container of the balm.

"You are not-"

"I need a shower," I interrupted, knowing she had begun to question our new alliance.

"Okay," she replied, lifting the first aid kit. She headed for the door, and as she reached its frame, she halted and turned to face me. "You and I are going to get along just fine, Meraki." She smiled as she closed the door behind her. "Silas will be here soon to help."

I turned my back to the camera and smiled. Now all I had to do was get Silas to either offer the same deal or appeal to his baser instincts.

Silas sauntered into the room not too long after, dressed all in denim with a white fedora hat. It was clear that the younger Kingsley was a playboy used to getting his way with women and didn't take life too seriously.

"Brielle said-"

"I'm not here for Brielle but for my own amusement." He tilted his hat forward.

"I need the restroom!" I belted the words out with sheer desperation.

"And what's that to me?" He leaned his weight against the door, unmoved by my plea. I wasn't usually wrong with my hunches about people, but right now I had to question whether I had misread him.

"Do you want me to shit in the middle of the damn room? Because one of you would have to clean it up," I retorted, and his gaze swept over my body as if seeing me for the first time. The sight of it made my skin prickle with unease, and I couldn't understand why. The same look from his brother had elicited a different response a few weeks prior. I pushed the thought to the back of my mind, not wanting to analyze it too deeply.

"Stop staring at me like that." I stood from the bed and stepped forward brazenly.

"What are you on about woman?" he leered, his attention turning to the smartwatch on his wrist. "How am I staring at you?" He raised his head, his eyes briefly taking me in.

"Like a seedy pervert?" I replied hastily. What was wrong with this guy?

He rolled his eyes and released an exasperated breath. "I thought Brielle was delusional, but clearly I should add you to that list." He shook his head. "I have my sights set on only one woman-" He halted, his eyes bulging as if he had shared something he wasn't supposed to. I stored the information away, knowing an opportune time would come when it could be of some use.

"Oh, do tell?" I sauntered to the middle of the room, struggling to stand with the restraints on my legs.

"This is not what I signed up for," he muttered under his breath as he blurred before me and removed the rope with a single swipe of his elongated nails. Relief flooded me, and I stretched my legs forward and out wide to shake away the cramps.

"What about my hands?"

"Don't play smart." He motioned for the door. "And don't ask me any questions."

"I can see you're the more mature brother," I mumbled under my breath, following him down the now dimly lit pathway. The patter of my bare feet echoed off the walls.

"Here." He stopped outside a large door. "You have five minutes and be quick about it. I have plans as you can clearly see," he noted, pushing the door open.

The midsized room, like the one I slept in, was bare, consisting only of a toilet on one end and a shower on the other.

"Beggars can't be choosers," I mumbled as I walked into the room. The facilities weren't the greatest, but I could at least finally get this wig off, get myself cleaned up, and feel remotely human again.

"Yes?" I turned back to face Silas who stood pressed against the doorway, refusing to close the door.

"You didn't think I was going to leave you in here without watching? I've seen you with a weapon, and my sister may be swayed by you but I'm not." He pointed toward the toilet with a showerhead built into its wall. "And don't think I've forgotten or forgiven the fact you shot me right here." He pointed at his chest and sneered, making it clear exactly how he felt about the situation.

"Are you looking for an apology?" I replied, making no effort to conceal the fact that if I had more time, I would have shot more than his thigh. Something told me Silas preferred the direct, cutthroat approach, and his laughter was all I needed as confirmation.

"At least I can say now I've been shot by a human. There's a first for everything." He walked away from the door, looking too at ease for someone who claimed to not trust me.

"So, not to be ungrateful for your kind and gracious hospitality, but how am I supposed to shower?"

"What do you mean?" I raised my hands, indicating the cuffs that served as a hindrance. He simply shook his shoulder and raised his hand dismissively.

"How am I supposed to pull down my pants or clean myself up?" I pressed my hands forward, waiting for him to remove the restraints.

"That stays on. Quillian's instructions-"

"And this is also part of his instruction?" I motioned to the space around us, knowing that wasn't the case.

"I'm soon to be on my brother's blacklist. Let's not push it any further, okay? We are all just playing accompanying roles in his story." He dismissed me again, his voice filled with a twinge of unspoken anger.

I took a deep breath, knowing that this was a battle worth fighting. Going forward, I would have to learn to choose them wisely, especially since I was dealing with an insane family like this.

I stepped toward the toilet, thinking about how best to get my ass on and off the seat without making a complete and total fool of myself. Silas looked back and forth between his smartwatch and me, then exhaled loudly.

He stepped toward me, his face a mask of indifference. "These go back on in five minutes." He took out a key from the back of his dark denim pants. I squealed with excitement, reminding myself of the absurdity of the situation. Kidnapped by a vampire and the high point of my week was being afforded the luxury of a shower.

My life had hit a new low.

I quickly scrambled to the toilet, doing my business while stretching the cramps and aches out of my wrist.

"How long have I been here for?"

"Five days," he replied calmly.

"Five days," I repeated, my skin tingling with discomfort. The realization that if I didn't find a way to update the Alokari within the next six days, then death at the hands of the renowned vampire family would be a walk in the park compared to what awaited me.

"You have a date you need to attend to?" Silas laughed under his breath.

I gasped, catching a glimpse of my mascara-stained face, receding frontal wig, and chest smeared with cuts and bruises. I should have felt anger and rage, but all that raced through me was a silent growing interest in the depths this family is willing to go to in order to obtain information. Perhaps we may be of use to each other, and they could be the key I need to access Esneoh.

A few seconds later, Silas walked back into the room armed

with a towel, body wash, shampoo, conditioner, and a brush. He placed the items on a small railing on the wall.

"Four minutes. You've already wasted one on the mirror," he noted, stepping back to the door and perching himself on the entryway. "The water might remain hot for a few minutes. You might want to take advantage of it."

Turning my back to him, I quickly stripped down from my underwear and torn shirt, placing them beside the items he had brought in. I turned on the shower and moaned. Who knew having a warm bath every day was a blessing we took for granted?

I aimed the shower head, spraying it directly on the outer hairline of the lace frontal wig. I scooped large splotches of shampoo and slathered it on until the wig fell off and the glue holding it intact washed away.

My attention briefly turned to Silas, who made a feeble attempt to keep himself occupied with his smartwatch. I undid the two large braids that kept the wig in place. My hair fell over my back in loose waves, and I hastily washed it with the shampoo and conditioner. I then did the same with my face and body. By the time I was done, I didn't feel completely clean but clean enough to think straight and perhaps survive a few more days of whatever awaited me in this basement.

"Why are you helping me?" I asked, my head tilted up.

"Maybe I'm doing it to get a reaction from brother. I did always enjoy testing his boundaries," he replied, and though I couldn't see his face, I could sense his smile.

"I might just like you after all," I replied, turning my head to face him. Silas laughed, and a moment of companionable ease transpired between us

"What do you need from me?" I proceeded, sensing his need to make a request, just like his sister. He raised his head, training his attention away from the smartwatch. And in my fully naked state, he made no attempt to stare down. His eyes glinted with the knowledge of an unspoken secret, one he hadn't yet put a face to.

"Your assistance on a series of matters when the time comes," he answered solemnly.

"You could ask your kind for that, no?" I replied, testing the edged of what is left unspoken.

"If that were the case, we wouldn't be having this discussion," he replied, his attention turning back to the watch.

"You and your sister seem headstrong in your convictions. However, Quillian seems intent on making me bleed to death." I turned off the shower and reached for the towel.

"You worry about staying alive. My brother can be reasoned with," he replied coyly. I smiled in response, my chest expanding with relief. My gut instinct about the siblings had not been wrong.

I wrapped the towel around my body and reached for my underwear and the torn shirt, not particularly excited to wear the same dirty clothes I had been. "What are these *matters* exactly?" I asked once I finished drying myself. A slow smile tugged at his lips, and like his brother, a prominent dimple formed on his cheeks.

"I can see you're good at what you do."

"I didn't survive this long by not weighing my options. And right now, I need to know whether dying here is better than whatever you have planned for me up there." My eyes landed on the corridor.

"Whatever is up there cannot even compare to what is down here. My brother hasn't even pulled out all his cards, and I'm not sure if you want to find out what he is truly capable of," he stated, tapping on his watch to remind me that my time was up.

"You didn't answer my question," I stated, sensing that his request might not be so straightforward, unlike Brielle's.

"All you need to know is that it might involve some sort of undercover work. The rest you'll find out when it's time." He raised his hand dismissively and motioned for me to hurry up and get dressed.

Once I put on my clothes again, he strode into the room with the handcuffs, and every instinct in my body told me I could use this moment to run away. But I hesitated, knowing any false move on my part now would ultimately lead to my death. I had come this far. I just had to bear a few more days.

"It was nice doing business with you, Meraki." He beamed as he bound my hands again.

We walked back through the passageway, and as Silas opened the door to the room and waited for me to enter, his gaze turned to the rope on the floor. He hesitated for a time, looking back and forth between me and the rope. After a while, he tilted his hat back and closed the door, leaving me standing in the center of the room.

As I made my way back to the bed, my gaze turned to the evident wet spot on the floor that had almost dried up. I followed the water trail to a small drain in the far corner of the room. I leaned down and pressed my ear to it, listening out for any familiar sounds.

The drainage system in Jersey Hill was interconnected to a larger system on the outskirts of the city, which meant that it was constantly under maintenance and could be accessed at certain intervals. I had used it numerous times when trying to mask my scent or remain low after a *sneps or sners* job. I was more than familiar with its echoes and the recurrent whistles that its walls created.

A low humming sound echoed back, one distinctively unlike the one I had grown familiar with.

Could it be?

I rose to my feet, my mind reeling from the realization that I might no longer be in Jersey Hill. There was only one other place they would have taken me to.

Esneoh. The city that held all the answers regarding Alessia's killer.

Lying on the bed, I curled my body into a ball and turned my face to the wall, unable to hide the glimmer of a smile that now curved my lip.

Getting kidnapped by the reigning vampire family of Esneoh wasn't so bad if it ultimately brought me to Esneoh and a step closer to my sister's killer.

THICK, CALLOUSED HANDS WRAPPED AROUND MY mouth, jolting me from my sleep. My eyes darted open as Ryder's face loomed over me with a grimacing smile. My body had been thrumming with anticipation for his next visit, especially since my last conversation with Brielle and Silas. The other two Kingsley siblings may have been swayed to my side, but something told me Quillian was not yet fully convinced and was bound to send his henchman to see if he could extract more from me.

As he pulled me from the bed, I raised my feet and kicked from his chest all the way to his groin.

"There you are. You've been hiding, haven't you, ma cherie? Don't think I'm fooled by the veil you've put on," he laughed mischievously.

His gaze turned to my unbound feet, and something about the predatory movement of his eyes told me he hadn't anticipated them being unbound. He twisted the cuffs on my hands, releasing a series of electric shocks. I laughed out, feeling weakened from lack of food and liquid.

He twisted my feet aggressively as he reached out for the rope that still sat on the center of the room.

"Now behave before you experience pain you've never felt in the entirety of your useless life," he breathed, binding my feet together. The need to fight back thrummed within me, but my body no longer had any fight, and he knew.

Once bound, he carried me off the bed and dropped me. The cracking sound of my head hitting the floor and blood soaking my hair in its wake was the only sign I had to know that this was no longer an interrogation. Ryder was out for blood. My blood.

"You are going to pay for this, I promise you," I spoke

through gritted teeth. I no longer cared for the facade. It was evident that the camera could only record the room, but the audio didn't channel through, otherwise Silas and Brielle wouldn't have been so forthcoming.

Who the fuck manhandles someone out of bed without the end goal of an orgasm?

Ryder slapped me across my face, the sound echoing off the walls of the room. Blood trickled from my nose, filled my mouth, and poured down my throat.

"I'm looking forward to inflicting pain on that sharp tongue of yours. Meraki, wasn't it? Or was that a lie?" he grunted under his breath, and I decided then and there thatonce I escaped this hellhole, he was going to be my first kill. And I was going to take my sweet time with him, plucking out his fingernails and gouging his eyes from his body.

The thought stilled me, releasing the tension knotted around my shoulders and the dull ache that throbbed in the back of my head. I was going to take whatever pain he planned to inflict on me, but when my time came, I wasn't going to be merciful with his life.

He dragged my body through the room in a loop, his morbid attempt at letting me know who had the upper hand here, and I made no effort to fight back. If my predictions about the siblings were correct, they would ensure their brother would intervene. Whether I was dead or alive by then was another story altogether.

"Tonight is going to be a long night for you, no?" He smirked, wrapping the excess rope left around my neck and tugging at it as if I were a dog he was trying to tame.

"Now let's start again." His focus turned to the camera briefly, before tugging at the rope. The simple act let me know that even though he wasn't here, Quillian still called the shots. Ryder had been given permission to inflict pain, but not kill. That I could work with.

His hold remained on the rope as he spun me around,

ensuring my face and body directly faced the camera. This was a show, an act of defiance, and I was the sacrificial lamb.

Ryder tightened his hold on the rope, tilting my head back, until I choked for air. "Now, be honest. What is it you wanted with the necklace? Who sent you?" he spat, tightening his hold on the rope until the air in my lungs burned. He loosened it slightly, his hands pressed against my cheek as he waited for me to respond.

"I steal, that's it-" My words were cut short as his hands made contact with my face again. I coughed blood, and the side of my face tingled with an unknown ache. I kept my eyes trained on him, refusing to close them. Doing so would imply weakness, and Ryder thrived on the weakness of others.

"In case you're unaware, which I think you are" - he pulled on the rope again, his eyes glistening with a depth of darkness I had missed in our last encounter - "I'm known for removing the tongues of thieves and assassins...humans. After cutting them into pieces." He laughed, his mouth resting against my ears in a wet whisper. I flinched, recoiling at his touch.

"I've grown quite infamous for it. Something tells me you may know about it and the name I go by outside of this realm." He loosened his hold and lowered himself so that our eyes locked in a battle of wills. I choked back a cough as the rope loosened, my eyes straining with tears.

"Who am I?" He spat the words out as a low warning sound. I kept my eyes hooked on his, my body buzzing with a sense of awareness. "The Butcher," I answered slowly, watching as the light in his eyes intensified, confirming what I had suspected all along.

The Butcher was a name that haunted every agent in the Alokari. No one knew who or what he was, but there had been enough dead bodies and memorabilia left behind to warn us that this was someone who took joy from inflicting pain on humans, particularly women. Women that looked like me.

These women were usually assassins who had made an

attempt to infiltrate Esneoh. They were usually found dead, their bodies and limbs mutilated to the point that it was almost impossible on some occasions to get accurate DNA. Some of the best assassins had fallen to him. He was the living embodiment of the devil itself, and I had crafted many of my interrogation methods to follow what I had read about him in reports.

I hated, despised, and admired him all at once.

This changed everything.

I was no longer dealing with a reasonably sane person. I was staring at death itself, and if I wasn't careful, he would fuck up all my plans with a single blow.

"So, you know what I'm capable of then." His hands ran rough strokes around my cheeks. I bit my lip to hold back the rebuttal sitting on the tip of my tongue. I had to remind myself that this game of cat and mouse wasn't for him but Quillian. My focus was Quillian and getting back the pendant from his family. Ryder was simply a bump in that road, and giving in to his taunts was the quickest way to end up in the morgue.

The master had taught the student, but the student will inevitably surpass the master.

"I see you refuse to speak," he growled menacingly as he squeezed my chin, forcing me to face him. "If I don't get what I want from you today, I won't be sated." He paused, stared into the camera, and softly whispered into my ear. "When I don't get my way, I like to tear, break, and peel the skin off my prisoners until they can no longer be put back together. Is this the plight you want to follow?"

He pulled my head back, searching my eyes for some morbid response, perhaps an increase in my breathing or my heartbeat. When he seemed to note neither, something flashed through his eyes. A dark vacuum I was familiar with. A call to violence, one that knew no bounds nor peace until blood had spilled and nothing remained. I stared back, my eyes widening at the realization. And in that moment, I knew I had given too much of myself away. Ryder recognized the familiar darkness. He pulled back, releasing a slew of curses.

"You and I are alike," he commented.

"We are not," I choked. "You're spurred by rage and the thrill of a kill. My convictions are rooted in something else entirely," I spat, blood oozing from my lips.

"You think you're better than me," he chuckled, reminding me of my current place. "Who do you work for?"

"Myself," I replied brazenly. Ryder's gaze hardened as if my defiance enraged him. His hold on the rope tightened, and this time he tugged the rope back with my hair, grunting and muttering more curses.

"You're lying!" he shouted, releasing his hold on my scalp. He reached for his pockets, removing a plastic bag from its depth.

"Whatever you're looking for, Butcher, you will not find it here," I continued, knowing that offering the name of the Invisible Sun was not an option. Doing so would imply I was a snitch, and no one respected a snitch or wanted to do business with them.

"Something tells me you're lying, Meraki. And I'll make it my mission to get the truth out of you," he continued, loosening his hold on the rope slightly as he placed the bag over my head.

I knew what came next. I had used this technique countless times. I wasn't going to bend.

I raised my chin in defiance, keeping my head up so that my eyes remained locked with the camera. Ryder wrapped the handle of the bag around the rope, ensuring that as he pulled the rope, the bag would tighten, suffocating me.

If I didn't hate his guts right now, I would have been thoroughly impressed.

Warmth and heat flooded my face, and my body shook in response as I struggled to gasp for air. Ryder groaned as he kept tugging at the rope. After a few seconds, he loosened his hold and removed the bag from my face. Saliva dripped from my mouth as I gasped for air, my gaze never wavering from the camera.

My ears rang until everything around me became a series of indistinguishable sounds. Ryder hovered over me, his mouth moving, but I was unable to make sense of his words. I arched my head back from his vision, trained it on the camera and smiled, knowing that behind the lens Quillian was watching. My message was simple. *I may be a thief, but I do not cower in the face of adversity. I'm the type of person you need on your team.*

Ryder slapped me again, and the bag followed before I could register it. My lungs burned as tears stained my face and cheeks. He stopped, removing the bag again, his intent no longer to gain intel but to inflict the maximum amount of pain possible.

Figures my idol is a complete idiot. I need to find better idols.

Ryder continued with this, giving me a few seconds to breathe, then placing the bag over my face again, just as my breathing was beginning to steady. Each time he pulled the bag back, his laughter filled the room, followed by grunts and snarls of irritation.

With each passing moment, my body grew limper, the room spun, and my mind became a discombobulated convulsion of uncertainty. Had I overestimated the hold the Kingsley siblings had over their brother? Had I underestimated Quillian's cruelty?

Slowly, my body began to succumb the weight of it all. It was only a matter of time before I crashed.

Black dots covered my vision, and I coughed profusely as he removed the bag for the tenth time. "A thief who can withstand pain?" he whispered. "Who are you really?" he asked, his voice a steady warning.

"The Burning Sun," he finally muttered under his breath, testing the name on his tongue, as if needing convincing. He was good, that I couldn't deny.

Time for the final act.

I turned my gaze to him, widening my eyes as if the name itself was something familiar. Yet I refused to speak or publicly acknowledge it. "I have no idea what you're talking about," I replied, facing him head-on. "You might as well kill me because there's nothing else to share. I work for myself," I spat as blood trailed down my nose.

"Hmm. Ma cherie, what you don't say is as potent as what is said," he stated, his eyes sparkling with some unspoken knowledge.

Bingo. I had him where I wanted him.

"I'm sure the Burning Sun would no longer have any use for you. Your death is inevitable. What say you, ma cherie?" he whispered into my ear. The air sparked with electricity, his words carrying a weight they didn't before.

He was going to kill me.

The bag returned to my head, and this time I chastised myself for ever believing the words of two vampires. I knew better. Desperation can cloud the clearest of minds.

My eyes watered, my throat burned, and rage coiled around me at the fact that everything I was boiled down to this moment, to my inevitable death and failure at the hands of someone who could be my sister's potential killer.

Any other time, this would have been poetic. The student dying in the hands of their mentor. Today, it served as a bitter reminder that I was fucked.

Darkness played in the recesses of my mind, and I took one final breath. The room erupted into chaos, and my body fell to the ground, enveloped by Quillian's scent. It was a reminder that I may have survived death today, but I should never lower my guard around him, or else it could be my undoing.

I passed out somewhere in the midst of it all, thinking about plucking out those beautiful gray eyes and keeping them as memorabilia of my most infamous kill.

I had survived the test. Now it was time to face my new reality.

10

A NEW PLAN

Quillian

"What are you doing, brother?" Brielle asked, looming in the doorway of the security room.

I raised my head to take her in briefly, then turned my focus back to the screen, unable to take my eyes from the hellion before me.

"Meraki," I rolled her name on my tongue, savoring it like the warmth and lingering heat of liquor.

"She's a thief," Brielle said confidently as she strolled into the room.

"So, she says," I retorted, watching as Meraki lie splayed out on the bed. Something told me she wasn't sleeping. I had watched her countless times over the last few days and barely saw her sleep for more than two hours. Then again, that was my goal, mocking her with a lack of food, water, and access to any type of hygiene. I needed her completely broken before I had my way with her, but that was proving difficult. Practically impossible.

Meraki was strong and resilient, and the fact that after almost six days of interrogation she had not succumbed spoke to her character. I was impressed. Too fucking impressed.

Images of her coming over the gun I had aimed at her pussy

resurfaced in my mind, and I clenched my fingers, fighting back my growing erection.

"You don't believe her?" Brielle asked, drawing me from my frenzy.

"She's too well trained at combat and weaponry. What kind of thief do we know capable of that?" I noted, turning my attention away from the screen before my interest in her aroused Brielle's suspicion. My sister was too observant for her own good.

"Or she is who she says she is and is well trained at her job? Aren't agents from the Invisible Sun infamous for being well versed in weaponry and martial arts?" Brielle noted as she perched herself on the sofa chair directly opposite me.

"What's the sudden interest in our prisoner, baby sister? I know you, Brie-"

"Maybe I'm interfering before you straddle the line of obsessive. We paid dearly for the last one," she answered, her nails tapping the arm of the chair.

"You propose I kill her?" I turned to face her. Brielle loved carnage as much as I did, but unlike me, she used it as a last resort when she was unable to get her own way.

"Now you ask that? When Silas and I told you to leave her body on the roof and only take the pendant? You insisted on bringing her here, even knowing all the dangers."

"You're making it sound like she's some victim in all of this." I motioned to the space around us.

"She is far from a victim." Brielle pointed at the screen. "In fact, it's evident she's good at what she does. But, Q, I know what you're like when you become fixed on a thing or person-"

"This isn't the same!" I cut her off as a fresh wave of irritation washed over me. "Did you miss the part where she shot Silas? Or the part where she shot me?" I sat forward in my seat and reached for my glass of liquor.

"So all this is simply to feed your ego? Nothing else?" she pressed, her eyes swimming with a sea of accusations.

"Is there something you're trying to say, baby sister? Why

don't you say it out loud?" I sat back in my seat, giving her the floor to say what she really wanted. I was more than sure that Enzo would have dropped the bomb about the fact she was at the club the evening he had insisted on taking me out. It didn't take a genius to add the pieces together.

"Q..."

"Brielle..."

She exhaled loudly. "We just got back. Stuck under a spell for a millennium. Am I not allowed to be worried or question everything around you...us? Especially the small decisions that can ultimately become bigger in the future?" She leaned forward in her seat, and her brown eyes illuminated the haunting and harrowing truth it wasn't just me who had experienced the *silence* and the hollow emptiness that came after being trapped in a cave for so long.

Saying no to Brielle had always been a weakness of mine. She knew what to say and how to get under my skin in a way no one else could. But this case wasn't one I could easily ignore.

"Besides, I need a new friend," she remarked, the weight of her voice laced with a hint of sadness I couldn't comprehend.

"What about-" Brielle raised her hand, dismissing me altogether.

"What? It's not like I'm drowning in a sea of friends. We've been gone for a long time, Q...Things have changed," she replied, her voice strained. She reclined back in her seat and slowly ran her left hand over her wrist, a move that usually showed her unease about a topic.

"Baby sister." I attempted to reason with her because I knew she was someone that was hard to deter, especially once she had made up her mind about something. She always saw it through to the end.

"You were there when she tried to kill me. Several times, in fact."

"You survived. Don't be such a baby. It takes more than silver to hold you down." I chewed on her words, recounting the arsenal of weapons Meraki had on her. There was nothing remotely normal about my supposed little thief. Nor was her pursuit of the pendant coincidental. She knew more than she was letting on, and I was going to make it my job to get to the heart of her deceits.

"She shot Silas too. She would have killed me if I were a lesser man," I remarked as she rolled her eyes. "You're not listening, Brie," I added, attempting to keep my voice even.

"Come now, brother. It was barely a scratch." Silas strolled into the room and headed for the seat beside Brielle.

"A scratch? It took you an hour to get your wits back," I shot back.

"I'm a big boy. I can handle myself." He smirked mischievously. "Besides, I think I like her." His familiar gray eyes went to the screen, and he stared intently at her. All I wanted to do was punch him in the face for the length his gaze lingered.

"Of course, you do, baby brother. You fucking pervert," Brie chuckled. "You love anything moving with legs." She shook her head. "We've been back for almost two weeks, and in that time, you've fucked half the incubi here and certainly picked up some diseases along the way."

"Come on. You think so lowly of me." He smirked teasingly. "Not just incubi, Brie. I don't discriminate. I love all-"

"I'm not having this conversation with you, Si. I'm still reeling from the shock that they want to sleep with my baby brother." Brielle made heaving sounds, and her face morphed into a look of disgust.

"That's the problem, Brie. You still think I'm a baby," he added coyly, flexing his muscles.

"What's going on here?" I reclined in my seat, getting a better reading of them. "You two agreeing on something means that either you or you" - I pointed at them both – "is up to something, and don't play me for a fool." I took a sip of my drink, waiting for them to divulge.

"Not everything is about you," Brielle chided.

"You know he thinks the sun, moon, and stars revolve around his every whim and command." Silas shook his head, leaning forward to reach for a glass and filling with liquor.

"In case you're forgetting, she's also human," I added dryly, refusing to fall into their trap. "If there's anything I know, it is that they can't be trusted. Every single one of them."

"Q, what happened with-"

"Don't mention that name here," I bite back.

"Then can we talk about Alaric at least?" Silas' hold on his glass tightened.

"What's that supposed to mean?" I sat forward in my seat, planting my legs wide.

"It means we can't discuss one without the other," Silas shot back, placing his glass back on the center table.

"This is my point. She's barely been here a week, and she's already manipulated you into siding with her. This is what her kind is capable of," I shouted, my fingers pointed to the screen.

"You really just missed everything else I said before that?" Silas remarked, shaking his head as his lips flattened.

"And you both forget the fact the last time you both insisted on something, we allowed a she-wolf into our home, and now...."

"And now?" Silas arched his brow, taunting me. "Say it, brother," he barked, standing on his feet.

"Can we ever have a conversation without shit blowing over with you two? Sit, Silas." She reached out for his hand, pulling him back down on the seat.

"Alaric wouldn't have wanted this." She motioned to the brewing tension in the room.

"He wanted a lot of things. Those things led to his death," Silas mumbled under his breath. Brielle reclined in her seat, releasing her hold on him. I took another shot of my drink, unable to come up with an argument to state otherwise. But the truth stared us all in the face. Alaric's need for change played an underlying role in his death. And we lost him in the process.

"Which one of you allowed her to shower?" I finally spoke

after silence had lingered for too long. My eyes turned to Silas, already knowing he was the mastermind behind the stupid idea.

"What? She begged to use the restroom, and I couldn't turn down a pretty face," he replied, and I squashed the need in my hands to wring his neck.

"Which part of 'Ryder will be interrogating her' did you miss? That was part of the fucking plan, Si," I remarked with my voice elevated.

"The plan wasn't working," he snarled in response. "You're wasting your time. It won't take a genius to work that out," he hollered.

"And why is that? Please explain it to me, baby brother. Since when have you become the expert on women? When did you become the specialist on interrogation methods?" I replied, trying to remove the sarcasm in my voice. "Last I remember, we" - I pointed at Brie - "seem to be the ones cleaning up your woman problems." I rose, rolling the last word off my tongue to emphasize my point.

We may not have been in each other's presence for a long while, but the familiar irritations were now more prominent than ever before. "Alaric cleaned up my shit! Not you." He jumped from his seat, the air between us sparking with anger.

"If only you knew," I laughed and shook my head. Even with him gone, I was still living in the shadows of the impossible expectations and reputation he had left behind. Alaric was everything I wasn't, and this moment reminded me of that cold truth.

"I was with her for six minutes and could tell there was nothing normal about her. That isn't going to work." He pointed at the image of Meraki on the screen. Ryder now had her bound to a chair.

"That I will have to agree with," Brielle stated, her attention briefly shifting to the screen. "Is that necessary, Q? You know how I feel about him and his techniques." She pointed at Ryder. "He would have killed her yesterday if I didn't intervene."

"He isn't going to kill her. I gave him strict and clear instructions not to-"

"And what happens after?" Brielle asked.

"After?"

"The interrogation is done, and you've got what you want. What happens then? Her death?" she pressed, and something cold settled within me.

"You know I can't allow her to walk out of here alive," I replied, the words warring within my chest. It was the rule, our rule. Changing that now or ever would allow our enemies to come knocking on our door with no fear of the repercussions.

"She wasn't expecting us to show up that evening," Silas intervened when it was obvious, I was still deliberating on the question. I recounted the startled look on her face as those hazel eyes, like orbs of the deepest shades of green and amber, turned to stare at me.

"What are we going to do about the pendant?" Enzo interrupted, and we all turned to the door to face him. He stepped into the room, reaching for a glass and pouring himself a drink.

"Any news or updates since yesterday?" I asked. He shook his head hesitantly.

"Hera is still working on it," he answered as he took a seat beside me.

"Can we trust Hera?" Silas offered, stating the obvious.

"Can we truly trust anyone right now? Especially since we don't know who placed us under the hold, we were in." Brielle responded. "As grateful as I am to her for freeing us, I don't trust her coven. A pendant like that? Imbued with such magic that it had to have been crafted by a witch?" she noted as if thinking out loud. "For all we know, she could have even been the one who spelled the necklace. Have you checked into this?"

"I did. She wasn't in Esneoh at the time," Enzo answered, taking a sip of his drink.

"At least that's one witch we can eliminate from the equation," Silas offered.

"I still don't trust her," I remarked.

"You don't trust anyone." Brielle rolled her eyes.

"That's not true-"

"Me, Brielle, and Enzo do not count, brother," Silas intervened mockingly.

"After years of searching, failed intel, and a lack of response or support, she was the only one I found who was willing to help, or who even believed you all didn't just decide to leave out of choice," Enzo added, making his stance on the matter clear. He was on Team Hera, and nothing could persuade him otherwise.

"Whoever had us bound in those caves was powerful and had planned to do so for a while. The execution was too flawless. I don't think it's a coincidence it happened a day after Quillian won the trials and would have been crowned King over Esneoh," Silas offered. "We should be focused on those demons then. Who else would have benefited the most?"

"What would they have gained at that time? We had a good relationship with them. We were even getting ready to swear an oath of partnership with each other on the eve of his coronation," Brielle noted, biting the bed of her thumbnail.

"Gain? They had everything to gain. The law stated that if anything happened to the initial winner, then next in line will be the runner-up," Silas answered.

"That is true," I noted, thinking back on the eve I would have been crowned leader of Esneoh. I had completed every trial with blood, sweat, and tears, only to be cheated out of what was rightfully mine.

"The demons took the position when you disappeared," Enzo intervened. "And for the longest time, I chased leads on that but came up empty. Their circle was always the hardest to penetrate."

"But we can't deny the most obvious fact. Like Silas said, they had a lot more to gain than the other houses," I stated, leaning my weight on the arm of the sofa. "In some way or form, they were involved."

"Something is off about the whole thing, and I can't put my

finger on it," Brielle muttered aloud. "What about the others? This doesn't seem like something that could have been done solo. Where were the witches and shifters in all this?" Brie turned her gaze around the room, her eyes bulging. "How do we know it wasn't one of our own that sold us out?"

"We can't start to do that," Enzo stated, arching his chin toward her. "If we start distrusting even our own people, this can get messy. However, to ease your worries, I'll rally some of our most trusted men to keep their ears open. If anything comes up or seems out of the ordinary, I'll let you know," Enzo concluded.

"He's right, sister. If we start suspecting each other, the discord will destroy us. Let's focus our energy and drive on something else moving forward," Silas added. The tension in his shoulders and the tightening of his hand on the glass were a clear indication that if he had his way, we would simply pretend that the last millennia never happened.

Unfortunately, life wasn't that merciful.

"Our second priority for the next couple of months is finding out who was involved. I want names, details, and locations. This time I'm not planning on taking prisoners. I want blood, screams, tears, and to see them suffer," I said, wringing my fists on the chair. "I will bathe Esneoh in blood to get to the heart of the matter."

"What's our first move?" Enzo asked, placing his glass down and turning his full attention to me.

"Entering the Dark Crown Trials again and taking back the victory that should have been mine. Ours," I stated, feeling my chest tighten at the prospect.

A smile broke out on Enzo's face, one I was too familiar with and knew only spelled trouble. "I'm already one step ahead of you, old friend," he expressed vividly, the sparkle and excitement in his voice unmissable. "I may have already been one step ahead of the game," he added. Brielle and Silas keep their attention trained on him.

"What do you mean?" Silas asked.

"Well, the laws were slightly changed by Loki a few years ago during the time of your imprisonment." He flinched at the mention of the word.

"How?" Brielle asked. "We've clearly missed a lot and have to catch up on everything," she noted disdainfully.

"A clause was added," Enzo replied, going silent immediately after.

"And?" Brielle pushed, motioning for him to get to the point.

"He always did have a flair for the dramatics," Silas chirped mockingly.

"And this is coming from you?" She turned and stared down at him.

"And here I was trying to defend you. A man tries to help a woman, and this is what he gets. Don't say I didn't try."

"Contrary to popular belief, women aren't asking to be helped or saved, baby brother. We can do bad all by ourselves. Now hush." Brielle raised her hand dismissively.

"Well?" I asked, waiting on him to fill in the missing details.

"The leaders have to have a partner," he replied briskly.

"A partner? You will need to be more specific, Enzo," Silas chuckled lightly. "As in a girlfriend? I'm sure we can find someone. We all know he's incapable of keeping any relationship longer than a few weeks," Silas continued, and the need to fling him across the room pulsed through me. Unfortunately, this thing called family...

"No. That's not what I meant," Enzo answered quickly.

"If not, then what?" Brielle pressed, her frustration mirroring mine. "Oh...wait...oh." Her eyes widened, and a pyramid of emotions passed through her features. Silas and I exchanged confused glares.

"You now have to be married to participate." He spoke so quickly that the words would have easily been missed had I not had sensitive ears. Silas burst into fits of laughter, and Brielle's face went stark cold like the idea of me being in a relationship with someone was absurd.

"Is this some sort of joke?" I shouted, twisting my fists into tight balls.

"Let's forget about the trials then and focus on revenge instead," Silas continued to laugh.

"Not a joke, unfortunately," Enzo answered, his eyes moving across the room unsteadily.

"You're being serious?" I muttered, sensing his discomfort. I rose from my seat again and ran my hands through my hair.

My attention turned back to the screen as it zoomed in on Meraki, who now stared candidly into the camera as if she were directly in the room, listening to our every word. I watched as Ryder placed a bag over her face, and she sat still, not making a single effort to fight him. When he removed the bag, her eyes were still trained on the camera, a devious smile curving the corner of her lips.

The little hellion knew she was being watched and was getting off on it. She was putting up a show for my viewing pleasure, and something about the whole act made my fingers itch with the desperate need to tie her up and choke her as she came all over me.

"Well, brother?" Brielle spoke. Her gaze flickered to the screen and then back to me.

"How the hell is he supposed to find someone?" Silas asked his voice steeped with disdain. "The last woman died-" I blurred before him, my hands around his throat as I lifted him into the air.

"Watch what you fucking say," I spat, irritation coursing through me.

"Is that so, brother?" He arched his brow, refusing to back down. "What are you going to do? Kill me? You want to put another brother to the grave?" He taunted, and I knew I should not give in, but Silas always knew what to say or do to get under my skin.

"Stop!" Brielle shouted, stepping between us. I released my hold on him, dropping him to the floor. Silas immediately picked himself up, making a beeline for me.

"Why should I? Who put him in charge? Last I checked, I only reported to Alaric," he spat, and something about the words set me into a tailspin, and my vision blurred, rage coiling around my every thought.

"Alaric is gone, Silas, and he's never coming back. The sooner you get used to it, the better," Brielle spoke, her voice pained. Silas only seemed to be spurred on by this.

"I'm glad we finally mention his name, Brie." Silas stepped back, a dark glint illuminating his eyes. "Or are we going to just keep pretending he didn't exist? Like any of this shit is normal?" he added as he shook himself from some invisible weight.

I stepped toward him, my fangs elongated. "You have done enough. Continue with this conversation, and I will end your existence," I snarled. "You will not continue to keep disrespecting me. You will either follow the fucking protocol or get in line. If you don't like it, you know where the door is." The words hung in the air like a noose around our necks.

"Let's all calm down." Enzo stepped into our midst, reaching for Silas.

He jerked from Enzo's hold and snarled. "I know my way out," Silas said. He turned and headed for the door.

"Si, wait. Don't," Brielle shouted after him.

"Leave him. He's been babied for too long. And we've encouraged his bad behavior for far too fucking long. No more." I gritted my teeth, unable to control the wave of anger coursing through me.

"Quillian..." She exhaled a breath.

"I'm back to being Quillian?" I answered, knowing she only called me by my full name when she was irritated with me about something.

"I'm doing this for Alaric. I'm honoring his work and legacy." I gritted my teeth.

"I know, brother. I know," she spoke lowly, her shoulders hunched. She stepped back to her seat, reaching for a glass and reclining as she filled it up. Enzo reached for me and lightly tapped my shoulder in a show of comradeship. He knew the weight I carried since Alaric's passing and the burdens that came with the responsibility of it all.

"What did you have in mind for this relationship *thing*?" I blurted out the foreign words.

"A marriage," he answered.

"A wedding. To whom?" Brielle looked from him to me, her face void of any emotion.

"A human. I believe it would-"

"Stop right there." I dismissively raised my hand. Enzo was known for his absurd plans and ideas, but even this was a stretch.

"Enzy, baby. Are you sure about this? You know how he feels about humans," Brielle teased, her eyes locked with mine. "And why not another vampire? Or even a girl from one of the other houses?" she teased.

"Having a human would make his proposal for the throne more legitimate," he countered, now having my full attention. It was no secret how I felt about humans, but I was smart enough to know when to tolerate them to get what I wanted.

"How so?" Brielle asked. This was news to me.

"When the Nephilim initially founded Esneoh, they wanted to make it a haven for supernatural beings. They also desired for it to be a bridge between us and the humans."

"Okay. And?" Brielle pressed.

"The goal was never for there to be such a huge separation between Esneoh and the human realm. They envisioned the joining and crossing of both worlds." He sat forward in the chair, his hands resting on his thighs.

"But over time, those relationships the Nephilim's built with the humans withered as those mortals died. The newer ones that came into power either lost touch with us, feared us, or craved the power that could be found here. The gap between them and us has grown exponentially," he added.

"What does this have to do with me?"

"Well, what if your plea was rooted in bridging the gap?"

"How?" Brielle and I both asked together. Enzo smiled, looking between us both.

"Inviting a human into the realm under your protection. That hasn't been done in-"

"Eons," Brielle replied, seemingly on board with whatever Enzo was trying to relay.

"By marrying one, you will appeal to the more seasoned veteran beings from each house, especially the demons. You will also appeal to the younger shifters and vampires who have been growing more vocal about changes within the realms. They seek for more intermingling with the other houses, even more so with humans," he added coyly.

"And this human you're suggesting for marriage? What role will she have in this? What becomes of her after?" I questioned, my mind an inferno of raging thoughts. "What human would be crazy enough to accept the terms, especially when dealing with our kind? She would forever –"

"I have two. Two I've been preparing for this moment," he replied, quickly reaching for his phone. Brielle, who was usually the most talkative in the group, sat back in her chair seemingly contemplating the idea.

"She will inevitably become an easy target for those who despise our family. Even if we had security around her, it could still pose a problem and a weakness in the long run," Brielle mumbled, shuffling in her seat.

"I will have to agree with Brielle on this. The idea is sound, but there are too many underlying issues."

"But..." Brielle trailed off, her eyes turning to the screen behind me. "What if? What if she wasn't a normal human? What if she were someone well trained and could fight and protect herself? What if she was someone who would comply because she had something to gain from the partnership?" she continued, her eyes glimmering at the thought.

"And where would we find such a human?" Enzo questioned, falling right into her trap.

"We already have one," she offered. She rose from her chair, walked toward the screen, and motioned at the image of Meraki.

"No," I answered without thought. I wasn't sure what I wanted to do with the hellion yet, but I knew allowing her access to my space spelled trouble.

"No?" Enzo frowned, rising from his seat to join Brielle. "I think it might actually be an amazing idea. This could work in our favor." He stared at his phone, then looked back at the screen.

"I don't trust her-"

"And anyone else we bring here you won't trust. That's the point. You don't have to trust her. You just have to ensure she plays her role well. Think about it..." Brielle trailed off, turning her gaze back on me.

"She's well trained in weaponry and combat and was able to sneak into a top-security gallery. This could definitely work," Enzo noted, gazing at Brielle with a smile. "She could even be of help to us as we find out who was involved in your abduction."

"How so, brother?" I asked, my interest now piqued.

"She's human. And no one would suspect her of-"

"Breaking into our enemies' lair, gaining intel, stealing important relics that could help our plight," I interrupted Brielle, the weight of my own words dawning on me.

"We might have a problem, though," Brielle noted with caution.

"A problem?" My focus turned to the screen, and the image of Ryder looming over her magnified. My skin prickled with agitation as that familiar hollowness in his expression stared back, the same one I had witnessed multiple times when he went into one of his blood rages. No one usually survived that.

"Get the witch. Now!" I screamed into the hallway as I made my way down to the basement to put an end to him. How dare he ignore my instructions.

The haunting sounds of her screams followed by fits of laughter could be heard from the foot of the basement stairs. Ryder stood over her body with blood-covered hands. Scars marred her body from her breasts to her feet. The scent of her blood mixed with wolfsbane muddied the air, suffocating me.

"Stop!" I roared, rushing into the room. Ryder did not flinch and continued tightening his hold on the rope around her neck.

"You won't get shit out of me, asshole," she mumbled, her eyes falling in and out of consciousness. He pulled tighter on the rope, and her body fell slack against the chair.

"Enough!" I pushed him aside, ripping through the ropes around her. Anger boiled through me when she fell into my chest. And though the rational part of me screamed that this was my doing, this was my plan. Another part burned with rage at the idea of someone else inflicting this sort of pain on her. It should be me - and only me - that makes her existence unbearable.

"My liege, you said to interrogate her and get the information you require," he spoke solemnly, yet his hands remained gripped on the end of the rope, and those familiar blood-thirsty irises stared back at me, unshaken by my request.

"I didn't say kill her," I hollered, lifting her in my hands. "You were trying to kill her. You went against my word." I continued, knocking his body across to the far end of the room. "Enzo, ensure he waits for me in my office," I instructed as I stepped out of the room.

"Hera is on her way," Brielle noted at the top of the basement stairs. She motioned for me to follow her. We bounded up the stairs to the second floor as Meraki moaned softly into my chest, her breath coming up uneven with each passing second. Her blood dripped along the staircase, her nakedness a warm reminder that a few seconds ago she was my prisoner. And those roles were soon changing.

My fingers trailed the outline of her cupid's bow, remembering how her lips felt against my cock. And the sight of her scarred body covered in blood elicited more than rage within it. Her heady scent wrapped around my cock, making even thinking straight difficult.

"Place her in the guest room," Brielle instructed, moving toward that path.

"No!" I grunted, continuing up the spiral staircase to the next floor, which led to my section of the house. "She stays in my room," I ordered, letting her know this wasn't up for negotiation.

"After all that, she still didn't give him what he wanted, huh?" She scrunched her face, her eyes following the series of knife marks and wounds across her body. "I think I may like her even more," she added, her tone filled with admiration.

Now I was intrigued.

"The witch is here," Brielle announced as I placed her on my bed. "She's on her way upstairs now. You speak with Ryder. I've seen some of his work, but this? This looks personal. Something tells me he knows more about her than he's letting on," she commented, biting her lower lip.

"So, it is true death and bloodshed always follow your family?" Hera strolled in, her eyes locked on Meraki's body.

"Deal with her!" I instructed, not having the patience to explain myself. I headed for the door, ready to drain the life out of Ryder.

"She's human," Hera muttered, her eyes widening at the realization. "This is crossing a line, Quillian." She halted in her steps.

"What line would that be, witch?" I turned toward her, now more irritated than before.

"Witches like me do not harm humans. I'm willing to help with most things, but this? No friggin way."

"You are not harming her." I exhaled a frustrated breath. "She is under my protection-"

"If this is what your protection looks like, I want out of our alliance," she shouted, stepping toward me.

"I need her healed, or so help me I'll tear the limbs off every member in your coven until someone does what you refuse to do."

"Do your worst," she spat back as if the idea of me enacting that was what she desired.

"Q, you see to Ryder. Hera and I will talk. She's going to calm down. Right?" Brielle intervened, moving toward her and wrapping her hands around her shoulder. Hera hesitated for a second, looking from Meraki's body to me. Hesitantly she nodded and allowed Brielle to lead her inside.

"If he did this-" Hera's voice trailed off, laced with disgust.

"He didn't," Brielle's voice echoed as I left the room.

Ryder had a lot of explaining to do, and if I wasn't satisfied with his answer, there would be blood spilled.

"I DON'T KNOW WHAT SHE IS. I'VE DONE EVERY CHECK imaginable. The only intel I could find on her showed that Meraki Irinhera was an orphan, and she died in a car accident a few years after her parents. But we know that's not the case," Ryder announced, sipping on the glass of liquor in his hand with a slight tremble. He was smart to be afraid. I didn't let disobedience go unpunished.

"My sister believes this may have been personal for you. This was beyond the remit of your job," I added, ensuring he heard the irritation in my voice. "You were going to kill her even though I had instructed you not to." I stated it as a fact rather than a question.

"I was intrigued. She isn't like any that I've interrogated before. How is it possible that a human would be able to deal with that level of pain inflicted upon them and still not divulge everything? I know some beings here that would have confessed during the first few minutes," he replied.

Enzo's attention turned to me, his hands resting awkwardly on the arm of the chair. I could see the wheels turning in his head as he weighed the pros and cons of what we had previously discussed.

"You think she's hiding something?" Enzo questioned. Ryder shook his head.

"She's more than a thief. I've interrogated agents from the Invisible Sun, and none lasted this long, and they weren't as well trained as you described," Ryder continued, his head still bowed in an act of submission. Enzo turned to me, acknowledging the possibility of that being true, and silently motioned that he would look further into it.

"I cannot let your insolence go unpunished," I spoke after a moment of silence. Killing him would be too easy. I needed him to suffer, and Enzo had ensured that a surprise awaited him upon his arrival home. Blood was not going to be spilled in this house. "But you are of value," I stated, rising to my feet, my attention trained on the image of the empty garden area.

"You do not speak of her or what happened in the house," Enzo instructed, leaning forward in his chair, and motioned for him to leave. He knew me well enough to know that if I had to stare at his face any longer, I would do something drastic.

Killing him now would not reflect well in my quest for leadership.

"My liege." He bowed, his eyes moving erratically across the room as if anticipating my attack. "What will become of her?" he asked, a little eager for my liking.

"That's not for you to worry about. You may leave," I answered flatly. "And, Ryder, if a rumor gets back to me about this, I will personally ensure your death," I spoke slowly, wanting him to understand the seriousness of the predicament he was in. As much as I needed his services and called on him more frequently than I would like to admit, I wouldn't hesitate to be the reason for his demise.

"Of course," he answered calmly as he opened the door and made his way out. Enzo stepped in immediately after.

"You did what I asked before?"

"Of course," he replied, rising to his feet.

"I also need him trailed and followed. Report anything out of the ordinary," I instructed.

"You think he's hiding something?" Enzo queried as he sat opposite me.

"I agree with Brie's assessment. This doesn't feel like his usual job. He knows something, or he has become even more twisted than I remember. I need more information on Meraki. I need intel on any friends and records we can use to our benefit. Also, keep an ear out about agents from the Invisible Sun. If Ryder's suspicions are true, we might be dealing with more than a thief."

"An assassin or assassin," Enzo whispered. I nodded, not wanting to expand further. Dealing with Vera was one thing. The possibility of another killer was another thing altogether.

"So, we are going ahead with the plan?" Brielle strolled into the room. "Hera just left. She healed her and made a potion to help relieve any symptoms of pain." She sat down on one of the chairs facing my desk. I turned, giving Enzo the ground to expand on what came next.

"We are going ahead with the plan," Enzo answered, clapping his hands together as he sat down.

"Do share more, Enzy baby," Brielle chimed, moving her seat closer.

11

THE LIFE IS IN THE BLOOD

M*eraki*

LIGHT HEATED MY SKIN, AND THE STEADY SCENT OF freshly baked bread filled my senses, making my stomach grumble in turn. Soft cashmere sheets pressed against my skin, and a bed of pillows kept my head upright. I ran my hands through my hair, anticipating another long day of interrogations.

My eyes slowly peeled open as an immaculate room overlooking a large city landscape came into view. The room consisted of hanging ceiling lights above an elevated bed and was complete with a mid-sized open-plan seating area. Large railings covered the four corners of the bed. The view outside was made even better by the round jacuzzi at the curve of the balcony.

I inhaled the scent of the sheets, and my nose was hit with the familiar scent of Quillian's woodsy aroma.

My plan had worked.

I rushed out of bed and made my way to the balcony as the warm summer air bathed my skin.

If I had qualms about whether I was in Esneoh, those were now laid to rest.

A jolt of excitement buzzed through me, and it took everything within me to squash down the need to jump and scream with excitement.

I was here. I was finally here after a decade of persistence.

This wasn't how I anticipated making it in here, but I was grateful. I just had to ensure I played my cards well and got to the heart of what the Kingsleys wanted from me.

If that want came with the possibility of staying in the city, it was one I would utilize without thought.

"You're awake," Quillian said, startling me from the depth of my thoughts. His eyes heated, and his gaze trailed over my body, setting my skin ablaze.

"You changed my clothes," I noted, realizing I was no longer naked.

"We also cleaned you up," he replied. I made a note of the fact that I no longer smelled like sewage. My skin and hair were freshly cleansed, my body well moisturized.

"My cuffs are off," I said, playing along with this game as if I was oblivious to the obvious.

"Perceptive," he replied, walking to the center of the room, and perched himself against one of the gray accent chairs.

"I could kill you within seconds," I spat, taking note of the various things around the room I could use as weapons to hold him down temporarily before I gained access to my equipment again.

"I could snap your neck right now, and no one would hear about it." He arched a brow. His eyes followed mine as they landed on the silver bedside table.

"Silver doesn't work on us, my Little Hellion. My family and I had years to train our bodies against its effects." He smiled tersely. It wasn't in a mocking manner, but rather one of a tiger assessing the weakness of its prey.

"Why am I no longer in the basement?" I asked after a

moment of silence. It was clear that Quillian was waiting on me to make the first move, asserting his dominance. I leaned against the glass balcony, wishing I had wings. Now more than ever they would have come in handy.

"I have a proposition," he said, leaning back against the chair, his movements calculated and domineering.

Never give your enemy a vantage point against you.

"And why would I adhere to any proposition?" I asked, keeping my eyes trained on the subtlety of his movements, anticipating his next move.

He rose, taking calculated steps toward me. I stepped to my left, my hands resting against the railing.

"Don't tell me you're afraid of me," he laughed with that undermining air of arrogance about him. His nostrils flared and his pupils dilate as each step carried the weight of a battalion. "Though I don't think you're capable of such an emotion," he continued, stopping before me, his height blocking my view of the room.

He reached for me, and I bypassed the movement by lowering myself to his waist and angling my body outward. I stepped back and made a beeline for the silver lamp at the center of the sitting area.

"I know better than to trust any man, let alone your kind." I gripped the weapon, my hold on it tightening. "This may not affect you and your siblings as you claim. But it still does." He blurred into the room, circling my movements with amusement and irritation.

"I saw the way your pupils widened, and your body slackened every time I shot you with one of my bullets."

"Is that so?" He crossed his arms over his chest.

I stepped forward. "Should we test it?" I asked, pressing the tail of the lamp against his abdomen. He wrapped his thick hands around it, beckoning and daring me to do so.

Remember your plans, Meraki.

I smiled, loosening my hold on the weapon. "Why am I here?"

I motioned to the room, dropping the weapon to the floor. He stared down at it, then back at me.

"Sit," he stated, the word a forcible command.

"I'll stand," I offered, stepping out of the way. A low rumble emitted from his chest, and it was obvious Quillian was not used to his requests being denied by a woman, let alone a human.

"A partnership." The words were like a sword pressed against his tongue.

"Why would I –"

"Either the partnership or death. You choose." He motioned to the window. I took a few steps back, giving myself a safe space not to inhale the familiarity of his scent.

"I'm not afraid of death," I replied hastily.

I wasn't afraid of death, but I was scared of dying without avenging my sister's death. Those were two different things.

"What are you afraid of, Meraki?" he replied, his tone flat, his legs outstretched. "Or perhaps I should ask what it is you desire?" He pointed at the scenery of Esneoh. "I watched you look out there. I heard your heartbeat increase. The first time since you've been here, may I add. I saw the eagerness and determination in your eyes when I caught you. There's something here you desire and are looking for. Perhaps we may be of some help to one another."

My mouth grew dry, the reality of his assessment making my skin tingle with discomfort. I should have been on guard, anticipating his next move.

"And what is it you want? What is so pressing that you would rather lay with an unknown enemy?" I asked. He laughed, rising to his feet.

"A wife," he answered plainly. I stepped back, almost tripping over myself. "For pretense obviously," he added, eliminating the space between us. Laughter bubbled up inside me, and I couldn't help but chuckle aloud. Was this another part of the interrogation?

"All right, joke's over-"

"Do I look like I'm joking? Do I look like someone who makes insignificant things like jokes?" he questioned, his lips curled, and the veins on his hands becoming more engorged.

"Wait, you're serious!" I stepped back, frazzled. This I wasn't expecting. "I'm human, remember?"

"How can I miss how repulsive your kind is?" he deadpanned, his eyes cold and flinty. Blood pounded in my ears, and I clenched my fists, reminding myself to stay cool.

"Then why would you want to marry someone so repulsive?" I pointed at his chest.

"Pretend-"

"Oh, for god's sake," I stepped back, realizing this wasn't someone to be reasoned with. "No!" I stated plainly.

"No?"

"Death seems more fitting than marriage to you," I replied, the words making no sense in my ears, but I could not for a minute see myself bound to this asshole of the highest order.

"Little Hellion, I didn't make myself clear before. You have no choice."

"And this" - I motioned between us - "is a death trap." I snarled, making my way to the balcony.

"You're not afraid of death, remember?" His eyes turned to the field ahead and back to me.

"Yes-" My words were cut short as he blurred before me, and a sharp object pricked my neck. "What the actual fuck?" I jerked back as warmth filled my skin. "What did you do to me?"

"I infected you," Quillian stated, throwing the syringe.

"You what?" I shouted, my hands fixed on my neck.

"A mixture of my blood and a witch's spell, ensuring you and I are bound."

"You asshole." I lurched for him, releasing a series of blows and kicks. Rage and anger boiled inside me, mixing as one heady potion.

"It's simple, really. In two days, your organs will continue to deteriorate until we enter a Blood Oath." He stepped back, his face marred with amusement.

"A Blood Oath?" I repeated the words, trying to make sense of what the hell I had gotten myself into.

"We swear an oath to one another, binding ourselves to whatever terms we both agree on. When those terms are fulfilled, then the bond is broken, and you can leave here after, like we never met-"

"And the pendant?"

"That, Little Hellion, you can never have," he replied, an edge of warning in his voice. "You have two days to think on it. I'll be back for an answer," he added, the echo of his voice trailing along the walls of the room as he disappeared.

I fell on the chair at the center of the room, contemplating what had just transpired yet unable to really do so as my stomach rumbled nonstop.

The door creaked open, and I jumped to my feet, anticipating another showdown.

"It's just me!" Brielle called as she strolled in with a tray filled with steak, potatoes, vegetables, cheesecake, and a side of freshly baked bread.

"Well, I guess I came at the right time?" She smiled as my stomach rumbled in that moment. She placed the food on the center table and sat across in the adjacent chair.

"I take it your conversation with my brother didn't go well?" She arched a brow, beckoning for me to eat.

"He injected me," I answered, easing into the seat beside her.

"And what exactly did you say to him for him to do that?" she asked, her demeanor a subtle giveaway that this was standard behavior.

"No to his offer," I answered, my eyes now focused on the food.

She laughed, and a bemused look stretched her lips. "He's definitely going to stew on that for a while." Her eyes followed mine, stopping at the food displayed before me.

"You should eat. You'll need the energy." She motioned to the food.

"Nice try. You can go poison another helpless human," I responded, stealing my gaze from it.

"My offer still stands. Poisoning you would be of no benefit to me," she stated, pushing the tray toward me.

I wanted to argue, but I had two choices right now. Die by hunger or by poisoning. I reached for the cutlery and bit into the stake and potatoes, groaning from the texture and seasoning.

"I'm glad you like my cooking," she laughed.

"You cooked?" I asked, buttering the warm bread.

"You sound surprised."

"Don't you guys just drink blood and kill people? Why cook?" I asked through a mouth full of food.

"I like the taste of food. I don't need it, but I like its taste," she answered truthfully.

"You're weird," I replied, continuing to stuff the remainder of the food into my mouth.

"For someone who doesn't eat, you sure know how to cook a mean steak," I commented, wiping the remnants of food on my mouth.

"Some could say that steak is like-"

"All right. Don't ruin this meal for me. I plan to continue eating steak after I leave this place." I raised my hand dismissively before she could go any further. The last thing I needed was the imagery of stake and human meat.

"Under different circumstances, you and I would have been friends," she stated simply, and a look I couldn't name crossed her features.

"Maybe," I replied, not wanting to get into the semantics that under normal circumstances she and I would have never crossed paths. There was a world of difference between normal humans and her kind. I was simply the exception.

"Quillian isn't as bad as he seems-" She stopped herself

midsentence when she saw the look on my face. "Okay, fine, he is an asshole, but he also has redeeming qualities," she pressed.

"Are you trying to convince yourself or me?" I laughed as I bit into the cheesecake.

Brielle released an exasperated sigh and stood. "Take the offer. I'll ensure he adheres to his promise," she stated as the door closed behind her, leaving me to wonder what came next.

12

OATHS CANNOT BE BROKEN

M*eraki*

"What's your answer?" Quillian strolled into the room, his imposing presence taking all the air out of the room.

Warm hands trailed my body, starting from my stomach and resting against my chest. I leaned into it, allowing myself to indulge in the sensation. When I opened my eyes, I found myself in the darkened room.

"You're up," Quillian said, the outline of his shadow blending and merging into the door.

"Why me?" I asked the question that had been an impending thought throughout the day.

"You're strong and can look after yourself," he replied, making his way to the sitting area.

"How romantic," I mumbled under my breath as I rose from the bed and took a seat in the chair opposite him.

The air in the room strummed with energy, and I leaned back

in my seat, my guard lowered, open to negotiating his previous offer.

"So, you're saying you need my skills," I said after a moment of silence. "And if you need my skills, you're trying to obtain something," I continued, playing into the narrative.

"Correct," he answered, his eyes dancing across my bare legs. "I need someone versed in playing a role," he continued, his tone accusatory.

"And?" I motioned for him to continue, sensing there was more here that I wasn't yet privy to.

"Every millennium, a leader is chosen from the four houses in Esneoh. They compete for the Dark Crown."

"Okay, and what are the benefits of the Dark Crown?" I sat forward in my seat, my skin buzzing with an unknown awareness.

This wasn't information known to the Alokari, and I had read everything they had on record about Esneoh.

"The ability to be the one supreme leader over all the other houses. The other houses will pay a tax to the king and follow the laws and rules created by them."

"What else?"

"The land imbues the king with strength," he finally added, and I shook my head.

"The land. What does that mean?" Quillian sat forward, the moon casting a shadow over his face.

"What do you know about Esneoh?" he asked hesitantly, the light drawing attention to the sharp edges of his face.

"Nothing at all from the looks of it," I replied, motioning for him to continue.

"This land was created from ancient magic."

"The Nephilim's?" He nodded.

"Magic runs through the land, revitalizing it. And each house is like the vessel that keeps it running."

"The land is like a living, breathing entity in itself?" He shook his head, and another reality dawned on me. "The leader will have access to that power source?" I stated, not needing his response.

"And my role in this?" I questioned, still not quite comprehending how this all ties with me.

"The law now states that every party that seeks to enter the trials must be married," he answered, his eyes absorbing my every movement.

"And you need me because-'"

"Our marriage will legitimize my claim. You will be the first human married to a leader, the first given access to the land that isn't because of some ancestral oath," he continued, his hands resting on the arm of the chair. "I might also need you for more skill-related things."

"Such as?"

"Ones I cannot disclose until you are under oath."

"Why?"

"Because whatever I share with you, you will not be able to share it with anyone outside these walls," he stated, pointing at the space between us.

"So, you need three things from me, not one," I noted, running my hands through my hair. This could work in my favor. "And what do I get out of this?" I pinched my nose, waiting for his response. This would determine how we moved forward.

"Three things. One of your choosing, your life right now, and the ability to leave Esneoh once our alliance has been fulfilled," he added, and the tension on the final part of that sentence told me that was a lie. "What is it you desire" - he pointed to the landscape outside -"out there?" His gaze never left mine.

"Something I can only tell you when under the oath," I replied, my mind assessing and calculating how to best use him to attain information about Alessia's killer.

"How can I be sure you will stick to your promise?" I questioned, realizing there was too much on the line to trust his word for it.

"A witch will bind our agreement. If I fail to deliver on my end, I'll become indebted to you."

"What does that mean?"

"It means I become like a slave to your wishes. Anything you say, I will have to fulfil."

"And me?"

"The same applies. Your soul becomes tied to me. I can demand you do what I please, and you won't be able to fight it," he added solemnly, and I swallowed hard at the implication.

"The witch is here now," Quillian spoke after a brief moment of silence. "She's outside the door." I nodded, unable to find the words to agree to the madness but straying away or saying no wasn't an option.

The door opened immediately after, and light flooded the room. A slim-figured woman with hair as thick as the morning fog strolled in, seeming exasperated.

Quillian rose to his feet, his jaw tensing at her presence.

"How are you feeling?" She turned her warm eyes toward me. "The potions worked. You feeling, okay?"

"Thank you for helping me." I rose to my feet, standing a few feet beside Quillian.

"Hera..."

"Quillian." She turned to face him, defiance in her eyes. She turned back to me. "Are you sure you want to be tied to him? A blood oath is-"

"Don't test me, witch. You won't live to talk about it," Quillian spoke, his voice filled with unspoken power.

"Don't worry about me. I can hold my own," I replied, returning her smile with another. "I'm Meraki."

"Hera. You and I will be seeing a lot of each other," she commented, her eyes briefly turning to Quillian. It was evident that there was no love between these two.

"Blood," Hera muttered, reaching for his hand, and pricking his thumb with a blade. She repeated the same movement with my hand.

Hera chanted a series of incoherent words, and rays of amber light flashed across the bedroom walls. The wind outside stilled, and an eerie silence descended, followed by a quiet *pop*. Warmth flooded my body, and an unexplainable feeling locked in my chest, making goosebumps rise across my skin.

She pulled back the dagger, and her gaze flickered back and forth between us. She reached into her purse and pulled out two vials, handing us one each. “Once you’ve both stated your terms, drink this. The binding will take effect then,” she noted, making her way to the door before I even had time to say thank you.

Quillian and I stood, facing each other in the room, the atmosphere charged with unspoken power.

“To be my wife and to help with requests to uncover who had us imprisoned for a millennium,” Quillian said, drinking the entirety of his vial. My eyes widened at the implication of his words.

“To help me find my very close friend’s killer,” I half lied, twisting the truth of our relationship. Years of assassin work had taught me one vital lesson.

Never show your enemy all your cards.

I drank the contents of the vial, the same warmth that rested on my chest now making its way across my body.

13

GROUND RULES

M*eraki*

"Is my sister-in-law awake?" Brielle's singsong voice startled me from my sleep.

"What time is it?" I asked, my head throbbing. "What did you call me?" I turned to face her in her black bodice and lavender high-waisted pants.

She walked into the room, her heels echoing on the tiled floor. "My sister-in-law. What do you call the woman who's engaged to your brother?" She sat on the edge of the bed, seemingly at ease within my space.

That was a weakness.

"If you and I are going to be friends, we should probably never discuss your evil brother," I stated, running my hands over my wrist. "Speaking of the devil, where is he?" I rose from the bed, feeling more energized and like myself than I have for the last eight days.

"Meeting. He will join you later. When did you move into

this room?" she asked surveying the room I had moved into last night. After the oath, I had insisted on space, and Quillian was all too willing to get his room back. The rooms were identical in nature except for the missing jacuzzi and city view.

"Last night."

"I see," she stated blandly. "In the meantime, I volunteered to shop for you." She smirked, clapping her hands. Two elderly women walked into the room, pulling behind them metal wardrobes. The clothes ranged from long gowns, dresses, shirts, pants, and shoes to swimwear.

"Only the best for my sister-in-law." Brielle smirked, and I couldn't shake the feeling that she was enjoying this way too much for someone who knew the whole thing was a farce.

"Can I shower first? I stink and-"

"Say no more, sis-in-law."

"Brielle-"

"Okay, fine, I'll stop," she noted. "I just never thought those words would ever leave my mouth. I had to test it out at least." She laughed as she motioned for the elderly ladies to step forth.

"This is Eugene and Elena. They help with maintaining the house. If you need anything, these are my two favorite ladies to ask." She pointed at the women with deep frown lines and heavy skin.

Eugene and Elena introduced themselves and left us to rummage through the items.

"There're a lot of gowns and dresses," I noted, running my hands through the materials ranging from silk and chiffon to cotton.

"Well, there's going to be a lot of events. If there's one thing Esneoh society is good for, it is hosting events," she stated dryly. "Besides, my brother will want to showcase you across Esneoh to legitimize the whole affair."

"There're also pajamas, underwear, and anything else you may need already placed in your wardrobe." She motioned to an empty wall to my right. Brielle pulled out a black bodice gown, pressing it up against my body.

"What do you think?" she asked excitedly.

"Everything looks good," I replied, unsure what to make of her yet, especially as she hadn't mentioned the proposition we discussed in the basement.

After some time had passed, Brielle walked to the empty wall on the far right, placing her hand on the indented door that blended in with the walls.

The door slid back, and we walked into a gigantic glass wardrobe accented by grays, blacks, and gold furnishings. The end of the wardrobe led to a bathroom with a black marble floor, walls, and brass fixtures. Brielle sensed my desperation to get clean and left me to it after the tour.

I spent time in the bathroom recalling the events that had transpired and what that meant for me going forward. I now had access to Esneoh, but no pendant. Darya's warnings about the severity of this case were a subtle whisper at the back of my mind reminding me that returning empty-handed would have consequences. Unless I offered an alternative.

I also needed to get back to Jersey Hill as I had long extended my reporting frame for updates, a first in a decade. This was bound to set alarm bells blaring in the Alokari.

After I had showered, I walked back through the wardrobe, finding the clothes Brielle had bought had been hung, put on display for my viewing pleasure.

I changed into a black set of pants and a sheer top. Then I walked back, anticipating my next conversation with Quillian.

"You took a while," Quillian said, towering over the frame of the bed.

"Privacy is clearly not a thing in this house," I muttered under my breath.

"Yes. I needed to clean a week's worth of mental and emotional filth," I replied accusingly, closing the door behind me.

"Hmm," he mumbled, his gaze raking my body.

"Do you need something?" I asked, stepping into the fray and taking a seat at the foot of the bed, directly facing him.

"We need to talk-"

"A woman's four favorite words," I nodded, waiting on him to take the floor.

"I don't respond well to sarcasm, human-"

"My name is Meraki, vampire." I rolled my eyes. "You should probably start calling me sweetheart or honey soon. You know, to make this whole thing believable?" I motioned to the space between us.

He snarled and stepped toward me, eliminating the space between us. His eyes radiated a lighter shade of gray under the morning light.

"The marriage takes place today in the courts of Kinavari," he stated, a tinge of threat behind his words.

"This proposal will go down in history as the most romantic, Mr. Kingsley," I replied, enjoying pushing his buttons as fury radiated through him. I was under no illusions. Quillian Kingsley was dangerous, but I did enjoy the sight of him trying to restrain himself. With his eyes locked on me, he stepped back and sat on the chair facing me.

"Let's set the ground rules in my house," he stated, reaching for the assortment of drinks on the side table. Hesitantly, I make my way toward him and reclined on the sofa opposite him.

"Rules," I repeated.

"Number one: never leave this house without being accompanied by someone."

"And who would accompany me?" I asked, noting how this could pose a problem for later.

"Me, Silas, or Brielle. There will also be security around the house. Two specifically set to follow you," he added, grinding his teeth.

"It feels like I'm a prisoner-"

"Because that's what you still are. My prisoner. And in case you're unaware, your kind is more food and entertainment than beings to be wed and showcased." He sat forward in his seat, his voice deepening.

"Aren't I just lucky? I get to marry you," I interrupted, his arrogance irking me.

"You have no idea-"

"Are we going to discuss the ground rules or how much of a catch you are in Esneoh? Or is caring part of my role as your accessory?" Quillian rose to his feet, turning to face the view ahead.

"Rule number two: mind your business, and do not get involved in any of my family affairs." The muscles under his shirt flexed with each word.

"Noted. Mind my business. Though legally they will technically be my family once we are-" He blurred before me, his hands wrapped around my throat. He snarled, his fangs elongating. I kept my eyes trained on the red edge of his iris, smiling as his hold on me tightened.

"Rule number three: remember what this is." He pointed at his chest, then mine. "You are disposable. There are millions of your kind who could be in your place and be more compliant. Don't test my patience, human. I am not nice when pushed."

"Oh, nice." I choked, wrapping my hands around the outline of his hands, and my legs around his waist. Resting my weight on his body, I curled my legs around him, pushing him to the chair until I sat on top of him, straddling his waist. His breathing hitched, and his teeth clenched.

"Don't underestimate me, vampire. Too many of your kind have, and they haven't made it out alive," I breathed, unwrapping my legs, placing them on his chest, and pressing down until his hold relented.

I stepped back, readjusting my attire. "I have rules also." He laughed, leaning back in the chair.

"Rule number one: don't touch me," I bit, folding my arms across my chest. My eyes scoured the space, looking for a weapon.

Always be armed in anticipation of an attack.

"I think you're misunderstanding this alliance, little human," he laughed, rising to his feet, his hands clenched. "You're my wife, remember?" He stepped before me, his fingers trailing my face with rough strokes. "And as my wife, I should be able to touch you." His hands lowered to my collar, his gaze suggestive. "Kiss you," he continued, his eyes focused on my lips. "Fuck you, as and when I please, like the little slut you are," he continued, his thumb caressing my lips, trying to force its way into my mouth.

Warmth flooded my body, and my breath quickened, memories of the night we shared flashing through my mind, a reminder of how my body succumbed to his demands, his needs, and my desires. I stepped back, pushing myself from his hold.

Quillian stood still, watching me, a knowing smirk on his face. "Look how well your body responds to my touch," he continued, stepping forward. A predator after its prey.

"Rule number two: the lines between us should not be crossed. This is a job, a business transaction, a façade for the world out there. Keep your hand, and..." My eyes briefly fell to his groin, and I licked my lips, remembering the salty aftertaste.

"And?"

"And your dick to yourself, vampire," I breathed, my mouth saying one thing, my body another. He laughed, his dimples becoming more prominent, drawing emphasis to the fullness of his lips.

"I don't beg for pussy. "

"How fascinating." I rolled my eyes, leaning on the arm of the chair he had previously sat on.

"It's in abundance, and I can get it as and when I please," he stated, stepping back into the seat behind me.

"Monogamy is not a thing with your kind then?" I asked, keeping my voice even as my hands stretched around the head of the seat.

"You don't expect me to remain monogamous for the duration of this farce, do you?" he laughed. "You can do whatever you want as long as you're discreet about your affairs. This isn't a jail sentence after all."

"Noted," I replied. I moved into the seat, contemplating the liquor after all.

"Since the oath is now in effect, there are a few things we need to discuss to give you a clearer understanding of what I expect from you. The oath stipulates that whatever I share with you can never be discussed with another that is outside my family. If you do, death awaits you. If you attempt to break the oath or run, you become mine, tied to me for an eternity," he reaffirmed what we had already discussed.

He reclined in his seat, watching my throat bob as I sipped on my drink. "My family and I have been missing for a millennium," he exhaled, his fist tightening, and his eyes closed briefly. "It wasn't by choice."

"What does that mean?" I sat forward, placing my drink down, training my attention on him.

"We were imprisoned in caves in the human realm a couple of days after I won the last Dark Crown trials," he added, cracking his neck.

"Why didn't they just kill you all instead of-" I stopped myself, realizing the implication of my words. They were unable to kill them, and the closest they could get was keeping them bound. "You can't be killed?"

His jaw tensed, his whole body going rigid. "That's not what I said." He enunciated the words as if uttering them pained him. My mind went back to the news of his older brother's death recorded in the Alokari's records. There was a way to kill them. It just wasn't public knowledge.

"Our family has been around since the inception of Esneoh. We were here during the times of the Nephilim and before that. So are the leaders of the other houses. We are immortal."

"But-"

"But even immortality has its weakness," he stated as pain flashed through his features and disappeared just as quickly. I knew that pain. I had lived and breathed it for the last decade. It was a pain that ate away the fabric of your being, a reminder that some part of you, someone you loved, was no more.

The need to ask about his brother sat at the tip of my tongue, but I knew doing so would expose that I knew too much about the family and doing so would only rouse suspicion.

"We also need to discuss your bargain, finding the killer of your family friend." He rolled the words off his tongue, letting me know he knew there was more there than I was letting on.

"What do you need?"

"Everything you have." His brows dipped. "Including all the intel you've already acquired."

"I will need my things-"

"I kept your weapons but destroyed every communication device I found on you." He raised the glass to his lips with a condescending scowl.

"You destroyed my things?" I asked, keeping the anger coiling through me at bay.

"You're lucky that was all that was destroyed. Your life could have been one of those things. But I've been known for my generosity," he replied.

"Then I will need to return back-"

"No!" He laughed, the words etched with warning.

"I wasn't asking." I tapped the arm of my chair. "Not doing so would put a hit on my life-"

"Then I guess you remaining here would do you favors?" His brows arched, beckoning me to argue otherwise.

"You have to fulfil my request," I stated boldly.

"I do? Do tell," he raised his hand, motioning for me to continue, a mocking undertone in his command.

"It's part of my bargain. You can't fulfil one without the other." He released a low growl, his eyes darkening. "Unless you want to go back on your promise? I'm more than happy to make you, bitch!" I smirked as he rose to his feet. I followed suit, anticipating a not so favorable response.

"Your kind repulses me," he stated calmly, the anger in his

tone filled with vitriol. His attention turned to the door, and he walked past me, bumping my chest in the process.

I ran after him, stopping him at the entrance of the door. "Move, human," he warned.

"We are not done. No agreement has been made." I remained unmoving, knowing that I needed to return today. Any longer than that would make me an enemy of the Alokari. Agents who were suspected of betraying the organization or tried showed up dead or were never heard from again. And I certainly wasn't trying to join that list.

"Do you want me dead before this even begins?" I motioned to us both. "The people I work with will ensure that's the case." I pressed my fingers to his chest.

"I need to leave today. I also cannot be here seven days out of the week. I will need to be in Jersey Hill at least two days out of the seven."

"Two days out of seven, nothing more. You can work out how to balance that," he replied, trying to maneuver past me. I placed my hand on his chest, blocking his path. "Saturday and Sunday," he exhaled in a frustrated breath, his hands pressed above me, tugging at the door.

"One more thing," I continued, pressing the entirety of my weight on the handle.

"Human-" Quillian growled, the sound echoing across the walls as a clear warning.

"I need the necklace," I demanded, knowing I was in no position to ask for it, but there was nothing wrong with trying. He stepped back, staring long and hard at me.

"What do you know about the pendant?" he asked, his hands clasped around my left hand, running circles around my ring finger.

"It's a job I was assigned," I replied, ensuring I gave nothing away about the little I knew of the pendant. He wrapped the entirety of his palm over my hand, holding my fingers in place.

"I see," he murmured under his breath as his pupils dilated, beckoning me to submit to his power and divulge more.

"That's not going to work on me, vampire." I jerked my hand from his hold.

"I know. I was testing how it would feel when I finally have you under me, submitting to my every whim and command without being able to deny me," he laughed, stepping back. "The answer is still no. But you already knew that."

"I can't have disappeared this long and return with nothing," I pressed, my mind coming up with scenarios and excuses to relay to Darya. Each one ended with me six feet under. "I've never failed a job. Going back empty-handed will send red flags," I added, keeping my voice even, refusing to beg him for it. Doing so would show weakness.

"Then you better start getting creative. And ensure you don't die. We still have so much to do," he answered. I stepped away from the door, my hands curling into fists, wanting to stab a knife through his chest.

"Now, get dressed. We have a wedding we need to attend in an hour," he laughed, walking to the door. "Go for the white silk dress. We need something that emphasizes how sweet, innocent, and untouched my human bride is, no?" His laughter trailed behind him as he left the room.

I slammed the door, not wanting to start another fight before the bargain had even begun. Besides, I had a wedding to prepare for.

14

THE SACRIFICIAL LAMB

Meraki

I DIDN'T WEAR THE WHITE DRESS. I OPTED FOR A cream-colored three-piece suit as a silent warning and reminder that no man owned me or told me what to do.

"Oh dear." Brielle smiled thirty minutes later when she came to collect me. "I see that one of you is going to kill the other before this is all over?" She motioned for me to follow her. There was no malice in the words, just an undertone of amusement.

I followed behind her, taking in the long white passageway adorned with art pieces and gold accessories. "The house tour can wait for when you come back," she stated as we reached the intersection of the passageway. "You and I are on the third floor, Quillian on the fourth, and Silas on this one." She gestured around as the stairs appeared, making her way down the pristine spiral staircase.

"The first floor is where everything else is," she continued, her steps halting as Quillian, and Silas came into view. Silas tipped his fedora hat back. He was dressed informally in black knee-ripped pants and a t-shirt.

Quillian's gaze fell on me, his pristine black suit clinging to every muscle in his body. "That's not what I asked you to wear," he gritted out, placing the phone in his hand in his back pocket.

"The day I start listening to you is the day hell freezes over," I replied, stepping onto the floor after Brielle.

"Now, brother, that's no way to speak to a woman," Silas said, turning to face his brother with a playful jab.

"You were supposed to wear a white dress-"

"Come on, Q. Since when did you start believing that bullshit? You can't control everything." Brielle rolled her eyes.

"He thinks he can, that's his problem."

"Tell me more." I stepped toward the youngest Kingsley brother, intertwining our hands together. "Brother-in-law," I added as Silas pulled me into the direction Brielle was heading.

"You and I are going to get along just fine." Silas lightly tapped my hands. Quillian released a low warning growl, one that only seemed to make Silas laugh even more.

"Did you know he-"

"Enough, Silas," he warned. Brielle opened the door ahead.

"You two can save your bickering for another day. Must you always embarrass me by acting like teenagers?"

"Now Brie" - Silas stepped forward, the smirk on his face still prevalent - "what fun would that be?" He unclasped our hands as we walked through the passageway into the garage.

"I'll take the human on the Aventador. You two trail behind. Enzo is at the courthouse ensuring there is no one else there," Quillian ordered, reaching into his pocket for the car keys. "We go in and come back out. No one sees us until I've called a meeting with the leaders of Kinavari in three days," he added, his accusatory gaze turning to Silas. Brielle pulled Silas to the left end of the garage where an innumerable fleet of cars was vertically parked.

Quillian turned to the right, and my eyes fell on a Cosmic

Starship and MTT motorcycle, and I almost drooled. Motorcycles were a weakness of mine.

He stopped, motioning for me to enter the car, and kicking off the ignition immediately after. Excitement bubbled in my stomach at the prospect of finally getting a glimpse of Esneoh.

The garage door opened, and Quillian sped down the driveway. My eyes fell on the rear-view mirror that gave me a clear view of the large estate, a classic royal mansion design, king-style canopy with a fountain, and additional adjourning houses.

The ride was silent, and I was appreciative of it.

We drove through woodlands with grand luxurious mansions to private streets and communal cul-de-sacs. And as we neared the heart of the city, large skyscrapers, boutiques, restaurants, and streets came into view, each emulating a similar dome-shaped architecture. The streets were packed with bodies of not just vampires but demons and other supernatural beings as well.

I looked over each building and street, keeping my eyes out for The Den, as that was to be my first pit stop in my search for the bearer of the ring.

"We are here," Quillian announced, bringing the car to a halt behind a Grecian building. Unlike the other streets we had passed through, this building and its surrounding area were empty and derelict, and only the sound of the sweeping wind could be heard from miles away.

Quillian exited the car and made his way to the back of the building where Silas and Brielle could be heard on the other side of its walls.

"Everything went well, Enzo?" Quillian asked as a tall man with an army cut approached us. He and Quillian were of similar heights and seemed to navigate around each other like old friends.

"Meraki." He stopped to take my hand and bow courteously. "I'm Enzo, a long-time family friend." He smiled, peering down at me with his green eyes, reminding me of a fresh lawn of grass.

"Brother." Quillian interjected, making it clear that this wasn't just anyone but someone he held dear.

"Thank you for helping," he continued as if Quillian's words didn't register.

"Not by choice," I muttered under my breath.

"Let's get this over and done with. I have things to do and leaders to snoop on," Quillian commented, straightening his cufflinks. Enzo walked on his right, and I remained at his left side as we walked along the long marble-floored pathway lined with rooms.

"Loki might suspect something is up. He had me tailed. Luckily, I had the two security you assigned for Meraki. Sol and Blaze lead his men on a wild goose chase. This will have to be quick, and it's probably best she's disappearing for the next few days."

Quillian kept his gaze ahead, refusing to acknowledge my presence. "You leave after the wedding and be back here no later than six on Monday morning," he said to no one in particular. I stopped, turning back and forth, acting oblivious to the fact the statement was directed at me.

"Do you know who he's talking to?" I turned my attention to Enzo, who seemed unsure whether to respond or back away.

Quillian halted, turning to face me. "The blood priest is here," Enzo said, trying to ease the tension between us.

"Should I make myself clearer, Meraki?" he spoke the words slowly, as if needing to ensure I grasped the weight of his irritation.

"You do have manners after all, vampire." I lightly tapped his chest, noting Enzo had strayed to an open room on the right. I followed him, not bothering to turn back.

"This is your fault," I hear Quillian say, his rage aimed at Enzo.

"Priest, keep this short and sweet," Quillian called from behind me as we walked toward the altar of the small room. Silas and Brielle had already arrived and were waiting by a scroll at the side of the room.

Near the altar stood a white-haired man adorned in gold, brown, and ruby-red apparel. "Your liege," he spoke, his hand visibly trembling. "This was unexpected," he continued, his eyes trailing to me.

"You are to marry us under the laws of Esneoh."

Brielle stepped away from the scroll, moving to stand beside me on the left side of the altar.

"Silas and I have signed as the two witnesses," Brielle stated, wiping her blood-stained hands on a handkerchief. My brows furrowed at the movement, unable to make sense of everything transpiring right now.

"Marriage is a blood-binding contract. Silas and I swore as blood witnesses. You and my brother will now drink each other's blood to seal the contract between you," she whispered in my ear as the priest stepped forward with a small knife in his hands. Silas approached and stood beside Enzo, whose attention was fixed on the door as if he were expecting someone to break into the room at any moment.

Quillian's face was a mask of indifference and an impenetrable cloak of guarded indifference.

"We are gathered here today-"

"Cut the speech, old man." Quillian dismissively raised his hand, turning to face me fully for the first time since we had left the house.

I was doing this. I was actually about to marry a vampire in order to have access to the City of Darkness. Hollywood could never prepare me for this shit.

The priest with trembling hands reached for two golden jugs on the pulpit and motioned for Brielle and Silas to help him. They each held one.

He motioned for me to raise my hand, and I did so hesitantly, my eyes scouring the room for a way out. Could I do this? Could I tie myself to a vampire and trust that he would help me find Alessia's killer? As the seconds ticked by, my breathing hitched and my vision began to grow blurry, the weight of the responsibility like a stone wedged against my chest.

"Breathe," Quillian spoke, his scent and the power behind his words like a cord wrapped around my heart.

"I would feel the same way being tied to him, Meraki," Silas snickered, and Brielle followed, calming the madness of everything.

"Your hand," the priest interrupted, taking hold of my wrist. Brielle placed the jug underneath my hand as the knife drew blood. I winced, the cold edge of the blade making my body still with unease.

The priest raised my hand, allowing my blood to coat and fill the jug. He then turned his attention to Quillian, performing the same rite.

Brielle handed me the handkerchief she had used earlier, pressing down on the cut to stop the flow of blood.

"The life of a being is in its blood. Blood ties, binds, and acts as an agent of flame and chaos," the priest said, stepping onto the pulpit. "By partaking of each other's blood, you agree to become a single flame, a single unit." He motioned for Brielle and Silas to exchange the jugs.

"You will drink at the same time, unifying this contract," the priest noted, directing Silas and Brielle to hand us the jugs. Quillian scrunched his face in disgust as he raised the mug to his nose, reminding me that the wolfsbane was still present in my blood stream.

"Something wrong, your liege?" I smirked. He tipped his head up, the twitch in his lip a silent warning for me to behave. I raised the jug to my nose, my stomach threatening to give way.

Quillian tilted his jug and drank. I followed suit, anticipating a salty, metallic taste. Instead, warmth flooded me, his blood an inferno filling my chest. Honey, summer fruits, and a light dusting of spices covered my tongue, nose, chest, body. Everything around me spun, coming to life as if being made anew. The room stilled, and the crashing sounds of wings against the wind made my eyes roll back. My heart beat out of my chest, paralyzing me in a state of unspeakable euphoria.

This was lust, chaos, vengeance, and desire intermingled. A potion, an elixir, a drug that would make a man bend his knee to continue drinking it.

"As the Nephilim long ordained it, so shall it be," I heard the priest mutter. The room began to rearrange itself, and my beating heart slowed.

"I'll take it that's her first time drinking the blood of an immortal," Silas snickered, bringing me back to the present. Quillian's eyes changed to dark orbs. His nostrils flared, his fangs extending and retracting in successive movements.

"We need to hurry this," Enzo commented, resting his hands on Quillian's shoulder. Quillian's eyes calmed, and he stared down at me as if unsure of who and where he was. Brielle and Silas removed the cups from our hands.

"Here," he finally spoke after the moment of silence had lingered between us all. He reached into the pocket of his suit, pulling out a ring box, and Brielle silently squealed beside me.

"My, Mr. Kingsley. This is so romantic," I remarked as he stepped in front of me, eradicating any space between us. He opened the box, pulling out a rounded, large ten-carat yellow diamond ring.

"You may be an asshole, but at least you have good taste," I commented. He put the ring on my ring finger. It fit snugly.

"Welcome to the family." Brielle stepped between us, admitting to what I could only guess was her handiwork. The priest stood at the alter awkwardly, soaking the whole exchange in with anxious trepidation.

"You three go ahead. I will direct her back to Jersey Hill," Quillian ordered, and Silas, Enzo, and Brielle immediately disappeared, leaving just us and the priest. Quillian quickly removed his blazer and placed it around my chest, covering me.

"What are you doing-" My words caught in my throat as blood splattered the walls of the room, and the priest's head rolled from the altar, landing before me.

"You couldn't give me a heads up?" I shouted. I stepped back, feeling the warmth of the blood against my cheeks. "Was that necessary?" I asked, using his blazer to wipe the wet warmth.

"No witness, no rumors, and no contradictory evidence," he answered dryly, his voiced devoid of any emotion. He stepped toward me, forcefully removing his blazer from my grasp.

"Stay still," he commanded, his voice a warm, hushed whisper. One hand cupped my face, the other the sleeve of the blazer, and he dabbed at the remnants of blood on my hair, nose, and ears.

He pulled me into his chest, his hold on my face tightening. My body heated up at his proximity, his breath, and lips against my skin.

"There is one way out of here and one way back. Since my blood now fills you, it is to me you will always return," he stated, lowering his blazer, whispering the words into my ears like a soft caress.

"Now, isn't it a human tradition that the groom gets to kiss the bride?" he mutters, a low laugh erupting from his chest.

"No." I stepped back, wanting no part of this.

Never mix business with pleasure. These two evils cannot coexist.

The words echoed in my ears as Quillian pulled me harder into his chest, lowered his head, and kissed me. I fought, pounding against his torso. His hold on me tightened. His kiss grew more hurried and forceful.

Quillian kissed me like my mouth was an enemy he sought to conquer, my body the sacrificial lamb on his altar, and tongue the vessel in need of purification. It was raw, brutal, dirty, and encompassing of the blood that lay at our feet.

"What the actual fuck was that, vampire?" I pushed from his hold, running my fingers over my sore and bruised lips.

"Unification. Now you smell and taste like me. There's no mistaking who you belong to," he replied, picking up his blazer from the floor.

"I belong to no one!" I snarled, stepping forward and refusing to allow my treacherous body to imply otherwise.

"Uh-hmm," he replied smugly, as if the scent of my arousal hung within the air. "Time to go," he announced, his eyes briefly glancing at the door. "Repeat this twice as you leave and twice as you return." He stepped forward, and the head of the priest rolled further away, a reminder of his cruelty and what could become of me if I wasn't cautious.

"Si erupẹ ni a yoo pada," he said, enunciating each vowel. I repeated the words with him.

"Si erupẹ-" He reached for me again, pulling my back flat against his chest.

"Now be a good girl, go home, and come back to your darling husband. The beast will be waiting for you." He pressed his erect manhood against my ass. "See you in two days-"

"Ni a yoo pada," I hollered, pulling out of his hold, and my body went limp. Everything around me became a blur of colors, movements, and sounds. A portal opened, and everything went black.

15

MISSION FAILED

Meraki

I SCANNED MY IMMEDIATE SURROUNDINGS, NOT putting it past Quillian to have me followed. The portal had dropped me back in Jersey Hill on the large greenway between the Upper West and East Side.

I walked along First Street, then followed the long path to Abel Road until I arrived at my apartment. I was a ball of nerves, unable to make sense of what had transpired within the last eight days and what was going to happen next.

Darya was not going to take this failure lightly, and I could think of nothing else to compensate for the pendant.

I walked into the main lobby and briefly smiled at the security guard, who I had seen on a few occasions. I made my way to the elevator, went up to the twentieth floor, and entered the security code on my front door.

The alarm system rang, and I immediately reached for the wall dial and entered the second alarm code.

There was no such thing as being extra cautious in this line of work.

I closed the door behind me and re-entered a new code, ensuring the security system was on standby, a preventative method to warn me of any suspicious movement inside or outside my apartment.

I immediately ran into my room and pulled out the extra comms device I kept in case of emergencies.

This was an emergency. A matter of life and death.

I logged into the Alokari system, signing into my personal portal, and hesitantly typing the words that made every hair on my body stand on end.

Mission failed

I watched as the system registered the update and another message appeared on my screen.

System updated.

I bit my lip and began to pace the room, wondering what came next. An idea began to formulate in my mind, and I raised the device again, entering the jobs section of the portal.

I typed the family name that had become the bane of my existence and waited as the search loaded up. Three jobs came up. All of them had been registered in the system within the last five days. I clicked on the first hit. It was for Quillian. Reading through the brief, the job was noted as a *sneps* and *sners*, offering half a million as compensation. This was big, the largest amount I had ever seen offered for a job of this caliber.

Someone wanted Quillian dead, and they were willing to pay a hefty amount to ensure it happened. I kept scrolling down, registering details and warnings about other organizations that had responded to a similar call and failed.

This was practically a death trap.

I quickly checked the other two for Brielle and Silas. The briefs were similar in nature, the price tags slightly different. The jobs included an additional price for insider information, equating to almost two million in total.

I returned to Quillian's, pacing the room as my thumb rested over the accept button. This was my only way out, my penance, my excuse, one that would allow me to kill two birds with one stone. I would have access to Esneoh and the opportunity to get my hands on the Alokari's biggest kill.

I clicked accept, pressed the comms against my chest, and exhaled. I returned to the call screen for Silas and Brielle, but when I attempted to accept the job, I was met with an error message for both siblings. The rules in the Alokari were simple. Each failed job came with a price, and more than five within a certain period of time would result in the dismissal of that agent, never to be seen or heard from again. There had been many agents that started with Iris and me. As the years passed, their numbers had dwindled.

My failed job ensured that I could no longer take on multiple assignments at once, something I had never experienced before.

Shit.

I turned the device off, needing time to breathe before I contacted Darya tomorrow and updated her on the full scope of the case. The same one I could not speak about because of the blood oath.

Double shit.

I went into the kitchen and opened the lower cabinet, taking out the emergency phone that Skye, Iris, and I had agreed could only be used for emergencies.

"The emergency phone? Did something happen?" Iris picked up on the first ring, her response followed by movement and shuffling.

I bit my lip, wanting to divulge all that had transpired, but the rules were clear. Confiding in Iris would only place her in danger.

"Raki, talk to me. Are you there?" she asked, her voice laced with worry.

"I'm here," I replied hesitantly, needing a calm and familiar voice to center me. "You watered the plants," I breathed, stating the obvious.

"Of course. Always," she answered, and a moment of silence passed between us.

"Something happened," I finally spoke, knowing that Iris was a worrier. If I didn't give her a few crumbs to hold on to, she'd drive herself crazy with worry.

"Okay," she replied with a deep exhale. "How bad on a scale of I'm fucked to hail Mary fucked?"

"Hail Mary, double fucked," I answered, recounting how we had come up with the measurement after we had been caught trying to sneak out of the Alokari orphanage by a nun. She had beat us until we couldn't move for a week. I still carried a scar on the inside of my right thigh as reminder of the sheer brutality. I felt a shudder course through my body as my hands instinctively moved over the scar.

"Shit!" She whisper shouted. "Do you have to run? I have-"

"No, I can't."

"We discussed this. I have passports with different names. We can go, disappear for-"

"I can never ask you to do that, Iris," I interrupted, warmth filling my chest at the mere fact she even offered.

"You never have to ask me. You're the only family I have, and I would do it without thought," she answered. A long silence lingered between us, as if she was waiting for me to give the all-clear.

"I failed the job," I confessed. My stomach sank at admitting that aloud.

"Was this a special assignment?" she asked hesitantly.

"Yes." Iris whistled low, and a flurry of movement continued.

"What are you doing?"

"Packing," she whispered, the sound of a bag zipping trailing after her words.

"No, wait." I took a deep breath. "I failed the job, but I may be close. Closer than I've ever been to finding Alessia's killer," I added, my breath hitching with each word.

"Raki," Iris called, her voice a low plea.

"I know, but I can't just let this opportunity pass. I've been waiting for this type of luck for ten years. I've come up with a plan." I paced the kitchen floor, running my hands through my hair. "We can't travel with Nelly and the other plants. You know how I feel about my babies," I added, hating that I couldn't go outside and draw attention to the fact someone was home. I needed to keep low.

"If it doesn't work?" she asked, the shuffling in the background halting.

"I leave-"

"No. *We* leave. Together," Iris stated, leaving no room for arguing.

"Together." I exhaled the breath I didn't know I was holding.

"By the way, what happened to you that evening we went out?" she asked, a sure ploy to distract me from the severity of the situation.

"The...phone...is...breaking...up...beep-"

"Raki!" she screamed. "You better spill the tea, bitch. You got laid, didn't you?"

"Ms. Brown, as a teacher this is not becoming of you," I chuckled.

"Fuck those kids. Now spill," she continued, and I could only imagine the glee and anticipation in her face.

"I got almost laid. Let's move on." I spoke so quickly that I was sure she didn't hear anything.

"Ermm, what the hell does almost mean?" she giggled like a high school student.

"Iris," I said, holding back the laughter rumbling in my chest.

"Okay, wait. So, no dick? Oh, oh, oh. Are you into kitty

Kats?" she whispered lowly, as if stumbling on a piece of information that now finally made sense.

"No Kats, Iris-"

"I know you're not opposed to it-"

"How the hell do you know that?"

"I know you. I know you like I know myself," she said mockingly. "So?"

I exhaled a frustrated breath. "We did everything but the D action," I replied, thinking back on how that one evening has come back to bite my ass.

"So, it was good," she offered, and I could feel her smile through the phone.

"Orgasmic," I confessed, seeing no need to lie that even without penetration, the vampire was able to get me off by playing into kinks I didn't know I even had. "I've met him again after," I confessed, the words leaving my mouth quicker than I anticipated.

"Do we like him?"

"No, he's an insufferable asshole."

"The plot thickens," she muttered. "What happens now?" she asked, her voice taking on a more serious tone.

"If all goes to plan, then I might be gone for the next five days."

"Keep me updated?"

"Promise." Iris took steady breaths.

"When you come back, let's go for lunch. There're a few developments in my life I need advice about."

"Okay," I replied, heading to the fridge, and taking out a water bottle. We exchanged a few updates and pleasantries before ending the call. I turned the phone off, placed it back below the counter space, and walked to my room, my body drained of energy from the anxiety of past and upcoming events. I removed my clothes, noting specks of blood that could easily be mistaken as food stains. I quickly changed and curled into bed.

Sleep first. Life after.

I was awoken by the blaring sound of the standby alarm system. Night had fallen, and the room was basked in total darkness, except for the small streams of light that infiltrated through the blinds. I jumped from my bed and reached for the loaded gun on the bedside table.

I leaned against the shadowed walls and tiptoed, waiting for my eyes to adjust to the darkened corners. With my gun aimed forward, I slowly crept into the living room, searching for anything out of the ordinary.

Deciding to stay here may not have been my smartest move.

I walked to the entryway and disengaged the system, as the alarm had grown louder by the second. As I stepped back, my eyes landed on a round object in the center of the kitchen counter. I made my way to it. It was a phone. It immediately began to ring, and I knew this was bound to go one of two ways: the vampire had tracked me down, or Darya was pissed.

"Hello?" I answered. Silence lingered as I anticipated my fate.

"Red," Darya spoke. That one syllable, hanging on a thread between us. She was beyond pissed.

"Darya," I called, allowing the name to serve as an anchor. I may have fucked up my last job, but I had a plan, and I could bide my time.

With the gun still raised, I placed the phone back on the counter, anticipating her next move.

That was the problem. Darya was the queen in this game of chess. The most powerful piece, able to move any number of ways at will. I was simply another pawn out of many that she could discard.

I continued to check the apartment, questioning why she needed to break in and leave the phone instead of addressing me directly

As I stepped toward the center of the room, my eyes landed on the shadowed outline of a man on the balcony, his movements slow and calculated. I moved closer to the wall, my finger pressed against the trigger.

The outline of another shadow in my peripheral vision halted my movements. I arched the gun, spun, and released a series of shots. Instantly, a needle pricked my skin from behind. I staggered forward, taking in the two beings before me.

"I don't take well to betrayal, Red. You know me," Darya spoke, the smoke from her cigar clouding the space all around me. My vision blurred, and I fell.

16

QUEEN MOVE

Meraki

"Red," Darya called, her face coming into focus as my eyes slowly opened. My muscles ached. It felt like I had been doused in hot molten liquid. "It's been over a week," she added, the fumes from her cigar hitting my face. I groaned, shifting the weight of my body, only to realize I had been tied to a chair.

"Eight days, to be precise," I replied, my throat parched. My eyes took in the desolate space, with towering rows of storage units covered in dust and the remnants of leaves from outside. Two of Darya's men stood to my left and right at a steady distance, each dressed in all-black attire.

"Imagine not getting an update, and when I do, it says mission *failed*?" she said, stepping forward. Her heels created a steady echo with each step. She exhaled a frustrated breath, using her free hand to move back the loose hair that had fallen from her ponytail.

"How? I hate being placed in this predicament because this is not what I want to do, especially to you," she continued, puffing more aggressively on the cigar. "But protocol, Red...Where have you been?" She asked, a sinister edge to her voice, one I had only experienced when I failed at a training session during my years as a trainee.

"Esneoh," I replied, training my eyes on her.

"Do you want to tell me where this ring is from? And-" She halted, dropping her cigar to the floor. "What did you say?"

"Esneoh. I've been in Esneoh," I repeated. As I opened my mouth to say more, the words refused to come out. "If you had given me more time, I would have reported what I could in detail," I added, the bass in my voice increasing.

Darya's demeanor relaxed, and the pacing she had been doing earlier halted. "The floor is yours," she stated, motioning for one of the security guards to bring her a chair. The tallest, with hair the length of a Greek god's, stepped forward and placed it directly facing me.

She leaned back on the chair, feet crossed, waiting for me to take the floor.

"I got the pendant that evening, but someone else was also after it that night."

"Who?" She moved forward.

"Quillian Kingsley," I answered calmly, watching as her eyes widened, her mouth opening and closing.

"They are out in public already? How is that possible?" she muttered under her breath.

"It's possible. Him and his siblings attacked me that evening," I replied hesitantly, thinking about how to bypass the stipulations of the oath.

"Why are you still alive, and what does it have to do with that ring on your finger?"

"Here is where it gets tricky, and I may not make sense," I said, shuffling in my seat.

Whatever I share with you can never be discussed with

another who is outside my family. If you do, death awaits you.

I recalled his words in my head repeatedly.

"Okay?"

Whatever I share with you.

The words echoed in my head. The loophole, the gap, my saving grace.

"I have to be careful what I say. I'm indebted to it." I made a feeble attempt to raise my ring, hoping she would read between the lines.

"I was kidnapped, tortured, and given a proposition," I announced slowly, testing the words in my mouth. "This was it." My eyes followed the ring.

Darya rose and lowered herself before me, raising my hand to inspect the ring. "He has good taste at least," she commented in passing. "Why?"

I opened my mouth and closed it again, knowing this information threaded too close to what he had disclosed.

"You can't say," she said, rising to her feet. "You've never held back on information, so I'm assuming they may have used some sort of spell on you."

"I had a choice. Lose my life and the pendant or bargain to stay alive and gain access to Esneoh."

"So, you were in Esneoh?" she asked again as if needing to ensure she heard correctly.

"His property," I added coyly, struggling against the bond of my restraints.

"This is huge," she muttered aloud as if adding the missing pieces of the scattered information. "Do you know what this means?"

"I can find Alessia's killer," I offered. She stopped, her gaze assessing as if seeing me for the first time. Her eyes softened at the sound of Alessia's name.

She nodded slowly. "Yes. It also means you are the first agent to have ever gone in and come back out of Esneoh...alive," she said, and a glimmer of pride flickered in her eyes.

Her hands reached forward, and she slowly began to remove the restraints holding my hands in place. Once my hands were free, she stepped back and motioned for another security guard to remove the remainder of the restraints. She reached into the pocket of her black leather pants and removed a pack of cigarettes, lighting one immediately.

"I thought you quit," I commented as the final restraint was removed.

"This" - she motioned to the space around us - "requires it." She pulled out an additional one and handed it to me.

I shook my head. "I've already been through the worst," I commented, making no effort to rise to my feet. I couldn't afford to do anything that would test the power dynamics between us, something Darya is very big on.

"You accepted the job." She inhaled and exhaled the cigarette quickly.

"Yes." I readjusted my position on the chair, stretching out my legs to regain feeling in them.

"Then you know he has been someone that other organizations have failed to seize since long before you and I were even conceived." I nodded in response. "This job isn't like the others you've done before, Red," she warned, her voice a steady mix of apprehension and tender understanding. A voice that's solely reserved for me.

Perhaps being the favorite has its benefits. Not getting killed is one.

"Are you sure?" she asked, one hand placed under her breast, the other in the air, her scrutinizing gaze taking me in.

"I have to," I said, keeping my gaze steady, refusing to show any fault.

"This job is your first priority, and if the hunt for Alessia's killer intervenes, you step back. Do not compromise this job, Red," she offered hesitantly, stepping into the seat directly facing me. "Your job is to collect intel on him. His strengths, weaknesses. Once we build the database for that we can think about the assassination job."

"Of course," I lied. Knowing my sister's killer trumped everything, even if it meant death awaited me after. It was a risk I was willing to take, one her life and legacy required.

The Alokari was my life, the reason for my existence. I owed my life and livelihood to it. Without it, Alessia and I would have become a set of statistics in the system, lost in a perpetual cycle of poverty. They gave me hope, a new purpose, drive. I lived and breathed for them, giving the entirety of myself to them without ever questioning or taking anything for myself. This was my one and only time to do so.

"I will have to deal with the issue of the pendant. Luckily, there are two different benefactors." She exhaled, her hands briefly running through the edges of her hair. "They will not reveal what they know...Not that it even matters now," she laughed dryly.

"Did he tell you how to go in and out?" she asked, dropping the stub of her cigarette, and stepping on it with the heel of her shoe.

"No, he said he will send someone when it's time," I lied, unsure of why I had concealed that piece of information. A part of me reasoned that it was so that my plans didn't solely rest on the Alokari. They needed to be focused on Alessia. A tiny voice in the back of my mind told me that was a lie.

"I came here today expecting to do one thing I never imagined," she swallowed, her nails tapping lightly on her thighs. She had come here today with the intention of killing me, and it didn't surprise me.

"We've been betrayed before," she stated calmly, her hands folded against her chest. "Since you will be taking a more active leadership role after this job, I might as well fill you in."

If we told the agents or allowed such information to spread, imagine the frenzy that would ensue. I did the honorable thing, maintaining their reputation in death, even when they weren't deserving of it. Darya wasn't without flaws, but are any of us? There were days and moments like these when I got a small glimpse into the weight of the responsibility she carried, and it softened my heart toward her.

"I will let the pendant slide. After ten years, you are allowed at least one fuck up, as long as one doesn't turn into one too many," she warned, her brows creasing together. "How long?" She motioned to the ring.

"I will be gone five days out of seven," I replied solemnly, the previous tension between us easing by the second.

"You still have to keep up the facade when you come back. You will have to pick up small heist jobs here and there. Otherwise, it would look suspicious." She said, letting me know that she had somewhat managed to add the pieces together. "Find a way around the gag order when you come back. I also expect weekly updates." I made no effort to answer. She and I both knew this wasn't a request. It was an order, plain and simple.

She slowly rose to her feet, tapping her toes on the ground. "My guards will take you back," she spoke, motioning to the two who had remained hidden in the shadows.

"Be careful, Red. The Kingsleys have a reputation for a reason. Don't allow yourself to get swept away," she added as she headed out through the door to my right.

I followed the guards out not too long after, pondering what my lie meant and what the way forward would be like. I couldn't imagine a life outside the Alokari and doing anything to disrupt that position did not sit well with me.

17

SAFE SECRETS

M*eraki*

I ARRIVED AT THE ESTATE FIELDS, REACQUAINTING myself with the stark difference in atmosphere. Here, the night sky illuminated and brought to life every celestial object in the sky, almost as if it were within arm's reach.

"Meraki, you're back," Brielle turned up behind me.

"You waste no time."

"I sensed your presence and saw the lights outside flicker nonstop," she pointed to the now darkened pathway. Her eyes briefly fell on my midsized black bag, and I clutched it tighter.

"I must ensure I'm prepared for whatever comes my way." I shrugged.

"I wasn't expecting any less," she noted, her eyes landing on the main floor of the house.

"Am I interrupting something today?" I motioned as my eyes caught the two housemaids' tables and chairs being shifted inside and out.

"No, Quillian wasn't expecting you this early."

"I'm sure he was hoping I didn't show up, so he could have the upper hand in this whole arrangement."

"I can't argue with that," she laughed, heading toward the house's side door. She suddenly stopped as we neared the door. "There will be vampires here soon," she stated, then continued walking. "We are having the first meeting tonight. My brother was hoping not to make a formal introduction today," she noted as we walked through the main floor of the house.

"So, stay hidden?" I asked, hoping she said yes. She nodded hesitantly and continued ahead from the main floor to the first.

"Where is Quillian? Somewhere on the grounds. I'll advise that you stay out of his way. He seems to be in a mood." she rolled her eyes.

"Tell me something new!" I answered, my eyes taking note of each floor. I had intentionally shown up hours before, wanting to give myself enough time to snoop around the various rooms. And something told me today was the only day I could do so without being followed or stalked by my soon impending security personnel. And my instincts had been correct. This meeting was the distraction the family needed for me to snoop through and try and gather as much intel about Quillian as possible.

Brielle and I landed on our floors, excusing herself to her room. I headed for mine and rushed to place the midsized handbag on the bed. I scanned through the series of weapons and masking sprays. I knew without a shadow of a doubt a time would come when I would need to use it.

I removed my comms device hidden within the bag's pocket and attempted to see if I could pick on any data. As anticipated, it was futile. It was a well-known fact that Esneoh operated on its data and security systems, which were superior to what we were used to in the human realm. I just had to ensure I found a way to record everything, so I missed nothing.

I turned off the device, entered the wardrobe, placed the bag and weapons at one end of the room, and walked around looking for the perfect spot to hide the device. I settled on a small opening between the shoe racks and inbuilt jewelry cases.

Noise filtered from outside the building, and I turned the lights in my room off, watching and noting the faces and bodies of each individual who entered the house. As time passed, the numbers dwindled until the house's front entrance lay covered with fleets of cars and motorcycles.

I waited an additional ten minutes and briefly changed into a silk night robe and a camisole, wanting to ensure that if I got caught, I could blame it on getting lost.

I reached for a book near the bedside table on gardening and peeled back the bedroom door, ready to go through each room on the third and second floors. I was familiar with the fourth floor, as I had taken a quick inventory while locked in Quillian's room.

The third floor harbored a home theatre and a small library space. Me and Brielle's room sat on opposing ends.

I went to the second floor, where there was a larger-sized family library and an entertainment area crammed with gadgets, games, and equipment that made no sense to me. Silas' room was in the middle.

A room between the library space and Silas's room caught my attention, and I snuck inside, facing a large monitor screen with angle views of the passageways on each floor. I stepped deeper into the room, navigating the monitor's panel, and taking note of each angle, needing to ensure I moved with caution when I reached those key points in the future.

Enzo and Quillian's voices and footsteps outside the door drew my attention. I peeled the door back and headed toward their voices, stopping a few feet away.

"I do not need to be reminded of my mistakes," Quillian bellowed, echoing through the walls.

"Mistakes?" I asked, making my presence known before they picked up on it. Quillian's nostrils flared, his eyes bulged, and a flicker of surprise crossed his features.

Enzo and I exchanged quick pleasantries as Quillian's eyes

pierced through my clothing. "Go ahead; you were making a lot of noise, don't let me disturb you." I moved away from the library's door and turned my attention to the entertainment room at the far end of the corridor.

"You're back early." He stepped toward me, partially blocking my path.

"I take my jobs very seriously." He snickered in response. "Having meetings without me? What a shame; perhaps being your wife would be easier than anticipated?" He folded his hand against his chest as Enzo stepped back and watched with mock interest.

"I mean, show up in white, don't speak, and flash this ring. I missed my true calling as a sugar baby."

"We need to find a better way to use that mouth of yours. Maybe fuck it into submission?" His hands grasped my face. "Now be a good girl and stay upstairs so that your husband doesn't also include you on the list of dead bodies tonight?" He smiled coyly, yet there was no jest behind his words. His scent wafted through my nose, and I cringed from his hold, refusing to acknowledge whatever reaction my body had to him.

"Of course, my darling husband. Enjoy your meeting with your *little* friends," I replied, giving him the middle finger as I stepped into the entertainment room. I leaned my ears against the door walls, waiting for them to move so I could make my way to the one place my hands had been itching to enter - his office.

Their voices filtered down the stairs, and just before I attempted to open the door, Silas and Brielle walked from Quillian's office and headed for Silas's room. I leaned against the door again and waited an additional five minutes before stepping out and making my way back to the office space opposite the library.

I pushed open the door, Quillian's masculine cologne pouring through the fabric of the walls. The office, with its large windows and front-facing view of the estate, oozed opulence.

A large black and gold glass table sat within the room with

gray accented chairs against the backdrop of faux doors and an overhead glass ceiling.

"As expected," I mumbled under my breath when my eyes fell on one of the faux walls differently than the others. Voices filtered from the ballroom, followed by shouts and gasps. I strained my ears, trying to sift through what was being said but could barely make sense of it.

I pressed inwardly on the door, and it moved automatically to the side, bringing into focus a small safe. I stepped back, running my hands through my hair, realizing I hadn't brought anything that could help me crack the code.

People are creatures of habit and will always subconsciously leave a clue behind.

My eyes screened through the office space, recalling Alessia's words. It fell on a miniature landscape portrait that was awkwardly angled. I stepped toward it, running my hands through the canvas. The painting was a blend of black and whites set before a maroon backdrop. The initial AK, followed by a set of numbers at its bottom, caught my attention. I walked back to the safe and entered the six digits, hoping my instinct was correct. The safe creaked and then opened with a soft thud.

"Yes," I mumbled as I pulled back its door. A single envelope lay at its center, surrounded by miniature art pieces. I ran my hands through its walls to ensure there were no hidden or secret compartments that could be missed. When my efforts came up empty, I pulled out the envelope.

More screams echoed through the walls, alerting me that the meeting was still ongoing. I carefully opened the envelope's content, finding a series of four images placed inside. The first two were of a full-figured woman with hair a deep shade of burgundy and eyes dark pool of brown orbs. Both images were taken of her, clearly unaware, yet her smile filtered through the camera lens, giving her a halo and angelic ambiance.

The other was of a man with full lips, familiar gray eyes, bronzed skin, and barely visible dimples. He was an almost identical replica of Quillian, but instead of dark lines and sharp edges, his face mirrored soft angles and faint edges.

"So, this is Alaric." I continued to mutter, understanding the fascination around him from the reports I read. He was the epitome of grace and eloquence. Broad shoulders, tall stature, and a smile that lights up a room. A stark difference from Quillian.

The final image was of Alaric with the red-headed woman, his hands wrapped under her waist, which could be misinterpreted as friends or lovers. Yet, the way Alaric gazed at her told me she was more.

I turned back to the two initial images, trying to weigh them against the latter two. The first two images seemed personal, intentional, as if carved from a lover's heart.

The sound outside had quietened, and something told me that wasn't good. I quickly placed the images back on the envelope and closed the content, berating myself for not bringing my comms device to take images. I had been back less than twenty-four hours and was already fucking up everything I learned during training.

"Meeting finished," Enzo's voice filtered through the walls, and an onslaught of incoming footsteps caught my attention. I ran and hid behind the long drapes pooled at the windows' far end. The door of the room slammed open a few seconds later.

"What the hell did you think you were doing?" Brielle shouted, followed by Silas's laughter. "You're drunker than you were before. Are you kidding me, Si?" she persisted. From the window, the reflections of the movements played out. Enzo stood between them, trying to tame Brielle's anger.

The door opened again, and silence followed as Quillian stepped into the fray.

"You stepped into that room to sabotage us? Because of your hate for me?" He stated the question as a fact, yet it seemed to fall on deaf ears as Brielle and Silas continued arguing back and forth.

I expected a rebuttal, a fight to demand that his presence be acknowledged, but Quillian did neither. He exhaled long breaths and moved to sit on his office chair. His shoulders hunched, his eyes clouded over, and I saw vulnerability there for a brief second. It disappeared immediately after when the hard-edged contours of his face fell into the light. He uttered no words; instead, he filtered the whole room out until somewhere in the midst of Enzo, Silas and Brielle. He did not attempt to move; he kept staring ahead as if lost in his thoughts.

After some time, he stood up and reached for a rocks glass and a bottle of liquor. The door opened, and his footsteps filtered through the house. I stepped away from the window, catching sight of him through another window as he headed for the glasshouse.

I snuck out of the room, ran upstairs, and locked the doors to my room. The smartest thing at this point was to end my snooping for the day and not draw any attention to myself, but I had seen too much in the depth of those gray eyes, to let it stop me from investigating further. This was part of the job, and there was no time better than the present to push for intel.

I ran into my wardrobe, changed into a form-fitting swimwear that barely concealed anything, and made my way downstairs, intending to lure intel of him.

18

MEETING OF THE MINDS

Quillian

When the little hellion left, she didn't anticipate I would be watching her every move from the shadows. I placed a tracker on her and had two of my most discreet men trail and follow her.

The tracker showed that she usually kept to herself and only left her house in Jersey Hill for brief moments. However, there was a glitch in time that ended with her on the outskirts of Jersey Hill at an abandoned warehouse. She had somehow bypassed my men, but when they caught up with her again, they found her leaving the warehouse with me.

"Two fucking men."

Less than twenty hours after she had left Esneoh with my ring on her finger.

"They're here, brother," Silas mockingly hovered over me as I perused some images of her in her apartment, the gym, and the balcony. Ironically the blurriest of the images was of her outside the warehouse. Her makeup streaked, hair roughed, she looked like someone that had been fucked. Thoroughly fucked, and the sight of it enraged me.

A gentle knock on the door, alerting me that all the players in Kinavari had been called.

"You're having her followed? Some could say this is bordering on obsessive, won't you?" Silas said. I raised my head, releasing strains of my power, alerting him that I wasn't in the mood. Not today, not with the weight of the responsibility that awaited me in the ballroom.

I sneered in warning, unable to find the words to tell him to fuck off. Unfortunately, my baby brother wasn't someone who cared to read a room or heed warnings. He reached for the image that had riled me up, a smug smile on his face, as he placed it down and looked down at me.

"I'll advise that you keep her at arm's length. The last time you turned your focus fully on a human, she died along with Alaric. Coincidentally, not too long after that, we all ended up as captives," he stated, a subtle warning in his voice.

"How she conducts herself here and out in her world is important. What if someone was watching her-"

"Who?" His brows creased, stepping back. "Last I checked, no one had even caught on to your plans. You killed the priest, remember? So, who would be watching? This isn't about others; this is about your need to control everything and everyone," He stated plainly, and the need to grab him by the neck and throw him out of the window became an overwhelming thought.

He was right. I shouldn't care. I hated her and despised her kind even more. But her scent, and the taste of her blood...

"Is everyone here?" I ignored him, packed the envelope's content, and locked it away in the drawer space behind me. Silas stepped back, and I caught a whiff of the scent that clung to him.

"They are all here, waiting," he answered with a depth of seriousness in his voice now. Brielle and Enzo strolled in immediately after, the atmosphere thrumming with anticipation.

"Our family had been gone a long time," Brielle said, sitting beside Silas. Enzo leaned on the arm of her chair, and the same questioning gaze illuminated his face. What happens next?

This meeting was a way for us to reestablish rules, create new groundwork, and break down the joke that the leaders of Kinavari had become.

Was there likely to be bloodshed tonight? Yes. Was I anticipating this to go smoothly? No. There was nothing my kind loathed more than unexpected change. It fucked with some part of our psyche; we like order, a clearly defined way for things to be done. Any changes in that routine kindle our desire for blood, lust, power, and chaos.

Tonight was bound to be those nights; that is why I ensured the meeting was happening at one in the morning on a Monday, hours before Meraki returned.

"Without leadership, there had been a division among the different vampire sets. Each had fought for power, neither succumbing to the need of the other. The north under Ferguson's leadership has been the only ones who've held some ounce of dignity and made several strides to unite the other three," Enzo said, recalling what we had previously discussed.

"You're drunk," I turned my attention to Silas when the stench became unbearable. Getting drunk for our kind was supposed to be an impossible feat, but thanks to the demons, that shit had gone out the window. They had somewhat crafted Mallanga, an elixir that truly allowed you to loosen your inhibitions. Unfortunately, it had turned Silas into a raging teenager who couldn't hold his liquor or dick in place. Even after all this time, nothing had changed. And the prospect of cleaning his shit all over again infuriated me.

This was a reckless move that could not delegitimize our claim tonight.

No one could trust a leader whose house wasn't even in order.

"He's not," Brielle quickly intervened, trying to cover for him like she usually did.

"He is," I snapped. She stared at him long and hard as her nostrils flared. Silas stepped back and sat on the chair opposite me with a cockily smirk on his face.

"Tonight is one of the most important nights for our family, and you chose to do this now?" I clenched my fist, holding myself back from what I really wanted to do.

"We can fix this; he can miss out on the first part while he sobers up," Enzo offered, rising to stand beside him. Brielle continued to stare at him as if staring at a stranger.

This evening was not going according to plan.

"You will not ruin this by saying or doing the wrong thing. You will not be coming in there with us. Do I make myself clear?" I spoke through gritted teeth. He shrugged and leaned forward, wanting a reaction out of me.

"And what will you do, Quillian?" Silas spat.

"Enough, Si," Brielle warned. He turned to face her briefly, shook his head, and turned his attention back to me.

"Well? Lock me up and pretend I also no longer exist?" he laughed, rising to his feet. Enzo clasped his hand around him to force him back down. Once he got into this stage of drunkenness, it was usually hard to reason with him.

"Don't touch me!" He shouted, shrugging from Enzo's hold.

"Do not bother with him," I dismissed Enzo's efforts.

I had hoped our years of imprisonment would have quenched his self-detective habits.

I was wrong.

It had revitalized his hunger, and none of us was safe from his path.

"Out," I warned.

"No!" he yelled back, and my vision blurred. I quickly reached for him, wrapping my hands around his throat.

"Q! No," Brielle screamed, placing her hand over mine.

"You will not disrespect me. Do you hear me?" He choked and hesitantly shook his head. "Get yourself cleaned up and stay out of my sight before I'm forced to do something I regret," I added, loosening my hold on him. Without waiting to hear Brielle's chastisement or reasonings, I walked out of the room, needing a moment to steady the anger boiling inside me.

Enzo caught up to me before I made my descent down the stairs. "Hold on, brother," he called, holding me back by pinning my shoulder in place.

"Say what it is you need to. Once I go down there, I no longer care to hear it." I shook myself from his hold, my hands clasped around the railing. "He is so reckless! And I still don't understand what his issue is."

"He's hurting. "

"And what the fuck are Brielle and me?" I spun around to face him, needing to get this moment and this conversation out of the way. I refused to bear the burden of Alaric's death. Not anymore.

"I know, but Silas isn't like you and Brielle," he exhaled, hesitantly taking a few steps back. My gaze turned to the door, realizing that Brielle had not left the room with us. She was most likely babying him like she usually did.

"He needs to toughen up and act like a man."

Enzo's bass rose. "Last I checked, that isn't who or what we are," he continued, his anger irking my skin. "He processes things differently, he expresses himself differently. That does not take away from his strength or who is. He is very much a man, more so because he is able to show some emotion." He hesitated, running his hands over his head. "If you all would just sit and talk...You can all shoulder the burden and help carry it for one another."

"Enzo..." I warned, allowing the depth of my rage to permeate around us.

"You need to be gentler with him, Quillian." He stated hesitantly. This time his voice bore no anger, or forewarning, just an air of calm and understanding from one friend to another.

"Cleaning up his shit since... wasn't me going easy on him?" I stumbled, unable to find the words to say Alaric's name out loud.

"You and I both know Silas has always been a prankster.

Willing to test the limits, but he was never like this when Alaric was alive," Enzo continued, his palm resting on my shoulder.

Silas and Alaric had always been close. They held their relationship so far removed from Brielle and me. Alaric was his rock, the anchor that always pulled him back. I was the cleaner whose silent worries and clear-outs of his fuckups were never acknowledged or discussed.

"He lost Alaric," Enzo stated, and the words rippled through me, making breathing, or seeing straight difficult. I wasn't ready to talk about it, so I refused to acknowledge it.

"I lost him too," I screamed, the words piercing the space between us, shaking the ground in a silent rumble.

"Old friend," Enzo exhaled, placing his hands on my chest, a show of solidarity, a reminder that this moment wasn't about drawing blood. "This is not an attack against you or me questioning you as a leader; I have no worries you will excel. From one friend to another – family trumps all," he spoke slowly, his eyes falling to the space downstairs. A gentle reminder, attaining everything that awaited us would mean nothing without family.

I inhaled and exhaled steady breaths, acknowledging what he had said. I was still not in the right frame of mind to hear or receive it fully, but I was willing to listen. Enzo had always held our family's well-being above all else.

The familiar scent of jasmine, vanilla, and cedar caught my attention, and I quickly turned to find where it was coming from. As if picking up on it, Enzo stepped back, a look of amusement marring his expression.

"Human." My eyes turned to Meraki standing at the far end of the passageway, perched beside the library door, a book in hand.

"Vampire," she mocked, tugging at the hem of the red silk robe barely covering her. "Is everything okay?" She asked, something akin to worry hidden behind the question.

"When did you get back?" I asked, the words coming across angrier than I intended.

"Do you ever answer a question with an answer?" she rolled her eyes, making her way toward Enzo and me.

"You're early; I said to be back nine, not one in the morning," I pointed.

"You're awfully perceptive," she replied. "Hi Enzo," she turned to face him, the scowl on her face now replaced with a genuine smile. Her disdain was what she evidently saved only for me.

Enzo returned her greeting with a warmth I had never seen in the years I had known him. I pulled him back, blocking his view of her before he made a complete fool of himself.

"Stay upstairs until I say otherwise," I instructed, but she ignored my warning and bumped past my shoulder. My eyes followed the swell of her breast, the dent in her calves, and the fullness of her lips.

This woman was a siren that had evidently brought many sailors and warriors to their feet without even trying. An enchantress, a seductress, one the heavens had placed in my hands as a punishment for all the blood that covered my fingers.

They clearly underestimated my resolve.

She halted and turned to face me. "Was that an instruction or suggestion, vampire?"

"Don't push me, human," I warned, wanting to step before her but thinking against it. It was bad enough Silas had rattled me, i couldn't allow a small insignificant human to do the same. I was not in the right state of mind, and I refused to argue back and forth with her today.

"Run along and meet with your *little* vampire friends" she raised her hand dismissively, her back now turned to me.

"Little?" Enzo echoed the words holding back his laughter. She disappeared into the entertainment room without a response.

"What?" I turned back, finding Enzo's accusatory gaze watching me. His gaze flicked back and forth from where she stood.

"I haven't said anything."

"Then wipe that smug grin off your face, asshole," I warned, stepping before him and making my descent down the stairs.

"Her scent needs to disappear," I instructed. Enzo nodded, pulling out a small bottle from his pocket. As usual, always one step ahead.

"I had Hera create one. Just in case" He began to spray the staircase and continued as we landed on the main floor. "She said a few spritzes of it should suffice." He placed the bottle back in his pocket and pulled out his phone. "Brielle will join us in there." He turned left, heading for the ballroom.

"Showtime!" I beamed, my fangs throbbing in anticipation.

"Ladies and gentlemen," I announced as I pulled back the door, elevating my voice.

The room went eerily silent as all eyes and ears trained us. I walked through the sea of bodies as Silas followed.

I stopped at the head of the room, an elevated stage for acts that used to perform here during some of our many extravagant events. Three chairs were sprawled out, one for me, Silas, and Brielle. Enzo usually preferred to stand for events like these or make his way through the crowd.

Murmurings and whispers erupted, the tension and fear in the room palpable. I savored it, allowing it to strengthen the roar, bursting to gain sound in my throat. These imbeciles, within a short time, had fucked up what my family had spent thousands of years building.

I paid their murmurings no heed; instead, I kept my eyes focused on the door, waiting for Brielle to make her debut. My sister, as much as she annoyed me, was my person. In many ways, we were more alike than I was willing to admit. Like Alaric was Silas' anchor, she was mine. She was the quiet, steady voice that made it her mission to humble me constantly.

Brielle strolled in a few seconds later, and a trail of eyes turned to face her, then back to Enzo and me on the stage. Disappointment coursed through me when my eyes followed the door after, realizing Silas wasn't with her through it all. He had not tried to sober up or used the witch for a potion that would expedite the process. He simply didn't care.

"Quillian?" Ferguson, the leader of the northern region of Kinavari, stood up and took cautious steps forward. The northern part of Kinavari comprises winged vampiric beings like me. Ferguson had always had an amicable relationship with my family and was someone whose voice and ideas I respected. The same couldn't be said for the others.

"It's me, old man, in the flesh," I replied, my legs outstretched, and my gaze briefly turned to face him. The few beings scattered in the room standing before had now sat, waiting.

"It's been-"

"You disappeared for millennia, and you show up now?" Amma, the leader of the eastern region, interrupted him. She governed the hybrid vampires resulting from interspecies marriage over the centuries. They had been growing in numbers before our imprisonment, and from Enzo's report, that had continued to be the case. They were now the most populous within the regions.

"Is that a question or a challenge," I asked, lacing my voice with the steady flow of my power. I rose to my feet and stepped forward, ensuring they could all see me. Amma had always been a loose cannon who only ever stopped talking and making demands when she had a dick in her mouth.

"Q..." She fumbled, her long braids swaying as she rose, letting me know that her initial question was more personal than professional. Amma had been granted the privilege of sucking my dick for some time. And heavens were those lips carved from the pits of hell itself. Her only problem was that she had become too attached, demanding formalities, and making statements about who and what we were. To me, she was a good fuck, but to her, I was the lord that would elevate her to ladyship.

"Quillian, overlord, you choose," I warned. "And to answer your question, no one disappeared," I replied curtly, waiting for the rest to note their grievances.

"What happened?" Hakim, the leader of the west, spoke. He

sat to the far right, his table surrounded by four domed bald head beings with visible veins on their faces. Even under artificial light, their skin glimmered the purest shade of white.

"We searched nonstop for you and your family. We just had to accept the rumor that you were dead...all of you," Makeba, leader of the southern region, sat perched on her seat. I sensed from the thrum of electricity in the air that she liked how her followers used their psychic powers to heighten the emotions of the others in the room.

Brielle briefly laughed at the visible lie. Makeba made no such efforts. According to the report, he was the first to make a play for the throne and even threatened to storm this estate to acquire it.

How Enzo had ensured that didn't happen was something he had refused to discuss. Enzo wasn't one for blood, but I had amassed enough intel to know blood was spilled that day.

"You have some nerve to show up here today, you venomous leech," Amma interrupted him before I even had enough time to address him.

"Venomous? Have you seen your followers? I do not engage with beings that are not even pure-blooded," Makeba spat, and a long-drawn-out screaming match with raised voices and shuffling ensued.

"You will not speak to her like that," Someone from Amma's side called.

"Make us take it back," Another from Makeba's. Ferguson shook his head and sat back down. It was evident that the years of warring and trying to bring the regions together had worn him down.

"Sit!" I commanded, elevating my voice. The leaders and their second in command, whom I was acquainted with, sat down. However, a small number didn't, opting to remain standing.

I guess blood was going to be spilled tonight.

"Who are you? You don't just show up and think you can tell us what to do," a young fair-haired boy under Amma's delegation said.

"I shouldn't have worn white today," Brielle whispered under her breath.

"And you are?" I called, searching the crowd, ensuring I remembered where he was sitting.

"I'm Jayden, Amma's fourth in command," he boasted, his shoulder arched with pride.

"I assume you're new to this?" I pressed, keeping my voice calm.

"Does it matter?" He raised his voice, and the tension in the room grew even more heightened.

"Anyone else disagrees? Make your plight known now like Jayden. I'm more than willing to listen" I turned my gaze around the room, waiting for the others, who refused to sit, to speak.

A small set of people from each region still standing echoed Jayden's view; no bars were held. They each turned to Jayden after they had finished speaking to acknowledge him as if he was the preordained leader of this rebellion.

"We can govern ourselves and have been doing fine since you all fucked off and disappeared." A slim build, woman from Makeba's region shouted from across the room.

"They should have stayed dead, to be honest," another voice rose, yet there were so many others; it was hard to distinguish its source. I smiled, allowing every single one to speak, marking their faces.

"Why don't you give him time to speak, so he can explain what happened?" Ferguson stated, turning to face the others in the room.

"Here we go again with him." An unknown voice from Hakim's tabled spat, their tone laced with venom.

"Give it a break, old man." Another voice called out from the same side.

I blurred through the room in the blink of blood, enraged haze ripping each of their hearts and throats out and laying it before their leaders. The room erupted; sounds and echoes of shock, and dismay, filtered through, shrouding my better judgment.

I finished with Jayden last, ensuring his death was slow and drawn out. His statement was a carefully concealed threat about what things will be like going forward. Either shut up or follow a similar fate. The Kingsley household did not take disrespect well.

The room fell silent, and the stench of fear reverberated throughout. Jayden's body fell; I lowered myself to it, ripped out his heart, and placed it before Amma. I then reached for my pocket handkerchief and wiped the remnants of the blood smeared across my hand, face, and suit.

I stepped back onto the stage, waiting for any other interruptions before proceeding with what I needed to say.

"Is no one going to speak up against this-" Another young man at Makeba's spoke, but before I could get to him, Brielle had already reached him and dismembered his body with her clawed nails.

An eerily calm followed, no one uttering a single word or making any movements. Brielle walked back, wiping the aftermath of the blood from her white dress. "Anyone else has anything to add?" she raised her head and turned her attention to the crowd. When no one spoke, she returned to her seat and motioned for me to continue.

"Brother, please continue," she gestured, pursing her lips.

"What happened? Where have you been?" Ferguson asked, seemingly unmoved by the violence that had just ensued. The room settled, their attention moving from the carnage around the room back to the stage.

"Thank you," I briefly nodded to him. "Now that I have all your attention, I can start by filling you in on where my siblings and I have been for the last millennia.," Brielle rose, opting to stand beside me on the stage. Silas's absence was evident with the raised brows and the look of confusion on those whose faces I could identify at the front.

"My brother, Silas, will join us at the next event hosted here,"

I stated, ensuring to maintain a united front. "What I'm about to share with you will stay in this room. Each of you here plays an active leadership role, and the mess was to ensure the weeds planted were rooted before we progressed further." Silent mutterings ensued.

"For many of you, the last time you saw me, I had won the Dark Crown Trials, and we had celebrated on the eve of my coronation. Unfortunately, I never got to take on the mantle. Our people never got the opportunity to be at the forefront of Esneoh politics and development," I motioned to the familiar faces and leaders who had cheered for me and had offered advice and support during the period.

"We couldn't take on the mantle because my siblings and I were kept in captivity," Brielle spoke, her hands resting against my shoulder. Loud chatter, whispered gasps, and looks of shocks transpired in the room.

"What do you mean?" Ferguson asked, his face aghast.

"Captivity?" Amma hyperventilated, her eyes softening as they made contact with mine.

Other voices filtered around the room until the room erupted into a chorus of whispered hushes and sirens. I raised my hand, waiting for silence to descend. "After the celebratory event, we all woke up and found ourselves not in Esneoh but scattered across the human realm. As we couldn't be killed, we were placed under a spell, keeping us conscious but bound," I continued keeping my voice distant and aloof.

"How is that even possible? It must be the demon king?" Amma spoke, the tension in the room palpable. "Who else had the most to gain?"

"That we are not yet sure of," I turned to face her.

"They couldn't have been working alone. What you're describing sounds like something that entails magic and a vacuum of power," Makeba noted, and the room turned to him, following his train of thought.

"The witches!" Someone in the crowd spoke.

"If they were able to do that, what does it mean for all of us?" Ferguson asked, as usual getting to the heart of the matter.

"How did you escape?" Hakim asked, his hand tapping against the table,

"How long have you been back?" The questions continued as I observed the leaders in the room, scenting fear, or anything out of the ordinary, that could point to someone knowing something. Brielle lightly tapped my shoulder twice, signaling that she could not pick up on anything.

"Enzo found a way," I answered, ensuring I didn't give too much away. "We were able to find the item that held us bound and destroyed it," I lied, needing to ensure that I kept a tight leash on the situation. Outlining a problem without stating a remedy was the surest way to start an upheaval.

A leader who wasn't seen as competent was one whose position would also be contested by the masses.

"For those of you who know us, you know my family doesn't take too well to betrayal," Brielle stated, her hands in her pants pocket. "We are working on whoever did it. They will be made an example."

"That isn't the main topic at hand in today's meeting." I stepped into the audience reaching for one of the hearts placed before Makeba. "I had anticipated coming back to a united people" I exhaled a frustrated breath, toying with the heart in my palm. "Instead of uniting and fortifying your strength during that period of uncertainty, you fought against one another. You were soo distracted with your internal strife, and you missed the clues that something was even at play when the key leaders disappeared," I said, keeping all emotion from my voice.

The possibility that our time in imprisonment could have been shorter had they perhaps been more observant and attentive to everything around them had been a recurring thought since we had been freed.

"Wait for a second, we can't" I moved toward Hakim, anticipating what came next.

"Think carefully before speaking because I'm not feeling very understanding today. A long time in imprisonment can ware on someone's patience." I dropped the heart in my hand on the floor, ready to rip another one out. "You've all been elevated to positions that have served you for far too long. Question me, and those roles also come into question." Hakim opened his mouth and closed it again, and I corked my head waiting for one false move.

"Now, as I was saying, did it make any sense to endure the series of crippling tournaments in the trials to emerge the victor and future king of Esneoh, all but to disappear with my siblings?" No one spoke. I stepped back, walking to the stage to join Brielle.

"Going forward, there will be changes in the infrastructure and distribution of goods and services from one region to another. If anyone causes issues and refuses to heed the changes, I will personally ensure your heart is delivered to your constituents and allow them to elect a new leader." I raised the pitch of my voice, needing to ensure they all fully grasped that nothing going forward was up for negotiation.

The leaders of each sect nodded in agreement stiffly, and though their movements said one thing, I was more than convinced this wasn't the end of some of the issues I would have to face later.

"What happens now? The next trial is upcoming in a few weeks. Will you be taking part?" Amma volunteered after a moment of silence. Her eyes glimmered familiarly. She was up to something, and experience had taught me no good could come from it.

"Quillian will be running again," Brielle intervened.

"That might prove hard, as there have been some modifications to the law," Makeba stated. Enzo stepped forward to intervene and lay out our strategy. I raised my hand and motioned for him to hold back.

"Is that so? Please do tell."

"Well, the leader needs a partner, a wife beside them. The

demons added it as a stipulation as they believe a settled leader was a stable one," Makeba relayed, his voice filled with myrrh.

"Well ..." I reached for a napkin on one of the tables and wiped my hands. As much as I enjoyed the sight of blood, dry cleaning didn't always agree with eliminating its remains.

"You don't fit that bracket. Since that's the case, one of the other leaders here should enter," Makeba continued, his hands resting against the table.

"And who said I didn't have one? You seem very eager, Makeba," I smiled, needing him to squirm in anticipation for a bit.

"You're married?" Amma questioned, her brows furrowed.

"Yes," I answered simply, and the room erupted into another series of gasps and whispers.

"You've just informed us that you were imprisoned; now you're saying you're married. Is there something you are hiding from us? How long has this marriage been legalized, and when do we get to meet this being?" Hakim spoke up, gritting the words through. His ploy was simple, get the room to question the legitimacy of my claims.

"I've been married for over six months, and it was legitimized not only here but also in the human realm," I replied, unable to keep the smug grin from my face.

"Human realm?" Amma and Hakim asked unanimously.

"My sister-in-law is human. Any other questions?" Brielle asked, stepping forward as if anticipating more opposition.

"She will be introduced to you two days from now, just before the official trial announcement in Aarin," Enzo said, clapping his hand, alerting them all that the meeting was over. "If you have any further questions before then, book a meeting. I'll advise each leader to reach out and do so. Quillian and I have another meeting to respond to." He motioned for Brielle and me to quickly head out of the door, and we followed without question.

"We have an issue," Enzo whispered in my ears as we made our way from the stage to the congregation of people.

"Handle it. I need to make a brief round." He nodded hesitantly, his brows furrowed. He turned to Brielle and muttered something similar in Brielle's ears. Her eyes widened, and without so much word, she hurried out of the room, Enzo trailing behind her.

"Quillian," Ferguson stopped beside me." It's good that you are well" He smiled warmly, his white hair seeming to emphasize the joy behind it.

"Old man, you and I have much to catch up on. Enzo has updated me on how you helped and took him on like a son. However, not tonight. Something urgent has instead come up."

"Of course, I will have the Mallanga in hand. I may be old, but I could always outdrink you." He laughed.

"Don't be so sure of yourself," I smiled as I hurriedly made my way through the crowd. I followed their scents up to my office.

"Enough!" Brielle screamed as I walked into the room. Silas stood beside her, Enzo near, as if trying to intervene. "Have you lost your mind, Silas?" she continued, her usual calm and grace replaced by an anger she kept carefully concealed. "He tried to get into the room; luckily, Enzo had warned the guards you selected for Meraki to update him if he moves. He's intoxicated and..."

"What was your goal, brother?" I stepped into the room keeping my eyes trained on him.

"Join in, of course," Silas answered, visibly more intoxicated now than before.

"Do you know what we would have looked like to them if you had shown up how you did? Do you know what contention you would have ensued," she shouted, pointing to the door.

"You wanted to go in there and sabotage all our labor intentionally? Because you despise me so much?" I accused, waiting for him to deny it.

His eyes dilated, and he stumbled on his words for some time. "I just needed to silence the voice in my head. I've been unable to shake her," he answered, and the depth of hollowness that stared back let me know that Silas, unlike me, had most likely experienced more in those caves than words could surmise. I clenched my fingers and slid into my seat, knowing anything relayed now would be pointless.

I blurred out the argument and exchange of words between all three of them and poured myself some scotch. I turned my attention to the outline of the moon ahead as flashbacks of my time in the cave played in my mind. The dark, the hollow void of emptiness, and that haunting silence jarred only by the echo of dripping water. And an unending cycle that I could not escape.

After some time, I turned to note they had all left, and the room had grown still, and I was left with nothing but a desire for something new to replace that gaping vacuum.

I lifted a bottle of scotch and walked down the stairs to the back end of the house. I crossed to the glasshouse and headed for the familial jacuzzi area, which I frequently used when I needed space from the noise.

I put down the bottle and glass, stripped to nothing but my underwear, and turned on the settings. I closed my eyes as my attention fell onto the subtle sway of the wind, the echoes of crickets in the empty green space head.

"Oh," Meraki said, her voice and scent calling to some primitive part of me. I opened my eyes, taking in the yellow barely there swimwear she had on. "I can come back when you're gone."

"Stay." I closed my eyes again, not wanting to entertain the thought of running my hands through her body. "It's large enough, and there's enough space for us to keep our distance," I added when I sensed her still looming over me hesitantly.

"If you insist," she replied, stepping into its pool.

"Why are you here so late? I'm starting to think you have a thing about following me," I noted, my eyes still closed. I reached for my drink beside me and lifted the glass to my lips.

"It must be nice to think everything revolves around you..."

"Do you ever answer a question with a clear answer?" I shot back, my eyes opening in turn. Her eyes widened at the realization that I was now accusing her of the same thing she had accused me of not too long ago. "You were also warned to stay upstairs."

"I waited for everyone to leave before coming down." She moved to the farthest end of the tub, ensuring a steady distance between us.

"I struggled to sleep," she offered after a moment of silence. The moon basked her skin in its warmth as she turned her back to me.

"It seems we have that in common," I confessed, taking another sip. She tilted her head, and the gold flecks illuminated the pools of green in her eyes.

"How was the meeting?" she asked, her hands lightly tapping the tub's board. I moved toward her eradicating the space between us.

"You know how it went, Little Hellion, I whispered over her ears. "Do you think I haven't carved your scent into the deep recesses of my mind? Even with all Enzo did to erase it, I could still smell you throughout the hallways." I continued wrapping one hand against her waist and used the other to tilt her neck back. She licked her lips, not attempting to squirm away from my hold.

"Careful vampire, that might be mistrusted as you liking me."

"The only thing worth perhaps liking is that warm cunt. And perhaps that mouth, when it's used for anything else but talking. Perhaps, a gag around it will spare me listening to the bullshit that falls from it." I tightened my hold on her neck, enjoying her defiance. "I'll repeat my question Little Hellion, what were you looking for? Or to be more precise, what were you hoping to hear?" My grip around her waist tightened, pulling her flat against my chest.

"I needed to know what chaotic mess you had gotten me into," she answered, her ass pressing against my dick, which seemed to have a mind of its own.

"And?"

"I was thinking I should have chosen the death route.," she answered, an undertone of sarcasm in her voice.

"Hmm," I muttered around her earlobe as I slipped my hand away from her waist and reached for my glass of liquor.

"Open," I instructed as I drank its content. She eyed me warily as if unsure what I was relaying. I loosened my hold on her neck and used my thumb to coax her mouth open.

I spat the content of the liquor into her mouth, expecting her to retract; instead, she opened wider, swallowing every single drop. My cock immediately shut up at the sight of it.

"Quillian..." She called, her eyes glistening with lust.

"Hmm," I growled, turning her back around and nibbling on her ear.

"Fuck. Why does that feel so good?" she writhed as goose-bumps rose on her skin. "This, us, is not a good idea." She slid from my hold, brushing her curls from her face. "I don't trust you."

"I don't have to trust you to fuck you. Sex comes with no attachment. Just pleasure." I pushed back the loose strands of hair falling on her chest and squeezed her visibly erect nipples.

She moaned in response, her eyes rolling to the back of her head. My ears strained to listen for Enzo's incoming footsteps.

"Remember that as you get yourself off tonight." I released my hold on it and stepped back. "Next time Little Hellion when you decide to look through my office, make sure not to leave your scent behind?" I drew back, watching her mouth turn into a scowl.

"You think you're smart trying to bypass me? You're in my terrain, under my house. I can rip that throat out and fuck your corpse if I will. Pray I find nothing moved or missing."

"You're a bastard, a sick bastard." She snarled.

"The same bastard whose cock you wanted to ride not so long ago?" I replied, stepping out. She immediately followed behind me as if anticipating a sparring match.

"It would be good for you to remember that other women can take your spot. Do not overestimate your importance, darling wife." I tipped her lips with my thumb. "I could snap your neck-"

"You seem to have an obsession with a such said neck." I step closer, erasing the space between us.

"That's because, darling." I wrapped my hands around her neck, "it's one of the weakest spots on the human body. And it fits so well in my hands." I tightened my hold on it as Meraki made no effort to fight back. Instead, she stood still and watched me through those thick lashes, her silence beckoning me to continue, to squeeze a little tiger. "If I squeeze hard enough, you'll be dead." I loosened my hold a little to give her the illusion of freedom, then tightened it even further, ensuring this time I placed enough force behind it for her to gasp.

"Wife, If I did squeeze too tight, you would not be the first woman to die in the hands of her husband. History has seldom favored women." She clasped her hands around mine, straining my hold against her throat, her pulse a quiet beat against my fingertips.

"History has never favored women, but that has never stopped women from slitting the throats of their sleeping husbands. It has never stopped them from lacing the food and drinks of those who wielded power over them. Neither did it quench their thirst for more. We are fighters, and we never stop fighting. Remember that darling husband when you threaten me again?" She smiled, her palms slamming against my chest.

"Now I'm glad we have our boundaries set. Why don't you clearly outline what my role going forward entails? Since you've had your fair taste of blood tonight," she eyed, ran her thumb through my hair, and lowered her hand to show me the remnant of blood that lingered. She smeared it against my chest without a shroud of fear.

This woman...

"We have three days to get tongues wagging across the realms, of my angelic-faced wife, with the mouth of a demon." I shoved her back, needing space. "Tomorrow, I showcase you to the gossip hub of Esneoh; the following evening, we host an event for my people here. And you will be at my side, fawning over how amazing my cock is." I cup my manhood, emphasizing my point. "We then attend the official announcement celebration for the trials, but before that, you will need to complete a job," I note, towering over her.

"What job?" Her eyes glint with excitement, and something about the sight of them stirs something within me.

"You're going to infiltrate the demon king's lair and place listening chips all over it, ensuring you don't get caught, and we can reach the event on time." A devious smile sprawled across her face, and my heart somersaulted at the sight.

"Finally, something to sink into."

"Hmm," I replied, stepping back, and heading for the house. I didn't turn around; the last thing I needed to do, was to sink my cock into her tonight. No, I had plans and punishments set out for her. Before that, I needed to gather intel.

19

A FAILED ATTACK

Meraki

"Good morning, beautiful people" Silas walked into the dining space, casually dressed in a navy-blue fedora hat to accompany. His face was freshly shaven, and his eyes were a transparent shade of gray, juxtaposed to the drunk man I had witnessed last night.

"What are you two arguing about now?" Brielle strolled in, wrapped in a black silk nightgown. There was a strained silence for a moment, but everyone skated around it, acting like it didn't exist.

Enzo followed the train of my sight from the other end of the table but made no effort to call it out. He shook his shoulder and reached for some bread and butter instead.

"I'm grateful there's another woman in this house because I'm quite frankly sick of all the testosterone I have to deal with," Brielle rolled her eyes as she sat beside Silas.

Brielle and Quillian engaged in conversation about the event last night, looping Silas in on what had transpired. "What's wrong?" Brielle turned her attention toward me as I zoned in and out of their conversation, distracted by the low tick of their alarm system.

"Is there a way to turn that sound off?" My hands float around the air.

"What sound?" Quillian asked, taking a sip of the drink before him; I arched my brow, trailing my gaze around the table.

"The ticking sound," I waved my hand in the air, the loud growing more intense. My eyes trailed the confines of the room, trying to locate its origin.

"Meraki-" Brielle called, gently dropping the butter knife in her hand.

"What sound?" Enzo rose from his chair, and the room turned to face me, waiting for me to expand.

"The sound that's been going off since I woke up this morning. Though it seems to be picking up now," I continued, filling my plate with eggs, bacon, and toasted brown bread.

"Where's the sound coming from?" Quillian and Enzo exchanged weary glances.

"Wait, you really can't hear it?" I halted in my descent of the bread before me. They each shook their heads. "Then there's some sort of timer in the house-" I stopped and rose to my feet, realizing the implication of my words. "There's a bomb in the house," I announced, turning my attention to the door.

"But why can't we hear anything," Brielle rushed to her feet, her robe swaying with the swiftness of it. "I can't scent anything out of the ordinary either."

"That might be the point?" I noted, following the sound trail, across the corridor, to the house's garage. My stomach sank, recalling one type of weapon capable of bypassing the ears of even the sharpest supernatural beings. One that was directly created and sold by the Alokari.

"It's somewhere here." I walked into the white-painted garage space filled with a series of high-end luxury cars. I walked around the area, straining my ears for the exact spot.

I stopped by an Aventador, pressed my head against its windows, and lowered myself to its boot. "Don't freak out, but-"

Quillian moved to stand beside me, his eyes falling on the device wedged on its bumper. A small gray box was a timer attached to it that drew my attention, and I lowered myself to get a better glimpse. Quillian stood directly behind me, watching with his nostrils flared

"Wolfsbane," Quillian said, his face set into a scowl.

"Call Enzo and ask him to send the security intel we discussed." he turned to face Silas. Silas stepped back, pulling out his phone as he spoke in hushed whispers.

"How?" Brielle asked. No one gets through the premises without me sensing it."

"I don't think they got into the premises, "I replied, studying the angle and effort taken to set this up correctly. "This looks like it was attached outside the premises. I've used this type of detonator before," I spoke, immediately regretting the words as they left my mouth. Quillian and Brielle watched me with morbid curiosity. I shrugged, not wanting to draw too much attention to it. "It leaves a mess behind. Who last had the car, and where did they go?"

Quillian and Brielle immediately turned to Silas, who had just gotten off the phone with Enzo. He walked back toward us, his face masked with indifference.

"Where the hell did you go last night?" Quillian asked, the tension oozing from him in waves.

"A club," Silas replied, turning from one sibling to another.

"A club, baby brother? We were supposed to keep a low profile. No one was supposed to know we are back yet, you idiot!" Brielle yelled, turning to press her long manicured nails against Silas's chest. Her height compared to his made the whole scene almost comedic.

"I was cloaked Brie," he shot, dismissing her hand.

"Clearly, you weren't as cloaked as you thought." she chimed, stepping back from him, and running her hand through her short finger wave curls.

"Who was there?" Quillian's deep baritone voice echoed a silent warning behind it.

"It was a mixed club, more a bar, meant to be a space for all the sects to intermingle," Silas spoke. "it's the latest crave in Esneoh." He continued.

"And you took my fucking car? Are you looking for a death wish or trying to find a way to destroy any plans we have?" Quillian stepped toward him, the heat from his words like a whip across my skin.

"The car was also cloaked."

"Clearly, that was not the case. Someone saw through the charade. So, this could be anyone," she pointed at the explosive.

"We've barely been back a week, and my patience for your reckless behavior is reaching its peak," Quillian chimed in as they argued back and forth between themselves.

"There is a bomb here," I announced, stating the obvious. "It needs to be deactivated otherwise, there'll be no house left to stand in," I pointed at the ongoing timer that seemed to only speed up with each second.

"Someone is trying to send a message," Brielle finally spoke, pacing the garage as if she had completely missed what I just said. This family was a mess, one that I was now stuck in.

I turned back to the device and an idea formulated in my mind. Quillian was still apprehensive and suspicious about me, and to fully sway him to my side; I needed to earn his trust by winning his favor.

"Blowing up the house would have no impact on us directly. It's not like it can kill us," Silas turned his gaze to Brielle, ignoring Quillian's scowl.

"But it could derail all our plans?" Brielle offered, pacing the space between us.

"A message received," Quillian mumbled.

"Erm...hello? Where are the keys to the car?" I stretched out my hand, waiting by the car's door. "The keys, Silas," I repeated with my hands outstretched. He stepped to the right corner of the garage door and reached for the key perched on the side wall. He threw it to me, and I opened the car, rushing to get into it.

"What do you think you're doing?" Quillian asked, stepping forward; his hand rested against the steering wheel.

"The time just jumped to one minute," I pointed at the bumper's reflection from the wing mirror. I turned the ignition on, and the garage door opened. I pressed down on the ignition and sped out before Quillian could get a word in. As the car steered through the entryway of the estate, I opened the door with one hand while keeping the other on the steering wheel.

"Twenty," I mumbled, passing the house's main gate. "Ten," I fidgeted, as the outline of the house could no longer be seen through the wing mirror. "Ten," I continued ahead at full speed as a bayou came into view ahead. I pulled the door up.

"Five," I continued, nearing the water that covered the surrounding area. "Two," I counted out loud, seeing the plains of the bayou becoming more apparent by the second. I pressed harder on the gas and jumped out. The car steered forward, leaned against the lake, and exploded.

The large explosion ricocheted as I fell on the grass, twisting my wrist while my body rolled over. "Just my luck," I mumbled numbly as parts of the car flew into the air missing me by a few inches.

Dark wings hovered over me, blocking the sunlight and the growing body of smoke and flames emitting from the car. "That was a stupid thing to do," Quillian stated, lowering himself beside me, and stretching out his hand for me to take.

"That's my middle name. I think I twisted my hand?" He raised it into the air for inspection.

"This isn't twisted; it's broken." He stated, his brows furrowed. "You're in pain; why can't I sense it from you?"

I jerked my hand from his hold, realizing I was giving myself away. "I can fix myself." I stepped forward, gazing toward where I had just come from. Quillian pulled me back, swept me from the floor, and curled me against his chest. "What are you doing?" I fought his hold as the adrenaline rush from earlier began to wane.

"Relax," He answers, his wings outstretched as he takes flight.

"The car..." I stumbled, trying to find a distraction. Being taken care of after a high like that wasn't something I was used to, and the attention on me made me want to crawl out of my skin.

"Silas has it," he replied, turning me around to see the carnage behind us. Silas stood beside the car from a distance, his midnight-colored wings outstretched. He pulled me deeper into his chest, an unfamiliar softness in his approach.

"Is there anything you're afraid of, Little Hellion?" he asked, his gaze focused on the outline of the house ahead.

"If I tell you, then I'll have to kill you," I laughed awkwardly, knowing there was an ounce of truth behind those words.

Quillian descended, stopping at the front step of the door. Instead of placing me down, his hold on me tightened as he retracted his wings and made his way through the corridor.

"My hand is twisted, not my legs," I noted, unable to think straight with the weight of his warmth pressed against me.

He released a soft chuckle as if my words were somewhat amusing. He continued walking up the stairs to his office and placed me on one of the front-facing chairs. He turned his back to me, shuffling through several drawer spaces behind him. He turned back to face me with a small vial in hand. "Drink." He opened the vial and pushed it before my lips.

I hesitated, my brows dipped, and my eyes searched his. "If I wanted to kill you, you would be dead already." He arched his brow in a questioning manner. I pondered on the question and tipped the tip of the vial against my lips, drinking the full content in one go.

"What the hell is that?" I coughed, staring down at the bottle, its bitter aftertaste still lingering on my tongue.

"Something I had Hera create for you," he stated, not emphasizing further.

"Me?"

"In anticipation of anything going wrong."

"That almost sounds like you care, vampire," I replied as a warm sensation bubbled inside my chest and stretched through my body. My hands and fingers tingled as if something was being set into place. Trying to read this man was like deciphering a series of hieroglyphics.

"You saved my family," Quillian noted, ignoring my prior statement. He sat on the chair beside me, that permanent scowl etched on his face.

I smiled meekly, fist-pumping myself internally. My plan had worked. Family was everything to Quillian, and to breach his sea of barriers, I needed to tap into that family bond.

"No, I saved myself in particular. My brain matter was more likely to be sprawled on the floor than any of you." I dismissively raised my hand with ease.

"Hmmm," he muttered aloud, taking hold of my hand, and pressing lightly on my wrist to check whether everything had settled.

"If you want to thank me, you should release me."

"Nice try, but you already know the answer." He searched my face and released his hold on my wrist when satisfied he got what he was looking for.

"How does it feel?"

I moved my wrist slowly in a clockwise motion to demonstrate. "Healed."

"Good," he replied, his fingers lightly brushing against the skin.

"Word got around quicker than anticipated, and someone isn't happy about it," The door opened as Brielle walked into the room.

Her gaze briefly fell on Quillian and his proximity. If she saw anything out of the ordinary, she acted like she didn't. Instead, she moved to the seat beside her brother, her legs crossed.

"Do you think it was smart to tell the leaders the truth about our disappearance yesterday?" Brielle Turned to Quillian. He leaned back in his seat.

"It was intentionally, and I suspect word about it will get out once the leaders update their constituents. But that wasn't the point; word would have returned to those who had a role in our imprisonment. It was also a warning that our family always prevails regardless of what anyone may try. Those smart enough will be weary."

"Silas attended the club before the event. No. That means they were already aware of your escape or someone else was and guessed you would make a claim for the trials and want to sabotage that." I offered.

"Whomever it was wasn't one of ours. Each of those leaders last night seemed genuinely surprised. And either they were all great actors, or they were equally surprised about the news," Brielle said. Quillian frowned and ran his hand through his subtle stubble.

"You think otherwise, Q?"

"IT would be easy not to suspect our own. But too many things to point out that someone within our group played a role in it. The last thing we all remembered was Silas driving us from the celebratory event in Aarin. Someone had to have been aware of our plans and movement that eve. The whole thing just seems too clean."

"That's a big accusation," I interfered.

"It's pretty huge. Who do you have in mind?" Brielle asked, leaning forward. Quillian followed suit.

"Makeba would seem the most obvious choice." Quillian offered.

"Or Amma," Brielle said, folding her hands at the mention of the name.

"Who is Amma?" I asked, struggling to keep abreast of the names and details thrown around.

"Yes, brother, who is Amma?" She rose to her feet, her laugh ringing in soft echoes. Quillian's demeanor grew rigid, his jaw tightened, and his eyes narrowed.

"A friend, baby sister."

"Is that what we are calling it nowadays?"

"Don't you have somewhere to be?"

"No," Brielle laughed even more and turned her gaze to me. "Alright, alright, next time you decide to stick your dick somewhere, you'll hopefully not pick a psycho bitch." She raised her hand in mock surrender and made a beeline for the door.

"Well," I shuffled awkwardly on my seat as unease settled within me. This was good, and I was finally getting glimpses of his previous life, aspects worth reporting back to Alokari. Right?

Quillian rose and reached for an envelope on his desk. He sat back down, pulling his chair closer, eliminating the space between us.

"Security intel and images of the demon king's house." He placed the envelope on my lap, and I picked it up, shifting through its content. The images comprised of a Grande chateau compromised of several floors.

"What about security cameras?" Detailing vital strategic points that would be best for optical sound and audio.

"Of course." He rose again, turning to face the faux door opposite where the safe had been. A transparent screen opened, and he placed his thumb over the sensor. A low humming sound followed; he raised his hand and bit down his wrist. He then placed the blood flow over the same spot where he had placed his thumbprint, and I watched on, utterly fascinated. I had hacked enough safes and bypassed many systems with Skye in the past. This was by far the most outlandish.

The safe did not have that level of security; whatever had been there were things close to him, not things that bore secrets or held more significant consequences.

I needed to find a way to access it. I needed to know what dark secrets he kept hidden in there.

I tilted my head, trying to get a peak of anything from my vantage point, but the interior of the space was too deep to see clearly. Quillian reached down and pulled out a tablet. He closed the drawer, and a silent buzzing sound followed behind it.

He turned back around, his eyes assessing my curiosity, but he made no effort to heed it for too long. His stride spoke of his confidence, convinced it was impenetrable. He had never met me before.

He sat back down on his chair, his legs outstretched, and as he shuffled, his legs touched mine. This man either didn't know about personal space or was unaware of the weight of his presence, scent, and power.

He sat forward, fiddling on the screen for a few seconds. "I was able to hack into his security systems. What do you need me to do with it?" he placed the tablet in my hand, scrolling through the live feed.

"Who knew the vampire overlord was a tech geek?" I muttered aloud.

"Some would say genius." His palm rested against my knees, watching as it filtered through the house's four levels.

"Someone is fishing for compliments. Let's go for geeky tech genius then?" I arched my brow, and his eyes studied me, lingering long on my lips.

"How long?"

"Two days from now." He removed his hand, leaving in its wake a cold emptiness.

"Three days? This job takes a week of scouting, tracking, and observing."

"And?" He reclined back on his seat, turning the full extent of his body toward me.

"And there are factors like security, time, proximity, my scent, for one? It cannot be rushed." Quillian stared at me with narrowed eyes and glared back.

"We don't have a week. We have what we have. That celebratory eve is the only night that would be a good opening. He won't be at home, and his security intel would have significantly decreased, as most would be at the event."

"The time?"

"Would corroborate with his schedule." He argued.

"How do you know that?" My eyes narrowed into slits. Quillian watched me pensively as if he was aware of some insider information I was not. "You have someone on the inside?" I state it as a fact rather than a question. I was impressed. Quillian had planned this move to the basic minuscule details. No one would dare point a finger or suspect him of foul play if the fool's plan went awry. Everyone would be at the event, and it would be hard to account that he wasn't there otherwise.

"You are searching for more information than we have here," I mentioned, my gaze moving from the tablet screen to him. My gut was telling me this was more. It wasn't simply a job to observe the going in and coming outs of the king of Esneoh. This felt strategic, almost personal in nature. He was looking for something.

"What are you really up to, vampire?"

"I don't trust you."

"Didn't we establish this already?" I retorted.

"You're bound to me," he stated ominously, and my mind registered the words as some uncut threat.

"I belong to no man," I replied as the warmth of irritation coursed through me. Quillian leaned forward and arched my chin, his gaze communicating a secret code I couldn't decipher.

"You are mine. Mine to do with as I please." His thumb lightly stroked against my neck. "Mine to possess, mine to destroy, rebuild. Mine to devour. Mine," he enunciated every word, and my pulse quickened at a depth of power behind it.

"This," I moved to the space between us. "Is a transaction, a farce I've been forced into. To the outside world, I am yours," I stumbled on the words, gritting my teeth at its aftertaste. "But here, your existence still irritates my soul. Let's not confuse the two." I motioned to the space around us. His face morphed into a frown, and he stared long at me as if trying to communicate something.

"Hmm," he responded in that familiar dismissive manner of his. "Continue with what you were saying." He raised his hand, beckoning me to continue my line of questioning.

"How do you expect me to get through the walls?" I placed the tablet down and picked up the series of images now resting on my lap. "These look like they are electrically wired for trespassers," I note, running my hands through the never-ending wall that seemed to cover the full scale of the chateau.

"I can drop you on top of the property and pick you back from the same spot,' he noted casually, as if this was a straightforward task.

"I need more equipment; I don't have everything I need." I raise my hand, exasperated at the back and forth.

"I also have your weapons from the night we brought you back here."

"Brought implies consent. Kidnapping is a more fitting word," I replied brashly, not attempting to hide my contempt for the situation.

"To-may-toes, to-ma-toes. They all mean the same thing. It changes nothing."

"Do you have an answer for every insufferable thing?" I took a deep breath to stave the anger bubbling inside.

"Genius, remember?" he replied, mockingly reminding me of the words I had used to describe him not too long ago. I regret the words now.

"Get acquitted with the set-up," he pointed at the tablet. "And wife, don't do anything I won't do." He rose to his feet, leaving me in his office space.

I immediately turned my attention to the tablet and scrolled through, noting that it had been wiped clean.

That bastard.

20

AWARD-WORTHY PERFORMANCES

Meraki

"I'm hosting a welcome back event, and the leaders in Kinavari will be in attendance. They will get to meet you tonight," Quillian announced, strolling into my room without even knocking. I shifted under the silk sheets and rolled up leaning the top half of my body against the headboard.

"Good morning to you too," I mumbled under my breath while trying to make sense of the fact he was casually dressed in gray sweatpants and an accompanying shirt. Heat warmed my skin, and I struggled to focus my attention anywhere else but the long and thick stick poking through his pants. Gray sweatpants were a vice, my kryptonite, and my downfall.

"Is this a human trait? Do you plan to sleep all day?" Quillian stepped deeper into the room, oblivious of the fact I was ogling and admiring his manhood. The natural musk of his scent filled the space between us.

"It's six in the morning. I slept one hour ago! What the hell are you complaining about," I yelled, unable to hold back my irritation. Who the hell makes accusations this early without first even offering coffee?

"You're lying." He stopped midtrack, his gaze scrutinous.

"Excuse me?"

"Do I have to repeat everything, human? You lied; you've been in bed since eleven. You have about an hour to get ready for bed after leaving my office. He folded his arms and placed them against his chest.

"You were following me?" I pulled back the cover and slid from the bed, ready to stab a stake through his obnoxious mouth.

"This is my house; I know your kind doesn't exactly have a lot of sense." He shook his head. "I didn't realize your case was this special." He rolled the word in his tongue, needing me to grasp exactly how he felt about humans and me in general.

I stood at the foot of my bed and inhaled and exhaled loudly, refusing to give in to his bate. I smiled and turned my attention fully to him. "Well, husband, I was looking through the Loki's setup and strategizing how best to place the devices without one being detected and two getting my ass caught. Since I all but have less than a week to do it." I found my voice getting louder.

I turned and pointed at the tablet on my bedside table. "The tablet stopped being used just after twelve," he continued, his tone accusatory.

"And?"

"And you lied." He pointed at the tablet. "And there's nothing I hate more than-"

"Let me guess, humans?" He snarled, eliminating the space between us.

"There's nothing I hate more than humans. Yes, but a lying human? Even more so." He pulled the bonnet from my hair, and it spiraled down my shoulders. "Now be a good wife, get dressed, show up and shut up?" He snickered, lifting a curl into his hands, and placing it behind my ear.

I pushed back his chest and glared. "Be careful; your misogyny is showing," I stated, feeling my nose flare. Under any other circumstance, I would have shared that sleep and I were naturally opposites, and with the added benefit of staying in a new environment, a different world for that matter - was too much for my body and mind.

"You aren't denying it."

"Deny, I'm a liar, or all humans are liars?" I arched my brows. "Unfortunately, I'm not the United Nations and cannot stand as a representative for all humans."

"Yes, husband?" His cold, flinty eyes moved through my now exposed chest and bare legs in the silk night dress. I quickly wrapped the robe on top of it into a knot.

"Be ready for seven tonight," he stepped back and headed for the door.

"I need a car today," I called, wrapping my hand against my chest. Quillian turned back sharply as if I had just asked for a million.

"No!"

"No? Last I checked, I wasn't a prisoner!" I pointed to the space between us with one hand.

"You are and will always be a prisoner, human," he answered, a tightness in his expression.

"I want to get acquainted with Esneoh-"

"Which part of no, do you not understand?"

"The part you stated." I deadpanned. Quillian stepped forward and pulled open the door and turned back around.

"Not today; it's not safe yet. Tomorrow," he gritted the words through his teeth.

"That wasn't so bad now, was it, husband?" I mocked, watching the vein on his forehead and neck bulge. He stormed out of the room, shutting the door behind him.

I quickly changed and headed for the glasshouse toward the gym facilities in the adjoining building.

I spent a short amount of time on the treadmill and most on

weight training while incorporating isometric and ballistic exercises along the way.

"Meraki," Silas smiled, adorned in all-black workout wear. "Damn woman, you kick ass in the gym."

I shrugged. "All the better to kick your brother's ass," I replied nonchalantly.

"Now, that I won't be mad at seeing. Then again, Brielle said you had done before he sedated you." He shook his head at the thought.

I continued with my press-ups, pushing myself even harder to starve the unease of unfamiliarity of this new world. There were only so many reports and files I could read on it to be prepared. Being here right now felt like an out-of-body experience, making my skin prickle and my heart lurch by the quietest sound.

"You don't agree," I stated.

"I'm more of a lover. Quillian and Brielle love the fight and spilling blood," he noted, lowering himself down on the ground to join me.

"You don't believe in using force?" I grunted, my arms aching from the strain of each pull at a push.

"Don't go putting words in my mouth," he said, his gaze now focused on the floor and the steady movements of his hand. "The Kingsley love nothing more than spilling blood. I just prefer to do only if necessary." I nodded, watching his movements' fluidity and the bulge of his veins in his hands with every movement. Silas was different from his siblings and wore that with a badge of honor.

"Now, let's see what you're made of without a weapon," he smirked, making me recall our earlier encounter on the roof.

"What do you suggest?" I beamed.

"Attagirl, that's what I like to see," he laughed when I rose to my feet, my excitement palpable. "Boxing and long run?"

"None of that vampire shit; it needs to be fair." I arched my brow in warning, heading to the far wall with inbuilt clear storage, and pulled out boxing gloves for him and me.

"Vampire shit? You mock me." He placed his hand on his chest, feigning mock hurt. "But yes, I won't use my powers if that's the shit you're implying." I threw him his pair of gloves, fastened mine, and motioned for us to use the further end of the room, which had less equipment, and more space to move around.

I turned and faced him with my feet shoulder-width apart. Silas repeated, his frame blocking most of the view behind him. "Pretend I'm Quillian and don't hold back," he offered, the jest in his tone hard to miss.

I stepped forward, starting with a series of quick jabs. Silas kept his hands pressed together to block my movements. As I waited for him to make a move, I changed my moves, combining uppercuts and hooks.

His right hand lunged forward with quick, easy steps, and I slipped past his shot by bending my knees and rotating from the waist to the left and then right with each blow. Silas came at me hard, giving me no breathing ground to even collect myself.

Sweat beaded my body and clung to my clothes, but I persisted, ducking, and countering each blow. "Remind me to never let my guard down around you?" he threw a jab and quickly wiped the sweat on his forehead with his forearms.

"Same," I breathed, noting this wasn't even him at his full capacity.

"There she is," he commented when I stayed on the offensive by throwing punches in bunches to dictate the pace. I grunted, unsure of what he meant by the comment but kept my focus on his abdomen. I pounded his chest with one arm to slow down his offense. Silas seemingly caught unaware, attempted to correct this by counteracting it with a series of blows. While ducking, one caught in directly on the chest, and the air left my lungs. Giving up now wasn't an option.

I grunted and heaved out loud, refusing to dwell on the light throb left behind by its impact. My reflexes kicked in, and I waited for him to make the next move. As he did so, I ducked, counting the small opening on his chest when he raised his hand. I seized the opportunity, using the full weight of my strength, and pounded forward mercilessly.

I slipped back when he attempted to fight back as we both fought to catch our breath. "I haven't trained like this in a while," he stated, wiping sweat from his forehead. His low fade hair glistened with each movement.

"Because you were held…" I trailed, unsure how he would react to being privy to perhaps the most harrowing experience of his life.

He laughed. "You can say it, imprisoned?"

"People can be sentimental about shit like that," I commented, following him. He removed one glove, reached for two water bottles to his right, and handed me one. I removed one glove and reached out for the black bottle. I drank the full content once, taking a breather.

"Don't worry; I won't take offense. It happened, trying to pretend it didn't only dishonor the experience," he shrugged, tilted the bottle, and drank. "And no, that's not what I meant, even though that's one of the main reasons," he breathed, wiping the remnants of the drink from his lips. I didn't press for more information; the air charged with the answer already.

Since Alaric.

"I hope your body hasn't given out already?" he joked, placing his bottle down. "I know your bodies can be frail; I don't want to push you too far." He winked, squelching the retort I had.

"Don't worry, little vampire; this human has handled bigger dicks in her lifetime." I followed with a wink of my own, placing the bottle to the side and refastening my gloves.

Silas laughed, the deep baritone of his voice filling every corner of the room. "Attagirl!" He commented. "I'll try not to be offended by that emasculating comment." He refastened his glove and got into a boxing stance.

I snorted, feeling the previously felt discomfort starting to fade. "Well, they say if the shoe-"

Silas threw a punch before I could even finish my sentence.

"Don't you dare finish that," he growled; the subtle smirk tugging at the corner of his lips told me he wasn't offended but seemed to be enjoying our little spar.

I weaved and ducked under him, rising back up with counter-attacks of my own. "I went soft on you earlier. Don't hold your breath this time." I scuffed and shook my breath.

"The male ego is so fragile." I rolled my eyes. He jabbed forward, catching me unaware. We kept going for what seemed like hours, neither of us resting or giving the other more than a few seconds to catch our breath.

"What's the plan for today?" Silas asked when we had both worn each other out.

"I'm being locked away in the big scary tower, from the huge overwhelming world outside," I stated, taking a sip of water.

"I would support a rebellion on any other day, but today might not be the best in Kinavari," Silas stated, gloom clouding his face, and I wanted to reach out and soothe him as I would Skye or Iris, but the thought baffled me. Even though Silas is different from his brothers and battling several demons, he is still a Kingsley. I have read and heard enough about their family history to know that he has a hand in the chaos-seeking tendencies that his siblings have. I chastise myself inwardly, reminding myself he was still a liability, regardless of how open, kind, and frank he had been since I met him.

"Why is that?" I wiped the sweat from my face with the lower end of my loose-fitted shirt.

"Quillian didn't update you?"

"Does your brother look like someone capable of engaging in a conversation with a human?" I rolled the words in my tongue how he usually did. "I was hoping Brielle would before I went in there completely unaware."

Silas nodded, his hands briefly running through his hair. "As expected, there's been a lot of grumbling from some of the leaders in Kinavari. And you might... let me correct that. You will meet hostility tonight," he forewarned.

"And what advice would you offer me to navigate around it?" I asked, the strain of how hard I had pushed myself weighing against my body.

He stood still watching me, the depth of those familiar gray eyes probing and questioning my sincerity.

"Act human!" He stated.

"You may have missed me with that one." Silas laughed haughtily and motioned for us to call it a day.

"They have preconceived notions about how humans act and behave. Play into it. They'll back off if they don't see you as a threat. You'll simply be seen as someone under my brother's protection. If they, however, see you as a threat, regardless of my brother's protection, they will find a way to come at you," he added as we walked into the garden space and headed for the house.

"Act human," I reiterated the words, realizing his advice was sound.

"I know, I know. Being handsome isn't my only redeeming quality," he beamed from the periphery of my vision.

"Stop fishing for compliments," I lightly dabbed his muscled hands.

"Nothing wrong with hearing one from a beautiful woman." He reeled back, pretending that the pitch had caused him serious pain. I stopped before we reached for the door and turned my gaze toward him.

"Why are you being...this," I flicked my hand in the air, unsure how to describe the ease and comfortability I felt around him.

"This?!" he repeated my movements, a sly dig in action.

"You know what I mean!" My voice grew more serious, and my hands rested against my waist. Silas stepped back and ran his hands over his lower lip.

"Let's just say you remind me of someone, a friend. A ghost that won't stop haunting me." A brief smile spread across his face and retracted, followed by a deep scowl. I wanted to ask if, by any chase, it was the red-haired woman I had seen from the series of images in Quillian's office. But I knew doing so would ruse suspicion.

"This friend, she was a woman, I take it?" I questioned cautiously.

"Stop fishing for information," he replied, using the same words I had used just a few minutes prior. I knew it was someone he cared about because of the way the stillness lasted. What were the chances the Kingsley brothers were all in love with the same woman? Where was this woman now? And what role did she have in Alaric's death?

Since it was assumed that she was the human who was continually being called a dishonest liar, the question was, what had she lied about, and why was he angrier than Silas than Brielle? Or was Silas referencing someone entirely?

I nodded and followed him inside, concluding that this was a story worth unmasking, and I wasn't going to rest until I got to the root of it.

The house was bustling with movement, decorations, and freshly baked bread. Eugene and Elena ran around the passageways, consumed the act of preparing for tonight's event.

"There's food out in the kitchen," Eugene, the eldest looking of the two, stepped forward and motioned to the dining area. She hurried off before I could even thank her.

"Where do people go for fun here in Esneoh?" I asked Silas as we headed up the stairway.

"What kind of fun are you looking for?" He furrowed his brows.

"The type you get up to that leaves you slurring your words?" His pace picked up until he reached the landing of his floor.

"I have a few places," he offered deviously. I opened my mouth to ask about The Den yet thought otherwise. Though Quillian had sworn to help me find Alessa's killer, I was smart enough to know that nothing truly came without a cost. This was my fight and waiting or entrusting that responsibility to anyone else fully would be my undoing.

"I know who to seek out when I'm ready to shake a leg," I replied, heading up the stairs.

"You and I will get on just fine," I heard his voice call out from a distance. I smiled as excitement bubbled inside of me. I would allow some days to go by and approach the topic again; this time, it would draw less suspicion as he and I would have naturally built some rapport over time.

I continued up the stairs, showered, ate quickly, and made myself scarce in the library to learn more about this new world and everything it had to offer.

I found books on the landscape of each region and detailed accounts of the local politics and its backdrop. Most importantly, I was able to get some clarity on the history of Esneoh itself.

The land itself was birthed from magic, and with each new leader, it imparted some of that power onto them. Every millennium, power begins to diminish until the land calls for another Trial to balance the distribution of power. Without active participation in the trial, Esneoh itself would cease to exist.

Very little was known about the Nephilim, whose magic had been imbued into the very soil. They were mentioned as residing in Aarin and acted as the sounding board over the other beings. They were also recorded, as kings over the land at intervals, after winning the trials. They were, however, recorded as being wiped out over time due to internal strife and intermarriages with humans. Over time, those relationships weakened their powers, leading to their ultimate extinction.

With each page read, I found myself lost and longing for something I couldn't yet name.

I fell asleep not long after, lost amid the books, dreaming about a world born in magic and governed by powerful women.

The trail of warm hands against my lips, neck, shoulder, and thighs jolted me from sleep. In the morning, I awoke in a library, which was unusually dim due to the absence of light.

I scanned the space, convinced that someone had been here and had touched me. Warm, familiar hands I had felt before. I shook my head, convinced it was simply a figment of my imagination.

I reached for the lights to the far right of the wall. I stepped back, startled by Quillian leaning against its walls. "If you're trying to kill me, this isn't how to go about it," I stated, my hand clasped around my chest.

"Did you...?" I trailed, thinking better of asking the question. Quillian had made it obvious that my presence alone repulsed him, and whatever we shared in the restroom in that toilet was a one-off mistake with two horny people. And I had too much pride to push further.

"You have two hours to get ready," he briskly said, as if the idea of entertaining a conversation longer than thirty seconds was burdensome. "Eugene will help you get dressed. You and I will walk in together," he added, fastening his cufflinks. The move drew my attention to the rest of his body which I had missed, lost under his gaze.

Quillian wore a tailored to perfect three-piece velvet tuxedo tailored to adorning loafers. The desire to draw closer and draw my hands through his body kept me paralyzed, with my mouth unable to formulate any response.

"There's nothing I hate more than tardiness; he stepped back, stick to the time, human!" he spoke, and whatever lust had seized me immediately disseminated, and I was reminded that the vampire was a cold-hearted asshole—a good-looking one, but an asshole regardless.

"Yes, vampire," I responded, the sarcasm dripping from every pore in my body. I headed for the door, not wanting to give him time to catch on to my moment of stupidity.

True to his word, I walked into my room with Eugene setting up the vanity table on the far right of the room with enough makeup and hair products to pay the tuition for the kids in the orphanage.

"There you are," Brielle immediately followed in behind me. Her small, framed eyes and lips are accentuated by a subtle smoky eye and nude lips. Her short finger wave hair was curled and held in place by duckbill clips.

"Where were you? Q was looking for you everywhere and almost lost his mind," she rolled her eyes.

"I fell asleep in the library," I yawned, trying to process the dresses on the bed and the noise filtering in from outside. I walked toward the bed and ran my hands through the dresses laid out.

"Eugene helped me get ready. Choose your dress, and she'll help ensure the makeup matches," she offered, moving to stand directly beside me.

"Any advice for tonight?" I asked, my gaze falling from the dresses to the selection of shoes on the ground beside them.

"Only drink champagne. The wines are usually laced with magic to loosen people's inhibitions." She shivered as she spoke.

"Speaking from experience?"

"Don't make me dig them up; I'll rather they stay buried."

"Anything else?"

"Be on the lookout; you have a sharp eye and seem to be good at reading people. Note down anyone you see that seems suspicious," she said, her shoulders brushing against mine.

She wrapped her hand around mine, her excitement and glee palpable. "What are you thinking?" she stared down longingly at a black off-shoulder ensemble guaranteed to get every neck turning.

My thoughts went back to Silas's advice, and I opted instead for a gold tasseled beaded cocktail dress coupled with black ankle chained open squared toe heels. This dress was sexy and provocative, showing enough skin to make heads turn but not enough for them to dig past the surface.

Brielle left a few minutes, and Eugene took over, making it obvious she wasn't looking for input from the get-go, just a clean canvas that doesn't speak.

"It's time," Quillian knocked after some time had passed, and Eugene was placing the final touches on her masterpiece. She quickly applied my lipstick, opened the door, and held it open for me to pass.

"You look..."

"If you say human, I'll walk back in that door," I said, pointing in the direction of my room. His eyes roved through my body, and though he attempted to keep his face stoic, a satisfied grunt emitted from his chest. Butterflies swarmed my stomach; my breath caught in my chest as a strong spark of static electricity passed between us.

I closed my eyes briefly and inhaled deeply, taking in the fresh undertones of his masculine scent, and wrapping it around me. The desperate urge to touch him and feel his lips against my skin became overbearing. I was convinced I was losing my mind because I hadn't eaten for hours, right?

"You look beautiful," he commented, ignoring my previous comment. My eyes widened at his compliment, and those carefully placed guards around him lifted for a moment, giving a glimpse of his deep, dented dimples and the warmth behind his eyes.

"You don't look half bad for someone your age," I smirked, waiting for his reaction.

"The age jokes, I should have expected them," he replied, eliminating the space between us. "What would you call this between us then, since I'm so old?" He asked playfully while reaching out to move loose strands of my updo behind my ears.

"Robbing the cradle," I replied as I tapped his chest in jest. Quillian laughed unguarded without restriction, and my skin heated at its allure.

"Remember to be cautious of what you say when you're in the hall. Every being down there will be listening and looking for flaws," he remarked quietly once he had reassembled his composure. He lowered his hand from my ears to my neck, then lightly trailed the dress's corset with reverent awe.

"Like, what you see?" I corked a brow, and a smug look plastered over my face. Somehow realizing that he was attracted to me as much as I was to him quelled the fire within me.

"Always," I muttered so low that it could have been easily missed. He retracted his hand, and a coldness lingered where his touch had been.

"We should go," he offered, though I wasn't sure whether that comment was for him or me. He reached forward and took hold of my right hand, wrapping it around his. "The top floors are soundproofed, but the main floor, minus my office aren't," he added, pulling me along with him down the stairs. I nodded, already knowing this, but hearing it out loud was the confirmation I needed.

"Are you ready for the performance of a lifetime?" I asked as we descended the spiral staircases, and his hold on my hand tightened.

The passageway of the lower floor was empty, but the noise from the banquet room filtered through the walls. Laughter, chatter, and a backdrop of instrumentals caught my attention.

The doors opened, and Quillian and I walked into the large airy space now filled with an innumerable amount of people draped in elegant attire. One end of the room contained a seating area consisting of rows of carefully decorated tables with food on top. In contrast, the other end held a large center space assigned for dancing. The surrounding space where people had gathered saw servers filter through with drinks, and groups of people stood deep in conversation.

The entire room turned when we stepped in, their eyes assessing, probing, and accusatory all at once. Quillian seemed oblivious to it as he continued ahead with me in his hands.

"You clean up well, Meraki," Silas walked toward us as we walked through the sea of bodies. He lowered his head and planted a light kiss on my cheeks, soliciting a low grumble from Quillian. "I can look after her while you give the introductory speech?" Silas continued, and something told me he wasn't offering out of the sincerity of his heart. He somehow got a fix out of pushing Quillian's buttons, and I couldn't even fault him. I was the same.

"Behave," I tapped his chest warningly but could not conceal the smile on my face.

"Si..." Quillian warned, pulling me into his chest. Silas laughed; a knowing smile flashed in his eyes; he raised his hand in mock surrender and motioned for us to walk ahead.

Most people had picked up their conversation again and attempted to look inconspicuous, but I could tell their ears were alert to everything else.

Silas remained on my left, his shoulder brushing against mine in a protective stance. At the same time, Quillian on the right kept his face passive as we walked toward the stage. When we arrived, the small orchestra stepped back, giving us ample space to walk on the stage while they continued their ministration.

Brielle joined us a few seconds later with Enzo beside her. She was dressed in a sheer lavender lace dress with a train that demanded the room's attention.

Two attendants strapped before the stage handing us glasses of champagne while more walked around the room, ensuring every single person had one in hand.

"Thank you all for coming tonight. There have obviously been some changes since the last event we had like this," Quillian's voice boomed, followed by peals of laughter in the room as all eyes turned to face me.

I smiled into the crowd as Quillian locked our fingers together. "My family and I are back, and our goal is to reclaim what was rightfully ours. Tonight, we celebrate family," he raised our interlocked fingers in the air.

"Tonight, we celebrate friends and the leaders of this region who have worked to keep the needs of its citizens above their own tirelessly," Silas said, raising his glass.

"Tonight, we celebrate unity. Reuniting broken bonds and rebuilding broken ones," Brielle spoke, following Silas's move.

"Tonight, we celebrate each leader here. Each face here. Each of you took time out of your day to attend. We appreciate you," Enzo chimed in.

"Most importantly, we celebrate this, my union to this amazing woman, the newest member of the Kingsley and the Kinavari family. My wife, Meraki," Quillian said, tightening his hold on my hand even more. "Those that honor her show me honor. Those that protect her have the covering of my family. Those that hold her in esteem will be celebrated accordingly. However, those who oppose her will feel the fullness of our wrath," he concluded, turning to peer longing down at me.

I stared agape, coiling down the beat of my heart while subconsciously chastising my body for its lewd response to his possessiveness. Quillian had given a stellar performance, and I just wished my body knew the difference between acting and the truth.

"To family!" I said, raising my glass into the air, and the room followed.

"To family." The words echoed throughout the room, followed by the clinking of glasses. Unlike our initial entry, the atmosphere had become more mellow, charged with anticipation, promise and hope.

Regardless of how I felt about Quillian in particular, there was something here beyond the remit of a leader and his subjects. I searched through many faces in the crowd, who looked on with adoration and intrigue. There was something unique about the Kingsley that drew them in, and maybe it was the seemingly iron-clad family bond or what they represented.

This was a family, birthed through generations of built and broken relationships, promises, hopes, dreams, and blood. And they had earned the fear and respect of their people along the way. And in some ways, human or vampire, we all seek to have people who can call out our bullshit privately yet protect, guide, and love us regardless of all our flaws.

"Come, let me introduce you to the different regions," Quillian whispered in my ears; the warmth of his breath fanned my skin and heated my body. He removed the glass from my hands, handed it to a passing attendant, and reached for me, tugging my body closer to his and raising my chin until our mouths were inches apart.

"You look good enough to eat," he whispered, and from the periphery of vision, I saw the small attention we had garnered. Quillian lowed his mouth to mine, wrapped his hand around my waist, and kissed me. The kiss was gentle, demanding, and possessive offering me no room to pull away. And in the heat of it all, I wasn't sure I wanted to.

His mouth opened for me, owning, and claiming my tongue with urgency and biting, sucking, and swallowing the sound of my pleasure. I lost track of where we were, allowing myself to savor the warmth of his body, the firm caress of his hand against my ass, and the forceful pull of my body against his.

I was prepared to put on the performance of my lifetime tonight; I had not anticipated how great of an actor Quillian himself could be.

"I like this look on you, Little Hellion," he smiled. He pulled back, his eyes glazed with lust. His thumb ran around my swollen lip, and his eyes followed the movement with pride.

"Get a room, please," Silas intervened and stood before us, pulling me back into the present. When I turned back, I noted Brielle and Enzo had left the stage and were now deep in the crowd conversing. The small orchestra had moved back into position, and the room had been relegated to food chatter and alcohol. Yet some eyes remained on us, watching with scrutiny.

"Don't you have somewhere to be, brother?" Quillian tugged me against his side, his hands resting on the small of my back. The move alone deserved an academy award.

"Do I?" Silas arched his brow, a playfulness in the tone of his voice. I chuckled, unable to help myself. Anyone capable of putting Quillian in place and leaving him stumbling for words can easily win me over.

Quillian stared at me and snarled, his eyes propping me to

take his side. I shrugged and reached for Silas, lightly tapping his chest.

"Down, boy," I teased.

"Attagirl, I knew you would inevitably realize I was a better fit."

"Leave!" Quillian warned, and Silas raised his hand in mock surrender as he stepped off the stage. He turned back and winked at me, letting me know the move was intentional, a ploy to almost humanize his stiff and rigid brother.

Quillian's possessiveness did not seem to go undetected, drawing gasped stares from someone within the crowd.

"Come along, troublemaker," he instructed, leading me from the stage with a snarl that stoic expression back in place.

"As my wife, aren't you supposed to take my side?" he commented when we reached the bottom of the stage, his clasped around my waist.

"There's never any side to take when it comes to your family." he nodded as if impressed by the response.

"But Silas is your favorite" he continued, and if I weren't convinced this was all an act, I would have almost guessed he was jealous of the budding relationship between his brother and me.

"My favorite is who keeps me warm at night," I replied, tipping up to plant a kiss on his lips. Quillian stiffened at my touch on his chest for a brief second, but I kept it guarded, catching sight of the woman in yellow whose gaze had remained on us since we walked into the room.

She smiled stiffly and strolled toward us after the move. Something about her demeanor, and the way her presence carried power had forewarned me of who she was.

"Your liege," she beamed, full attention on Quillian's face and his hand around my waist. "This event was long overdue," she continued, and her hand casually moved to his shoulder in an all too familiar move.

Quillian had lied. Amma wasn't a friend; she was more. She

wanted more, and from the unchecked way she caressed him, it was evident they shared something at one point.

Quillian made no effort to move from her embrace; instead, he leaned into her like it was the most natural thing to do. My stomach twisted, and the sight of it unsettled me.

"Amma is the leader of the eastern region of Kinavari," Quillian spoke, confirming my suspicion.

"Amma, this is my."

"Meraki," she interjected, evidently not wanting to illiterate the obvious. Her eyes fell on the blinding yellow diamond ring, and her jaw tensed. Something told me Amma was going to pose a problem later. "It's good to meet you," she smiled with a pinched expression.

"I've heard a lot about you," I smiled in response, letting her know through my eyes that I could read through her bullshit and smokescreen, but I was willing to keep up the pretense.

Quillian's attention turned to a figure ahead, and his hand soothed my back affectionately as he did so. Amma caught the move, and she carefully concealed her mask fell before she forced it back into place when she saw me staring.

"We need a meeting to discuss some matters soon," she stated, her hands moving up and down his shoulder. "When can I come to see you?" she continued, trying to conceal the meaning of her words.

"Enzo can help with that. And when you visit, we should get acquainted," I stated, my hands resting against her wrist in a subtle warning. She glared at me and hesitantly pulled back her hand, knowing this wasn't a winning battle. You can't win against the wife.

Quillian nodded, tugging at my waist. "I'll get Enzo to arrange it." He stated, pushing me toward the man who had caught his attention.

"Quillian," the elderly vampire turned his attention to us, a warm radiant, inviting smile on his face.

"Ferguson!" he lightly nudged the man's shoulder in a gentle show of comradeship.

"And this must be Meraki. The woman that finally tamed the illicit bachelor," he laughed, intel the jab as a compliment. "I can see why." he nodded approvingly.

"Ferguson is the leader of the northern region," Quillian stated, natural ease around his presence. "And one of my oldest and most trusted acquaintances."

"Esneoh is a far cry from Jersey Hill. How are you finding it?"

"I still haven't had time to see all it can offer, but Q has promised I will this week," I replied. "But I'm excited to make it home with my new family."

"Make sure to visit the north, we are the scholars of Kinavari, and if you enjoy reading and the arts, you will feel at home," he answered, falling into my hands.

"How do you know?" I stared down at both my hands, wondering whether there were stained remains of paint left behind.

"Know what?" Quillian furrowed his brow.

"That your wife paints," Ferguson reached for my hand. "One creative to another. I've been doing it for eons, it's easy to recognize others who do," Ferguson added, his attention now solely focused on me.

Quillian's hold on me tightened, and from the intensity of his grip, he was surprised about this key fact. "What do you specialize in?" I question, feeling the ease that comes with navigating around familiar territory.

"Abstract. You?"

"Landscape, and the occasional portrait." Ferguson continued smiling at me, and I winced internally at how easily I had given that intel.

"I'm hoping to see your work."

"It's not worth seeing; I don't particularly think I'm good..." I stumbled, recounting my previous conversation with Iris and the anxiety that came with that. "But I would love to see yours?"

"Of course, whenever you both visit, I would love to." His attention turned to Quillian, and they shared pleasantries. Quillian continued to pass me around the room, but his demeanor had grown more rigid, and his expression plagued with questions.

"Makeba and Hakim." The introduction continued, and like my introduction with Amma, these ones were strained and rigid.

"I'll be back," I rested my hands on Quillian's chest. Before he asked where I wanted to go, I mouthed the restroom. We had been inseparable the whole night and mingled with everyone in the room. My mind was foggy with names, faces, and stories, and I needed fresh air to clear my mind.

"Find Silas," he instructed, lightly tapping my ass and drawing the attention of the vampires before us to the move.

I headed through the bodies of people, made my way toward the main passageway of the house, and headed toward the garden space near the glasshouse.

I turned left before the glasshouse and followed the lighted path to the wooden bench placed in the darkened area of the open garden space. I sat down and exhaled the air I didn't know I had been holding in.

"That was a stellar performance, ma cherie." Ryder hovered over me and clapped.

"Ryder," I replied, making no attempt to keep the facade of our pretense. If he was brave enough to antagonize me outside the house, then I wasn't going to cower.

"For a thief, you certainly know how to perform. Is that also part of the new syllabus of the job?" He laughed, and I made no effort to rise from my feet.

"What happened to your face?" I asked, my eyes locked on the bumped skin that looked like it had been cut with a knife.

"You will find out," he snarled, his hand moving to the scar. "Want to hear something funny?"

"Ideally, no, I came out for fresh air, not to share stories about how much we dislike each other," I rolled my eyes and leaned forward, knowing he wasn't going to give up soon.

He stepped forward, and I snickered and rose to my feet. "You want to do this here? I never penned you for a complete fool. In fact, I even admired your work." I corked my head, knowing I was provoking him but unable to help it. My sight was still set on killing him; I just had to play my cards well when the opportune time came.

"Ma cherie," he cackled, yet his expression remained rigid. "I'm never wrong about my victims. Enjoy the glamor, your day of reckoning will come, and I'll be there to finish my job," he stated, moving closer. A set of incoming footsteps and voices caught our attention, and he stepped back. Hesitantly, he walked away, turning back briefly with a mocking smirk on his face.

I ran my hands through my hair, turned, and lowered myself on the seat again. I leaned back in the seat, closed my eyes, and inhaled and exhaled steady breaths.

When I opened my eyes again, the innumerable stars that lit the night sky caught my attention, illustrating the beauty of Esneoh yet the reality of how far I was away from Iris and Skye. It also reminded me that my life would never be the same once I completed this job. Living in Jersey Hill and continuing like before would be impossible.

I was now compromised and exposed to too many beings ever to be safe.

"Not the smartest, are you?" Amma's voice filtered through my thoughts, and I turned my head to stare at her.

"Smart enough not to practically drool over a married man," I offered and rose to my feet. Finding a moment of respite tonight wasn't going to be an option.

"You dare, human?" she pounced forward with her fangs elongated. I lowered myself and maneuvered my body before she could reach me.

"Careful, Amma, your desperation is showing." She lurched forward again and halted, her mouth pinched in a tight frown.

"I can see why he may be fascinated. I expected..." her hands waved in the air, to signify the word she was trying to recall. "Boring, scared, maybe even a reserved plaything." she snickered at her own words. I chastised myself internally for not having my hunga munga. One clean throw with it would be enough to cut her head off and silence her annoying voice.

"You're no threat. Quillian has a reputation for picking up strays, building them up, and destroying them after his need has been sated."

"Is that what he did to you?" I asked, cloaking my voice with genuine concern.

"Who said anything about not continuing to see each other? You hold on to that beautiful ring human and your false ideals. I'll keep him warm while he governs this region."

My body heated and tensed at her words, and I fought the need to hold back my anger because reacting was bound to end in one way, and the last thing I needed was to garner more enemies from those that followed her.

"We've been seeing each other since his return, and I'm sure you're smart enough to read between that." "Let me guess; he told you we were friends?" She echoed Quillian's words, and I couldn't understand why this argument bothered me or why the thought of him laying with her even more so.

They will come after you if they see you as a threat, regardless of my brother's protection.

Silas's warnings echoed in my head, and I flattered in my rebuttal.

"Thank you for telling me," I sniffed, pretending to wipe a streak of tears from my eyes. Amma's countenance immediately changed as she fell into another one of my performances.

"Is that all?" I stepped past her, seemingly distraught.

"If it makes you feel any better, he never told me about you?" she continued, and I desperately wanted to roll my eyes at the fact she even thought for a second I would believe that.

"Thank you for telling me," I whimpered and continued ahead. "I'm off to find my husband," I added, implying I was going to confront him.

From my peripheral vision, I saw the smirk that tugged at her lip, and I beamed in response, knowing I had fooled her. She would rather that I am perceived as a fearful, foolish person rather than as someone who might cut off her head from her body.

If I were to navigate this new world as the wife of the vampire overlord, I would have to dust up on my acting skills.

21

ALL WORK, AND ALL PLAY

M*eraki*

"Where are we going?" I asked after being in the car for over an hour. Quillian's hands moved to the steering wheel as he reclined on his seat.

"Oloh." He answered, and my brows furrowed.

"The demon's territory?" He nodded, and that familiar smirk tugged at his lips, and his dimples followed. I watched, transfixed on the movement, unable to look away. "You're taking me on a date into the demon's territory? Just you and me, no backup?"

As he turned the car to the left, homes and structures resembling those in Kinavari were visible. However, this place had unique architecture. The gothic-arched structures varied in size and complexity. Their pallets ranged from the most vivid blues, oranges, and greens to the monochromatic shades of grays, magenta, and browns. Each building is comprised of a series of emblems by the building's flying buttress.

"Who said anything about not having a backup?" he asked,

his grip on the steering wheel tightening. I turned my attention to the rearview mirror to see if any other car was following us. His eyes dilated, and his head bobbed up. I then opened the window and leaned my head out to get a better glimpse of the winged vampires whose dotted outlines I could make from above us. Each of the vampires was dressed in all black attire.

"Those are your new security and will follow you around Esneoh," he replied. I moved my head back inside the car, opting to keep the window open.

"I don't need it," I answered as I reclined on my seat, lifted my green silk ruched skirt, and flashed him the dagger I had strapped around my thighs.

"I can't have you going around stabbing other beings in Esneoh." He shook his head, attempting to seem stern, but I noticed the small form of dimples threatening to take form.

"Why not?"

He slowed down the car as we approached a traffic light and turned his head to me. "Because they think you're human-"

"And humans can't stab vampires?"

"Yes, no, and yes," he replied, the amusement in his voice hard to shake. He lifted the steering wheel and continued driving ahead, taking a few turns through several streets.

"That makes perfect sense," I answered mockingly. I slowly pulled down my dress yet kept my hand clasped around the dagger now on display. Esneoh was still an unfamiliar territory, and even though I had the covering of the Kingsley's, I wasn't stupid enough to completely let my guard down. This wasn't Jersey Hill; I was dealing with an entirely different breed of assholes, and lowering my guard was a matter of life and death.

"They think you're human, and we should keep it like that?" His gaze turned to me, and an unfamiliar warmth I couldn't place followed.

"They underestimate me."

"I underestimated you, and look where we are? You managed to sink your claws into me, and I ended up giving you a ring, a vow, and now I'm even taking you on a date. Life can come at you hard sometimes." He deadpanned.

I struggled to hold back the laughter that had been bubbling inside of me. "Wait, was that your attempt at sarcasm?" I held my chest while struggling to control myself. "What was it you said about sarcasm?" I leaned forward. "Something along the lines of."

"Okay, Okay. Occasionally, I might entertain it when I'm in a good mood." He smiled, and it made my chest heat with warmth.

"A good mood? There's always a first for everything. Please share; why are you in a good mood?" I asked, my hand motioning to his now stoic expression.

"The fact, all of Esneoh underestimates my wife," he replied, the word a silent echo that lingered between us.

Wife.

I blinked twice, wanting to ensure I heard him correctly. Quillian and I had used the term mockingly to test one another's patience. Now there was affection in his tone that couldn't easily be ignored.

"Oh," I mumbled as I squashed the small trickle of guilt that threatened to seize me.

The car slowed as we approached the front entrance of a skyscraping glass building near a riverbank. Unlike the surrounding architecture, this building stood in length and width above the rest. The sun illuminated the building creating beams of light as it touched its left side. Bathing the river in a halo of rainbows.

The entrance of the building was filled with an array of luxury cars parked at strategic spots, and as Quillian drove closer, an attendant walked from the shadows of the building.

"You ready?" He stopped the car by its entryway and turned to face me fully. The winged security guards descended before us, catching the attention of the dozen people making their way into the building. I locked eyes with the tallest, with long blonde hair and alabaster skin. He smiled and nodded briefly in acknowledgment. His red-haired companion beside him did not try to do the same; instead, his focus turned to Quillian. They exchanged silent words, and within seconds the two guards stepped toward the entryway of the building.

I leaned back on my seat and reached for my small orange clutch bag in the passenger seat. An attendant stepped to my side and opened the door.

"Thank you," I smiled at the hooved incubus, who stretched his hand for me to take.

"Welcome to The Ace," he smiled, his eyes widening as his nostrils took in my scent. Quillian walked to my side and snatched my hand from his hold.

"Apologies, overlord. He is new here," another attendant dressed in a similar navy-blue attire stood beside the passenger side. His attention briefly turned to the attendant beside me, a warning glare in expression. The attendant beside me stepped to the right, creating a sizeable distance.

"It's okay; he was just helping" I turned and smiled at him. "You are?"

"Taiwo," the attendant answered cautiously. Quillian moved instinctively, a low growling noise emitting from his chest. Was this part of the act? Because I had clearly missed the memo.

With one hand on Quillian's chest as a silent warning, I smiled at Taiwo. "Nice to meet you. You can take the car," I instructed, giving him room to get away. The blonde-haired security guard snickered from a distance.

"That's Sol and Blaze," he stated, his eyes following the direction of my gaze.

"Fitting names." I turned back to face him, realizing my hand had somehow made itself home on his chest. A subtle beat rested against my palm, and for a moment, I considered what his carved-out heart would feel like in my hands. Would his splattered blood be warm against my skin? And why did the idea of that more turn me on?

He stared down at me, his eyes assessing me with piqued interest. "It's either you want to kill him, or you're planning my death," he whispered into my ears as he pulled me into his chest.

My eyes widened, and I tried reeling my hand back, but Quillian kept it in place, drawing attention to us as more cars entered the fold.

"I can scent you, Little Hellion, and the idea of blood seemed to spur you on?" His tongue lightly probed into my ears, and my body tingled.

"I have no idea what you're talking about, husband," I smiled, slowly pulling myself from his hold and drawing his attention to the people around us. His eyes glimmered a darker shade of gray, as his left hand wrapped around my waist.

"I know" he smiled down at me, letting me know all this was part of the act.

Taiwo coughed, drawing our attention back to him. "Sorry to disturb but please follow me. We have the table you requested." He motioned us through the main entryway. Quillian nodded, lowering my hand from his chest, and interlocking my fingers with his in the process.

Sol and Blaze entered the elevator first, doing a quick scan of the small space. Once satisfied, Sol motioned for us to enter. Taiwo selected the sixtieth floor on the panel, and the elevator shot up, giving me a panoramic view of Oloh and the surrounding areas over the mid-afternoon summer sky.

Quillian pulled my back into his chest while leaning against the left wall of the elevator. His nose settled on my neck while his hands ran steady strokes in my hair. The room was still as he exasperated, inhaled its scent, and a low growl emitted from his chest.

"Q..."

"Hmmm," he mumbled into my neck, and my body heated in response. Taiwo kept his gaze focused ahead while Sol and Blaze tried looking anywhere but directly where we were stood.

"We have guests," I laughed awkwardly, my hand tapping against his hand now resting against my waist. The mouth flickered through the arch of my ears, and I fought everything in my body to hold back the moan threatening to spill. The vampire was a great actor; I just needed my body to know the difference.

"We are here," Taiwo announced, pulling us from the moment's intimacy. The elevator opened, and Taiwo stopped at a large, elegant estuary filled with vibrant colors, chandelier ceilings, and a view of Esneoh that was beyond words. As we departed the elevator and made our way into the restaurant, Quillian's hands rested on the small of my back.

The moderately packed room initially paid us no heed, but as we walked deeper to its core, eyes and ears trailed our movements, and the low rumbling of whispers followed until silence filled the entirety of the space.

Sol and Blaze remained behind, trailing our steps while keeping carefully guarded faces. The room was comprised of all types of beings in their finest attire.

"Did you get the table I asked for you?" he asked as Taiwo led us through rows of tables to the far end of the restaurant, where a singular table was set, a small distance from the bustle of the center. The window view would allow us a full view of the restaurant and vice versa. The irony wasn't lost on me.

"Of course, that's how I knew it wasn't a prank call. The requirements for it were too specific. Only you would request this space set the way it is," Taiwo noted, turning to look at our hands, then turning back as if realizing he had said something wrong.

"And here I was feeling special. But this is where you brought all of your dates," I shook my head, unable to ascertain why that even mattered or bothered me in any way.

He pulled back my chair, not muttering a single word, and motioned for me to sit. "I don't do dates," he replied, the words echoing through him like a loud growl.

"I can pull the blind?" Taiwo offered awkwardly, standing a few feet from Quillian. I arched my brow looking around the restaurant space at the other guests who could not peel their eyes from us.

"Yes," Quillian stated sternly. I turned around, searching for the veil. Taiwo stepped back, and the subtle chatter that echoed around us subdued. "You can't see it," Quillian pointed, taking a seat on the opposite side. "For privacy, we can talk without the whole restaurant listening to our conversation." He pointed to the assessing eyes.

"They can still see us?" He nodded, turning his attention to my face.

"I didn't bring dates here," he reclined on his chair, his legs outstretched.

"Semantics...date then?" His jaw tensed, and the muscles around his hands flexed as if he was biting down his tongue. I pressed through a large part of my subconscious that was telling me to let it go.

My mind moved back to the image of Alaric I had found in his safe and the additional images of the woman, the pieces slowly adding up. Had he bought her here before? And how the hell was I going to find out who she was without drawing too much suspicion to myself?

"You don't have to tell me anything," I replied, preferring he didn't, and someone else did; disclosing that information to the Alokari without breaking the oath would be easier.

"Good, because if it's a heart-to-heart you were looking for, you are greatly mistaken," he answered, his features tightening and the easygoing presence he had around him earlier disseminating.

"A heart-to-heart will require you have one. I may not know much, but I've worked out that's something you don't have," I retaliated, though a small part of my subconscious screamed at me to stop. This was not the place nor time to push his buttons, as tempting as it was.

An unfamiliar look crossed his features, and his hands tightened on the arm of his chair. He bobbed his head to the side as if weighing the words. "I'm glad we can both finally agree on something, human," he stated coldly, an icy chill behind his words. A solemn reminder that I was dispensable, and I should remember it.

I exhaled a frustrated sigh. "Who was she?" I asked. It was evident that some human had hurt his feelings, and something told me the red-haired woman had some sort of role in it. I reached for the water on the table, finding no better time to have this conversation.

"Who did what?"

"The human that hurt you. You insist on reminding me I'm on the bottom of the totem pole in Esneoh. When I'm more than capable of killing your strongest men in a short period." I placed the glass down, refusing to cower at how this conversation could go haywire. "Because it's evident you have a stick up your ass about the fact Taiwo outed that you may have brought her here before and have resorted to that." I pointed to his tense jaw and the tightness in his demeanor.

"Because having any feelings is clearly some sort of weakness for you. And showing any emotion beyond anger, rage or blood-lust would make the whole of Esneoh fall on its feet." I rolled my eyes, anticipating the harshness of his words.

Quillian's jaw tightened as he sat back on his chair and stared, as if peering into my soul. "My brother died because of one, and that was enough of a lesson for me," he spoke through gritted teeth, and each word carried through the space like an eerie chill.

I tightened my hold on my chair, surprised that he would even share something so intimate with me. "And I don't need your sympathy," he added, the evident disgust in his tone.

A server walked into our fray, halting my response. His eyes remained downcast as he filled the one wine glass before me to the brim and placed a rocks glass filled with liquor before Quillian.

"Is that what the trials are for? A way to keep his legacy?" I asked opting to steer the conversation in another direction. If anything, I understood loss, and no matter how I felt about Quillian I knew there was nothing I despised more in the aftermath of

Alessia's death than people's sympathies and condolences. They were futile and brought no respite despite their best intentions. Quillian was all about action, and movement. A defensive mechanism to fill the void left behind and to sate the discomfort of losing a piece of yourself. What would I know? I wasn't exactly a shrink.

"Hmmm" he replied, lifting his glass, and sipping on his drink.

"Then I have no choice but to play the role of the best wife possible?" I corked my head while smiling playfully. My revenge consisted of placing a dagger in the heart of my sister's killer. Quillian's rested on honoring the legacy of his brother. I might find him insufferable, but I could respect it.

"And what do you propose, little human?" He asked that playfulness in his voice again. He placed his glass down and ran his hand briefly through his hair in a slow hypnotic gaze, the subtle move drawing attention to the fullness of his lips and the sharp edge of his jaw. He was beautiful, and there was no denying that.

I stood and slowly walked toward him, hovering over his body as he searched me for some sort of understanding. "And as your pretend wife, it's my prerogative to put on a scene" My hands rested on his shoulder; his eyes glimmered and danced with mischief as a slow sensual smirk tugged at the corners of his lips.

"How exactly are you planning to do that?" he asked, pulling back his chair to give me enough space to settle between his legs. I lowered myself between his thighs, my hands wrapped around his neck, my gaze locked on his iris's deep gray clouds.

I ran my hands tenderly through his loosely curly hair and lowered my lips to his. With slow, teasing strokes, I ran my teeth through his bottom lip, enthusiastically nibbling and sucking on it. Quillian groaned, lifting my legs and wrapping them around his waist with a single movement.

"For comfort, obviously," he mumbled into my mouth.

"The blinds," I Instructed as I separated my mouth from his, his growing erection leaving dents on my thighs. He raised his hand, and the familiar low mumbling from prior grew in intensity.

"I'm hungry." I groaned, running my hands through the outline of his carefully tailored suit.

"Food will soon arrive," he answered, pulling me deeper into the throws of his erection.

"I'm not talking about food," I smiled. Lust blazed in his eyes, and his hold around me tightened almost threateningly. Silence echoed around us, the knowing awareness of being watched and listened to.

"Well, I can't say no to my wife now, can I?" he arched a brow, the thrill of playing to the audience around us evidently turning him on. Though my back faced most of the restaurant, I could feel the stares penetrating my back at mentioning my humanity. This was bound to reach the rumor mills going and get tongues wagging, and Quillian enjoyed every moment of it.

A possessive, territorial move that claimed his stakes over me. He cupped my face and drew my mouth to his again in a passionate kiss, offering me no breathing room. Warmth flooded my body, and my body heated at the caress of his hands through my head, hair, breast, thighs, and legs.

He raised his hand again, and the noise around us lowered.

"I think we've given them enough to talk about today," he spoke when he parted our lips, mine swollen from the intensity of the singular moment. And I found myself asking the question again.

Are we still acting? And if not, this was bad, pretty fucking bad.

"Don't," he warned, pulling my back into his chest when I threatened to run from his lap a few seconds later. The waiter arrived again, filling the table with innumerable food and delicacies, most of which I had never seen before.

My eyes fell on Sol and Blaze, who had moved to a distant table to our far right.

"I don't know what most of this is?" I commented as my stomach made loud rumbling sounds.

"I'll teach you...through taste," Quillian said, moving the fullness of my body to his left leg.

"I am never saying no to that" I clapped my hand, my skin buzzing with anticipation.

"He cut through a plate with roasted vegetables drizzled in oil and a brown substance I couldn't name. "This is Gidi, a famous dish in Oloh." He raised the fork to my mouth as the mix of sweet and savory flavors burst through my mouth.

"Oh yes, hell yes to that," I moaned through a series of bites. "What?" I asked after we moved to another dish.

"Nothing," he beamed, wiping the remnants of some of the crumbs on the corners of my mouth and licking it from his fingers. "This is Kukhri, a rice and red sauce dish infamous in Kinavari." I opened my mouth and moaned as an array of flavors and herbs from the seasoning touched my tongue.

"I could get used to that sound," he mumbled, placing a glass of water against my lips. I took the glass from him and drank slowly, making no heed the butterflies that threatened to swarm my stomach at that promise.

"Who knew? The only way to get you to shut up is to fill you up with food, Little Hellion." I coughed in response, almost choking on the water.

Quillian took the glass from my hands, a snicker bubbling from his chest. He turned his attention back to the table, taking his time to serve me pieces of every dish on the table while giving me intel about the region it came from and any background facts behind its roots.

We had become so consumed in our company that we had missed the lowering of the sun and the shift in the atmosphere in the restaurant. "It's getting late. Should we go back?" I offered after finding myself back in my seat.

"A little while longer," he stated, stretching his hand to draw a server's attention for another drink.

"I'm enjoying the view here," Quillian stated, and my attention turned to the cascading view of yellow and orange hues the sunset over the city.

"It is," I murmured, finally taking a moment to appreciate the beauty that is Esneoh. In my years of trying to find a way here, I had imagined the worst possible scenarios and habitats.

The image before me was a far reality from that. My skin heated at the thought, and a warmth settled in my chest, at the sense of feeling at home, instead of out of my elements.

"I'm not talking about that view," Quillian noted with a depth of sincerity in his voice. A warmth of sensation filled my chest and spread to my stomach. I swallowed the lump forming in my throat as my eyes turned back to him.

"This is all pretense."

I alliterated to myself as my body struggled to decipher the truth from lies. The veil was raised, and this wasn't a conversation for listening ears but mine alone, and the thought somehow rattled me.

Resisting him was not part of my *how to survive Esneoh* guide. This wasn't a stumbling block I anticipated, and my heart and body reminded me constantly.

I could resist him by trying to keep our interactions to a minimum, but I was only human, and some persevere untapped part of myself enjoyed the charade. This was the most alive I had felt in a long while, and it didn't involve blood or murder...yet.

But I also knew nothing could ever become of this because a point would come when I would have to betray his trust, and if there was one thing, I was more sure about now than ever before, it was that Quillian held on to grudges like a badge of honor.

Our charade was bound to end with sex, blood, and carnage, and not the pantie-soaking type.

22

A DEMON PIT STOP

Quillian

"LET'S GO THROUGH THE PLANS ONE MORE TIME," I said, turning my attention to Meraki sitting beside me in the back of the car.

Her nostrils flared; she took a deep breath and mumbled curses. She trained her focus on me and scooted closer, eliminating the intentional distance I was keeping so my hands didn't end up in places they had no business exploring.

Her eyes turned to the tablet in my hand, and she reached for it, bringing up images of the demon king's lair. "Four floors cover over ten bedrooms, several workout areas, a ballroom, and an entertainment space. I'm going to place one device on each floor," she noted, stopping on an image of the outline of the house. "Here, here, here, and here," she points to the selected room on each floor.

The smell of her floral perfume, combined with her body's natural scent, whiffs through my nose, and a low rumble emits from my chest. Meraki looked up at me, brows arched, letting me know I had somehow given myself away.

"Continue," I pointed to the screen, beckoning her to go ahead.

Tasting her again had only deepened my thirst for her.

A human.

I repeated it in my head over and over until my mind recoiled at the thought. Alarm bells blared in my head, but I convinced myself it was a mere infatuation. She has a warm cunt; I hadn't sunk into one for over a millennium. Perhaps reaching out to Amma wasn't such a bad idea.

"Are you listening?" her voice hitched with irritation. "I'm not repeating myself." I nodded, my eyes roaming the fitted all-black active attire she had on. The spandex material clung to the curves and dips on her body, especially that ass. An ass that had probably been the downfall of many men, and I was soon steering toward becoming one.

"Your role is important. You are the eyes and ears of the house. I need you to be vigilant, warning me of any potential issues."

"We are here." Lucas, the driver for tonight, announced as the car stopped. Lucas was Ferguson's eldest son and the most trusted man on his team. He had loaned him to help with the job once I had filled him in on my plans.

I had instructed him to park miles from the house to ensure that we stayed clear from any footage or prying eyes.

Meraki placed the tablet down and picked up the small backpack she had carried containing an arsenal of weapons and the miniature listening device.

She opened the bag briefly and reached for the same gun she had shot me with when we initially met. "I've missed you, baby," she mumbled against the handle. I wondered if this was the same gun that evening.

Nope.

I shook my head again, refusing to go down that road.

She removed straps from the bag, placed weapons and potions into their compartments, and strapped them on her waist and ankle. She followed it with the cloaking spray I had given her from Hera, dousing her whole body in it, and then placed it inside the car.

I stepped out of the car and reached for her hand. He hesitantly placed her palm against mine. Once her feet touched the floor, I pulled her into my chest, wrapping my hands around her waist. She stilled at my touch, and her eyes widened almost as if she was anticipating some attack.

"Relax," I mumbled. I pulled out her part of the communication device and placed the earpiece on both ears, fastening them around her earlobe. I stretched out my wings and ascended into the air. Her hands tightened around my neck, her breath inches from my ears.

I scanned the horizon ahead, avoiding the hidden camera spots she had identified from her study of the property. Once the building came into focus, I flew forward swiftly, landing on the roof as we had planned.

"I'll direct from here. Meet me back here once you're done," I instructed, releasing her from my hold. "You have ten minutes before security does their usual round," I added, stepping out into the open space while she stepped through the door.

I reached into my tablet, bringing the security system into view. "I've changed the time frame on the camera. So, if it's being watched, they can only see the last five minutes," I noted as her form came into the screen of the fourth floor of the house.

"What's the security like?" she whispered. "I'm sure I can hear demons on the lower floor?" I briefly scanned the floors, taking an inventory of each room and the bodies.

"There are."

"How many and where?"

"Three, altogether. One on the main floor and the two others on the third floor. When they move or get close, you'll know."

She stepped into the long, red-painted passageway adorned

with the intricate gold statues of men, women, and demons in compromising positions. It was no secret that the demon king, an incubus, had a weakness for women, particularly human women. He was infamous for stepping out on his marriage, and with the intel, I had also gained on his wife, the word was that she also kept a harem of demons, vampires, and shifters on a rotation to keep her bed warm.

"He's an incubus demon," I relayed when her eyes stayed on the statues for too long. Her gaze particularly lingered on one of a human restrained and hanging in the air and a demon directly below her, his gaze over her cunt.

"Like what you see, Little Hellion?" I whispered the words into the speaker. My eyes bore into the screen, expecting her to cringe, but her gaze remained unwavering, analyzing the pose as if recounting it for another time. A time to enact it on a man, a human man? My body recoiled at the prospect, and I tightened my grip on the tablet, watching, anticipating her response.

"Maybe," she breathed, her voice hitching.

"Maybe?"

"Maybe, I aligned myself with the wrong house," she whispered the words like a secret confession, her voice laced with an undertone of lust. A snarl left my lips before I had enough time to register it.

"No demon can ever plow into your cunt as I can." The words come out strained and pained, and from my monitor, I could see that she was frozen to the spot, her hands trailing the curves of her breast.

Fuck, this human was going to be the death of me.

"They can tease you and create an illusion of a good time. But can they lick every part of you until your body becomes a quivery mess, a wanton of desperation?" My breathing hitched, and a subconscious part of my mind told me to stop. I was crossing dangerous territory, but this hellion was my undoing.

I should have fucked and plundered her that evening at the bar. Maybe, just maybe, then my need for her would be sated.

"They can't choke you until you're gasping for breath, and the only vision before you is me, begging to be consumed, bent over, owned, and possessed." I spat, the words unconstrained.

She releases a low moan letting me know all I needed to know. "Raise your top. I want to sink my face into your chest," I commanded. This was not the time nor place to cross these blurred lines, but I needed to see. I needed to know how far she was willing to take this.

At first, she hesitated, then she slowly turned and directly faced where the camera was located, her shirt raised above her chest, revealing a white lace bra.

"Fuck."

"And what do I get for this?" she teased, her hands running trails around her now evidently erect nipples.

"What do you want?" I breathed.

"I haven't decided yet. I'll tell you when I decide," she laughed feeling her breast release from the restraints of the garment

"Make yourself come, show me what you do when no one is watching, and maybe I might agree," I replied, as the need to own and possess her clawed at my chest.

"Yes, husband." She purred, the silk hum of her voice wrapping around me, and my cock begged to sink into her.

"Fuck, you're dirty. Be a nasty slut for your husband. Show him what is rightfully his," I continued, my eyes flinting from the image of her before me to the other cameras.

Meraki pinched her breast, moaning and caressing herself in the middle of the hallway.

"Good girl. Lower the pants," I growled the words out, my desperation getting the better of me. One part of my mind screamed for me to end this. Fucking up this job wasn't an option.

Her hands lowered to her cunt, and all the restraints I had gone out of the window. Everything stilled, and only the sound of her moans as she thrust in and out of herself with fast strokes could be heard.

"Taste yourself." I encouraged watching as her face set aflame. She raised her hand from below and smirked as she placed her fingers inside her mouth, tasting and drinking herself.

"Yes."

"Yes?" she questioned, her hands returning, her pace intensifying.

"Whatever it is, the answer is yes, if you let me taste you," I replied, one hand on the screen, another shuffling around the band of my pants. She mewled in response, her pants and groans becoming more strained.

"Tell me what you're thinking," I demanded as her eyes closed.

"I imagine being chained up as you eat me out and make me beg for your cock." she whimpered. "Soo close...."

"Would you relinquish control?"

"Hmm," she mumbled in response.

"Do you want me to gag you as I remind you that your pleasure belongs to me as my wife? Your orgasm is for me to give or keep?"

"Quillian. Fuck," she muttered, her body shaking in anticipation.

"Do you want me to gag you with my cock? Force it down your throat while you swallow every seed like the nasty slut you are?"

"Hmmm...hmmm"

"Words, Little Hellion, I need to hear them."

"Hmm...yes. Yes, yes, fuck yes." The promise echoed over the headpiece as her hand quivered, her legs shook, and she gasped her release, holding her in place. She was a fucking vision of beauty.

"Fuck," I cursed, noting the sudden movements of a demon walking up to the fourth floor. "There's a demon coming toward you. Loki's room is to the right," I stated, the possible outcomes playing in my hand.

"What are you doing?" I asked, watching her move into his room and make her way to his bed. She released a low grunt in response, and I couldn't decipher what she was trying to convey.

Why did this conversation, this call feel like this wasn't her first rodeo in a case like this?

The demon stepped into the fourth-floor hallway and halted where she had been standing a few seconds before.

"He's outside." I relayed, wanting to keep her updated about what was playing out. The demon's direction turned to Loki's room; his nostrils flared. I opened my mouth to update and realized she was no longer within the room's feed. She had disappeared.

"He's coming your way; where are you?" I questioned the line, deathly silent. The demon entered the room and stood at the entrance as if looking for something, and as each moment passed, anxiety settled in my chest.

He walked to the far right of the room, picked up what appeared to be a remote control, and then strolled back out. Within seconds he headed back down the stairs.

"Hel-" my words cut short when her small frame dragged itself from under the bed.

"The device is locked under the bed," she said, stretching her body. A beeping sound on the tablet's screen alerted me that the device had now been activated.

"I underestimated you, Meraki."

"Most people do," she replied, rising to her feet, refastening her hair again. Those words ring in my ears, a taunting reminder that there was nothing ordinary about this siren before me. She was all hard edges and soft curves, a far cry from Vera.

"You will have to be careful on the third floor," I alliterated, watching her pull back the door slowly, walk through the corridor, and down the staircase to the next landing.

"Turn left; his office is the third door." Meraki sprinted through the space and walked into the large double mahogany doors.

"I see he has a thing for the color red," she murmured, a tender affection behind her mention of it.

"You like the color red?"

"Something like that," she replied. "You could say it's my favorite color."

"I guess it is mine too," I responded, reading between her words, and knowing we were no longer talking about the color, but what it represented.

Meraki walked through the darkened office space, lowering herself beside the desk at its core. She angled underneath it so that her head was facing the table's ceiling. She locked the device at its top right corner.

Another message appeared on the tablet's screen again. "Two more to go," she noted, wiping a bead of sweat from her forehead.

"How am I going to go to the event, a sweaty mess like this?" she muttered.

I shot the driver a quick message, requesting he fly back to pick up sanitary wipes, warm water, and a wet cloth.

"What are the rest up to?" Her hands reached for the doorknob, and she walked into the open space again.

"Busy playing video games." My gaze was drawn to the demons sprawled on a sizeable S-shaped sofa in the other room she was exiting.

"The lounge area is the first door to your right," I announced, scanning the other rooms for any movements.

"Anyone on this floor?" she asked when she reached the second floor.

"No. The rest of the job should be straightforward from here," I said as a message from the driver came through.

Once she arrived on the second floor, Meraki ran into the lounge area and placed the device above a large decorative shelving unit that filled the room's entryway.

"Done," she exhaled, moving swiftly through the room with efficiency. Watching her move was like looking into her past but being unable to piece together her present or future. She pressed herself against the wall, slowly making her way unto the main floor of the building.

"Hallway is empty, nothing out of the ordinary." I waited. "There are two guards outside the premises. I'm not sure how opaque the glass might be on that floor," I added, noting the two demons seated outside playing a game of cards, their bodies directly facing the dining area.

"Be careful!" I anxiously wondered whether she could finish this job with no hiccup.

"Not so easy is it, vampire," she whispered, a burst of low laughter following.

"You steal?" I stopped hesitating about how best to frame the question.

Did I believe that? "You've done this for years?" I asked, desiring a better glimpse of who she was. I craved it.

"A long time," she replied, pride radiating from the words. Her shoulders straightened, her chin held upright, and her steps grew more confident in their strides. Those little details told me all I needed to know. Meraki was deep, knee-deep in this world, and it was evident she enjoyed what she did. She was good at it, hell a master of the trade.

"And you like it? you enjoy it?" I asked, ensuring there was no condemnation behind my voice. Men's behaviors were weird to me, but I'd lived long enough to realize that uncontrolled circumstances might occasionally drive individuals down unexpected routes.

Meraki opened the door to the dining space, her movements slowing. "Where are the guards now?" she asked, intentionally refusing to acknowledge my questions. It was intentional, but I didn't mind; it was only a matter of time before I got the intel, I needed about her.

"Yeah, definitely see-through," she mumbled as she swayed to the right, keeping herself hiding behind the wall shelving units.

The brightly lit dining space was stark different from the

other rooms with its white walls, gold ornaments, and furnishings.

"Loki has an interesting taste in deco." She stopped at the center of the room and slowly lowered herself, crawling under the table to the large white angular dining table. She fidgeted under the space for a few seconds, and her back turned from the demons.

One of the demons erupted into laughter, while the other rose, hand raised into the air, as he tugged at the other collar. Slowly, his attention tilted to the room.

"Move from there, now!" I growled into the device. Meraki rolled to the far left of the room, her body covered by the ornaments around the storage unit. Her hands rested against her chest, her breathing quickened, and the commotion outside continued for a few minutes until the demons settled back down in frustration.

"That was close." She crawled from the floor; her movements were swift and coordinated. She proceeded to the door and lowered herself just enough to twist the door handle and slide through the opening without calling attention to herself.

She leaned against the door, inhaling, and exhaling steady breaths as she wiped more trails of sweat from her forehead.

"I'll be up to you in a minute," she relayed, sprinting through the floors, not stopping for a single moment until she reached the roof. "I need to be paid for this shit," she stated, rushing into the open space, her hair clung to her forehead.

I placed the tablet inside my pocket, elongated my wings, and strolled toward her with a simple goal in mind.

"What..." her words were cut short as I lowered myself to her mouth, allowing my lips to trail through her. My lips sealed with hers, and I kissed her, swallowing her moans. My tongue probed into hers with the zeal of a man in his final days.

Meraki kissed like the wanton thief she was, cunning, sharp-focused and filled with unrestrained enthusiasm. She was going to be my undoing.

"We need to finish what we started, Little Hellion," I lifted her, her legs wrapped around my waist and my hands gripping that ass.

I needed this.

I moved her to the door wall, allowing her back to rest against it as she straddled me.

"We haven't officially consummated our marriage yet, wife. In some cultures, without doing so, do you know the marriage isn't seen as fully legal?" I breathe into her neck, breaking from our kiss.

"Then we should fully legalize it then." she watched me through her thick lashes, lust brimming in her eyes.

I released her hair from her ponytail until her soft curls fell over her heaving breast. "Off, I want it off," I commanded, lifting the shirt back, enjoying the view of her luscious breast.

She instantly follows, dropping her shorts and exposing herself to me. I toss the shirt on the floor and cup her breast, caressing her now pebbled nipples with my mouth. My tongue lapped at its core, savoring the taste of her sweat, scent, and body.

"You smell so fucking good, little human," I mumbled, sucking on one of her breasts through the material.

"Too much-talking vampire," she grounded harder against my cock, moaning and whimpering, trying to seek her relief. I moved on to the other breast, and my senses heightened to the sounds, scents, and movements around me.

"I want to bite you and leave my mark all over your body," I raised my head, trailing my fingers through her exposed body, chest, neck, and every piece of her flesh available for viewing pleasure.

What the fuck was I saying?

Without warning, I released her hold from around my waist and turned her face to the wall, her ass resting against my evident, erect cock. Using my legs, I spread her legs out wider.

My fangs elongated without my bidding, and the need to mark her, claim her became insatiable. I held myself back, knowing this wasn't a woman that could be claimed or marked without wars breaking out.

Using the tip of my fangs, I gritted my teeth against her back, scenting her and savoring the warmth of her flesh and the scent of shea butter and eucalyptus oil that followed.

"So fucking soft," I muttered, pulling her pants down to her knees.

"Fuck Quillian," she muttered, arching her ass higher.

"Beg!" I commanded, my claws running soft strokes on her back, breast, and ass. "Tell me you want this," I moved close, rubbing the print of my cock against her ass as the remnants of her juices soaked through it.

"Beg and tell me how much you want to be fucked and plundered by this vampire dick," I pressed, watching as goosebumps speckled against her skin.

Meraki mumbled and moaned aloud, releasing a series of incoherent words. "No words?" then no pleasure," I gritted the words as I lowered my pants fully.

"Quillian. Please..." Using its tip, I ran it up and down, allowing her to feel its length, width, and girth.

"Holy shit!" She groaned. "Fuck you, vampire. I still hate you," she whimpered, her voice laced with desire, desperation, and anger.

"I hate your fucking kind even more," I replied sharply. That's what this was, a hate fuck. This was sure to be the quickest way to get her out of my system.

"Stop talking, god, I can't stand your voice!" she arched back.

"That's not what your body is saying," I laughed against her exposed back. "Only sluts that beg get a feel of this dick." My fingers ran circular strokes around her clitoral region. With each stroke, she loudly groaned, bringing her ass back to crush against my cock.

"Whose dick do you want, Little Hellion?"

"Any dick," she answered, evidently not yet ready to succumb, but I was more than sure if pushed, she would.

"Then I guess we can end this," I trailed, pretending to reel back.

"Do not fucking dare, asshole!" she commanded, pulling my chest against hers.

"Whose dick do you want?" I slapped her ass, refusing to concede. She had been too much of a mouth the previous time in the basement, and now I wanted to remind her of her own words.

"Quillian," she warned, moaning, and heaving with each beat. One part of her fought against her body, another against relinquishing control to me.

"I need the words." I palmed her ass and cheeks, spread them wide, and used the head of my cock to strike her clit in slow rhythmic strokes.

"Yours!" she croaked, and I placed two fingers into her pussy.

"Good girl," I whispered, fucking her with my fingers. I lost myself to her pleas of desperation, her juices soaking and swallowing my fingers whole.

"Stop teasing me and fuck me already!" she met my thrust without holding back. I laughed, removed my fingers, and plowed my dick into her. The warmth of her wall's warmth swallowed me, pulling me deeper into her orbit.

"Fuck, you taste like trouble," I groaned aloud as I raised my fingers to my lips, testing, scenting, and savoring her.

"Fuck me," she mumbled through groans. I moved my hips arching her back further down with my hands pressed against the dimples in her back.

"You taste so fucking good, and I can't wait to eat you."

"Oh my god, harder, deeper." She challenged, meeting each of my thrusts with another of her own. "Fuck, fuck," she cursed.

"Do you want to be caught?" Her pussy clenched against my cock in response. "You like that, don't you?" I slammed into her with unrelenting force as I slapped her ass harder.

"So deep, oh god." My hands rested on both sides of her waist, digging deeper into all cravats of her body.

"You like the idea of being heard, seen, caught, here right now, my dirty little slut?" I pulled back her head, my hand cupping her breast as she ground her hips against mine. "Tell me, is that what you like?" I pinched her breast, leaving no room for debate. "Too many barriers."

I spun her around while she was still hooked to my cock, shredding her trousers with a single stroke of my claws. Her legs wrapped around my waist as I pulled her into the air. Her eyes rolled to the back of her head, and her chest beaded with sweat. I kept pounding within her, giving her no reprieve.

"Yes, yes, I do," she answered, her eyes locking with mine, that familiar defiance blazing through her eyes.

"Fuck me, show me how much you don't trust me. I want to feel it," she pleaded. I grasped the back of her head with my hand and pushed her mouth into mine, fucking her with my tongue and cock.

I continued slamming into her. "Look at you taking my cock, like the good little heaving thief you are." My mouth swallowed her moans, and her hands curled securely around my neck as her body trembled with the force of her release. My release followed after hers as endless spurts of my release filled her and trickled down her legs, marking her with my scent. There was no way she could deny that tonight.

"I...my clothes?" She exhaled loudly, her head resting against my chest.

"Rest!" I instructed, my cock still inside her, enjoying her body's warmth.

"Hmm," she answered, her strength waning. I reached for the remnants of clothes and materials on the roof and ascended into the air.

"Yeah, definitely just joined the mile-high club," she teased, tightening her hold on my neck. I laughed, a lightness filling my chest.

23

HIGH SOCIETY

M*eraki*

WHEN QUILLIAN HAD STATED THIS WAS AN ELABORATE event to showcase wealth, accolade, and strength, he wasn't kidding. Kinavari was the definition of luxury itself, but the heart of Aarin was incomparable.

The exterior of the large dome-sized building that served as the intersection of the various regions was the living and breathing embodiment of luxury. Its long marble pathways showcased a large water fountain at its core, surrounded by an endless display of plants and trees in colors, length, width, and dimension.

The drive to Aarin was a jarring reminder that I was no longer in Jersey Hill and needed to keep my guards up in Esneoh. It was also a reminder that getting dicked down by the same vampire that had kidnapped me was me perhaps straddling the fence of some severe Stockholm syndrome. I shook my head, relinquishing the thought tonight. I needed to be on my

A-game and thinking about Quillian's dick was not a good start.

"When we get inside, keep conversations and questions to a minimum." Quillian said, curling his fingers through mine as we drew nearer to the growing bodies of people further down.

"You like your women seen and not heard?" I teased, waiting on him to explain further.

"I like my women's ways; quiet and docile is certainly not one of those ways," he replied, his hold on my hand tightening. "The whole room will be on alert. Most beings generally tend to have sensitive ears."

"What If I have questions?"

"Then you can wait until we return or when we move to the Great Room." His thumb ran a steady stroke over my fingers. We may have just had spellbinding sex, but the lines between us were more blurred now than before, and it was evident neither of us knew how to navigate this problem.

"The Great Room?" I asked as we continued ahead.

"A room on the far right of the large communal event area." His thumb ministration seized, and his focus now solely on the view ahead.

I lightly tapped his hand, plastered on a tight smile, to prepare myself for the performance. Tonight wasn't meant for fun and games. I needed to learn more about Quillian and his relationship with the others. It would also be the perfect opportunity to spy and see if I can gain any intel about Alessia's case.

Hushed whispers and silent mutterings caught my attention as we reached the entryway of the building. In this state, it was hard to differentiate who was a shifter, vampire, or demon.

Everyone ahead stepped back, giving us access to long hallways ahead.

"Brother," Brielle called and motioned for us to join her ahead. Silas stood beside her. Both their eyes fell on our interlocked fingers, but neither spoke nor mentioned it.

"Meraki, you look like a vision," Silas's hand playfully reached for mine with a curt bow. "Lavender looks good on you," he added, twirling me around in his hold, oblivious of the growing body of eyes on us.

"She does," Quillian responded, his hands resting on the small of my back.

"Game time," Brielle whispered, her hands lightly trailing her tassel gold and silver dress. Quillian motioned for her to lead the way.

Marble and sandstone walls complemented by intricate flower designs brought the dome's interior to life. High ceilings, chandeliers, and accompanying block towers seem to hold the structure of the building in place. Each block glimmered with hints of jade, crystal, and turquoise.

Silas moved before us, his hand gently guiding Brielle through prying eyes and whispers. This was a message, a united front; many of the leaders were shocked to see them or surprised by my presence.

Light penetrated the lengthened hallway, and the onslaught of sounds and scents grew closer the further we walked until the sound of an orchestra became hard to miss. More beings stepped back, giving us access to a high staircase guarded by a being I couldn't place. His long white hair and perfectly asymmetrical face stopped me in my tracks. His cold gaze shifted to me, and he fixed it on me for a considerable time as though he saw parts and aspects of myself that were unknown to me.

"Overlord, Quillian of Kinavari, and his wife Meraki Kingsley," he announced into the widened space and stepped back. As he did so, the room swirled, and everything shifted under bright sparks of light. Quillian's hand wrapped around my waist as everyone focused.

Meraki Kingsley. Who would have guessed?

We stood at the intersection of a ballroom staircase—the large open room brimming with life, food, and drinks. Quillian moved me forward, keeping his hand on the small of my back; the beings below spun, turned, and trained their gaze on us.

"Not creepy at all," I muttered, a smile tugged on the corner of Quillian's lips. We descended the stairs; Silas and Brielle followed behind, their faces stoic, giving nothing away.

The stares continued when we reached the bottom of the staircase, but everyone around continued with their conversation, their eyes and ears trailing our movements.

"Silas and I are going to make ourselves busy," Brielle stated when they reached us. Her focus turned to the corner of the room, and her eyes widened briefly, but I could not take note of who or what she was looking at. "I'll be with Enzo," Silas pointed in the direction Brielle was headed.

"Don't do anything I won't do, Si," Quillian warned.

"Well then," Silas clapped his hands. "That leaves room for a lot of things." He smiled playfully and followed behind Brielle, leaving Quillian and me alone to face the questioning gaze.

I clung to Quillian's hand, feeling out of place. Everything was foreign, the people, the sounds, the scents, even the orchestra on the center stage.

As if sensing my unease, his hands ran soothing strokes on my back, grounding me to him.

"Quillian!" a voice called from behind us. And from the thick locks of hair, full face of facial hair, and deep amber eyes, I knew it was Thale, the leader of the shifters. Quillian's hands' ministrations slowed yet remained there, a reminder that somehow, I wasn't on this journey alone. Thale stepped before us, and his face scrunched into a tight pinch.

"You're here," he said with a subtle tone of apprehension behind his voice.

"Hi, I'm Meraki," I stretched my hand forward when Quillian refused to utter a single word. Thale stared down at my hand, then back at me, as if the idea of touching me was incomprehensible. This was something to be written in the book of awkward interactions.

"You're human," he murmured under his breath, and though

the music had picked up momentum, it was evident every ear in the room heard him.

"Thank you for pointing out the obvious," I answered in response, trying but failing to keep the sarcasm out of my voice. I kept my hands outstretched, scanning the signet of rings on his fingers yet wanting a better glimpse from up close.

"My wife's hand Thale," Quillian pointed, drawing the stares and interest of more people in the room. "Any dishonor to her is a direct attack on the Kingsley household," he added, power oozing from his words.

Thale hesitantly stretched out his hand, and I took hold of it, noting the emblem of each ring, but finding nothing that satisfied my needs. Like his demeanor, his hands were cold, clammy, and held enough grip to make me feel unease.

"Well, introduce us, my love," A tall redhead woman with the height and physique of an Amazonian warrior stepped from behind him into the fray. Thale retracted his hands and reached forward to pull her in.

"This is my wife, Althea. But you would have known that had you been here for the wedding."

Quillian pulled me into his chest and planted a kiss on my forehead. The act was so gentle and out of his character that it startled me. "Althea and I are well acquainted," Quillian replied, a hint of unspoken history behind those words. Althea stiffened beside her husband and smiled meekly, yet it did not reach her eyes. There was history here, and I could only deduce that my husband had slept his way through half of Esneoh.

The tension between us was stifling. Althea swallowed at the implication and leaned against her husband." It's been a while, Quillian." was her humble response. Quillian grunted in response, tightening his hold around me. "You always did have a peculiar taste," she said, eyeing me briefly.

"Oh, that he does. I'm learning." I smiled up at her, keeping the trainwreck of a facade going.

"We had assumed you had met your demise, and the same fate

that met Alaric had become yours?" Thale reached for a passing tray of champagne and passed one to Althea.

"I told him that wasn't possible; you weren't someone that could bond with a human," Althea's gaze condescendingly turned to me. My hands balled into fists due to knowledge and sensory overload. However, I could not ignore the most significant point here. Alaric's death was linked to a woman, a human, and something told me she was the woman whose pictures I had come across in Quillian's safe.

"If there's something you want to ask, you should have balls enough to ask it outright. No?"

Quillian's hand moved higher on my back, resting there as if needing it to keep him in check.

"Of course, you know I'm glad to see you. I'm just wondering what everyone else here is thinking." Thale took a sip of his drink and briefly exchanged a look with Althea. "Aren't we, dear? We are all wondering how he got up and left after winning the trials?" He motioned to the room of people who were terrible at acting occupied.

"And you came back...married," Althea added, her tongue curling with evident disgust.

"If you were worried about where the family disappeared, perhaps you should have gone looking for them?" I stepped in, unsure whether they were just very good actors or knew more at play than they were letting on. Distraction from one's actions was a ploy I was familiar with.

"Oh, she also meddles in affairs?" Thale took a sip of his drink. "I had always assumed your kind were well versed in the art of knowing when not to speak. Perhaps that's why vampires and demons favor you as a snack." Althea winced at his evident sexist comment.

I bite my tongue, holding back my retort. My report on this asshole was going to be at least four pages long.

"She speaks like all the women here. She can also be a great snack under the right balls. Then again, all balls aren't created equal. Right, Althea?" Her eyes widened, and she blinked twice, almost as if ensuring she heard correctly.

I needed to speak with my husband about broadcasting his past indiscretions.

Thale's eyes darkened, jaw twitched, and his eyes fell around the room, to the body of eyes and ears listening. His expression immediately changed as he straightened up and rewarded me with a fake smile.

"So, Quillian, want to share where you've been? We can't seem to get a straight answer." Althea interrupted when she realized her husband wouldn't continue initiating the conversation. Quillian's claws extended and moved around my back, stretching toward my stomach.

"My siblings and I took some time away, wanting to fulfill my brother, Alaric's final wishes," he lied, his claws retracting.

"For a millennium? That's a long time to fulfill..." Althea trailed, raising, and motioning with her hand for him to finish. I rested my hands on his chest, hearing the low growl growing deep within it.

"Hmmm, what an unfortunate request Alaric must have made?" Thale commented, placing his glass over a passing server's hand.

"You mock it?" I questioned, tenderly running my hands through Quillian's chest, silently beckoning him to calm down. This was not the place nor the time to make a scene. "Last I checked, Esneoh was built as a midpoint between the human and supernatural, or did I hear you the wrong baby?" I smiled at Quillian, hoping he would pick up on the queue I was giving him.

"That's right," he answered, his gaze over me this time a stark difference from what it had been before. It was possessive, proud, and filled with something else I couldn't yet name.

"And if the reigning winner could step away from all that for family, some would say it's admirable, no? Be able to hold the highest position in your palm yet walk away from it without turning back." I continued, realizing the chatter in the room had quietened, and some of the bodies were no longer pretending not to be listening.

"I suppose," Althea replied, corking her head to the side. She and her husband knew I had them where I wanted them, and if they pressed further, it would only make Quillian and his family look even better. The goal was clearly to challenge him and question his integrity.

"You're back, permanently?" Thale asked after a moment of silence.

"Right in time for the upcoming trial, of course," Quillian quipped beside me, his eyes laced with familiar mischief. "I won the first time, which would be no different this time."

"Please excuse us. I must ensure my in-laws are not trying to spill any blood before the trials even begin." I moved in the opposing direction before they could even respond.

Quillian pulled me flush against his chest, and though no words were exchanged, I could read his emotions as clear as day. I may have taken one for the team. He raised my chin and lowered his head, his mouth threading gentle kisses over my lips.

"Little Hellion," he breathed low enough to hear before he kissed me, disregarding everything and everyone around us. His mouth was forceful, leaving no room for discussion. This kiss was an open claim, warning everyone else watching that I was his property. I moaned aloud, unsure where the acting ended, and truth lay.

"Dance with me," he instructed, and the floor gave way as the music began to change tempo.

"Erm..." my skin grew flush, recounting the first time we had met and how that ended. He laughed, seemingly picking up on my reserved expression.

"Not that kind, that one, we reserve for the bedroom," he whispered. He held me close, and I rested my head on his chest. My waist was encircled by one hand while the other gripped my hand tightly.

"Q-" he moved around the room before I could even get my

words out. And as if on cue, the others followed his lead and joined the floor, dancing, smiling, and enjoying the moment. The tension and apprehension in the room had dissipated, now replaced with one of interest and intrigue.

"Relax." He breathed into my hair as I struggled to relinquish control. "I've got you." And that right there was the problem. I didn't need him to because it made some distant part of me, the one growing used to this space, this world, this family, feel guilty. And guilt wasn't an emotion I could afford in this job.

"Just for today," I mumbled. I relaxed into his hold, allowing him to lead and direct my steps.

After some time had passed, and we had disintegrated from the now packed dancefloor, Quillian pulled me back, reaching out for a drink and placing a glass of champagne in my hands.

"Quillian, it's nice to see you again." A woman with a long aquamarine gown stepped before us.

"Meraki, this is Valeria, leader of the Aldrata," he motioned as she drew closer. Her presence spoke of a wealth of power, while the soft lines around her mouth and under her eyes talk about wisdom.

"The witches?" she nodded.

"I had assumed it was just another round of rumors when I heard of your reappearance," she noted. "Have I introduced you to my better half?" she raised her hand as the woman moved a few feet from her to stand beside her.

"Ahhh, Hera," she smiled. And my attention landed on the witch who had perfumed the blood oath. Now I wasn't expecting this.

"Oh?" Quillian coyly asked, stretching his hand toward her. Hera kept her expression blank, giving nothing away. Quillian and I were not the only actors here tonight.

"I don't remember you?" He arched his brow, taking a single sip of his drink. If there was one thing that Quillian was good at, it was putting on a show, and this moment served no differently.

"She came just before your departure. She and...well, that

doesn't matter now; It's been a long while," she added, locking her fingers with Hera.

"Quillian Kingsley, your reputation and that of your family precede you." Hera smiled tight-lipped.

"A lot has happened and changed since we've been gone," Valeria interrupted.

"Nothing you can't catch back up to?" I offered, tapping his chest.

"Meraki?" Valeria asked, training her attention on me, but unlike Thale and his wife, hers wasn't condescending. It almost carried an element of remorse. The poor little human had somehow got herself with a vampire. Woe is me.

"Yes."

"May I ask how you met?" She questioned as Hera shot her a wary look. Something was off about these two.

"And how does this question serve you?" Quillian asked as I sipped on my drink. No one in Esneoh was versed in the art of minding their business, and it was exhausting.

"Don't be so hasty, baby," I laughed idly. "I can answer questions about us. I'm sure she meant no harm?" I tapped his chest again, my jaw aching from all the fake smiling.

He took the half-empty glass from my hand and motioned for an attendant to collect it.

"Just over six months, In Jersey Hill," I replied, deciding to keep the answer the closest to the truth to make remembering and recounting the lie easier.

"Interesting," she mumbled under her breath, her hand briefly running against the front fabric of her dress. My eyes fell on the rings on her fingers.

"What beautiful rings," I pointed to the gold ones on her left and right hand.

"Oh, this, just an old witch heirloom, passed since the creation of this realm," she moved her hands before me, and I lightly reached for her fingers, awing with feigned interest.

Though the structure resembled the ring I was searching for, the markings and engravings on these were different.

"Is that a common thing here? Rings as heirlooms?" I questioned, releasing her hand.

"Yes. Something like that.," she answered dismissively. Hera followed the train of my vision, and though she did not comment, I was sure she had stored that information somewhere in her mind.

"Anything else, Valeria?" Quillian pressed, his hold on me growing more rigid and restrained. I kept my smile plastered, leaning into his body.

"Perhaps you should visit me soon; I would love to hear more about this match," Valeria offered, her smile terse. "And perhaps we can discuss other things?" she continued as she squeezed Hera's hand tightly. The move was so subtle that I would have missed it if I wasn't paying attention. Hera winced in response yet made no effort to release herself from it.

"I'll consider it," Quillian replied. "Now, I would like to show my wife more of Aarin if you don't mind?" he motioned to the sea of bodies ahead, and Valeria stepped back, her eyes digging into our backs as we walked past them.

The next couple of hours were spent with further introductions and long-strained smiles beside Quillian. We had bumped into Enzo, Brielle, and Silas along the way and separated again.

"Excuse me, I need the restroom," I pulled out of his hold when we came to another stop for further introductions. There were too many names and faces and trying to keep track of them all soon became a daunting task.

Quillian stepped back and hesitantly released me. I walked through the sea of bodies and made my way through the crowd adhering to the signs pointing toward the bathroom.

When I neared the restroom, the unmistakable outline of Thale and another shifter beside him caught my attention. They continued ahead, following the sign that led to the Great Room. I stayed behind, slowly following their steps at an even distance.

The long hallway came to a halt when a large white door came into view. They pushed their way indoors, and I stood outside wearily for one minute to give them enough time to get situated without drawing attention to myself.

The Great Room wasn't just another room but a huge garden space within the dome itself. The ceilings bore images of dark angelic beings at their peak, and sketches of the other supernatural beings surrounded these Nephilim beings.

The large garden space was covered with an endless flow of plants and flowers, alluding that we were entirely somewhere else.

I observed the horizon, and I caught sight of Thale. The shifter beside him turned toward my direction, and I lowered myself, almost caught in his gaze.

"So, the reports were true," Thale spoke, lighting a cigarette.

"This changes everything." the shifter beside him, dressed in a similar all-black suit, spoke, his hair pulled back in a ponytail.

"I don't trust his story."

"Which one, about the human or his disappearance?"

"Both," Thale said, inhaling large gulps of the cigarette in his hand. "The others probably think the same, but you know those fuckers will never outrightly say it."

"You think he's faking it for the trial?"

"Without a doubt, Daniel," Thale replied without hesitation. "Proving it will mean he can be eliminated from the game."

Daniel smiled deviously in response. "I agree. I can set something up."

"His time from Esneoh has dulled his senses and weakened him. Having a human by his side is a weakness instead of a strength. If anyone wanted to make a play against him, the human would be an easy target," Thale proposed as he and Daniel exchanged an unspoken look.

"And they will; it's only a matter of time," Daniel added as Thale took his final cigarette round and dropped the stubs on the floor. "I want to be ready for anything that may come up during the trial. We cannot afford to lose, not this time."

"We won't; as your right hand, I'll ensure it," Daniel replied as they stepped deeper into the garden. I allowed them to walk ahead without following, knowing if I continued, I was bound to be caught. I had heard enough to report back to Quillian.

"Meraki," Hera said as I turned the curve to head outside.

"You followed me," I started it as a fact rather than a question.

"I came out for fresh air, and yes, maybe to follow you," she added, a warmth in her smile.

"So, Valeria?" I let the question linger in the air and turned back, weary that the others may be able to hear us.

"They can't hear us, just as we can't hear them," she noted, and I arched a brow wanting to tell her that wasn't the case. I was more than able to hear their conversation a few feet away earlier. But I hesitated, storing this information out to study at another time.

"Marriage for witches is different..." she trailed. "We align ourselves for power." She walked in the opposite direction, and I followed out of curiosity to see if she would offer me insight into how to free myself from this oath.

"That sounds very normal to me. Humans do the same, and from what I've gathered tonight, many of the other beings here do the same?"

"I guess we are all more similar than we like to admit," she laughed. "I proved myself to be the most powerful witch in the coven and could become tied to its head."

"Can't you fight for the leadership position then?" I asked, unable to make sense of it.

"It's not that straightforward, unfortunately; many have died trying that."

"I guess you and I are similar in many ways; bound to people, and spells we are unable to break," I noted, leaving the words open for interpretation. Hera's eyes shifted around the space, and though she had a warmth around her, something else lurked within its pits, something I couldn't name yet.

"You already know what I'm going to ask."

"And you already know what I'm going to say. I cannot break the spell I cast. It needs to fulfill its course." She continued ahead, her pace quickening.

"Then someone else who didn't cast it can break it?"

"Another witch of a similar standing can only do it."

"Valeria," I murmured, biting my lip.

"You have enough sense to know that doing so would have consequences for us all," she added, the subtleties of her threat evident in those words.

"Why should I care if it frees me?"

"Because I saw the way you looked at him tonight."

"Who?" I asked, and Hera slowed down, turning to face me fully.

"Quillian," she answered as if that name alone carried a thousand unspoken words.

"You saw wrong, I'm fulfilling my end of the bargain, but you and I both know that no good can come from fully trusting a vampire," I argued, though some part of me couldn't shake what she had just suggested.

"There is someone, a witch that lives in Jersey Hill," she offered cautiously. I stepped closer to her, my desperation palpable.

"Who?"

"My sister." Her hands formed into fists, and her gaze became distant.

"Your sister?" She nodded. "She lives there?"

"Not by choice; she was banished."

"Why are you willing to help me?" I arched a brow. My eyes fell on her fingers, trying to match the image of the feminine hands to hers. Luckily. Hers were slimmer in stature, and she bore a tattoo on her wrist that separated her.

"It's not a favor if I want something in return." She shot back, and I smiled, impressed by her bargaining skills.

"I understand," I spoke out loud, the pieces adding up. Hera had a plan for her and her sister, and it didn't involve Valeria in the fray.

"How could you? Do you know what it's like to be separated from your only family?" her words came out harsh, pained.

"Yes, I do," I answered, inhaling. If I was going to be here a while, I needed to form allies with unexpected sources, and Hera seemed like a plausible one. She was close enough in the mix to offer me intel but far removed enough because of her evident disdain for the system.

"Yours is still alive. Mine isn't," I stated, knowing it was a risk to share that piece of intel but a necessary evil to get what I needed. "Trust me, I understand what it's like having the only family you have ripped from your hands and working hard to avenge them, but nothing seems to be going in the right direction." I exhaled a pained breath.

"In a way, that's what I admire most about the Kingsley's," she spoke after a moment's silence. "They are willing to do anything and everything to protect each other, even if it means trampling on everyone else along the way."

"When you put it like that." I corked my head, and she laughed.

She clasped her hand with mine and muttered a chant under her breath. "Her details will be in your room when you arrive."

"And what is it you need for this favor?"

"An alliance" My eyes widened in shock.

"With me?" She smiled warmly.

"What's wrong with you?" She teased.

"Errr." I gestured to my body. "I'm as human as they come. Just in case you missed it."

"The trials have been known to include weird tournaments. Something tells me with you here; it might not be as it was in previous years."

"Oh? Shouldn't this be geared more toward Quillian? Aren't the leaders the ones who take part in it?" I questioned, eyeing her with suspicion. Hera was saying a lot without saying anything at all.

"I like to be prepared for the worst-case scenario. And if my predictions are wrong, then we can pretend this never happened?" She offered. "You might want to leave now; Quillian is looking for you," she turned her attention in the direction we had walked from, but I couldn't make him out in the distance.

"One more thing," I noted, turning to face her briefly.

"Yes?"

"How can someone kill an immortal?" I asked cautiously, hoping she interpreted it as interest regarding Alaric rather than Quillian. Her brows rose in a questioning manner, and for a brief second, she said nothing.

"Which immortal?" she asked, her eyes sparking with mischief.

"The only ones I care about at the moment."

"There are oaths and bonds. An oath is an agreement that a witch binds. Then there are blood bonds. Bonds cannot be created or bound by magic. They are shared between lovers and sealed by a pact."

"I don't understand" Hera smiled meekly, hesitant to share more.

"The simplest way to explain it would be like the mate bond shared between wolves. The vampires call it *yaera*; it translates as soul bond."

"What does this have to do with killing one?" I took a step toward her.

"A vampire having a soul bond with another vampire grows stronger, and the bond strengthens them. They can draw power and strength from each other. With humans, it's the opposite. It weakens them..." she stopped beckoning me to read between her words.

Alaric's bond to the mystery woman weakened him.

"Did he know?" I asked, making no effort to conceal who the question may have been about.

"Of course." She answered, and I turned my attention back to the entryway, biting my lip.

"And?"

"That's all I know about the case. The family has buried it so deep that no one can get to the heart of it. Though there were rumors when I first arrived."

"What types of rumors?" I asked, my ears perking up at the possible information.

"She may have been an assassin?" Hera's voice hitched, showing her lack of distrust for it. I hummed low in my chest, shifting through that information. The possibility of that is low, and if that were the case, the organization responsible would have claimed it. There was nothing of the sort recorded in the human realm.

Alaric was foolish, or something else was at play. Why would he have bound himself to a human if he knew the outcome?

"Thank you," I whispered as I headed out of the room, my mind racing with the possibilities of what it could all mean.

Quillian stood outside its doors, his expression filled with fury. He pulled me to down the hallways into an adjoining nearby.

"What the-" He placed his hand over my mouth, motioning for me to hush.

"Wife," he spoke after a few minutes. The word held a silent threat.

"Yes, baby? Do you think being in this room is a good idea? Won't the others hear us if we do it here?" I asked, making soft moaning noises, refusing to be manhandled by him. If he wanted to play this game, I could play it better.

He pulled out his phone. "You're irresistible," he murmured, pressing his hand against my chest. I stepped back, ensuring a steady distance between us, which only seemed to spur him on.

Where did you disappear to, human?

The message appeared on his phone. But I knew if he was asking, he already had suspicions. He was testing me, needing to see how much I knew or was willing to share. I rolled my eyes when my vision fell on the word human, realizing we were back to being strangers again. I took the phone from his hand and typed.

The Great Hall. I overheard something that might be of help later.

His eyes widened as he stared at the screen and then back to me.

"Hmmm, baby, that feels so good." I decided to push, watching his eyes glaze with anger.

What did I say about staying close, human?

He slapped his wrist, and the sound echoed, creating the allusion he had hit my ass. "Fuck baby, that's the spot." I continued breathing and moaning aloud, taunting, and bating him.

Your wife can't be chained to you all night, vampire. Last I checked, I was no longer a prisoner in your basement.

He gripped my hand, releasing a low grunt. Is this what married people do?

Please don't test me, little human, because you won't like my response when I bite back.

He stepped toward me, locking me against the room's door. I swatted his hand and pushed his chest, reaching for the knob of the door.

We are not finished.

He typed with a mischievous smirk on his face.

"I'm coming. Oh god. Oh god." A smirk tugged at his lips. He released his hold on, leaned back, and grunted loudly to signal his *finish*.

"That's my girl," he whispered, pulling me flush against his chest. I raised my middle finger in response as he dragged us out of the room to face a room full of supernatural beings who had just heard me pretend to orgasm.

I hate the bastard.

24

A CHANGE IN THE RULES

Q*uillian*

THE ONE ASPECT OF BEING IN ESNEOH THAT I DIDN'T miss was intermingling. It irritated me to have pointless chats with these idiots about things I don't give a shit about.

Right now, I had allowed the hellion beside me to get under my skin and over my cock before tonight's event. Was it a bad idea? Heck yes. Did I regret it afterward? No. I was now questioning why after finally getting a taste of her cunt I was still fascinated and drawn to her. The jury was still out on that.

Why was I hellbent on someone whose truths I didn't even trust? Meraki may have believed she fooled me with the lie about her being a thief, but after seeing her in action and pondering on it, I now felt that was a lie. I wouldn't have even believed she was human if it wasn't for her indistinguishable scent. Unlike most humans, she was too raw, sharp, fast, unrelenting, and unaffected by pain.

Something was not quite right about her, and not knowing all the facts was more aggravating.

Earlier she had roused my suspicions even more when she disappeared in the restroom. I had sent one of my men, who has been keeping an eye on her in and out of Esneoh. He found her in the Great Room, eavesdropping on Thale, then later saw her having a conversation with the witch Hera.

She had claimed to have overheard the shifter asshole share some interesting intel, but I was sure it was a ruse. Everyone knew that the Great Room walls were so heavily cloaked that it was impossible for anyone even to eavesdrop. It had been so since its inception.

No one can be trusted. The witch I planned on dealing with later. On the other hand, Meraki was becoming a thorn I regretted allowing into my space. She was still alive because we had come too far in our plans to go back now. I could not kill; otherwise, I would have to kiss the possibility of ever being king for the next trial, which I could not do.

"Having fun, brother?" Silas walked up to us after our stellar performance in one of the darkened storage rooms. I was more than sure that half this room had heard, but she was playing a devious game, and I needed to remind her that this was my game, my territory, my domain, and I held all the cards.

"Meraki!" He smiled, turning his attention to her and then back to me again.

"Don't even go there," she replied, cutting him off before he even had time to finish what he wanted to say. Some guests became fixated on her, listening to and watching her engage with my sibling.

Unlike me, Silas and Brielle weren't ones to hold on to grudges, and they had accepted her in our circle without hesitation. What still troubles me is how they made Vera's life hell. What was so different about this human?

"It looks like Loki and his wife have finally arrived," Brielle pointed as the music in the background began to lower, and the stage was being reshuffled for what could only be perceived as his big speech.

"He's here," I answered, eavesdropping on one of his security intel at the back of the room.

"Welcome all!" Loki's voice boomed over the room, and the room fell silent as everyone turned to face him on stage. The crowd split into two, one side sectioned for the various leaders in Esneoh, and the other for husbands, wives, and accompanying leaders.

Brielle and Silas moved to stand beside Meraki on either side, keeping her within their train of vision. I stepped forward, joining Valeria and Thale, whose tight-lipped expressions described precisely how I felt about the present moment.

Loki's eyes fell on me, my siblings, and Meraki. A smile curled his lips, and he reached for his wife Khadija's hand to draw her attention. He made no move to conceal the move, and the wary glances of the other guests watched hastily, drinking in the drama unfolding before them.

Our family wasn't infamous as it was for playing fair or being kind. They were anticipating me to attack or partake in combat or bloodbath. But I knew better than initiating a fight or coup against the reigning king. Doing so would set precedence for others to do the same. As much as his sight annoyed me, I was going to play the game, his game, even better.

"Welcome old... and new friends," he trained his attention on Meraki, then back to the room again. "Welcome to the official announcement party for the trials." Khadijah clapped, and the room followed suit.

"As the king, I've enjoyed my time within this role, so much so I don't want to let it go," he laughed. Who the hell laughs at their own joke? What a pompous asshole.

"I will be running again this time around. As will Valeria, Thale....and Kingsley." The room turned its focus on me. "It's been a long time, dear friend," he added, and irritation skirted my skin. I kept my face an expression stoic; there was nothing else after.

Loki was sending a message, an olive branch of a false truce and relationship to quench the gossip and whispers that may occur if I didn't arbor the resentment, I felt toward him as I did now. Perhaps I would have been impressed.

Control the room, control the narrative.

Loki and I had always had a cordial relationship. His people and I had built establishments and created businesses to enforce an unspoken bond partnership between our people. After I had won the previous trial, he vouched and offered his support to me as the next king.

Now I knew that was likely bullshit. To think he has a hand in my imprisonment wasn't far-fetched but was still disappointing. Regardless, once I got the confirmation I needed, I planned to enact revenge, one he won't even see coming.

"Tonight, will also be the night we discover what the first trial will entail and whether it will consist of three or two tournaments." He motioned to his son Tallen, who stood on the sidelines and rarely partook in Esneoh politics. He and Silas were alike, known for their squandering ways.

Tallen stepped forward with a triangular box in his hand. He stepped toward the bottom of the podium and placed the box at its center. Loki and Khadijah stepped down and stood over the box. The other leaders and I followed, creating a circle around them.

Loki opened the box and removed a rounded yellow ball with golden wings attached to its side. The ball, upon his touch, spurred to life and filled the room in a shade of yellow and orange as its wings began to flap.

"The gnet is the oldest relic in Esneoh and acts as the spear and anchor of the life force that lives in Esneoh. When the trial timing approaches, it calls to us and awakens the city." Loki said, stretching his hand out to hold the object in place. Following his action, the colors in the room grew brighter until every corner and space was left untouched. A map appeared, and the screen filtered through cities, animals, and greenery until it stopped on what seemed to be a maze.

"The Island of Labyrinth," Khadijah called. "This is where the first trial will take place." The screen moved again, displaying the island structured as a large unending maze. The screen froze again as replicas of the gnet fell from its sky to various corners of the maze.

"The competition will be centered on who can locate a gnet and escape the maze first.," Loki added, a smile marring his face. He began to step back, anticipating the end of the update. But the gnet did not halt, as it usually would have. It continued to filter through images of landscape, monuments, and plants.

The room started to fill with low murmurs and whispers. My palm sweated, knowing that whatever the next addition was, it had never happened before. The gnet shot into the sky, and gasps rang out. The images filling the room changed until Khadijah, Meraki, Hera, and Althea appeared on the screen beside each other.

"Erm... why am I there?" Meraki's voice filtered through to me. The room grew still, and the eyes of everyone turned to Loki, whose shock was obvious to the masses.

"It seems Esneoh prefers that the leaders' partners do the first trials.?" He looked around the room, unsure of what to do with himself. "This has never happened before."

The gnet had still not retracted and continued to buzz with power, showcasing the number two across the room. "There will be two tournaments instead of three? For the first trial," Khadijah chimed in, as her husband evidently could not find his composure.

The gnet began to lower itself, but its light still glimmered, and as it moved back into Loki's outstretched palm, another number appeared.

"Two. The first tournament will be in three days" His voice

boomed, and the lights retracted, leaving the room in a flurry of scuffles and wide eye surprise.

The other leaders' expressions lit up as they slowly turned their attention to me. My eyes were drawn to Meraki, who now held a glass of champagne in her hand, seemingly unaware of the eyes focused on her.

They will be in for the fight and shock of their lives when the tournament begins. If only they knew that the human who stood before me was far beyond what they anticipated; there was nothing weak nor fragile about her. She was sharp, twisted, and all fight. Underestimating her was for the best, allowing her to navigate the games more victorious.

"Thank you all for coming tonight." Loki seized the attention of the room. "This year, we will not be holding an introductory luncheon because of the unprecedented change. This is to give the contestants time to rest and be prepared for what's to come." He continued, stepping down from the stage.

"The contestant should use this time to train. Wait, that also includes me," Khadijah chirped, and the room fell into laughter. She smiled as Loki tugged on her hand and moved her from the stage.

I moved beside Meraki, watching her face's tight and rigid expression. She wasn't impressed and was pissed about the turn of events.

"No surprise there." Silas turned his gaze to Loki and Khadijah's security, who were now escorting them out of the premises.

"Hmmm," I hummed in response. Loki had always been a sneaky bastard; right now, he was running from a potential confrontation and its implications on the legitimacy of his rule.

The people in attendance carried on with the celebration as if nothing had happened. Nothing could get in the way of a party in Esneoh, not even a 180 turn in its trials after several millennia.

After a few more hours of formalities. "We all headed back home, deciding to address the next steps tomorrow instead.

"We chose well," Enzo offered as he and I walked into my

office before others joined us. Meraki had remained silent in the car ride, and something about it made me feel unease.

"If you had listened to my initial plan, we would have been screwed. This wasn't something any one of us could have anticipated."

"The beauty is that they'll expect her to be out within the first five minutes; they'll be in for a rude awakening." I smiled, pulling out two glasses and filling them with liquor. I spread it before us and motioned for him to sit.

"You believe she will win?"

"Yes. She single-handedly immobilized Silas, shot me several times, and was able to spar with Brielle and me together. She'll do well," I replied, my voice filled with pride I couldn't shake. Enzo caught on to it and arched a brow as he took a sip of his drink.

"Any news about her?" I asked, steering the conversation in another direction.

"Yes," he answered flatly.

"Well?" I raised my glass, signaling him to continue. He hesitated slightly and corked his head as if unsure how to relay whatever he was about to share. "Whatever it is, I am sure it's not something I'm going to like," I added, taking a full sip of my drink.

"She doesn't exist in the system. In the real sense, she exists in no system. There are no trails or records of her. It's as if she never existed," he finally spoke.

"Well, that's not surprising, isn't that normal? Didn't we experience the same when we dealt with members of the Burning Sun and the Grimm Hold?" He nodded, but there was something about the tension on his shoulders and the way he gripped his glass that let me know perhaps that may not be the case.

Now I was intrigued; who the hell was she?

"That wasn't a surprise for the Grimm Hold. Their members have no faces or records. However, for agents of the Burning sun..." He bowed his head briefly. "Their records can always be found. An early, unexpected death usually covers them during their primitive teenage years. ..." He stopped as I allowed his words to filter through.

"And?"

"I reached out to two sources from the Burning Sun." He sat forward on his seat, and anticipation gnawed in my chest. "They haven't sent out any agents on jobs for the last month. They've been on lockdown mourning the death of one of their leaders."

"Oh!" was the only word that could come to mind. I placed the glass in my hand, afraid if I held on any tighter, I would do more damage to myself than the person I wanted to hurt the most. "She lied." My tongue bristled at the words. What was I expecting? The truth, their kind wasn't remotely capable of it.

"She lied," Enzo reluctantly confirmed.

"I need intel. I need to know who she is. We do not want another case of Vera." I rose to my feet, my stomach in uncomfortable knots. " If she cannot be tracked through the traditional method, there is an alternative option." I walked to my office table and leaned against it.

"Track her through CCTV?"

"And the scent. It will require a lot of work and might take a while. I will need someone reliable on the job. Someone who can hide in the shadows yet proves effective behind a keyboard."

"I know just the right person for the job."

"Who?"

"Lucas," he offered.

"Ferguson's son?" Enzo nodded.

"Right now, I need us to keep our circle close until we are certain that no one in our midst had anything to do with your imprisonment."

"What about intel on the ring?" I asked, and Enzo trained his eyes on me. "There have been too many key figures over the years who could have worn it," he offered. "Each house has held it at one point or the other. Heck, it could have even been us," he added.

"It was recent."

"And that's the problem," he breathed.

"It's best she doesn't know, and if she asks, I'll create fake leads to keep her busy," I said, though the idea did not sit well with me. But I knew the implication of that ring and looping her in on what it meant could only cause further issues.

"For how long? She's smart. She'll catch on."

"Hmm," I murmured, pondering on possible scenarios. Enzo leaned back on his chair and drank the remainder of his drink.

"Q, if she lied about who she was, we could only ascertain that maybe she's lying. Perhaps the humans have come to find out about it?"

I shook my head. "No, I scented and tasted her rage when she spoke of it. The story regarding the killer is true. I just don't believe in the *family friend* aspect. It might be someone closer to home, sibling..."

"Or a lover," Enzo offered, and the words made my stomach recoil. "The answer to that might give us an indication of who she is." My hands reached for the tablet on my desk. I need to keep myself busy.

"There is the alternative," Enzo offered.

"What would that be?"

"She's an assassin?"

"Why would she then be stealing an artifact?" I ran my hands through my stubble, trying to make sense of all the pieces. "It's still something worth considering. Check into that. In the meantime, this stays between us" Enzo nodded.

"We also have to talk about the fact we have to align to at least one house," Enzo offered after updating me on the current dynamics between the leaders in Esneoh. The laws stated that another must vouch for the winner of the trial. This alignment was the cornerstone of the partnerships formed with houses. Whoever vouch for you would enjoy the spoils of your win. "Thale?"

"No, I would kill him before the conversation even started.

And there's just something about him that irks my skin." I gritted my teeth, recounting his magnanimous ego.

"Loki is clearly out of the picture. We are left with one choice, Valeria." He offered concisely, and his tone strained at the mention of her name.

"And what if the witches were the reason for our imprisonment? And we align ourselves to the same people that had a role in our exile?"

"Then we play along, take the crown, and deal with them in a public show of power.' He offered, motioning for me to pass him the liquor.

"You've changed, old friend," I smiled. Enzo wasn't usually one for violence; that was how he and Alaric had initially bonded. They believed in peaceful negotiations and conflict resolution without spilling blood, and we had clashed constantly on it.

"Sometimes force needs to be applied for a true change to occur," he answered as darkness flashed over his eyes.

"Arrange a meeting with Valeria. Since we have Hera in our arsenal, do we have the upper hand against them? Do you know what she might require from us in the future?" I asked, passing him a bottle of scotch.

"Support." He answered, filling his glass to the brim.

"Support? What does that mean?"

"I think she's vying for Valeria's role. The witch banished her sister; if my sources are correct, she wants to bring her back and lead. The laws there differ, so I'm unsure of the specifics."

"Cunning and calculative, fitting," I nodded, genuinely impressed by the witch.

"What about the shifters? We need a backup plan just in case." Enzo placed the bottle down and took a sip of his drink.

"If I have to see Thale's smug face one more time, the trials might end before they've even begun." Enzo laughed.

"You've hated him for as long as possible, but he's proven to be all bite more than bark."

"I'll think on it."

"Then that's my cue to leave," he said as he rose to his feet and drank the remainder of his liquor.

"Thank you, brother. For everything," I moved to my seat, allowing the sincerity of my words to pass between our bond.

"I guess I'm not the only one that's changed," he teased. "The old Quillian didn't know that word," he laughed, his eyes dancing with pleasure. "That's what family is for," he whispered as he headed out and closed the door behind him.

I reclined on my chair, reached for the tablet in my pocket, and connected it to the projector before me. I leaned back, shifting through the last hour's feed from Loki's house.

"Valeria," I called as Enzo, and I landed on the large residential field of her estate. The wide-open area was covered with moss and plants, leaving nothing but greenery from all fonts.

The distinct wooden and angular houses could appear as small dots on a map from a distance. Aldrata was the ideal combination of futuristic architecture and green space and being here felt like I was transported outside my body. However, I was still unsure if this was due to some spell the witches placed over the Pavilion.

Hera and a host of accompanying witches stood beside her, their expressions giving nothing away.

"Quillian, I was glad to hear you took my offer for a meeting," she beamed, stepping toward us.

"You know how much I love suspense. I could not say no." I stepped closer, taking in a dozen women of varying shades and builds. Hera stared right through me, her face a silent warning and reminder of our deal.

"Come with me to my office," she motioned as I followed beside her on a long footpath toward a geodesic dome house.

"I would like this meeting to be just us," she noted, turning briefly to Enzo and Hera behind us.

Knowing Hera, this came as no surprise. She was always one to keep everyone at a steady distance, and I had long concluded that there was and would never be anyone she could fully trust.

I nodded, letting Enzo know to stand watch. Valeria and I could engage in discussion without one of us attempting to kill the other.

Enzo nodded, seemingly hesitant but made no show of it. Instead, his attention turned to Hera as he made a feeble attempt at introducing himself to her.

Valeria and I entered the brightly lit house, compromising a singular floor with two rooms.

"This Is my getaway space," she announced, leading me into the first door to the right. A large office space adorned with a selection of books on one end and liquor on another came into view.

"I know all too well what needing a getaway feels like," I replied, unable to keep the dry sarcasm from my tone. She took the comment with a shrug of her shoulder, seemingly unaware of what I was trying to imply. I frowned, watching her move across the room. Either Valeria knew nothing about our imprisonment, or she was a damn good actress. Something told me it was the latter.

My eyes fell on the series of books far removed from the light magic theme the others followed. Human sacrifices, soul ties, and necromancy were a few that caught my attention. And I realized her request for the private meeting had nothing to do with the matter we were going to discuss but rather everything to do with hiding the dark arts she was most likely practicing without the coven's knowledge.

"See anything you like?" she asked, reaching for two glasses and filling them with liquor. She closed the unidentifiable liquor bottle and strolled to the center of the room, where a large accent table surrounded by two sofas sat.

"When did you start getting into dark magic? You were always particular about channeling light magic if my memory serves me correctly. Then again, it's been a millennia." I goaded and twisted my neck, picking up on her discomfort through her lingering scent in the air.

"Time can change a person," she trailed. "But there are certain things I can never introduce to all my people now, can I?" She answered. "You of all people should know about the importance of upholding your power, which sometimes involves making decisions contrary to your belief systems," she added, a faint smile tilting her lips.

She motioned for me to join her and sit. "Scotch," she stated, placing the two glasses on the table.

"You have questions," she noted as I took my seat opposite her.

"Let's cut the formalities, Valeria. You and I have known each other a long time, so there's no need to beat around the bush." I pulled one of the glasses on the table toward me and reached for it.

"I'm sure you've been updated on the politics of Esneoh since you've been back?"

"I can't say I have or haven't. What does that have to do with us?" I raised the glass motioning back and forth.

"You know the demons are many things but discreet or having any form of decorum is not one of them." She sat back on the seat, her legs crossed, her yellow summer dress lightly trailing on the floor. "Every law passed during their time has only elevated their need above us all. They collect extortionate tax way above the usually agreed threshold. They've also opened establishments within our regions and have pocketed more money while trading narcotics. You and I may have our issues, but when the witches last reigned, we factored everyone in Esneoh, even when we could barely stand its leaders," she said, a probing reminder of our standing relationship.

"Hmmm." I took a sip of my drink, listening and gauging what she was trying to say without explicitly doing so.

"In their time governing Esneoh, we've also had the most cases of missing witches, shifters, and vampires."

"Enzo and I have briefly spoken," I nodded, motioning for her to continue. The cases Enzo had updated me about raised my suspicion, but our kind was infamous for leaving the plains of Esneoh and living with the human realm for some time and then returning. Most did so without leaving forwarding details because they did not want to be tracked.

Valeria shook her head, releasing a silent snicker. "Under Loki's reign, I suspect that an undercover assassination agency may be thriving," she mocked, trying not to hide her evident disdain for him.

"And you came to this conclusion how?" I sat forward on my seat, my interest piqued.

"What else can explain the number of missing bodies and people? Especially for those who publicly stood in opposition to him."

"That's a big accusation that needed backing up with facts," I offered. Humans had long been aware of and fascinated by the supernatural. That fascination had come with the hunting of our kind. We became accustomed to it and ensured we were conscious of our steps when intermingled in their world. We kept a low presence and ensured we covered our tracks well.

"I've not been able to get evidence, but I know," she tapped her nails on the glass in her hand. "My instincts are never usually wrong, Quillian. Someone or something is hunting our kind, and my instincts tell me there's more to the story."

"And what is my role in all this?" I gestured.

"We may have a long history of distrust and tension between us..."

"So that's what we are calling it?" I corked a brow waiting for her to expand more.

"We have both mistrusted and betrayed one another...but I

have more faith in you than any other leader. And I hope vice versa?" she paused and slowly drank her drink. "And if you were to win, I would vouches for you." She placed lowered the glass and ran her fingers through its rims.

I studied her cautiously. "Why do I feel like there's something more you're not saying?" I replied, searching her emotions for anything out of the ordinary. Then again, Valeria was skilled at disguising and hiding her feelings.

"My cards have been laid. You will need to decide before the final tournament for the first trial."

"You sound very confident for someone who hasn't won yet. Is there something you know that I don't?" I placed my glass down and sat at the edge of the sofa.

"Isn't everyone's goal to win?" she replied, too quickly for my liking.

"One could say you're asking for a vouch because you don't see me as competition?"

"Why would I do that?" she replied earnestly, her eyes glimmered with an unspoken myth.

"Because my wife is human," I stated, the word like a stone in my mouth.

Wife.

Silence lingered, and I allowed the unspoken message to transpire between us. Valeria had only invited me here because she was under the illusion that Meraki would be the first eliminated from the trial. I would no longer be a threat to her. Aligning with me now to vouch for her was a strategic play. One that mocked my intelligence and undermined me as a leader.

I rose to my feet. "Offer the same terms again after the first trial, then I would know if you were being sincere here," I said as I headed for the door.

"Your problem was always that pride," she scolded in that undermining way she usually spoke. She rose to her feet, her hand pressed against her chest.

Pride. That word had haunted me until Alaric's death. She

had uttered those exact words about my family after Alaric's death, and I didn't deal with it then.

I blurred before her, my fangs elongating without my doing. "The only thing keeping you alive is the law of the land," I snarled, and she raised her hand as magic strummed through her fingers.

"You won't be as stupid to make a move against me in my land," she stated boldly.

I nodded ominously. "Careful now, witch, my wife is going to lose, remember? And you seem to need my support more than I need yours," I answered, keeping my expression stoic. There was no need to correct her assumptions; her thinking the way she did might work in my favor.

I smiled and slowly stepped back, enjoying the restrained look on her face.

"We will speak soon," she stated dismissively, her back turned to me. I scoffed, slowly stepped out, and shut the door behind me. Enzo and Hera stood outside, a few feet from the door. While the other witches now filled various vital spots in the large field.

"The meeting went well?" Enzo asked as he walked toward me. I took flight, and he followed beside me.

"It will be once Meraki wins the first trial," I answered as I caught him up on what had just transpired.

"Esneoh isn't ready for the Little Hellion," I muttered as I ascended higher into the sky, the wind beating through my wings.

25

ONE STEP CLOSER

M*eraki*

SECURITY NOW COVERED THE OUTSIDE OF THE HOUSE from the garden to strategic entry and exit points. The event at Aarin had changed the atmosphere in Esneoh, the true depths of the oath were beginning to take root, and Quillian was on high alert.

"What's the plan for today?" I asked, throwing a series of hits and punches into the punching bag over my head. "Or are you planning to watch me like a pervert?" I halted for a brief second, turning my focus around on him. Quillian moved from the darkened corners and stepped into the center of the room. I had felt his presence hovering, watching, and assessing me for the last hour.

He had something on his mind, but the broody asshole would instead hover and make me feel uneasy than disclose his problem directly.

"Just enjoying the view and thinking about the tournament." he stepped closer, his movements fluid and intentional.

"That wasn't part of our deal, vampire." I turned my back to him and refocused my attention on the punching bag. As exciting as the idea of entering the trials was, it wasn't part of my job description nor a requirement for the hit-on job.

"See, that's where you're wrong. Because it is." My fist connected with the bag, and I repeated the move alternating my hands. I halted, then turned to face him. Perhaps my boxing focus today shouldn't have been the bag but the conniving bastard before me.

"You needed a pretend wife, an arm candy! That has nothing to do with being forced into a trial that could consist of two tournaments." I stepped forward, erasing all the space between us.

He turned his head to the right, his gaze searing through my training gear. He took a step closer until our breaths were inches apart. "Is my little thief scared?" he teased, the warmth from his body distracting me.

"Scared of what exactly? Is it Surviving? Because I think I've managed that in my own life. Or killing? Because that ship came and sailed years ago. Getting my hands dirty is not the problem." The words flew from my mouth, and I regretted them immediately after. His eyes widened, and my gloved hands connected with his chest.

"Tell me, Little Hellion. How exactly has a thief dealt with bigger fish?" he stood immobile unmoved by my efforts to distract from what I had just shared.

"The same way she dealt with a vampire, who tried to steal something she stole," I replied, my tone and eyes trained on his every movement. "Unless there's something you want to say, you seem to be in an accusatory mood today for someone who needs my help to win."

If all else fails, distract and detract.

"Is that so?" He asked, the air thick with mistrust. His hand moved to my gloves, and I instinctively flinched back and threw a series of kicks and blows his way. He dodged them, stepping past me until my back pressed against his chest, one hand holding my waist and another around my neck with elongated nails.

"Careful vampire," I warned, freeing myself from his hold and getting into a fighting stance. "Many have died by my hands for making that same move."

He took two steps back, removed his blazer and cufflinks, and turned his attention back to me. "Prove it," he said, circling me. Every cell in my body knew this was another one of his mindfucks or was most likely a test to see me unrestrained but turning down a fight wasn't something I had ever done.

It had been more than a week since I had gone on assignment, battled, and seen the life drain from one of my targets' eyes. I circled him as sweat trailed down my forehead and beaded my clothes. I slowly removed the gloves, wanting to ensure nothing was holding me back.

He stepped forward, I kicked his chest, and he took two steps back, his eyes blazing with heat. Before I could think too long into it, he lunged forward, using his upper body to knock me onto the floor. I staggered to my feet and jumped back, giving myself enough time to reel from the after effect of the hit on my body.

He blurred before me, giving me no time to recover. His arms were bound around my neck, gripping me into a chokehold. "What were you saying?" He breathed against me as goosebumps erupted on my skin.

I leaned my head into his chest, looked up, and smiled. He stared down at me, a look of bewilderment filling his face. "Well..." I raised my head, aimed it toward his nose, leaned my feet on his leg, and thrust upwards.

His hold on me loosened, and he staggered back, his hand pressed against his nose. "You would do just fine for the trial then," he said. He removed his hand from his nose and reclined his head back to stop the bleeding.

"I didn't agree to anything."

"You did when you agreed to this," he motioned to the space

between us. He reached for his blazer and cufflinks and turned to the door, not sparing me another word.

"Where are you going?" I asked, not yet done with this argument. "Your nose!"

He stopped and turned to face me. "If you continue to act like this, people might believe you genuinely care about me," he answered. Before I could respond, his wings outstretched, and he took flight.

"Well, that went well?" I mumbled, refusing to feel guilty about how he had chosen to handle that.

I continued training, allowing ten minutes to pass before I headed back to the house to find a way to break into his storage unit, the one I had seen him open with his blood and thumbprint. The task was practically impossible, but nothing could be worse than not trying.

I made my way to the top floor, pushed open the large double doors, and was welcomed by his scent. It permeated every corner of the room like a thick impenetrable blanket. I walked to the center of the room, my eyes taking in the handrails atop of his bed. They merged with the bed from a distance, but as I walked closer, it was clear that wasn't the case. This time unlike the first, I was no longer a prisoner, trying to bargain for my life.

Its hollowed outline and the natural sheen it harbored gave the impression it was later added for other purposes. I swallowed, my body pulsing as images of being hung over the bed as Quillian fucked me on different angles flashed through my mind.

I shook my head. "Not a smart move," I muttered under my breath. I turned left, heading for his inbuilt wardrobe space that held the same dark touches the room had. Rows of suits, ties, cufflinks, and an endless collection of watches covered its expanse. I started from the deep end, opening every wardrobe space from top to bottom, looking for anything that seemed out of place or drew my attention.

"There must be something here; what am I missing?" "Of course, I had to marry a guy too smart to leave evidence behind," I grumbled after hours had passed and time was working against me. I walked back to the entryway of the wardrobe and took one final glance back.

I stepped into the bedroom, my hands resting on my waist as I scoured every nook and corner. My attention fell on two large paintings in the room's far corner. Unlike the neutral decor of the rooms, these two canvases held an array of colors that made them seem misplaced.

I reached for the first canvas and ran my hands through its body for anything out of the ordinary. I did the same for the second image, lifting it first, and then running my hands through its outline. My fingertips stopped at the bottom left corner, an uncanny bump drawing my attention.

"Bingo," I whispered, placing the canvas back on the wall and using my fingernails to brush away the layers of mounted acrylic paint lightly. A small key fell onto the carpeted floor, and I reached for it studying for anything that could give me a clue about what it was. The jagged edges and aged metal told me that it had been here for a very long time.

My attention turned back to the landscape painting, recalling that Quillian had briefly mentioned in a conversation that his brother Alaric loved to paint and did so as a hobby.

I stepped closer to the canvas, looking for a signature on its lower end. Every artist loved leaving elements of themselves behind in their work. For some, it was their name, while others were a symbol or hidden message within the art itself.

On the left corner of the canvas, the outline of calligraphy strokes caught my attention. "AK," I spoke the letters out loud.

Alaric Kingsley.

I quickly inspected the artwork again as my hands moved across the script, admiring the delicate line and brush strokes that had been angled with care and efficiency.

The longer I stared, the more questions swam in my head.

Why would Alaric hide a key in his painting, and what did this key open or lead to? Most importantly, did Quillian know? I shook my head at the prospect, noting it would make more sense for him to have hidden it in his safe instead of plain sight. It was out of his character. I paced the space

Brielle and Silas's laughter reached me, and my eyes fell on the carpet where the paint scrapes stood against the white and black rug.

I lowered myself and quickly scrapped the remains into my palm. What I could not gather, I angled vertically under the canvas, giving the illusion that it was naturally peeling.

I rose to my feet, closed the door behind me, and headed down the stairs to my room, ensuring I stayed on the corners of the lengthened passageway to steer clear of the CCTV key points.

Once I reached my room, I closed the door, my heart threatening to leap out of my chest.

My eyes fell on the key again as light sensations tingled my fingers. This house, like its owners, was shrouded and cloaked in secrets. Secrets I was more than convinced they weren't even aware of, not to speak of the depths they were buried.

This wasn't part of the plan but could perhaps lead to useful intel.

I headed for my wardrobe and buried the key under the hidden designated spot. I then ran into the shower taking my time to lather my skin with the shea butter mix Brielle had brought on my request. Once I was done, I hurriedly dressed and reached for the small notebook and pen beside the bedside table.

Images of the countless faces and leaders I had encountered played in my mind, and my fingers thrummed with the need to sketch. Something I hadn't felt an urge for in a long time. I leaned back on the bed and slowly dotted the faces of the Kingsleys and the other leaders. I finished with a partially done image of Quillian when the pen had run out of ink, and my fingers could no longer move from the strain.

These were the first portraits I had done in years, and it took getting into another realm, being kidnapped, and forced to spy on a family that would most likely skin me alive if they ever knew I was a double agent.

Life can be funny like that sometimes.

I placed the notebook under my bed and bit my lip, recounting the image of the ring on Elias's phone. My attention turned to Silas, who was likely to be the only person who might be able to know where The Den could be.

I rose to my feet, headed downstairs, and knocked on Silas's room. When no response came, I headed to the library, where I always noted him.

"Yes?" he called when I knocked. "I see my brother has managed to turn you into a prisoner even outside of the basement?" he laughed when his eyes landed on me. He tilted his black suede fedora hat back, his hands clasped around a book labeled 'poetic collections.'

I smiled and walked into the space closing the door behind me. "I'm looking to ditch the prison without the guards?"

"Oh, you have my ears," he motioned for me to sit beside him.

"How would you feel about going out to a club?" I offered, taking the seat directly opposite him.

"A club, you say?" he placed the book down and raised his brow. Light dotted his iris, and a contemplative look filled his features.

"I need out, and you promised last time?" I reached for the book in his hand, briefly scanning the pages. He laughed and wrapped his hand around his chest. His eyes blazed with a flicker of interest.

"Aren't you supposed to be training for a tournament?" I flickered through the series of classic poetry in the book and arched my brow at him.

"I have no qualms that I'm going to win," I replied, dismissing his question. "You were reading this?" I asked, trying to keep the intrigue from my voice.

"Someone has an inflated sense of ego?" he smiled, his eyes

falling on the book. "And yes, is it so surprising I like reading classical poetry?"

"I thought you would be more on the *I wanna slap that ass* instead of the *thy bosom bringeth me pleasure* type of guy." Silas roared with laughter as he leaned back on the chair. I placed the book in the space between us.

"I have someone..." he trailed, running his hands through his hair. "Someone who enjoys it, and I'm schooling myself in case *I might wanna slap that ass*...later, maybe," He laughed as he reached for the book, placing it back in line with the racks of books to his right. "So, the ego?" he turned to face me, a bemused smile on his face.

"What can I say? I'm unsure of many things but stealing and kicking ass isn't on the list."

"And my brother?" He leaned back on his chair, creating a table space between us.

"What about him?" I asked, my brows arched.

He peered down at me as if there was something he was aware of that I had somehow missed. He shook his head. "Nothing."

"If it makes you feel better, I'm equally competitive in all aspects of my life" Laughter bubbled in my chest as I thought about the countless board games Iris and I had played and refused to concede defeat.

"How long have you known them?" He reclined on the seat, making himself comfortable as if genuinely enjoying my company. "It's safe to say you have a life outside of all this?" he stretched out his legs, leaned further into the chair, and rested his head against the back pillows. "Tell me about them; what are they like?" He asked, his head facing the ceiling, an earnest interest in his voice.

After a brief moment of silence, he turned to me, and I contemplated how much to share. "I have two best friends. One I've known before I was even two digits old. They are my family." I noted, unable to hold back the smile.

"One thing I've admired about humans is their ability to garner relationships and friendships easily." His head turned to the ceiling, and I leaned back on the chair, resting my head against the cushions.

"Is he your friend?" I asked the question that had been bubbling on the tip of my tongue. Silas' expression tightened, his jaw clenched, and his hands curled into fists.

"My siblings," he stated, his voice filled with an array of emotions. "You've had a small taste of Esneoh. It's hard to trust anyone enough to let them close fully. Now more than ever...." he trailed, his eyes growing distant.

"What about Alaric?" I asked cautiously, knowing his name was a sore spot in this house. Silas's pupils dilated, and for a moment, I was convinced that I had managed to mess up our moment.

"He was my best friend," he answered honestly.

"What was he like? Did he like the classics too?" Si laughed, lightly jabbing his right hand.

"He was the embodiment of classical literature itself. He was the best part of all." Silas laughed, the tension in his body disseminating. "He was more of a critical reader. And most of the organisms and life sciences books are all his." He pointed to the far end wall of the room, covered with an array of science textbooks and journals ranging from human and animal anatomy to space exploration. "He did everything in excess..." he trailed, stopping himself from saying more.

"And who do you go to now?" I asked, recalling the earlier years of Alessia's death and how empty and hollow they were. Iris had been the glue that somewhat kept my mind intact. Without the constant presence, I would have lost myself completely.

Our eyes locked, and without uttering a single word, I could read the answer from his face. Silas was slowly spiraling, and he wasn't even aware of it.

"Having your siblings is great, but having people...friends outside of them, ones who are objective to your grief and genuinely care about you...seeing you whole, happy...that...that changes everything," I replied, as my voice shook in response.

"Are you looking to expand that friendship circle?" he smiled down at me, and though the question was teasing in nature, there was a depth of truth and longing behind it.

I swallowed hard as my chest tightened with guilt. "I'm not sure you'll be able to deal with my friends," I noted, coughing, and readjusting myself back on the chair. How could I deny such a request? Even if it meant I would become the exact thing he feared? I shook my head and looked up at him, reminding myself that this was a job, and all jobs, like relationships, had their expiration date.

"Now that I've never heard from any woman."

"Friends, Silas, for fucks sake," I shouted, throwing the cushion beside me on his head. "There's a lot you need to learn." I shook my head, a smile tugging at the corner of my lips. "So this club we are going to, what's it called?"

"Nope!" He rushed to his feet. "You should be training and preparing to win the trial." He tipped his hat forward.

"This is part of my training. In Jersey Hill, my friends and I would go clubbing to release tension. So, you taking me to one would be helpful for my overall mental and physical health," I offered, rising to my feet to block him from leaving the room. "Quillian will never find out. I won't tell if you won't," I continued, watching him run his hands through the soft stubble on his face.

"Hmmm," he bobbed his head, warming to the idea.

"Unless you're scared of your brother?" I said, relying on the other thing I was sure would further his movements. "If that's the case, then I get it. I just didn't take you as... you know." I slowly headed for the door; my ears trained on the sound of his movements.

"Scared? Really? That's all you could come up with?" he laughed, motioning me to come back and sit down.

"I had to try; you weren't budging," I mocked silently, squealing that my charms with him had worked.

"If we are to go, there are rules."

"Rules?" I beamed.

"Rule number one do not cockblock me. Keep yourself busy; I'm not babysitting you."

"Easy."

"Rule number two, be vigilant. You already know what happened the last time I was there," he added. "Q will lose his shit when he finds out." He smiled as he spoke the words.

"If he finds out, which he won't, right?"

"I, tell? I would never do such a thing, my fair lady," he headed for the door. "It's after six, be ready in two hours max. If you're not down then, I'm leaving without you," he stated with a glimmer of mischief in his eyes.

"You made me do all that begging, knowing you were already going there?"

"What can I say? It's a Kingsley pastime; we love watching women squirm a little before giving into them," he laughed, his deep baritone voice echoing through the walls like a melody.

"And I thought I would prefer you to your brother," I rolled my eyes teasingly.

"You better. I'm setting my life on the line for this," he mused, continuing to the hallway.

"Dress code is clothed but naked," he shouted behind him as I followed.

"What the hell does that mean?"

"You're a woman, work it out," he replied, dismissively raising his hand behind him.

"You never told me the name of the place?" I called from the other side when I realized I still couldn't ask him if he knew about The Den.

"The Den." My eyes widened, and I found myself momentarily frozen in place. My chest tightened like someone was crushing the air out of my lungs.

What were the odds that the last clue I had left to Alessia's killer was within range all this time?

I slowly made my way up the stairs to my room, anticipation bubbling in my chest.

One step closer.

"We need to get rid of your two lapdogs at the front of the estate," Silas stated as I stepped down the final staircase.

"What do you suggest?" I asked, placing the green gold studded bag on my shoulders. My hold on the bag tightened as I remembered that I had stuffed my comms device inside its lining.

"We leave through the garage. You hide behind the car seat, so I can distract them enough to sneak out," he offered as we made our way toward the garage.

Silas reached out for the Bacalar keys and made his way to the car, motioning for me to ride back.

"Stay low," he instructed mockingly as the car came to life.

"You don't have to tell me twice," I mumbled, angling my body between the chairs. Silas chuckled as the car sped forward and slowed down, alerting me that Sol and Blaze were nearby.

"Gentlemen, busy night?" I tugged on the hem of my lime green swing dress. Silas wound down the window on the passenger seat.

"Everything seems quiet," Blaze spoke, his voice filled with irritation. "Yours seems more eventful," he offered.

"That's the plan," Silas offered. "Meraki seems to be having an early night," He lied, his head turned back to the direction of the house.

"For a human, she's certainly restrained and boring," he grumbled, and I bit back my tongue to hold in the laughter.

"What would you prefer, her causing trouble, and we chase after her across Esneoh?" Sol laughed.

"You should be grateful she is reserved and isn't causing any trouble, fewer issues with my brother on your part," Silas noted, a teasing tone in his voice. I smiled, impressed by how believable he was. His chilled and carefree demeanor told me he enjoyed toying with them. I had a feeling that from now on, he and I would get along well.

"Protect the next queen," Silas added as he wound up his window and sped ahead.

"I hate you for that." I jabbed his shoulder and pulled down the front seat. I angled my legs forward and slid my body into it. I then lifted the head of the seat back up and strapped myself in.

"Buckle up," Silas stated, revving up the car, and I lurched forward before I had enough time to prepare. I had encountered my fair share of bad drivers in my life. Skye and Iris may even claim I was one, but nothing came close to Silas, and he lacked any road or safety laws - if they existed in Esneoh.

"Remind me to never do shotgun with you ever again. You're a terrible driver," I held on to the car's door, gasping for air, as the car came to a halt.

"I'm a bit rusty; it's been a while after all," he said, turning off the car's engine and stepping out. He tugged on his black and white striped shirt and tilted his brown suede fedora hat forward.

I closed the door taking in the streets buzzing with vampires and other supernatural beings dressed in their finest attire.

Silas motioned for me to follow him, keeping his steps and pace even with mine. We walked from the parking lot to the main street, making our way through bodies of vampires, demons, and witches. Silas would occasionally stop and exchange pleasantries with a few people who would bow in response when he introduced me.

"Kingsley," a large horn-rimmed demon, smiled, opening a red tapped barricade. "Back again already? I'm sure the leaders would love to see you," he winked, and Silas jabbed his chest teasingly. The demon's attention turned to me, his eyes glistening with unspoken interest.

"She's with me," Silas stated. The demon nodded, assessing me from the crown of my head to the sole of my feet. His attention ran up my body, stopping at the V-neck rhinestone spaghetti straps. His gaze remained on my chest for a few seconds too long, and Silas stepped forward, blocking his view of me. "Quillian's wife," he stated, the words carrying a subtle warning.

"I didn't touch, just looked," he laughed lightly, stepping back and opened a single discreet door for us to enter.

"Your hand," Silas instructed, leading me down the stairs, one step at a time. "These stairs go on for a while."

"Who knew the youngest Kingsley behind all the gruff was a gentleman?" I tightened my hold on his hand when we went across a series of low steps.

"Don't go telling my enemies that," he motioned for me to watch the next flight of stairs curve into the wall. With each step, the music coming from deep within grew louder. He released my hand when we landed on the final step, with The Den splattered on the world in a green calligraphic font.

My heart raced with excitement, and my grip on my purse tightened as I followed Silas into a darkened hallway filled with demons who clung to its walls, openly making out and having sex, without a care who saw or who walked by. Silas seemed unphased by it all and strolled into the space as if he owned it.

The music boomed when we walked into what could be described as a warehouse with ropes of hanging female bodies in the air at its core. The club and bar cascaded over two floors. The top floor comprised a private area blurred into the darkened walls, while the main floor contained a large disco-like center dance floor and bars stationed on opposing ends of the three walls of the space.

"Upstairs," he motioned, his voice audible and clear through the music playing. I arched a brow, and he laughed in response. "It's a staple for all clubs in Esneoh," he stated, leading us through a sea of bodies, up the stairs, and into the private area, gaining the attention and acknowledgment of some of the beings on the floor.

After walking past a series of reserved spaces, he stopped

before one of the open sections and slid into the curved leather chair. An attendant immediately arrived and filled the center table with an innumerable amount of liquor.

"Should I ask?"

"Rule number one, remember?" He stated, his eyes landing on the ropes of women performing acrobatics before us. "Stay out of trouble and make sure you're within eye length," he stated, motioning to the dance floor and back to our section.

"Hmm," I replied, serving myself a shot of liquor for courage. I made no effort to argue contrary because I had lied and told him I needed to get out of the house to have fun, and there were bound to be two things' people do in a club - drink and dance heedlessly. In Silas' case, three, not two.

I took a quick inventory of the space assessing cameras at key strategic points in the room. My attention turned to the crowded bar area and the growing dancefloor, evaluating what would be my best channel for gaining intel. Someone here had seen Alessia's killer before, perhaps even held conversation with them. The bar staff was going to be the best source of information.

I just needed to find out if anyone knew when the event on the picture had taken place and whether there was also CCTV I could view.

Silas disappeared when I turned my head back, and I was silently grateful for it. I needed to thread carefully tonight to get the information I needed, and him acting like my new security intel wasn't part of my recon attempt.

I slowly walked through the top floor, stopping at the intersections of the private booths. The initial ones were filled with shifters making bets about the outcome of the upcoming trial.

"I'm telling you, we have the first trial in the bag. The human will be out within the first five minutes. You already know they are of a fragile disposition." The loudest male of the group boasted, making the other erupt with laughter.

"The betting stations are going wild against the vampire house." another gruff voice chipped in.

"I may have put down a few thousand," a female voice chipped in, and I pursed my lips, taking in the information. Once I finish my mission here tonight, I will speak to Brielle and find out how I could go about betting on myself. If I was going to play, I might as well make money out of being underestimated.

I continued ahead, keeping my head down and not drawing any attention to myself.

"Remember, stay close," Silas's voice boomed behind me, his hand wrapped around two women.

The blonde-haired one who was the tallest sneered in my direction, staking her claim in the trio they had concocted.

"Down girl, she's my sister-in-law." He laughed as the dark-haired one clung tighter to him.

"Meraki, these are my favorite girls, Mila and Sinclair," he motioned to the blonde first, seemingly inebriated already.

"You're the human entering the trials?" Mila asked, her brows knit tighter.

"If she's his sister-in-law, then that would mean, yes?" Sinclair rolled her eyes, evidently the smartest in the group.

"I'm the one," I replied, my answer clipped. The last thing I needed to be doing right now was having small talk with Silas's muse for the evening when I had a more significant task at hand.

"My bet is on the witches," Mila fake smiled. I seriously needed to get my bets down too.

"I'm not so sure," Sinclair grumbled. "What do you think, Silas" she turned her mouth into a pout. Perhaps I was mistaken; not the smartest.

"You will have to see," Silas replied, tugging them ahead. I waved him away, turning my attention back to the room at hand.

I made my way to the bar toward the bottom of the stairs, reaching for my comms device in my backpack as I proceeded. The once busy spot had quietened down, and two ladies and one guy served behind it, dressed in skin-hugging leather attires.

I headed for the woman in the group. "Hey, I came here a few months ago and may have lost a valuable family ring."

"Do you have a picture?" she asked, leaning close. I placed the comms device with the image before her, and she leaned closer, scrutinizing the ring.

"Nothing from what I've seen in the lost and found section at the back. Something like that found would have been taken by someone. But there could be another stash I may not know about. I'm sort of new here."

I pulled back the device. "Who can help?"

"Eric over there has been here the longest. The rest of us are all relatively new. He might be the best person to speak to." She pointed to the bar on the right, consisting of two women and one man.

"Thank you," I smiled, slowly edging my way past the sea of dancing bodies.

"Eric?" I asked when I finally made it to the counter. "Your colleague over there says you've been working here a while?" I asked cautiously, trying to get a reading on what he could be. The orbs of his eyes glowed into a luminescent shade of yellow, alerting me to the fact he was a shifter.

He nodded, strands of his blonde hair falling on his forehead. "Yes, sure?"

"Well, my husband lost a family ring here, and I was wondering if you may have seen it here?" I lied and raised the screen of the device. His hand rested on it, and a flicker of recognition registered in his iris. "You've seen it?" I stated it as a fact rather than a question.

He released his hold on his phone his eyes turned to me. "I was here when that woman wearing it came In. I remembered it because it was...beautiful" he stated, though there was some hesitancy in his voice.

"A woman?" I swallowed, wanting to create the allusion to some sort of infidelity. "Oh," I added, looking downcast.

"Look, I'm sorry."

"I already knew. I didn't know he was this blatant about it. That motherfucking asshole. I'm going to rip him a new asshole and get all his money's worth," I continued, lowering my voice's octave.

Eric turned back to see if anyone was watching him. "Look, it was over a month ago. I didn't see faces; everyone was masked. But there was man and woman without a doubt. They took one of the VIP booths, and I served them that evening."

"Thank you," I stepped from the bar, watching the corners of the bar club's walls, and identifying the various places the cameras were angled. I needed to get my hands on that CCTV.

"Hey," Eric called. "This is none of my business, but if you're looking to get his pocket, you might be able to salvage the CCTV," he offered, pointing at the key focal points in the room.

"Yes, thank you." I turned around and pretended to wipe a tear from my eyes.

"The CCTV company is...." he trailed, rowing into his apron pocket to write A.V.R.L along with the date and the time the event started. He immediately turned his attention back to the growing queue of customers, and I scurried off.

My heart somersaulted in my chest, and it took me a few minutes to catch my breath. Finally. The closest trail of the ring that I had ever gotten in the last ten years. I placed the paper in my bag and turned off the comms device, making my way back to join Silas upstairs.

"Meraki," Brielle called when I stumbled into our booth.

"When did you get here?"

"A few minutes ago. You two didn't think I would let you party without me?"

"How did you know we were here, sister?" Silas asked the question sitting on my tongue.

"I hate to break it to you, brother, but you're rather predictable with your hangout spots. It took less than five minutes of poking around to find you here. You should be happy it's me and not Q, especially as neither Blaze nor Sol is here?" She stated a tightness in her expression.

"Let's drink!" Sinclair shouted, passing around shot glasses, and I couldn't have been more grateful for the interruption.

"Here!" Brielle took the glass from Sinclair and handed it to me. Brielle sighed, closed her eyes, and smiled. "I want to drink, dance, and not think about anything today."

"Shitty day?"

"The shittiest," she replied, sipping her drink in one go. "I don't want to think about it today." She motioned for me to drink and offered me another glass.

"Time to dance!" she announced, downing another set of drinks with me.

"You don't have to tell me twice." I took her hand and headed to the dance floor, which had grown more packed than it had a few minutes prior.

Brielle pulled me closer, and her hands raised high as she swung her hips. I moved in tandem, oblivious of everything and everyone around me. We danced, laughed, and enjoyed each other's company without the weight of the world's responsibility over our shoulders.

Bodies moved and merged around us until warm arms snaked around my waist. I turned back as my body shivered with unease at its roughened movements across my body.

Quillian blurred before me as I did so, knocking back the man with brutal force. His face was set in a scowl, and his eyes burned with rage.

This wasn't going to end well.

26

UNDER THE INFLUENCE

M*eraki*

"What are you doing," Quillian asked, his hand clasped around the neck of the man. Lifting his weight into the air, he stared from him to me, an icy chill passing between us. The music had long stopped, the sea bodies had halted in their movements, and everyone was now fixated on us.

"Everyone out," he shouted into the space, his eyes locked on me, filled with accusations and a hint of something else I couldn't name. The sight of it made the hairs on the back of my neck rise and my heart pulse with trepidation. Did this seriously turn me on?

"You don't own this club." The man in his arms choked. He wasn't only arrogant but also stupid—poor thing.

"I am lord over Kinavari if I have to repeat myself." He stopped, turning his gaze to the entire room. With one swift movement, he tore the man into two, and his blood splattered on the floor, against my skin, and every space within the distance.

Warmth spread through me, making me gasp for air I didn't know I needed. "The same fate awaits you all." He growled the words as he reached for the man's heart and dropped it on the floor alongside his body. The sudden movement of people as they hurried out shook the floor.

"Is this necessary?" I arched my brow, wiping the warmth of the blood against my chest. Quillian briefly turned to me, his nose flared, blood splattered across his pristine white shirt, pants, and one-half of his face, making no effort to address my question. Instead, his attention turned to Brielle whose presence I had lost in my dancing haze. Beside her was a horned demon, who had missed the memo about leaving the premises. His eyes burned with anger as he stared at the corpse on the floor. His hand, however, remained locked on Brielle's waist, who stared at her brother with heated anger.

Within seconds Enzo blurred beside her and locked his hand against the demon whose hand rested on her waist. "Leave! " He warned, his tone sharp.

"Not after what you've done to my friend," he replied, tugging at Brielle as if she was a child who needed to be carried. I watched, unsure why she allowed it to play out the way it was.

"Don't you dare!" Her words floated through the loud groan that left the wolf as Enzo dug out his heart while keeping his other hand against her waist.

"Have you lost your fucking mind, sister?" Quillian spoke, evidently missing the tension between his sister's best friend. Brielle glared at him, but her attention remained locked on Enzo in a stare-down.

Bodies still moved through the room, but from my peripheral vision, I caught sight of Sol and Blaze, who stood by the door, motioning to a dozen similar-dressed vampires to stand guard at key points in the room. I tightened my hold on my purse, prepared to fight if something was amiss. If there was one thing, I was sure of, it was that Quillian was always followed by blood.

Quillian stepped toward me, his eyes blazing with unshed

anger. "You are my wife. No one touches what's mine." Each possessive word echoed as a carefully cloaked warning, halting the movements of the small remnants of people still left behind.

"I belong to no man," I stated, though my heart, body, and chest strained to catch up with the notion.

He moved closer, eliminating the space between us. His body blocked everything before me until all that remained was him, his scent, his eyes. Those shadowed orbs remained fixed on my face exposing the darkness beating inside my chest. His gaze exposed the veil I had enacted around myself. Stripping me of all faces until nothing but bloodlust and rage stared back. And I hated him for it.

His hands rested on my chest and slowly smeared the remnants of the blood there all over my chest. A taunt, a warning, a silent message that I could perform for the world around me, but he saw through my darkness.

"Last I checked, this was an..."

"Don't you dare; you better not fucking say what I think you're going to say," he sneered, stretching out his hand to the room of small spectators watching the ghost of our performance. He cupped my face tightly, and I was more than sure his fingerprints would be left behind if he pressed harder.

"No man touches you," he raised my head, my chin, gripping it. "No one possesses you and leaves their scent all over you," he concluded, his nose flared, and his features contorted with evident disgust.

My heart lurched in my chest. This was nothing but another performance, an open declaration of his claim over me. And I had to tell my heart, pulse, and vagina to remain calm.

Control the environment of your job, and you will have reign over the situation.

Alessia's words rang in my ears, reminding me of what I initially came here for. Today was a good night, the fight night where I could get a tangible lead on Alessia's killer, and somehow Quillian found a way to dampen my mood.

I stepped past Quillian and moved toward Brielle, ignoring Enzo's towering presence. Where the hell was Silas?

"Brielle and I were having fun and will continue to do this. There are plenty of places we can do so in Kinavari. Or are you planning to shut each one down tonight?" I gripped, and she locked her fingers with me in solidarity.

"Remind me to kiss you after all this!" she smiled as we bypassed Enzo. He stepped back and rested his hand against his chest, watching.

"Let's go," I muttered, heading for the exit. As I did so, two sets of vampires stepped forward, barricading us. Anger coiled all around me, and I felt the small ounce of control I still held threaten to loosen.

"I will kill every single one of you if you stand in my way." I turned back, masking my irritation with a coy smile. "Don't test me, vampire."

"Really, Q?" Brielle spoke, unlocking our intertwined fingers. "This is ridiculous," Brielle stepped forward, and Enzo immediately moved beside her. Quillian's eyes darkened when she tried to lurch forward, and the surge of his power hold held her in place.

"You will not intervene," Quillian warned, and Brielle sneered in response.

"You used compulsion on me? I won't forgive you for this!" As Enzo picked her up, she spat and moved her to the far end of the room.

"You're going to allow this?" she looked to Enzo, then back to her brother, and I wasn't sure whether the question was about the fact he was allowing her brother to maltreat her or in reference to whatever game Quillian was playing with me.

I exhaled frustrated and reached for the lipstick container in my purse. I pressed on its cap, which expanded to the floor like a curved blade.

"I'm sure my wife can handle herself," he smirked, his gaze locked around the blade.

This was a trap, and I had fallen into it. If I refused to entertain the fight now, it would imply I was human, weak, malleable, and susceptible to his control. It would make me more of a target than I already was. With the trial so close, that was the last thing I wanted to be reiterated about me.

The small number of guests still lingering behind moved to the room's shadows, watching with unabashed interest as the events unfolded.

"Hold this." I threw my bag to Brielle with a simple goal: to preserve the information given to me tonight. Enzo caught it midair and clasped it around her hand.

The two guards around me took two steps back, and the sight infuriated me. With one hand clasped around the blade, I raised my dress and reached for the dagger I had hidden underneath it.

I threw the dagger forward; it landed on the vampire's chest to my left. Before the other could retaliate, I raised the sword and swiftly pressed it into his chest. He groaned aloud from the silver penetrating his skin. I twisted the blade, and his body stiffed. Drawing back the blade, he fell to the floor simultaneously with his companion.

"That was easier than anticipated," I smiled, taking a quick scan and inventory of the other guards sparsely spread through the room. Quillian's chuckle could be heard behind me, yet I made no effort to turn back. I stepped toward the first vampire with the stake fastened to his chest. I lowered myself, lifted it from his chest, carved out his heart, and tossed it at Quillian's feet.

If this is what he wanted today, to see me raw, uncontrolled, then I wasn't going to hold back.

Blood covered my hand and body and filled all the corners of my nose. Adrenaline pumped through me as if I was on steroids, and my hands twitched with each passing second, wanting to color this place Red.

The shocked gasps and whispers from the small crowd were the only sound that could be heard in the room. "Anyone else wants to get in my way?"

I rose to my feet, waiting on who was stupid enough to test

me right now. From my peripheral vision, Quillian motioned to two guards to my right, and they stepped forward, blocking my path.

My eyes locked with Blaze and Sol ahead, who were now watching me with a sense of interest, confusion, and pity.

The tallest of the two vampires stepped forward, and instead of waiting for him to make the first move, I kicked the tip of my heels into his calf.

He lurched back, and we both fell to the floor. He groaned aloud as I dug my heel deeper into him until a snap and crunch sound made me reel back. With the sword still in my hand, I used its blade to lift myself, carrying his weight with the lower half of my body. I raised the blade; I tore his feet off, jumping up and down on one foot until his remains no longer clung to my heel.

He whimpered and groaned aloud when his eyes caught the movement of his body, rolling across the floor.

The other vampire lurched for me, and without raising my head or turning back, I swung the blade, tearing his head direct from his body.

The warmth of his blood splattered against my back and the side of my face, covering me in a sea of crimson. The thud of his body hitting the floor made the vampire on the floor before me snarl.

"You...killed... him," he stumbled through his words.

"Kill or be killed," I repeated the words that vibrated through every cell of my body as a warrior's call. Tilting his ankle, he unexpectedly reached for me and attempted to drag me to the floor. I fell, clasping back my hand around the sword tighter. His hand squeezed my feet and scratched my skin with his clawed nails.

I lifted the sword and screamed, cutting off his hand, then repeating the same act with his feet and head.

"Fuck" an unfamiliar voice shouted, followed by more murmurings and a series of illuminated eyes from a distance. I slowly rose to my feet, feeling each eye in the room locked on me.

I knew I looked crazed and deranged, but I no longer cared. I had been pushed too far.

Blood soaked every perimeter of the floor, and my skin tingled with excitement. Using the sword blade, I removed the remainder of the vampire's limps from my six-inch snakeskin gold heels.

"Don't ever touch me without my consent, asshole," I spat; I lurched forward and dismembered the remainder of the body with two quick movements.

I raised my head from the body, not attempting to wipe the new splutter that covered my face. Instead, I licked the rims of my lips, allowing its metallic taste and scent to fill me. I slowly turned around the room, scanning the horizon and beckoning the others to make a move.

Brielle's voice could be heard from the distance as she released a series of curses and grunts toward her brother and Enzo.

I placed the sword down beside me and reached for the stake a few feet away, and two other vampires stepped from the left and pounced on me. Raising the hem of my dress, I pulled out the other stake on my left strap and turned my attention to them.

"I see you all want to die today" I corked my head, my voice sounding unfamiliar in my ears. The tallest stepped forward, and red blinded my vision as my heart pounded in my chest.

With both hands raised, I threw both stakes at their chest and turned my attention to Quillian. I made no effort to look back to check and see if they were still alive. I didn't miss my marks.

Rage coiled around my chest at Quillian's betrayal. He had sworn with his mouth that under him, I was protected and assumed by everyone else, but he had also forgotten to mention that involved him. And since we were in the business of breaking oaths, everything was off the table.

He walked toward the empty bar area and sat on one of the stools, his hand outstretched in that familiar, condescending manner. A few feet away, one of the guards followed him, reaching behind the bar. He opened a bottle of liquor, handed him a rocks glass, and filled it to the brim.

"All bets are off, asshole," I spoke, ensuring each word was enunciated enough for him to read between the lines. I couldn't kill him the traditional way, but I was going to ensure I dismembered his body and carried his remains back to the Alokari. Damn the consequences.

"Sister, would you like to have a drink?" he said, pretending he didn't hear me. He turned his gaze to Brielle, and a pearl of his power flowed through the space. Brielle pushed Enzo from her path and walked toward her brother. She took the glass from him and lurched the full content on his face.

"You will never disrespect me as you did tonight, ever again." Her hold on the glass tightened until it broke, and her blood smeared the remnants of the broken shards.

"Now, was that necessary?" he chided, motioning to the vampire on the bar for a napkin.

"You can go home now," he instructed, this time a long moment of heated glances and unspoken words transpiring between them. The heat in her gaze began to dwindle, and an unspoken understanding transpired between them.

"Fuck you, Quillian," she spat, turning to face the entryway, my bag clasped around her hand. "Kill every single one of them, Meraki. If you did the same with my brother, there would be no repercussions on my part," she shouted as Sol stepped from the door allowing her access to exit the building. Enzo followed behind her with a quick nod to Quillian.

I stepped past my sword, walked ahead, and retrieved the two stakes pressed over the hearts of the dead vampires. As I did so, another set of guards moved from the direction of the door toward me.

Quillian rose from his chair and slowly removed his blazer, placing it on the arm of the stool. The vampire behind the bar handed him another glass. His eyes remained locked on me, filled with lust, anger, and mistrust.

"Show me what you're made of wife. You are human, after all." He stretched out his hand and body in a mocking manner.

"Let's see what you're capable of," he tilted the glass to his lips and sipped the drink slowly as the remaining three vampires began to circle me.

"Perhaps when I'm done, I'll slit your throat, dismember your body and take your seat as head of Kinavari?" I voiced aloud, needing him to know that he was next once I was done with his men. "Any husband capable of ambushing their wife is undeserving of respect," I added as a lump formed in my throat. I swallowed hard, refusing to give into the raging emotions inside me. I should have known better; vampires could never be trusted.

The first vampire lunged forward, his feet landing on my chest. I staggered back, my hands clasped on my weapons. "You will regret that," I stated coldly. Decided that this one would be the one whose death I would drag out. I ran toward him and punched him directly on the nose. He groaned aloud, stepped back, and covered the trickling of blood with his hand. The others circled us as if waiting for the appropriate time to jump in.

"Bad move," he grunted, releasing his nose, and allowing the blood to soak his mouth, throat, and shirt. He lurched forward, and his hands clasped around my throat. Before it could tighten, I dropped the sword; arched my hand pressed the stake into his neck. He released his hold and clasped his fingers around his neck, tugging at the weapon. His blood splattered against my face, and I lurched forward with the other lunging it directly on his chest. He fell to the floor, and instead of waiting for the others to attack, I quickly gathered the stakes and turned my attention to them.

The other two stepped forward together, one angling himself behind me while the other now covered my view of Quillian. I trailed my steps after their movements, allowing myself time to catch my breath. As I did so, I wiped the blinding remains of the blood that covered my face with the back of my hand.

With my hold on the dagger tightened, I kept my gaze focused on the subtlety of their movements. The shortest of the two behind me made the first move by reaching for my neck with his elongated nails. When I bypassed his hold, he reached for the edge of my ponytail, pulling me flat against his chest.

I screamed out as he pulled my head back. My scalp tingled with a burning force, and the louder my voice grew, the higher his grip intensified. His hands clasped around my hands, rendering my movements immobile.

Never show weakness before your enemy; only show calm and poise.

I inhaled and exhaled steady breaths while focusing on the other before me. He moved toward me, a victorious smirk plastered on his porcelain face.

Quillian released a series of grunts as if he wasn't the one who had orchestrated the whole ambush. The vampire ahead of me lurched forward, and I raised my feet, hitting directly on the ground.

"Well, that's one way to go about it," Sol mumbled, a mocking undertone in his voice. The small group of people gathered in the shadows took a few steps forward, their eyes running from me to Quillian.

I leaned my head back against the vampire's chest and leaped upward, allowing the back of my head to knock back his chin. He staggered back, and his hold on me loosened.

The vampire ahead blurred before me; I arched my right hand as I lowered myself into a squat. I plunged the stake on my right toward the vampire before me, while the one on my left at the one that was behind me.

The vampire before me fell on the floor swiftly, while the one to my left leaned to the right, and the stake missed him by a few inches.

"Oops," I grunted, watching as the stake left a tear in his black pants. He sneered, and his fangs elongated. I stood on my feet, wiping my hair back and forth. The small body of the people still in the room stepped back, and silent murmurs and chatters ensued. The voices were filled with awe, confusion, and reverence.

None had expected the ambush, nor that I would have lasted this long.

I ignored the voices keeping my eyes trained on Quillian and the vampire now before me. Quillian sat forward on his seat, the dimples on him becoming more prominent with each passing second. One could almost confuse it as pride, but I now knew better. He could not be trusted, and I couldn't allow today to be like our first encounter. One of us was going to leave here dismembered, and it wasn't me.

The last guard before stepped forward, blocking my view of Quillian. His eyes dilated, and the wave of his power brushed through my skin. I laughed, knowing I looked crazed and deranged, but after all that he had witnessed, he still thought that compulsion would work on me.

"I underestimated you, human." He breathed the words through a series of grunts as if saying them out loud pained him.

"Most men do," I replied, taking a few steps back to pick up my sword.

"Any final words?" I smiled, clasping my hand around the pommel. "You touched me..." I mentioned nonchalantly. "There are consequences for that." I corked my head, and trails of blood fell from my head, coating my vision in crimson.

My heart stammered in my chest as light prickles set my skin on fire, making standing still almost impossible. A silent voice urged me forward to show no mercy. The only mercy tonight was red, crimson-stained walls and floors. I closed my eyes and ran forward, plunging the sword into his chest. His elongated fingers scratched my hand as his body convulsed. I pulled the sword from his chest and stepped back. I swung the sword in diagonal lines, and the remnants of his dismembered body fell at my feet.

My chest was constrained, my breathing heightened, and something tugged into my subconscious for a brief moment. I closed my eyes, the room stilled, and no sound could be heard apart from disgruntled breathing.

When I opened my eyes, my body froze, taking in the series of bodies all around me and the weight of blood that now covered the entirety of my body, making the green hue of the dress unrecognizable.

My attention turned to Quillian, who was now on his feet, heading toward me.

"Everyone leave, now!" His voice boomed across the space, and within seconds, every single being left the premises until only he and I remained.

"Red looks good on you, Meraki." He smirked, and my heart thundered in my chest. Did he know?

"I'll look even better once I've marked my skin with yours," I replied, trying to gauge what he knew.

He blurred before me and kicked my sword from my hand using the heel of his shoes. He then pulled my back to his chest, pinning me with one hand.

"Are you sure about that wife," he whispered in my ears as the sound of steel scrapped against metal. I shook from his hold but found he had bound my wrists with his hands while tightening the other around my waist.

Vampires were strong, but Quillian possessed strength and cunningness the others did not. Discovering his weakness was going to be my Christmas gift to myself.

"You're bound to me in more ways than one," he continued, his thumb lightly trailing the ring on my finger.

"What kind of sick game are you playing? You pulled this on me tonight?" I snickered, jerking my body against his.

"Now...now, Little Hellion. Don't change the conversation. All will be revealed in time." His mouth moved up to the juncture of my right ear, lapping it with slow trails of his tongue.

I shuddered, unable to hold back the moan that threatened to escape my lips.

"You and I are alike..." He continued, his tongue licking the remains of blood smeared on my neck. His fangs elongated, scraping the skin in circles. He lightly bit my neck on specks of blood. "You pretend the killing is for survival, a job of some sort.

But you and I know better. I see through you. I see how your pupils dilate, and your heart stutters with each kill."

"Even with the wolfsbane in your system. I can still scent some of you, taste some of you... and it's glorious!" He chuckled as if drunk from the haze of it all.

"We are nothing alike!" I groaned, using every ounce of my strength to shake his hold, freeing myself from his grasp.

He stepped back, watching me with bloodshot eyes, and his once white shirt was covered with the remnants of blood on my body. "There is still honor even amongst thieves; you know nothing about that!" I shot back, lowering myself to reach for the two stakes within reach.

I knew I couldn't kill him, but I was more than capable of inflicting pain, so he could finally get a taste of his medicine.

"There is nothing human about you, Little Hellion," he stated plainly, and the word shut through me, making the hairs on my neck rise.

"Is that so?" I stepped back, circling him with both stakes in hand.

"Right now, I can hear the irregular beat of your heart. I can scent you...your desire to inflict pain, enact revenge and bask in the euphoria of warm blood against your skin." He smiled knowingly, and my hold on the weapons tightened. My skin heated with recognition, knowing there was truth to his words. Admitting it out aloud would be conceding, accepting defeat.

"You set your men on me," I remarked, needing him to realize this wasn't something that was going to be swept under the carpet as his family did with most things.

"Little human..."

"You're good at that. Sweeping shit under the covers like it never happened. Never existed." He blurred before me, and I lunged the stake at his neck, missing by a few inches.

"Be careful; this is a road you don't want to go down," he sneered, following the sway of my movements, as I continued to circle him.

"I'm not your family...I'm not Alaric; you aren't going to sweep what you did to me here tonight under the covers," I spat, baiting him. His shoulder tensed, and the tightening of his jaw and clenching of his fist told me I had him exactly where I wanted him. "We are nothing alike. You seek to dismiss the existence of yours, and I seek to avenge mine," the words flew from my mouth before my brain could fathom what I had just spoken aloud.

His eyes widened, and his lips curled into a snarl. Understanding washed over the depths of his eyes as the seconds lingered. He now knew more than I had intended for him to know because the band aid had been ripped.

"Don't ever speak on him," he threatened.

"And what will you do about it?" I stepped toward him, my focus set on inflicting him with pain. I lunged forward with both stakes raised. Quillian's hand reached forward, holding both hands mid-air halting my movements.

"Enough, Little Hellion"

"You can't poke the bear and decide how it should respond." I thrust back, freeing myself.

"I didn't ambush you."

I choked on my laughter. "So now, I'm not just a weak human but a delusional one too?" I threw the dagger from my right, and it missed his abdomen by a few inches, leaving a tear on the fabric of his material.

"Think! Why would I do that now? When we both have to lose?" He began to circle me. His use of the word "we" did not go unnoticed.

"I was setting a presence for the tournament." His eyes fell to where the stake had left a tear. Ignoring his words, I ran forward and angled both daggers upwards. Quillian leaned back as I dragged the tips of both stakes through his chest. The sound of torn fabric and blood movement ricocheted as a soft echo.

"You needed-"

"Oh, you did this to save my honor?" I laughed, pointing at the sea of bodies all around thrust ahead, and he blurred out of my reach. He wrapped his hand around my wrist when he reappeared, pulling me into his chest.

The stakes fell as we wrestled. "Your honor didn't need saving, Little Hellion. They needed to know what you were capable of. They needed to know that you were not weak, frail, or remotely normal." My heart stuttered in my chest as he spoke the words longingly in my ears.

Warmth blooded my body, and I inhaled the heady scent of his aroma. The sight of blood, coupled with the slow, deliberate movement of his hands across my body, made me arch my body, wanting to lose myself in this moment. The fact that this turned me on made me consider getting a shrink when I left Esneoh.

This was the man that set his men on me and stood as they ambushed me one by one, yet my body moved like an instrument against his fingertips, desperate to smell, taste, and inhale his scent.

Nothing in my life made sense anymore.

He leaned his head in the crook of my neck, the spot he always seemed to gravitate toward. His fangs lightly trailed the skin there, making me moan out aloud without even realizing it.

"You are nothing short of a masterpiece. A vision bathed in crimson, lust, and force. A mirage plucked straight from my wildest fantasies." His right hand moved to the small of my back as warmth filled my body. His manhood pressed against my back as his voice grew hoarse with each movement.

"I promised you would be safe as long as you were under oath to me," he continued, and I couldn't help but pick up on the loophole in that sentence. He continued his hands slowly moving around my body, cupping my breast, and leaving the ghost of his handprints behind.

"There could have been another way." I struggled feebly to release myself yet finding myself being dragged deeper into his hold.

"No! There wasn't" his voice dipped, and I sensed the sincerity behind his words. "Loki's men were here, and key leaders from each house. This was the only way, a statement, a declaration of strength."

"I killed your men, Quillian."

"No, you claimed your role beside me as someone to be feared and revered. No one can question that, or you after. They will go back and relay the vision you were tonight." He continued, his words slowly soothing the sting of anger and mistrust built around me.

"Tell me what you want," he resumed forcibly, turning me around until our faces were inches apart, and his hands gripped the back of my head.

"Quillian..." I murmured, my eyes focused on his lips. Currents of electricity shot through my body, setting my skin aflame with desire. Now that the thrill of the kill was starting to wear off, lust reigned in its wake.

"I can scent you, Little Hellion," his hands continued to rove my body, making me arch into his hold. "Let me help you," he tugged at the straps of the dress, ripping it into tatters.

He reached for my ponytail, pulling it tight enough for me to arch my head back as his lips left trails across my mouth, face, and neck.

Each kiss was bruising as if he was marking me, mixing his scent with mine.

I couldn't trust him for shit, but it didn't mean I should turn down the chance of an orgasm.

Quillian released his hold on my hair, and with his eyes trailing me, he bit down on his wrist. Blood pooled from his hand, and without a single word, he raised it toward my neck, covering my chest, face, and breast.

"Mine," he whispered, a possessed and deranged look on his face. There was no point pretending that his possessive streak did not turn me on. It was the thing that assassins' kryptonite.

His palm smeared his blood on my face, and with each move and stroke, he grunted aloud and heaved silent declarations.

"Be a good girl, and open for me," He ordered, his blood-stained thumb pressed against my lips. I did so without hesitation, taking his hand into my mouth with an eager zeal. My tongue curled around it, nipping, and sucking on it with eager moans.

I licked the blood clean from his thumb, and the coppery and sweet aftertaste made me groan aloud.

Quillian's lustful gaze roved over my mouth, and the sight of it speared me on. How did we get from me trying to kill him to thumb fucking in the middle of a dancefloor?

He moved his hand in and out of my mouth, his movements picking up pace and momentum. I groaned out loud, visualizing my mouth around his cock and enjoying the pleasure for myself.

"Open wider," he commanded, removing his thumb from my mouth. The surge of authority behind the words shot straight to my vagina. I opened slowly, my response sparking a low grunt from his throat.

"Good girl," he praised, his blood-soaked fingers tenderly running strokes against the cupid bow of my lips. He moved his hand to my chin bringing my mouth to his. I whined, arching back and opening my mouth wider.

"Wider."

Saliva dripped from his lips, and he spat it into my mouth. I swallowed, groaning as he reached for my neck. The move was filthy, raw, possessive, the definition of everything that embodied us.

He bobbed my head, pulling me into an all-encompassing kiss that made warmth fill me and goosebumps rise against my skin.

"You're so submissive to my touch." He stated, lifting me from the floor. I wrapped my legs around him, and our mouths tangled into a deep, searing kiss.

"Not here," he pulled back and gripped my neck. "No one gets to see this body," his eyes rove over me, his expression more deranged than before. "No one," he added. He growled low within his chest and scanned the room now filled with the bodies of the men I had just killed.

"Little Hellion," he called, his voice filled with an affection that wasn't there before.

"Hmmm," I replied, unable to find my voice from the haze of the blood lust and the fire now burning between my legs.

"What should I do with all these bodies," he asked, a bemused tone in his voice. The question caught me off-guard, and I arched my head fully up to take him in.

This was the first time he had asked for my input about anything. I stared into the depth of his grey eyes, finding no condescension behind his words.

"Get one of your guys to clean it up and get everything running in two days," I answered, thinking about the staff who would go without employment if the whole establishment was locked down.

Quillian lifted me from the ground, and before I could get a chance to argue, we were in the air, his wings fanning over us. He gripped my waist, and the hardness of his dick pressed inside my thighs. I tightened my arms around his neck, straddling his waist, as I licked the trails of blood splattered on the collar of his neck.

Quillian grunted out aloud, the sound coming from deep within his throat like a wild beast possessed by some inanimate force.

"Meraki," he warned, tightening his hold on me, pulling me deeper into the outline of his bulge. He began to descend, the flight making butterflies erupt in the pit of my stomach.

"Hmmm," I continued as the wind flapped against my skin, and the warmth of his body set the lower part of my body on heat. Quillian grunted with each caress and lick.

Quillian landed on the front door of the house. His hold on me tightened, and I remained straddled around his waist, desperate for my release.

His hand moved to my cheeks, and he bobbed my head back. His mouth locked with mine, and he kissed me. His tongue made laps around my mouth, demanding access and letting me know who held the power at this moment.

The door of his room flew open and closed. He carried me into the room."I need you," I groaned as he placed me on his bed, his eyes roving over my blood-soaked body.

"Strip, I need you naked with nothing but my tongue inside your cunt," He growled. My head turned to the bed, catching sight of one of my nightgowns.

"Presumptuous or coincidence, vampire?" I crossed my hand against my chest.

"Neither." I arched a brow, waiting for him to expand. Quillian paid me no heed; instead, he kept his gaze locked on me and slowly started removing his cufflinks. "You stay here tonight and every other night until the end of the trial," he responded, unbuttoning his shirt.

"That wasn't part of what we agreed, Quillian."

"We have no choice, and I'm not asking."

"Yes, the fuck I do," I stepped from the bed.

"I have a word; Loki will send someone over to do an impromptu early visit tomorrow," he noted, stepping before me, the last button on his shirt falling open.

"And?"

"Someone questioned the legitimacy of our marriage. I know they've checked the courts, but all ends there were cleaned up." He tilted my chin up, forcing me to look at him. His bronzed and chiseled chest on display flexed with the subtle movement of his hand.

"Thale," I offered, without saying I told you so.

"It seems like it."

"So, you brought me here and planned all this?" I stepped back, feeling more exposed now than I did earlier. I knew I had no ground to stand on. This was the arrangement; this was my job. So, why did it feel like that truth hurt like hell?

"No, you're here because I'm selfish. I want more," he replied, leaving the word open for my interpretation. He took another step forward, eliminating the space between us. "I want you." Those words were my undoing.

He took hold of my hand and ran it through his chest, all the way down to his groin. "Does this feel like someone who doesn't want this?" I blinked, remembering how thick and long it was that evening I had been on my knees before him. My expression seemed to please him, and he smiled subtly, his eyes focused on my mouth as if recounting the same thing.

"Just for one night."

"Just for one night," I lied, knowing it wouldn't be enough, and it would make drawing the lines between us harder than it needed to be here.

"I can see your head clicking with excuses," he spoke, his eyes soaking in the blood still smeared over me. "Let me take the burden of responsibility and consent from you." He released my hold from his groin, pulling me closer to him. His hands trailed the peaks of my aching nipples, pinching them hard enough to make me whimper and send bolts of electricity to my core. My stomach quivered as I imagined them sliding down to another place completely.

"I can play the role of the villain, the beast who imposes himself on you" His hand hovered over my pussy, as he slowly played with the lace outline of my underwear. I pressed closer, beckoning him to continue. "Spread those legs," he demanded, and I immediately followed, panting loudly while moving to the beat of his fingers.

"So responsive," he moaned, and before I could follow his instructions, he used his knees to spread my legs wider.

"Quillian..." I called out his name as he ripped the fabric of my knickers from my body without hesitation.

"Fuck," I murmured. The pressure made my pussy spasm from the unexpected throb. He progressed to doing the same with the dress, leaving me in nothing but heels and bra.

"Keep them on," he stopped me when I attempted to remove my heels. He moved me to the foot of the bed and forced my chest down. He lowered himself to the floor, placing my feet over his shoulder, as he stared long and hard at me. "What a pretty pussy," he growled the words with reverent admiration, and my pussy throbbed in response. His tongue snaked out, running steady laps and strokes around it.

"You smell so fucking good, but you taste...like a drug I can't get enough of," he murmured, licking, and sucking my clit, as if it were an offering placed before an altar.

"Give me a safe word."

"A what?" I replied, leaning forward, and burying my hands in his hair.

"A safe word Little Hellion, because the depraved things I want to do so have no limit." His fangs brushed through the walls of my pussy, and words failed me. Where words even needed when you were getting the best head game of your life?

"I want to eat this pussy and fuck it so hard that you always remember who you belong to."

"Quillian" I groaned as he shifted two fingers inside me and moved them in and out with the sole intent to torment, and make me beg for his dick.

"I'm so close," I muttered aloud to no one. With both hands bumping in and out of me, his lips nipping and sucking like I was a feast to be devoured.

With each second, his pursuits grew louder and more desperate until he raised my hips and licked back and forth from my ass to my pussy.

"Who do you belong to?" He grunted with each pursuit.

"I...I...I" words failed me as my legs shook, and my mind went completely blank. I stuttered on my words, unable to control myself or make sense of anything.

Over possessive men with the good head game were my Achilles heels.

"Words, I, my little thief, I need words," he continued, his nails scraping against my thighs until I lost all control of my body.

"Fuck me," I screamed as he drew his mouth back, pinched my clit, and dragged his elongated nails from my thighs to my ass, drawing blood with each trail.

"Who do you belong to?" he asked again, a silent warning behind the words.

"You- you- yours...fuck, it's you," I screamed as his nails dug deeper, and my body shivered in turn. My mind left my body with one final scream, and I came with the heel of my feet digging into his back. Quillian groaned and moaned aloud, licking the remains of my juices that had now mixed with the trickle of my blood.

"You smell good but taste even better." He inhaled, humming as he did so. "A word, human," he commanded, and the sparks of the force behind it called to some primal part of my subconscious.

"I'm not done with you yet," he commented, removing the remainder of his clothes. Without warning, he swung me around until my head and hand rested against the bed, and my ass raised into the air.

"Hands," he called. With his erection pressed against me, he reached down and gripped my hands, ensuring my back remained against him. The rattling of locks caught my attention, and within seconds restraints were pulled from the top railing of the bed and placed over my hand. For a moment, my eyes widened, and memories of our initial week resurfaced in my mind, and my body stilled.

"Relax." He shooed, fastening the chains of the restraints, allowing me no room for movement. I eased back into the bed, reminding myself that this wasn't like our earlier encounter. I had enough power and bargaining chip in this relationship this time around. I was the queen in this game of chess, and there was nothing Quillian could do without my full involvement that wouldn't ruin his chances in the trial.

"Has anyone told you, you have an amazing ass?" he noted, cupping it with both hands and slapping it.

"Well, I know now," I laughed, feeling his dick pressed against my opening.

Slap.

The sound echoed in the room as he forced himself inside me. My breath caught, and I gripped the sheets, trying to accommodate his fullness. One hand pressed down on the arch of my back while another gripped my ass, pumping in and out of me with force.

Quillian fucked me as if he was going to war, and I was an enemy he needed to conquer. Each slap and thrust tightened the restraints leaving me gasping for air and cursing aloud at the fact that I was ruined.

Quillian had ruined me. Sex with a man, a human man, could never compare to this. It could never hit the walls and spots he could.

"Fuck." I arched further back, meeting each thrust with my own, deciding I wasn't going to be the only one who left this arrangement a fragment of herself.

"Look how your pussy, is clenching around my cock."

Slap.

"Look how well your body responds to me."

Slap.

"Quillian, please." I panted, unsure whether I was asking for release or for him to thrust deeper and make me forget the possibility that I would have to betray him and his family soon.

He read between my words and twisted me around. Raising one leg over his shoulder and holding it in place while he fucked me relentlessly. He thrust in and out of me without mercy or care. He cupped my breast, pinching and marking my skin with more marks and blood until the remnants of blood from earlier and mine became indistinguishable.

"This pussy is fine," he thrust again; this time, my pussy spasmed at the possessive behind the words. Quillian continued to pound until my release came, leaving me a quivering mess after. Quillian did not stop, he kept pumping into me until he finally came, and the warmth of his cum trickled down my legs as he massaged my breast.

He reached for the restraints, released me, and lightly massaged my wrists as he pulled me into the bed sheets. My brain was a quivering mess of stars and colors, unable to make sense of anything. The only thing that came to my head was one word.

"Nelly," I groaned the name aloud.

"Nelly? Who the fuck is Nelly," he asked, rising from his position and hovering over me.

"My plant..."

"A plant?"

"A ponytail palm plant. One Alessia gave me... a gift..." I shook my head, forcing myself to stand. His eyes widened slightly, and the realization dawned on me that I had yet shared another piece of myself he could use against me.

My mind told me to leave the room or come up with another cover, but my body and brain could not cooperate. I was fucked, literally and figuratively.

Quillian made no effort to pry and dig for more; he simply pulled me into his embrace as my eyes struggled to stay awake.

"It has a name?" He snickered.

"Don't judge me," I yawned.

"Rest!" he instructed, planting a kiss on my forehead. I mumbled a response, deciding tomorrow, I'll create distance again and remind him that this was a mutually beneficial relationship.

Tomorrow I'll find a way to chase up on my lead.

Tomorrow was the trial.

27

THE ISLAND OF LABYRINTH

Meraki

"THE TRIAL WILL BEGIN IN THE MAIN HALL IN FIVE minutes," Brielle announced, popping her head through the door of the empty small-sized room I had been placed into when I arrived in Aarin.

I strapped the stakes and daggers around my hips and ankles before raising my head to face her.

"You look ready," she commented, stepping inside the room. I read the accusatory tone in her voice but decided to play oblivious to it. Though the walls of the rooms in the house were soundproofed, I couldn't put it past Brielle to have heard more than she was putting on. The last thing I needed to do right now was to talk about her sleeping with her brother last night, especially after the blood ambush in the club.

"I feel ready," I responded, running my hands through my hair.

"So, about last night," she commented, resting her hands against her chest.

She exhaled and rolled her eyes. "Look, there's something clearly going on with you and my brother."

"There's nothing," I replied too quickly, and her brows arched in turn.

"Nothing," she repeated the words, taking purposeful steps toward me. "Family is everything... and as much as I hate Quillian right now, he is family. If you hurt him-"

"Hurt him?" I scuffed at the idea. I was most likely the one to have my heart handed to me figuratively. She placed her hands on my wrist and bit her lip as if debating what came next.

"Those who seem the most unlovable are usually the ones that need love the most," she murmured, releasing her hold on my hand. "Look, my brother has a type...he tends to go for women who are in some capacity unavailable." she stared hard as if daring me to argue otherwise. "The last and only time he entertained someone...a human, it destroyed our family."

"I didn't ask for this." I reasoned, swallowing back the guilt threatening to take me. Was I going to betray this family and mess up their perspective of humans all over again? "What happened?" I finally asked after a brief, tense moment passed between us.

"That's not a story for me to tell. He has to tell you. But it caused division with Alaric...He died when they were on bad terms."

"She had a role in his death?" I asked, knowing the answer but needing more intel. Brielle nodded hesitantly, and darkness flashed across her features as her fingers clenched.

"A blood bond?" I asked, recalling what Hera had mentioned in our previous conversation. She swallowed hard and slowly nodded as if the act alone pained her. I shook my head, knowing I now had the information I needed that could destroy them all, and I wasn't sure I wanted to disclose it to the Alokari

"I see you as a friend, Meraki, and in my way, I like you, perhaps more than experience has taught me. But after a millennium of being stuck with nothing but my thoughts and regrets, I didn't want to come back and be how I was before. Alone...shutting everyone and everything out." My hands reached for hers; without words, I could see the horrors of her time written on her face.

"Raki."

"Huh?" Brielle questioned with a confused stare.

"My friends call me Raki," I answered, the weight of my possible betrayal weighing more heavily now than before. Brielle beamed, repeating the nickname under her breath. A dinging sound from outside halted our bonding session and drew our attention to the door.

"Let's move on and finish this up. Oh, there were also last-minute additions," she mentioned as she walked toward the door.

"Meaning?" I stepped forward, trailing her steps toward the door.

"Apart from the leaders, regular people from the houses can also enter the competition," she mentioned casually as if this wasn't an important piece of information I should have long been informed.

"Wait! What?" My hand halted on the door as we stepped out of the room into the corridor. "How? And why am I only finding out about this now?"

"It's part of the founding law. It encourages even distribution of power. The law of the land requires it. What did you think? We aren't complete savages. We believe in a fair trial," she teased, motioning for us to continue working.

"Does this mean anyone from Kinavari can also enter?" Brielle tersely nodded as we walked through the dimly lit corridor space.

"Yes," she slowed her movements, turning to briefly face me. "The final entries are announced before the game commences. This stops any interference from outside forces."

"Is there anyone from Kinavari we suspect might take part?" I continued ahead, walking side by side with her.

"We have some guesses. My brother rules with an iron fist, but one thing he cannot stop is this," she noted in deep thought.

"Who did you have in mind?" As Amma was the first name, I asked what rolled through my thoughts. She halted and turned toward me, her face etched with caution.

"What? "Brielle bit her lip uncomfortably.

"Done," she noted, her hands resting on my shoulder.

"What is it?" I turned my head to face her.

"We made a bargain when you were in the basement." She hesitated, briefly reaching for the pockets of her dark high-waisted pants. "I'm asking for it now."

"Okay… why do you seem hesitant to tell me?"

"This wasn't how I wanted to use it, but the change in tournament rules means I have no choice," she continued taking a cursive glance behind her.

"Well?" I asked, trying to gauge what she needed to ask right before the tournament.

"Protect Hera." She stated, her face void of any emotion.

"Hera?" I repeated, wanting to ensure I heard her correctly and wasn't reading this wrong.

"I need her safe," she relayed cautiously, and I nodded, grasping the severity of what she was saying. If this were Quillian's plan, he would have conveyed this to me. This was outside her brother's jurisdiction, and there were only two reasons for it. One, they were close friends, or there was something between them. Something tangible enough to warrant the tightness in her demeanor and the frown lines around her lips.

"Oh…she's…you are?" I uttered cautiously, not wanting to offend. Brielle nodded, and the tightness in her jaw told me she did not want to go into specifics yet.

I nodded, ensuring I didn't give away the fact Hera and I had already come to our pact long before. However, getting one Kingsley promise out of the way would make me sleep better at night.

"This stays between us," she whispered, turning to face the

path we were headed. Now I was more confused than ever. Was there something between Brielle and Enzo or Brielle and Hera, or was I losing my shit altogether?

I followed her, passing through several long passageways with iron doors. As we walked, the first door to the right opened, and Hera stepped out with Valeria behind her. She and Brielle shared a longing look, and Hera stilled before Valeria whispered something in her ears. Hera's expression tightened, and she immediately sprinted ahead without another backward glance.

Brielle's expression morphed through a series of emotions, but true to Kingsley style, she buried it and plastered it on her don't fuck with me sneer.

The door to the left opened, and Althea stepped out, followed by a harem of five female shifters trailing behind her. She turned to briefly take me in, her lips set in a downward disapproving glare.

"Let's go," she murmured hurried to her attendants, who followed suit without question.

"Valeria," Althea acknowledged her presence with a heaved sigh.

"Good to see you again, Althea," I called cheerfully, knowing it would someone irk her. The others turned, including Hera and Valeria. "Nice to see you again, Hera and Valeria," I added as I continued walking ahead. Brielle chuckled her breath, picking up on what I was doing. If these women thought they would intimidate me simply because I was human, then they would be sorely disappointed.

"Meraki," Althea all but rolled her eyes.

"I know you're new to this world, human. But there's an order and way of doing things which it seems you've not been trained on," Althea spoke, making it evident her snarky comment was for Brielle.

"Careful, Althea, the last time you and I engaged in a battle, it was your blood I carried, not the other way around," Brielle moved, not attempting to mask her disdain for the woman before me. "Then again, the last time you tried to ride the Quillian train was because you had no name or standing to hold on to?" Althea's mouth hung open, and her skin turned the same deathly shade of red as her hair.

Something about the idea that Quillian had been with her or even entertained some sort of relationship with her made my stomach churn. I had no right but...

"We will see who will soon be humbled and how the tables can quickly turn," Althea replied, keeping her composure because of the women around her.

"I can't wait to see you be humbled on your knees," Brielle rolled her eyes.

"By whom? This human here?" Althea laughed. "Don't be ridiculous. But don't worry, I know how much she means to you and your family. I will take my time with her."

I corked my head to the side, resting my hands against Brielle's temple, who seemed ready to lunge forward for her. Something crossed Hera's eyes from ahead, and Brielle exhaled loudly and stepped back.

Valeria shook her head and motioned for Hera to follow. "I'll see you in there, Althea," I smiled, making a conscious decision in my head to ensure I kick her ass during the game.

Another door to the right opened, and Khadijah stepped out with an entourage of men and women around her.

"Ladies," Khadijah announced as she headed forward, not wanting to pay us any heed.

Althea turned with her harem and briskly walked ahead, following behind Khadija. Brielle and I followed the passageway and continued ahead, the haunting sounds of our footsteps echoing through the walls.

The hallway came to an end, and we moved into a large circular space with two floors, white walls, marble flooring, and a scattering of gold ornaments in the form of various creatures.

Quillian and the other leaders stood at the center, and a huge display screen stood above their heads. The top floor of the room was filled with an innumerable amount of beings from all four regions.

Valeria joined the other leaders as Brielle, Tallen, and Althea's attendants stepped back, leaving me, Hera, Althea, and Khadijah standing at a steady distance from the center.

Quillian's eyes landed on me, and a slow grin tugged at his lips, silent, observant, with an unspoken pride and message - *win*.

"Welcome, Esneoh, to those here in Aarin and others scattered throughout." Cheers and laughter erupted in the room, and images of the various regions flashed on the screen, showcasing bars and restaurants with beings glued to their screens.

"Today marks the start of the trials," Loki announced, waiting for the noise to quiet down. He motioned for Hera, Althea, and me to step forward.

"Before we begin, I must reiterate the rules. The first trial consists of two tournaments instead of three. Today's tournament will be something that showcases the participants' strength." His voice rumbled. Inciting more excitement.

"Now, before we begin, we must follow the laws on which Esneoh was built. And the law states that before any trial, we must open the floor to followers from all regions who seek to make a name for themselves by participating. If any of these individuals win, they will triumph over the current leader and rule as king over Esneoh." Silence echoed in the space, and a somber mood followed.

"Now is your time; step forward now, introduce yourself." The room went eerily still, and every eye darted back and forth between floors, waiting, watching.

"We seek to stand in line." India stepped forward, her sister Adelaide directly behind her. We are leaders from Aldrata," she added, and Hera flinched beside me. All eyes turned to Valeria, whose face remained stoic, giving nothing away.

"We seek to enter." Two other females stepped forward, one with deep mahogany hair that cascaded over her shoulder like flames. "My name is Esme, a dragon shifter from the Fleelens."

"And I'm Sierra, a Kitsune, from the Fleelens" The petite woman behind her with equally bright colored rainbow hair stood forward. Their eyes fell on Thale, whose fisted palms showed his displeasure. He nodded, immediately turning his gaze from them. Yet everything about his demeanor spoke of the rigid tension radiating from him.

Three female demons stepped forward, two-horned with deep brown skin, while the third had deep alabaster skin and raven black. Their gaze turned from Khadijah to Loki with caution. But there was something not quite right about the rigid exchange. And the subtle nod Loki gave them that seemed to have been missed by the entirety of the room only confirmed what I already suspected.

This was a carefully orchestrated plot to ensure Khadijah had a higher winning chance.

"My name is Ezri, and this is Yemi and Biola; we are here to represent Oloh." The tallest with alabaster skin and shoulder-length hair spoke on behalf of the others.

"You may all join the others," Loki pointed, and they stepped forward, moving to stand beside Khadijah, who briefly turned to face me with a coy smile on her face.

"Anyone else?" Loki called as all eyes turned to Quillian, waiting for someone from Kinavari to step forward.

"Well, since there's no one."

"I would like to partake on behalf of Kinavari." Amma, wearing a skintight black cotton body suit, moved forward. Subtle chatter filled the room, and Quillian kept his gaze on me, his features impassive. But my time with him had taught me that even his lack of expression spoke a thousand words. And right now, he was pissed, in fact fuming.

Amma's eyes followed Quillian's, and her mood soured when she noted where his attention was aimed. I could foresee she was going to be a big problem for me, and I just hoped she had enough senses to keep steady during the trials.

Amma stepped forward, taking a stand beside Khadijah's

entourage, a scowl drawing attention to the frown lines on her forehead

I briefly turned back to catch Brielle, seemingly shocked by the unexpected addition to the trial. It was one thing preparing to defend myself against Khadijah and her entourage, another also dealing with someone from Kinavari who I know hated my guts because I was human and had married her dick ticket. You can't make this shit up.

Tallen moved beside his father with a box in his hand. Loki opened the box and removed the gnet. When he touched the wings, the room lit up with that familiar shade of yellow and orange. An image of a maze appeared, eliciting whispers from the room.

"The Island of Labyrinth," Loki stated, his voice losing that earlier excitement. "The goal is simple, the four who make it out of the maze first with replicas of the gnet will amass points. And ultimately, by the end of the second tournament, the individuals with most points will be crowned the winner of the first trial, along with their region." He added cautiously. "You can use weapons, force, and strength, but you cannot use your powers to fight," he concluded with finality.

The room erupted into more shouts and cheers, and the screen displayed various images of the maze island from multiple angles.

"Good luck," Loki spoke, and a loud horn sounded off as the floor around me shifted, the walls shook, and everything around me seemed to turn upside down in a kaleidoscope of colors. I held my stomach to stabilize myself as nausea swam over me in a sick green wave, and I almost heaved bile.

When I was finally unable to walk any farther, I dropped on all fours and spent some time attempting to calm my raging stomach. The sun burned my skin and blinded me for a brief while as I struggled to my feet.

I found myself standing before a large golden gate. To my left and right, long, clearly defined paths curved the greenest plants and flowers, the path illuminated by a mixture of dark soil and white sand.

Hera appeared next to me a few minutes later, a dagger in one hand, while the other fell around the waist of her body suit.

"Wow!" She stopped taking in the height of the maze, which seemed to almost touch the sky. "They are really watching us," she commented at the innumerable drones around us.

I stepped toward her, and she jerked back. "What are you doing?" she raised her dagger toward me in a questioning manner. Her eyes glinted, and I recognized the mistrust there.

"Ensuring we don't get killed before the game even formally begins. Let's go," I muttered, bypassing the weapon in her hand, and taking hold of it. "You have to be on your guard and quick on your feet. That's how quickly someone who isn't me can get to you." I relayed, knowing that in the future, she was going to be my responsibility.

"I can defend myself," Hera stated, stepping back from me.

"That I do not doubt about, especially when it comes to magic. But there's no magic allowed here. Remember?" I exhaled, realizing every moment we wasted standing here was time lost to getting ahead of the others, who I suspected hadn't yet arrived.

"Okay, but if you," a small beam of light caught our attention, and I pulled her to a small curve ahead before she could finish her sentence.

Khadijah, Ezri, Yemi, and Biola flashed in the same space we had been standing. Hera and I peeked through the opening of the maze ahead and watched as they gathered themselves and briefly scanned the space.

"It looks like we are the first, your highness," Ezri offered.

"We need to find the human. She's the weakest link, then Hera," Biola chimed in.

"That may not be true, according to rumors." Yemi shuffled, taking steps toward our direction. Hera leaned into me, her eyes widening. I motioned with my hand for her to stay quiet and keep her gaze ahead.

"Rumors?" Biola asked, kicking the direct beneath her feet. Yemi turned back, and the others gathered around Khadijah.

"There have been rumors of her and Quillian at The Den. People swore she slaughtered a dozen vampires last night," Ezri said.

"Tallen mentioned it earlier today, but I paid no heed..." Khadijah trailed off, her hand now resting against her chin, in deep thought.

"I find it hard to believe the human is capable of that. Have you seen her? She's practically bite-size," Biola offered, and I fought down the need to laugh. It was one thing being underestimated by men, but by women, it left a certain sting. "Anyone that goes there is either heavily intoxicated or dealing in some questionable trade. Their words should not be trusted," Biola continued, shaking her head as if the thought was unfathomable.

"I don't have time for the long chatter. I don't have time for baseless rumors about the weak human that the vampire overlord now calls a wife," Khadijah shouted, drawing on all their attention.

"Your highness..." Ezri motioned for the others to station themselves around Khadijah. "We need to be aware of our enemy's strengths and weakness; it's the only way we will win all three trials."

Khadijah heaved a frustrated sigh, bit her lip, and nodded in resignation. "Where do you think the others are now? "Khadijah asked.

My head turned back, noting the long path ahead, and I tugged at Hera, my hand pressed on my mouth to warn her to stay quiet. I had seen and heard enough to anticipate their next move.

Hera nodded and silently followed behind, her hands clasped around her dagger.

"What do you know about this place?" I asked after we had walked for a while, and I was convinced we were a steady distance from Khadija and her followers. "Everything looks the same, and nothing seems to be changing?"

Hera studied the path ahead and turned to face me. "This island was once the home of gargoyles," she said, a crease forming on her forehead.

"Gargoyles?" I asked, wiping the sweat that now beaded my forehead. "What do you know about them? It could give us a clue about how the hell to get out of here?"

"They are territorial creatures of the night. There haven't been sightings of them for decades..." Hera's train of thought trailed with each step.

"But?"

"I was always told this land was created by them. Wouldn't the island disappear if they've become extinct?" I ran my hands through my hair, weight the weight of her words.

"Let's say they aren't extinct. Then we should expect them to show up by the time the sun goes down.?"

"Yes."

"Then we better be out of here within the next six hours, or we are bound to be dinner for a group of gargoyles, I suspect five to six hours." I continued ahead, my hands clasped around the weapons on my waist.

"We also need to find the replicas of the gnet," Hera added, a hint of uncertainty in her voice. More drones began to gather around us, and as I looked up at the sky and considered the probable length of the cave, the possibility of waking gargoyles coupled with finding the gnet, I estimated we were not going to be leaving here tonight.

After a few hours of struggling through the heat and the constant circles we had been walking around the maze, it came as no surprise when both our steps began to falter, and our movements became slower.

"A cocktail would be so good right now," Hera grumbled. "Scratch that; I'll settle for water."

I turned to face her as a thought registered in my head. "You genius. There must be water here, something that's keeping all this greenery fresh?"

"Magic?"

"And wouldn't the magic have created a green life to accompany it?"

"You think somewhere in here is another forest space with water?" I nodded, turning back, and noting the curves at the end of the pathways we had passed through the last few hours.

"Come." "One that's keeping this whole system running, for sure." My steps faltered, my eyes locked on the upcoming curve of the maze. I ran back ahead, needing to confirm if the pathway ahead followed the same pattern.

"They are here!" India called aloud, making Hera and I halt in our pursuit.

"Hera girl, there you are. So glad to see you." Adelaide chimed as she drew close to her sister. A tight-lipped smile curled her lips.

"Meraki, meet Twiddle Dee and Twiddle Dum," Hera announced, making no guise of the fact she evidently hated the sight of these two.

"Twiddle Dum? Watch who you're talking to, you murderer," India shouted, stepping forward.

"Witches do not kill their own," Adelaide echoed, my hands clasped tightly around the dagger on my waist.

"Murderer?" Hera repeated the word taking two steps forward.

"Like your...." Hera shot forward and lunged for Adelaide before she finished her sentence.

"And I thought high school girls were bad," I muttered, turning my attention to India, wanting to ensure she didn't attack Hera.

"This fight has nothing to do with you, human," She hissed as she drew a dagger in the direction of Hera. I jumped forward and kicked the weapon in the opposite direction before it could reach.

"Technically, it is. Any attack against her is one against me,"' I replied, falling back to my feet before her.

Behind me, Adelaide and Hera fought back and forth with blades in their hands. India stepped back, her attention wavering between her sister and me behind.

"India! Now," Adelaide shouted, and she raised a dagger, aiming it at Hera's back.

"Lean back, Hera," I called out, realizing I wasn't going to be able to stop the weapon. I threw one of my daggers at it, and the daggers collided, missing Hera's cheek by a few inches.

India ran toward her side, and I moved to Hera.

"How dare you!" India spat, reaching for her dagger a few feet from her. Adelaide exchanged a knowing look with her sister, and India grew quiet; a smirk formed across her lip. India's attention fell on her sister's powdered hand clapped on a small pouch to her right.

"Hera?" unease settled within me. I called to my left, to no response. India and Adelaide ran off, their laughter immediately echoing behind them.

"Hera?" I turned, watching as her eyes dilated and her breathing hitched.

"I can't feel my body" she stopped, her eyes darting back and forth with panic, while her body remained immobile.

"So much for no magic?" I shouted at the small drone that had now appeared from nowhere. "Do you know what they used?" I asked; her eyes widened. "Is there a way to fix it?" I continued, hoping that though she was unable to speak, she could communicate with her using her eyes. Hera blinked serval times in confirmation.

"Okay, it can be fixed with another spell?" I asked, and Hera's eyes remained locked on me with no movement. "Give me something here, Hera." I reached for her falling body as she struggled to remain upright. "Does the spell need time?" I pressed, and she blinked several times to confirm.

"Now we are getting somewhere. How long?" I asked, realizing that perhaps it wasn't the question that should have been communicated to someone unable to speak. "Two hours?" I paced my hand against her chest, thinking of how I was going to carry her through the maze.

"Four hours?" I continued, and Hera blinked several times, confirming my greatest fear.

Yeah, we were screwed.

Hera stared at me with heavy-lidded eyes; even within words, I could see the palpable fear reflected through them. "I'm not going to leave you here for the vultures," I made a feeble attempt at smiling to calm her down.

Slowly I lowered her body to the floor. "Stay here then," I started, laughing at the absurdity of my words. Hera deadpanned, clearly unimpressed.

"I need to find something to help carry you," I relayed, running back to the curve we had passed a few minutes prior and the alloy rods I had noted out of the blue.

I squinted, looking up at the angling of the sun, and my eyes fell on the watch on my hand that stated it was just after four.

I sighed, picked up the six moderately sized alloys, and dragged them to where Hera laid, praying no one else showed up out of the blue.

"Okay, I'm back," I mumbled as I reached her. Hera's pupils dilated, and streaks of tears fell down her cheeks. "Us chicks have to stick together; there's no way I'm leaving you here," I said, hoping my words would bring her some relief. I knew what it was like to feel powerless, and it wasn't something I wished on my worst enemy.

"Those two sisters seem to have a boner for you," I commented, reaching for the pouch she had wrapped across her chest. Hera blinked twice, and I laughed, grateful she still had a sense of humor at a time like this.

Reaching for the elongated branches of the shrubs before her, I fastened them around the alloys while using her stringed pouch to bind the metal together. I ran my hands through my forehead as sweat beaded my forehead and soaked my clothes.

The last thing we needed was to draw attention to ourselves. I took my time, wrapping the branches at key points on the metal, wanting to ensure when I dragged it didn't create a scraping sound. I used the remainder of strings to fasten at the top of the vertically lined metal and covered it with some displaced branches for longevity.

My mind warred with the responsibility of the task, knowing that Hera's predicament had slowed down our pace compared to the others. It also meant if the others caught up to us, it would leave us both at a disadvantage and make us easy targets for an attack.

I tugged at the placement and made a feeble attempt to pull and tug to ensure it was stable. "We might have to stop later for any branches and roots to tighten any loose parts." "I think I'm done," I said, watching Hera's eyes move with every movement.

I placed the placement closer to her body and rolled her body unto it. I then reached for more branches, fastening them around her waist to keep her from falling.

"Fingers crossed, we don't bump into someone with a boner for me," I mumbled as I pulled on the strings and dragged Hera's body forward.

After three hours, my back ached from the strain of it all. I had gone through the maze in what seemed like a never-ending circle and curve, with no gnet or sign of the green forest space with water Hera and I had guessed earlier.

The only consistent clue I had noted in our hours of traveling through the maze was that the edge of each turn curved, and the accompanying shrubs pointed eastward. Hera and I were still trying to decipher what that meant.

The sun had begun to set, and with each growing hour, I was becoming desperate to unravel the hidden answers in this maze; otherwise, the other contestants were the least of our worries.

Incoming footsteps from a distance caught my attention. "Look what we have here." Ezri's voice boomed as I turned back. With Biola beside her, they thrust forward, yet Khadijah and Yemi were nowhere in sight.

I dropped the placement and ran ahead, wanting to create a sizeable distance between them and Hera's body. Before I could do so, Ezri jumped midair, her feet landed on my chest, and my body flew to the far end of the open space.

"Well, that wasn't nice," I winced from the shock of the impact. Ezri and Biola laughed derisively, as they walked toward me.

"Oh, look what we have here?" Biola spoke, her attention turning to the placement with Hera. I jumped to my feet and reached for the stake around my waist. I threw the dagger at Biola, and it scrapped her hand, halting her before she reached Hera. From a distance, I could see Hera's enlarged eyes and feel the wave of helplessness radiating from her.

The dagger fell, leaving a small scratch on her right hand. "You will regret that," she snarled, turning her full attention to me.

"Shame isn't part of my everyday life experiences," I rebutted, reaching for two other daggers. I took several steps back, knowing they would follow. Biola edged toward me first and smiled drearily.

"Why don't you lower your weapons" she whispered sultrily, and goosebumps burst across my skin, a sure sign that they were using succubus allure to pull me in.

"Yes!" Ezri chimed beside her, her pupils dilated.

Deception is the surest way to lure any job.

Alessia's words echoed in my head, and I instinctively lowered my weapon, creating the illusion that I was under the allure of their power. The same power that was forbidden from being used during the tournament.

I was starting to realize the rules were simply a formality for this tournament because no one seemed to adhere to the rules. And whenever they did, there were no drones within the distance to capture it.

Ezri and Biola shared conspiring looks, and I continued to lower my hands yet tightened my grip on the weapons.

Hera moaned behind me, drawing their attention. I shook my head in warning, hoping she would pick up on the clue as her eyes locked with mine.

"Where's her royal highness?" I asked, drawing their attention back to me. "You two are out here doing her dirty work?" I smiled, knowing my words somehow irked them.

Biola stepped forward first, and I pounced, running into her but ensuring the dagger's blade slid through her chest. She howled, clutching her chest, as she stepped back.

"You bitch!"

"Thanks for the compliment, demon," I answered, catching sight of Ezri's to my right.

"You will pay for that."

"What? will you use your powers on me again?" I pointed to the drone above us.

"Get her!" Biola shouted as they both zoned in on me at the same time. More drones appeared above us. Ezri released her claws, which scrapped through my attire fabric, leaving their prints behind. Biola followed the same move; anticipating it, I lowered my body to dodge her blow.

I threw the other dagger in my hand, aiming it at Ezri's lower leg. Stepped back in time to miss the weapon by a few inches

I stepped back, and they both followed, predatory gleams in their footsteps. "It's time you be reminded of your place," Ezri spoke.

"My place?" I asked, keeping the condescension from my voice. My hands clasped around the hunga munga concealed on the side of my hip.

"Your kind is good for fucking, using, and luring for games, nothing else," Biola spat.

"And your kind?" I arched a brow, my fingertips stroking the outline of the weapon.

"What did you say?" Ezri continued trailing my steps.

"You can't both be that stupid-" I stopped as they both rose into the air, and thick leathery wings flapped against the darkening landscape. With synchronized movements, they lunged for me, Ezri ahead and Biola moving behind me. I pulled out the hunga munga to ensure I dodged each blow by lowering my body.

I twisted the weapon's body around my hand and swung it outwardly as it made contact with Ezri and Biola's wings. They both screamed in turn, ascending into the air. The weapon rolled back, and I jumped up, clasping it back in my hand.

Ezri descended first, and her feet landed on my shoulder blade, making me stagger to the floor, and the weapon fell to my far right. She instinctively flew toward it, and I rolled my body to the right reaching for it just before she did.

This time, I aimed the weapon at the juncture of her wings, knowing it would be enough to paralyze her flight and slow her down. The weapon landed with a thud, and she flew back and landed a few feet away with a thump.

Ezri groaned aloud, and Biola, whose attention was trained on Hera, ran to her. I edged toward Hera, looking for any sign of injury. Hera moaned, her eyes darting forward to where Biola was.

Biola threw a dagger in our direction before lowering herself to pick up Ezri's bleeding body. The dagger came at us with full speed, and I ran forward, throwing the hunga munga at the dagger, thwarting the weapon to our left. As both weapons fell, the sound of incoming wind coupled with Hera's heightened whining caught my attention; before I had enough time to digest what was happening, the blade of a dagger I had missed locked onto my thighs.

I groaned, the impact making me fall back. Blood spilled, a heaviness fell over the lower half of my body, and unease settled in my chest.

"This isn't the end; you will pay for what you did," Biola shouted, wrapping herself around Ezri's body and ascending into the sky without a glance back.

"Fuck," I mumbled aloud, frustrated at the fact I had somehow missed the second weapon before it made an impact.

I staggered toward Hera, whose lower arms could now move,

but everything else remained immobile. Her eyes moved from my face to my thighs, and her brows creased at the sight.

I removed the overlay of my athletic wear and folded it beside me. I slowly removed the dagger from my thighs and proceeded to wrap the cloth around the wound to stop the bleeding. Hera's eyes remained on my face this time, an array of questions radiating from her expression.

My eyes turned upwards, noting how dark the sky had become. When I looked at my watch and saw it was seven in the evening, unease settled within me.

"We are going to be gargoyle food soon," I muttered, staggering to my feet. I stepped forward and pulled on the placement, my pace slower now than it was before.

I continued for another hour until the darkness began making it hard to see anything.

I pulled the placement further down until I reached another curve and stopped. I placed the placement down and stepped back, assessing the area while trying to piece together what I knew so far. What was I missing?

The sound of shuffling caught my attention, and I reached for my dagger, anticipating another attack but unable to spot anyone around us.

Hera moaned aloud, drawing my attention to the moving branches from the shrub that were now tightening around the lower half of her body.

Using the dagger, I cut through them as Hera fought through them with her hand. Her voice came out in low silent whispers, and I knew it was only a matter of time before she would have control over her body and voice again.

"Go to Esneoh, they said. It would be fun; they said," I laughed awkwardly, trying to make light of the severity of the situation.

I pulled Hera's body from the placement as I cut through the branches that kept growing each time, I cut one down. "Lean on me," I instructed, noting that she had movement now on the lower half of her body.

A series of drones hovered over us, and I released a series of curses at their fucked-up timing. Wrapping Hera's hands around my neck, I stepped forward, finding myself unable to do so. A long branch fastened around my right leg and tightened its grip with each passing second. I cut through it with another dagger around my waist.

Hera groaned as I dragged the weight of her body ahead with me. I stopped again a few feet away, watching the curve of the turning. My eyes fell to a right shrub, which remained motionless, unlike the rest that moved and seemed to come alive. Understanding finally dawned on me, and I moved to the right.

Blood sipped through the fabric of my pants, trailing the floor. Each move weighed against my leg and body, but I refused to stop. This was a matter of life and death; dying like this wasn't how I planned to go out.

I wrapped my hands around Hera's waist and continued ahead, praying my instincts were correct.

Heat pulsed through my skin, and the branches scraped against it, leaving blisters in their wake. I continued forward as the weight of my body grew tired and rigid with each step. When I reached the maze on the right, I closed my eyes and walked into it, unsure of what to expect.

The branches slowly separated, making way for Hera and me. My heart pulsed in my chest as the sound of chirping birds and the subtle sound of water crashing against rock caught my attention.

I continued pressing ahead, ignoring the twigs that slapped against my skin with each movement. "Almost there" I strained ahead, unsure whether I was trying to soothe Hera or myself.

The further I pressed the branches, the more they gave way until everything behind me receded, and only the sight of a large open field beside a stream ahead could be seen. I stepped through the final branches, and my vision began to sway. My hold on Hera loosened, and heat flushed my skin as a deep burning from where the dagger had stabbed me earlier made me whine aloud.

"Meraki?" Hera's voice echoed through my haze from a distance. Everything around me began to spin, and I fell face down to the ground.

No, I can't die. Not now, not like this.

28

ISLAND EXPLOITS

Meraki

"Stay still... You're okay." Hera's voice filtered through the haze of my thoughts as I struggled against the weight of her hand pressed against my body.

I slowly opened my eyes and jerked back, instinctively reaching for my dagger. "Hey, relax, it's just me," she spoke, her hand resting against my thighs.

"My....my..." I stumbled on my words, staring down at my swollen leg and the trail of dried blood encompassing it.

"Yeah, that bitch used some sort of poisoned dagger to stab you. It seemed to have slipped into your system," she stated, cautiously reaching for my leg again.

"Am I okay?" I asked, scanning the empty, run-down shed we were in. "And where the hell are we?"

"Your predictions were correct," Hera replied, moving her hand to collect a string of carefully plucked leaves and a series of leaves I had never seen before. I played my dagger against the pouch on my waist and rested both hands on the floor.

"It seems like this forest, and the surrounding water give the maze life?" Hera placed the leaves in her mouth and chewed. She spat the content out into the palm of her hand and stared headlong at me.

"What are you doing?"

"Healing you."

"Now, you sound like a man. Your spit is not a healing palm." A tight smile tugged at the corner of her lips.

"With magic." She reached into her pouch, removing a single dried basil leaf.

"With magic? Isn't it forbidden?" I attempted to move my feet but found my right leg frozen.

"There's always a loophole around magic. We can't use our powers against each other. I'm using it to heal you instead." She stated, and a drone appeared out of nowhere, hovering above us.

"Those assholes are cheating." I spat, wincing when Hera's cold hands touched the warmth of my skin. "If I Knew the laws were up for interpretation, I would have planned better for the tournament."

"I'm surprised Quillian didn't encourage you to..."

"Perhaps he has too much trust in my abilities?" I motioned to the state of the lower part of my body. Hera shook her head, and amusement filled her features.

"Are you not in pain?"

"Of course?" I lied, not wanting to get into the specifics of it. Hera snickered, evidently not swayed by my answer.

"You're a bad liar."

"Isn't there some hygiene rules around wounds... and saliva?" I said, steering the conversation in another direction.

"True, but human laws don't apply to magic," she laughed, mumbling a series of incoherent words under her breath. The saliva paste in her hand glimmered for a few seconds. "Though my sister would have to disagree with you. My spit does have healing properties," she smiled and placed the paste on my thighs.

"That's what they all say," I chimed. The paste was cool to the touch, and with each passing second, the heat emanating from the wound pulsed with relief.

"Thank you," Hera said, spreading the mixture around the open wound.

"For?"

"Saving my ass."

"We made a deal." I shrugged, questions about Brielle sitting on the tip of my tongue.

"A deal you could have relented on. Especially when you had to drag my heavy ass across that damn maze, I wouldn't have even faulted you. Carrying me wasn't part of the deal," she added, followed by a series of whispered incantations. With each utterance, the stiffness in my leg began to wane until I could feel my leg again.

"I fulfill my promises." Hera raised her head; her brow arched mockingly. It wasn't too long ago I was indirectly asking her for a way out of the oath with Quillian.

"Sometimes?" I laughed. "When it doesn't involve a vampire that might break my neck once he gets what he wants from me."

"That, I can't argue with." She corked her head, then slowly removed the paste on my thighs. "You're good as new," she added, as only freshly healed skin could be seen from where the wound had been earlier.

"I told you, my spit is gold," she mocked, running her hands over the healed area. I stretched my leg, needing movement on it from all the pins and needles. I slowly rose to my feet, shaking the cramp in my body.

"If we are here, then I'm to assume the others found out about this place." Hera nodded, following my movements. "Then we can't stay indoors. It will leave us weak to attack, and I suspect those cheating bastards won't rest until you and I are out of the equation." I headed for the door of the shed.

The night sky filled the horizon, illuminating the forest in hues of green and turquoise. Fireflies danced over its horizons, and the subtle hum and chirps of the creatures woven with the place acted as a soothing melody in the backdrop, bringing everything to life.

"Wow. Minus the plants attacking us, I would say this place is beautiful," I commented, passing through the beaten path created by rocks outside the shed.

Hera followed beside me. "This place is like a witches' haven," she remarked, running her hands through the large body of trees and plants we walked past.

"Food is always a good idea?" Hera laughed, and I nodded, running my hands through my stomach. My stomach rumbled, and Hera's followed, a reminder that neither of us had eaten nor drank water since this morning.

"A bath is also a good idea," I stated in passing, scanning the horizon for where we could both rest, find food, and get cleaned up.

A large upside-down tree beside a stream drew my attention from ahead.

"We sleep there," I pointed to the opposite side of the tree. "It would be easier to see any attack from all directions. We can share guard duty, so we both get to sleep?" I commented, fixing my attention from the north, east, west, and south.

We walked toward our chosen shelter, which comprised of a series of adjoining upside-down trees. Hera placed the remnants of her pouch down, pulling out a dagger in the process.

"I'm going to see if I can find some food from the stream."

"I'll scan the area and find trunks we can use to heat the food. I'll also keep my eyes out for anything edible," I replied, heading in two opposing directions.

I followed the footpath ahead of me and took inventory of everything within the distance to be prepared for any unexpected attacks.

Green pastures went on for miles, encompassed by the never

stream. As the area was a large open field, Hera and I would have to be cautious and ensure we remained covered by the trees not to be spotted.

I continued ahead while running my hands through the plants in my path and feeling inspired for my next acrylic piece when I returned to Jersey Hill.

After almost thirty minutes of walking around in a circle and noting that the field broke into four paths further down, I returned to Hera, picking up a dozen branches for the fire.

Along the way back, I came across some mangoes, dug up some potatoes, and found what I assumed was spinach. When I arrived, I found Hera waiting with two large snappers in hand and her whole attire soaked.

"Don't ask." She shook her head. "Let's just say I tried using magic to catch these bad boys, and It didn't go down so well."

"Please tell me the drones caught it?" I laughed.

"Unfortunately, I'll be a laughingstock right now. Those hell-bent things are never around when they should be. They love popping up at the most inconvenient times."

"This should make up for it?" We set up camp by creating a low fire, skinning the fish with our daggers, and roasting skinned potatoes atop the fire. I pushed the items in my hands forward, and Hera squealed with delight.

Using the branches, Hera was able to create a holding rod over the fire so that the fish could cook without either of us having to hold on to it for a prolonged period.

Once everything was almost ready, I stripped myself bare and headed for the stream, picking up some wild elderberries, which Hera had turned into soap with her magic.

I washed the blood from my clothes and swam in the stream, cleansing my body from the remnants of the blood that remained and the sweat that clung to my pores.

Once I was done, I walked back to where we had set camp with my freshly cleaned clothes in hand. "You should get cleaned up; I'll watch over this in the meantime," I point my chin to the food while looming over her. Hera stares at me dumbfounded.

"Erm...Can you put on clothes?" She shuffled uncomfortably. I shrugged.

"My clothes are wet?" I pointed at the fabrics in my hand. I searched the tree before us, thinking of the best spot to hang it so it would dry before dawn.

"Are you into some exhibitionist stuff?" she asked, her skin heating up at the words.

"Stop being a prude; I'm sure you've seen women naked before." I raised my hand, dismissing her.

"Yeah, my sister."

"Then, pretend I'm your sister," I snorted, settling down before the fire. "Or dry those with magic?" I pointed at the clothes that now hung on the tree behind us. Hera wasted no time raising her hand and chanting over the materials. She handed the items immediately after.

"I grew up in an orphanage, and this was a common occurrence. Sometimes I forget not everyone is as comfortable with nudity," I replied, cutting the lower half of the pants.

"Oh," Her eyes widened at my revelation. Her attention immediately turned to the drone over us. "They don't record audio," she pointed out, sensing my unease.

"Stop staring, Hera," I joked, getting into my underwear. She awkwardly retracted behind me, then stopped.

"Thank you for sharing that with me," she whispered, her voice filled with emotion. My heart ached to recount her words in my head. "People here showing kindness or even uttered more than a few words to me is...rare" She fumbled and quickly walked to the stream ahead.

I watched her from a distance, recalling how similar she and Iris were when we first became friends. The kids at the orphanage at the time had picked on her continuously until she had lost her voice in the midst of it all.

After I had got into fights and beat some of them to the pulp, the bullying eased, and over time we found out that Iris wasn't mute; the bullying and her environment just wore her down.

I dressed and moved close to the flames moving the potatoes around to ensure they cooked on all sides. I hung the spinach atop the fish and fanned the flames with a large leaf.

Hera spent time in the stream getting cleaned up and washing her clothes. By the time she came back, the flames had died, and the food had cooked and cooled down.

And as she hurried and dressed, I caught a quick glimpse of the dented scars behind her back, as if she had been whipped with something heavy for long periods.

"What happened to your back?" I asked when she approached, making no effort to hide the fact I had seen it.

"Ermm, what mark?" She shuffled awkwardly.

"Did those twins do that to you? The ones on your back?" I pointed at her, rage bubbling in my chest at the thought someone had done that to her.

"I fell into something." She dismissed me, perching on the opposite end of the food.

"You fell into a whip?" I ran my hands through my hair, wondering why the hell I was so worked up over the welfare of a stranger.

"Not all of us are fighters like you, Meraki..." Her voice trailed.

"If it wasn't the twins, then your coven?" I stated it plainly, after weighing the options in my head. Hera's eyes dilated, and I realized that as much as a facade she put on, there was a twinge of fear when it came to her coven.

"I-I-I"

"Why would they do that?" I found myself shouting.

"It's nothing for you to concern yourself with; I can protect myself. They know not to mess with me now." She motioned for me to sit. She separated the fish on the two large leaves before us and followed suit with the potatoes and spinach.

"They call me half-blood," she finally answered after some

time. The fear I had seen in her eyes earlier had now been replaced by the boldness I had seen when she had interacted with Quillian.

"My sister and I have different magic than the rest," she started, and silence lingered between us. Using her hands, she broke the fish and potatoes and said nothing else, letting me know this was all she could offer at this point. I subconsciously made a note in my head to ensure I inflicted the same scar on India and Adelaide to avenge whatever the hell had happened to her.

"So, you need this win as much as I do then," I commented, the reason for her secret alliance with Quillian and his siblings now becoming clearer. This was beyond the scope of ensuring her sister was no longer exiled. It was about punishing the people that had exacted pain on her. And that I could respect.

Hera made no effort to respond but instead ate her food in companionable silence. A challenging feat to achieve, especially when most people find prolonged silence equated to awkwardness. Hera wasn't like that; like me, the silence served as a time of reflection and inner dialogue.

"What's it like growing up as an orphan in the human realm?" she finally spoke after some time had passed.

I lifted potatoes from before and, using the blade of my dagger, peeled back the roasted skin.

"I had my sister, so I didn't feel like I was alone or missing anything...for a while," I answered earnestly, unsure why I felt comfortable opening myself to her. I bit into the fish and potatoes and groaned aloud at the unexpected flavors. Having a witch on your side has its perks; this would have been a dry, stale, and unseasoned meal without her magic.

"And when she died, it was lonely... I went into a dark place. Until..." I bite my tongue, contemplating how best to go around the issue of the Alokari. "Stealing artifacts was how I fended for myself and found a new family," I added, sprinkling the lie of my current predicament with the actual truth.

"What about you and your sister in Aldrata? Where did the human part of your ancestry come from?"

"When the Nephilim reigned, many of the other beings intermingled with humans, and so did our people. Me and my sister's bloodline was one of the oldest surviving ones of that intermix."

"Okay..." I nodded attentively and continued to eat my food slowly.

"We lived with our human dad until his death. After, my sister and I continued to live in the human realm. It was all we knew. Esneoh was a far-away story my mom had passed down to my dad. We moved across countries and continents for a long while, keeping our heads low from drawing unwarranted attention to ourselves. It's pretty hard to escape the fact that aging doesn't come naturally to us. What takes humans a few years takes us decades."

"What happened?" Hera raised her hand, and two wooden cups appeared filled with water. She placed one before me and reached for the other.

"The coven happened. We accidentally bumped into someone from there, and they instinctively knew what we were. At the time, it seemed like it was a blessing, a chance at a family. Hera wasn't so trusting. But I insisted we come to Esneoh, check it out." She sipped on her water. "And they loved bombed us. Boy, did they love to bomb us? It was too late when we realized all wasn't what it seemed. And Hera being who she is, began to speak against Valeria."

"Why didn't you just leave?" I offered, chewing on the final pieces of my food. Hera raised her head and watched me as if I had asked the stupidest question.

"Because once you cross into Esneoh, you are tied to the land."

"Tied?"

"It becomes part of you; it lives in you," she stated cautiously. Unease settled within me, and my heart leaped in my chest as the weight of her words dawned on me.

"What does that mean?"

"It means the land recognizes you as its own. You can only leave if one of the leaders grants you domain."

"I don't understand," I stated, my hand raised, beckoning her to slow down with the information overload.

"It means you can go in and out as you please, but you can only be away for a set time. A week at best before your body fights against itself. Inevitably, if you refuse its call, you'll die," she answered, this time her words slow as if giving me time to savor the truth behind it. "Only the ruling houses can do so."

I rose to my feet and began to bite my lip thinking about what this could mean for me. Even if I broke the bond with Quillian, I was still bound to Esneoh. "Fuck." I ran my hands through my hair, realizing now recounting Quillian words about belonging to him.

"I take it you didn't know then," Hera commented, placing dirt over the burned remains of our fire. "Don't worry about it. That won't be a problem; he has enough enemies who would be more than willing to grant you that to spite him."

I slowed down my movements and weighed my options in my head. Hera was right; when the time came, I knew without a doubt I could get Loki, Valeria, or even Thale to release. They would be more than willing to do so to simply spite Quillian. So, why does even contemplating that idea make me queasy?

"We need to find the gnet replicas tomorrow," I said, not wanting to yet think that far. I needed to keep my mind clear and focused on the now. "Some may be placed some on this side?" Hera offered.

"And others close to the exit of the maze," I added. "We will have to be awake early to be a step ahead of the others in searching for the gnet first." Hera yawned, perching her body beside the large roots of the tree.

"Rest; I'll take the first watch," I offered, moving to stand beside the largest of the baobab tree a few feet from where Hera lay.

"It's time," Hera yawned, looming over me at a steady

distance. I slowly rose to my feet, more exhausted than I had been before I fell asleep.

"Anything out of the ordinary?" Hera shook her head, curling herself in the same position I had been in.

"I suspect India and Adelaide are close, though; I was able to pick up on the excess use of their magic from a distance," she noted, staring up at me.

"If Twiddle Dee and Twiddle Dum show up, I'll be sure to wake you up," I commented, walking in the direction she had stood guard. I leaned against the baobab tree, my thoughts briefly falling on Quillian, my impending attachment, and the guilt that followed my actions. Within minutes Hera fell asleep, and the soft hum of her snoring was heard from the distance.

When I got to Esneoh, I had anticipated my time here would be quick, and navigating around it to find my sisters would be brief and swift. I did not expect to fall under the Kingsley and find that I was drawn to them in some inexplicable way. I shook my head, knowing the direction my head was going would only lead to heartache and disappointment.

People like me did not believe in happily ever after's or even the possibility of being settled down with one person for a long period. People were liabilities to an assassin. We thrived on death and the thrill of a kill, which involved being in a relationship with the Alokari full-time.

I rose to my feet after some time had passed, taking a quick scout and inventory of the surrounding areas. Something flickered in the stream ahead and caught my attention. I walked toward it, ensuring my eyes and ears were focused on anything out of the ordinary.

I stared down at the clear water and the glimpses of fish and various other creatures I had never seen before. Perched on the mouth of a Devil's Hole Pupfish was a gnet. The metallic navy-blue fish with through the stream as its black finish and golden iridescence illuminated the gnet into a hue of colors.

I reached forward and stopped midtrack, remembering what

Hera had said earlier about struggling to fish in the stream. I searched my surroundings and settled on a twig a few feet away. Placing it on the top wing of the gnet I pulled it forward, separating the fish from it.

The fish continued ahead, not cognizant of what had just happened. Using the twig, I continued navigating through a series of other creatures until I found a more abandoned section that lacked any sea creatures.

A drone hovered over me as I lowered myself, reached for a lipstick container in my back pocket, and flung it forward. The container elongated into a midsize sword, and using its tip, I hooked the wins of the gnet and threw it into the air. The replica fell beside me; I rushed to it and palmed it, feeling the warmth of its heat against my fingertips.

I exhaled a sigh, grateful that one aspect of the tournament was fulfilled; my only goal now was ensuring we managed to get out before the others.

I corked my head, and my eyes fell on the outline of Hera's body. "Don't be stupid," I muttered aloud, running my hands through my head. I stared longingly at the gnet, hating myself for what I was about to do.

The drone flew over me and disappeared into the air. I scanned my surround and walked back to where Hera lay. Looming over her, I placed the object close to her head so it would be the first thing she saw when she woke up.

Attaining another gnet would be an easy feat for me in this tournament, but I knew without a doubt that Hera might not be so lucky without full use of her magic.

I stepped back, watching as she tossed in her sleep. After some hours had passed, she stretched her body and opened her eyes.

"Oh wow...oh wow," Hera screamed and jumped to her feet after a few hours had passed.

"What?" I turned around, already knowing what had caught her attention.

"It's a gnet." she raised the object into the air peering at it with awe. "Right here...how...," she spoke aloud as if trying to piece the object's trajectory together.

"Congrats. This makes today easier," I beamed.

"How?" she asked, her eyes assessing my every word and movement.

"All we have to do is find one more and manage to find our way out of the maze," I replied, ensuring my voice didn't give anything away. Hera stared at the object for a beat, then back at me with an unknowing spoken in the depth of her eyes.

"Meraki-"

"It's time we get going. The others may already be waking up with the same goal in mind." I turned toward the stream northward in the direction I had traveled last night to look for food. Hera rushed to her feet, placing the gnet in her bag.

"I have a feeling there might still be a gnet or two here," I commented as we made our way through the undefined path. After seeing the trajectory, the fish had traveled from last night, the thought had occurred to me that others may not have found it yet. I also couldn't explain that after holding the previous object, there was a knowingness that came with the tug of the others.

The further ahead we walked, the more the environment around us turned to shift. The plants and flowers surrounding us grew more distant until nothing but red soil and the branches of naked trees could be seen.

After walking what seemed like a few miles, a loud explosion followed by shouting caught our attention from a distance. Hera and I ran forward, catching sight of Esme and Sierra fighting against a monster formed from the red soiled ground. Sat on its head was the gnet, and with each strained attack, it refused to relinquish its hold over it.

"This is ours; don't even try it." Sierra dismissed us with the flicker of her hand.

"I don't think it works like that. First come, first serve, darling." Hera commented, flinging her dagger directly at the monster's head, but the weapon's impact did not impact the gnet.

The creatures still released a deafening howl, and within seconds two more of its kind rose from the ground.

"Smart," Esme commented, pinning her glare quickly at Hera. One of the creatures lunged for me, the other Hera.

"Whatever you do, avoid it," I called out to Hera as we both jumped in parallel directions. Three more creatures rose from the ground, flinging Esme across the threshold as they did so. A series of drones hovered over us, recording our current predicament.

The creature before me reached forward, and its body formed its outstretched hands. Running back, it took hold of my feet, pulled me to the floor, and dragged me toward its body. Reaching my dagger, I tried aiming for its hand, but the weapon seeped through the creature's body and fell to the other side.

"It's not affected by metal!" I shouted, unable to locate Hera. Esme and Sierra ran toward each other, tag teaming the monster with the gnet. The remainder of the monsters pounced on them, throwing them into the air in a chokehold.

"Erm, are you sure we want this particular gnet?" Hera spoke, the fear in her voice clear as the night sky.

"You ask this now?" I teased, keeping my evident discomfort at bay as the creatures continued to pull at me. I leaned forward, reaching for its hand, and was met with a solid form. At my touch, it released a loud wailing sound and pulled harder.

Panic pulsed through me, and a thought came to mind. My attention briefly turned to my surroundings and the lack of any life force. Keeping one hand on the creature, I reached for the stake on my right-hand side and threw it at the creature. The stake landed on its solid chest, and its hold on me released as it slowly disseminated into the air.

I pulled out the other to my left and threw it at the creature that now held Hera upside in the air. She fell on her ass as it disseminated.

"A warning next time?" she huffed, wincing loudly.

"Heads up?" I shouted, turning my attention to Esme and Sierra, who were now screaming their lungs out. "Wood seems to be their weak point," I commented as I collected my stake enroute to her.

Hera immediately ran back to the tree a few feet away. I stepped forward, drawing the attention of two of the creatures. They screeched and headed toward me like a whisp of mind. I threw both stakes simultaneously at their chest. The monster lowered itself from the incoming weapon to my right, while the one to the left immediately disseminated.

The remaining one screeched even louder, and the ground beneath us shook as the outline of more forms grew in prominence. Esme managed to free herself somewhere along its midst, and as she drew on the creature's attention, it released its hold on Sierra. "It's not worth it," Sierra called out with a choked sob, fighting her way through the creature's hold.

"Run," Sierra shouted once Esme was released. They headed in the opposite direction, paying no heed to me or Hera, who now headed toward me with four naked branches.

The forms of the creatures on the ground had not materialized but seemed to be connected with the two creatures before us, whose sole attention we now had.

"We have to be quick before whatever the hell that is they are calling wakes up," I pointed at the ten bumped ridges on the ground.

"You go for the one with the gnet; I'll go for the other," Hera said, handing me one of the branches, and ran forward. I did the same, picking up my daggers along the way. Before I could get close to the creature, it blew a gust of wind made from sand. The wind lifted me into the air and forced me to the floor.

The monster thrust forward and disseminated into the air before I could reach for my stake. "I'm not just good for carrying around," she teased, her hands reaching out to help me to my feet.

"Thanks for this!" Sierra said, riding on the body of a large red dragon and scooping down to pick up the gnet. Rage curled through me, and I grunted a series of curses out loud.

"Hey, that's cheating!" Hera called the body of the dragon a steady distance away from us.

"Remind me to slit both their throats when this is done," I gritted the words through my teeth, trying to remain in control. "What are you doing?" I asked, watching as she raised the palm of her hand into the air and drew circles around it with her thumb.

"Cheat," she stated simply. The discomfort in my chest began to ease, and I drew closer to her, watching as an orb appeared in her palm, giving us a glimpse of the island. "There's two left, closer to the maze's end."

"We need a quick way out of here."

"I got it," she mumbled, turning back in the direction we had come from. "There's a shrub midpoint here, and we can cross back over to the maze; the exit is closer there." The orb disappeared; she retracted her hand and began running ahead.

Like we entered, we pushed through the wall of the plants, feeling them pull and tug us backwards. As we pressed forward, the branches and roots released us, pushing us out into the familiarity of the maze again.

"It's close," I commented, running across the plains with Hera beside me.

"You can sense it?" I nodded hesitantly, knowing how absurd it sounded. Hera scrunched her face, seemingly digesting what I had just said.

We ran through a series of curves until we came to the end of the green shrubs to a similar gate to the one that had appeared before when we arrived on the island.

The gate opened, and I could see Khadijah's outline from a distance, followed by Ezri, Yemi, and Biola. Enzi's weight rested against Biola, who turned to glare at me before a mist covered them completely.

I took a step forward, and the ground beneath me shook, gave way to a large creature with the body of an enormous man, and a bull's head grew in stature. Its skin the shade of gingerbread, and the lower half of its body a midnight shade of black.

Rested on the top of each horn were the gnet replicas. A thunderous growl emitted from its chest, shaking the space around us.

"Holy fucking shit," I stammered, unable to comprehend how huge and ugly the creature was. Hera stood frozen beside me, her mouth agape. "Go through the gate before anyone else comes," I commanded, reaching for the lipstick case in my waist strap. Throwing it into the air, it stretched into a long sword, its blade glistening against the sun.

Hera hesitated, and I made no effort to turn back and face her. Once she passed that wall, my obligation to her and Brielle would have been fulfilled. Right now, ensuring she left with her gnet in one piece was more important than facing the creature before me. The creature raised one of its legs, and its impact knocked me back a few feet.

"We need to get the gnet from its head," Hera stated, coming up behind me and offering me a hand.

"Hera."

"You helped me, and I'm doing the same. We either argue about it or get this over with so we can leave this place. I don't know about you, but I'm, dying for an actual hot shower?"

"The shower part sounds good," I stated, turning my attention to the creature lunging toward us.

"I'll distract it while you retrieve the gnet," she shouted, running in the opposing direction. As the creature lunged for me, she chanted a spell aloud, and it fell to its knees, the impact creating a dent on the floor.

"Now!" I ran ahead and lunged into the air aiming my sword for its horns. Tilting my body to the left, I flipped the gnet upright and fell a few feet away with the object in my hand.

The creature released an ear-shattering wail, making my skin's hairs rise on end. "Run!" Hera exclaimed, and I saw her rushing toward the gate from the periphery of my eyes. Amma appeared from the depths of the maze without warning and jumped on the creature to take hold of the other gnet on its head.

With the gnet tightly grasped around my palm, I ran forward, the ground around me giving way with each step. "Fly faster!" I heard Althea's voice from behind me. When I looked up, I saw her straddled on Esme's dragon form with Sierra beside her.

I threw my sword overhead, aiming for the dragon's stomach to deter them from getting ahead. The dragon released a yowl, catching the attention of the creature.

I turned back around and continued running, noting that Hera had reached the outskirts of the gate but stood waiting for me. Something within my heart warmed at the idea. I had made a lot of assumptions about what people in Esneoh would be like, Hera was one of the best surprises to come from it.

"No, you don't," Amma screamed, hurling herself beside me. "You're not going to steal this away from me too." Her claws elongated and she tore at the skin on my calf in order to hold me back. I ignored the burn that followed and kept my focus ahead the threshold. With the final bout of strength, I had left, I jumped foreword, leaving her a few inches behind me.

Once I crossed the threshold of the gate, Hera followed behind me, and everything behind me disappeared. White flashes of lights blinded me, and loud deafening shouts and cheers echoed all around me until I found myself standing beside Hera, back in the announcement room.

Ahead, the leaders stood peering down at us, on the stage. The screen above them enlarged our images.

Khadijah - First

Meraki - Second

Hera - Third.

Amma – Fourth

Althea - Fifth

Quillian blurred before me, his face beaming with pride. My heart somersaulted in my chest at the sight. I knew then I was screwed, I was falling for my captor. This was some A-grade Stockholm syndrome type shit, but then again Beauty and the Beast had always been my favorite fairy tale.

29

RINGS

Meraki

"YOU DID GOOD YESTERDAY, LITTLE HELLION," Quillian whispered against my neck, as he pulled me against his chest. His hands tugged at the bed sheets, wrapping them around us like armor.

"That better be your phone?" I yawned and mumbled lazily. My eyes jolted, my muscles tightened, and my body froze at the realization we were in his bed together.

I slid from his hold and rushed to create space between us. Quillian growled and mumbled under his breath as he pulled me back into him, this time ensuring his hands wrapped around my waist and chest, immobilizing me altogether. I winced at his pull, my body sore from exerting so much energy from the last few days.

"Quillian," I grunted, unsure what exactly I was asking him for. "This feels-"

"What?" he turned my body around to face him, his gray eyes

searching, scrutinizing, and looking for something I wasn't sure of. "It feels like what?"

"Intimate" I relayed, punctuating each syllable as a reminder of what we had agreed on.

"Me fucking you on the roof. That isn't personal? Me taking you over the bodies of my dead men. That isn't personal? Me fucking you in my bed, while you screamed my name, wasn't personal? But this? Holding you, this is personal?" he asked, his thick masculine hands running steady strokes around my eyes, nose, chin, and lips.

My heart pulsated against my chest and my mouth grew dry acknowledging the truth in his words. But...this felt different.

"That was sex... it's different," I stumbled unable to find the right words.

"Huh? Continue," he muttered allowing his hands to trail the outline of my lips.

"...Its release. Its relief." the words failed me as his other hands lowered down to my breast pinching and squeezing my nipples through the cotton shirt.

"I-I...Can't think when you're doing that," I breathed opening and closing my eyes, my body heating at his ministration.

"This is personal," he lowered his head and sucked each nipple through the shirt.

"Quillian," I warned, moving closer. He laughed, his hands moving from my stomach to my thighs.

"I like when you say my name." he lifted the covers, spread my legs, and lowered his shirtless body in between my legs.

"Vampire?" I smiled, knowing I should put an end to this, but my wretched body wanted something else. I worked hard in the trial, I deserved this.

A small part of my brain relished this, his scent, the warmth of his body, the deep bass in his baritone voice. The other screamed in retaliation warning me to not get carried away like Darya warned, though I questioned whether that was already too late.

He stopped midmovement and pulled my body flat against

the bed, lowering me closer to his hold. "What are you thinking?" He stared down at me as if my next few words were gold.

"This is just sex right, some fun in the sheets with your pretend wife?" I voiced my heart stammering in my chest. Quillian's face tightened and irritation skirted through his tightened features. "You said-"

"I don't need a reminder of what I said," he replied, towering over me with one hand plastered on my exposed stomach, the other on my raised leg resting against his chest. "I just want to taste you, make you feel good. I can sense how tired, your body is," he confessed his eyes piercing and unrelenting.

My heart elevated at the considerate act, a far cry from the vampire I initially met. Yet another part of me felt a pang of disappointment, one I had no right to. I was leaving here tomorrow and reporting back to the Alokari everything that I had found out. I was going to report on his weakness, one that could have consequences for his family. The same family, I was growing fond of.

And right now, all I needed was something, a reason, something, anything to hold me back. He offered me no time to question his motive, he moved in and kissed me. I squirmed, as he wrapped my legs around his waist, the sheer size and height of him blocking everything within view.

I kissed him back, throwing my guilt along with it. I couldn't change what happened later, but I could be here, present, and enjoy this moment. He lifted my shirt, and cupped my breast with both hands, his lips never leaving mine.

"What are you doing to me?" He muttered, and I couldn't make sense of it. His lips ascended down my body, halting briefly at the scar left behind by the gun wound. He continued down my leg and halted. Rising he peered down at the inside of my thighs with a deep ferocity.

"What are these scars?" He gritted the words as if holding himself back. "This," he pointed at the one inside my thighs, and I winced. "This, he continued to the right side of my abdomen.

"Nothing!" I jerked back, feeling raw, and exposed, emotions I prided myself on not ever carrying.

"No!" His voice boomed, and the full weight of his power rested against my chest.

"This was a job, I got shot," I answered, knowing he wasn't going to let this go until he had an answer. He stared at me, long and hard, a series of emotions passing through his face.

"And this?" he pressed, his intent more on my thighs than the gun scarring.

"A childhood scar?" I offered, wanting to crawl out of my skin.

"Who did this?" he tightened his hold on the spot as if doing so would eradicate the burn mark. "Tell me or I will go into Jersey Hill and kill every human I come into contact with, male or female" he grunted the streaks of red in his eyes growing more prominent.

"A home I was staying in..." his hold on me loosened, his shoulders and every muscle in his body clenched. He nodded, motioning for me to continue. "I tried sneaking out...no, running away with a friend. We were caught. And they punished us for it-"

"They? There was more than one?" I nodded tersely, unable to comprehend why he was so angry. This was my scar, something that was done against me.

"Let's not talk about it, it was a long time ago and I would rather finish what we started?" I reached for his hand on my abdomen and raised it to my chest.

"No!"

"No?" I arched a brow, holding his hand in place.

"Why are you not angry? You've accepted this?" he asked, the words branded on my skin like an insult. I shrugged, unable to find the words to explain my childhood and everything that had shaped me into who I was today. How could I be angry when hunger and death were the other alternatives?

"They are family-"

"Family doesn't-"

"They became the family I didn't have. They clothed, fed, and trained me. I would be different...my life would be very different without this." I moved my leg slightly for his convenience. Quillian's blood-raged demeanor told me he wasn't satisfied by this response, and from the intensity behind his eyes, he was calculating who what and where. Fortunately for me, he was never going to ever find out those answers.

"Did you kill whoever did this?" he lowered his hand from my breast to the scar of the gun wound.

"Of course," I answered swiftly. He smiled, pride illuminating his features.

"that's my girl," he murmured, his movements no longer rough, and urgent. They were slow reverent, yearning, lustful, and filled with emotion.

Those three words branded every corner of my heart, making breathing, and thinking straight impossible. Quillian slowly removed my shirt, my pants, and underwear without once steering his gaze elsewhere.

"Everything about you drives me mad. Your voice..." He lowered himself between my thighs but took extra time to focus and kiss the scar.

"Your scent..." His mouth tugged at my clit, sucking and biting with a gentleness I wasn't used to. He lifted the lower part of my body and feasted on me as his hands roved all over my body, branding and marking me as his. His tongue ran circles around my clit as his mouth made itself at home down there. "Your mouth, your eyes, lips, and everything that makes you...you, makes me want to claim you," he continued, and the response died in my throat.

This was not another one of our intense fucking sessions, this was more. A sharing of body, secrets, hopes, dreams. A claiming, a promise of what was and what is to come.

My hands roved through the length of his hair, enjoying that this powerful masculine man was buried between me, and cared about nothing else but my pleasure.

"Shit, shit," I cursed, pressing his head further inside me, seeing how close I was. Quillian peered up at me lowering his mouth to his fangs and biting on his... finger.

He raised his blood-soaked hand and pressed it on my lips. My mouth tingled and skin prickled at what awaited. I sucked his thumb, as he continued to eat me like he was a starved animal.

"Fuck," I moaned aloud, from the sweet and tangy taste of his blood. My body exploded into bliss, my legs shook, my heart rate accelerated and the pressure from my legs drove me over the edge.

"I'm coming," I screamed out, losing touch with everything around me. The room blurred into a kaleidoscope of colors, and the need to desperately crawl out of my skin became unbearable.

Quillian's blood was an elixir I couldn't get enough. My body shook profusely as I finally came, screaming his name as tears streaked down my cheeks. Quillian refused to stop, even after I came, he continued eating and lapping at my juices like it was a matter of life and death.

"Q......," I muttered, my skin flush from the sensory overload. "I can't take anymore." I heaved, tugging at his hair, and scratching his skin in the process.

He raised his head, our eyes locked, and my body exploded from another release. I started to shake with adrenaline from the high his blood had offered.

"Why does it feel different than last?" I muttered unable to formulate clear sentences. Quillian raised his head, his hands running through my shaky body.

"Emotions, make the experience more heightened," he answered, placing steady kisses on my lips. "The soreness you felt earlier should be gone by now," he offered, his kisses moving to my jaw then eyes.

The scent of my release and the warmth of his body over me stirred something within me and all I wanted to do was continue and ride this wave for a little longer.

I pushed him down on the bed, and sat on top of him, needing release from this...Whatever this was.

"Meraki," he murmured my name, a warning yet there was reverence behind it.

I angled myself over his hardened dick and placed it into my opening. With my eyes closed my body arched back, and my hand pressed over his chest, I twisted my hips and began to ride him. My movements slow at first giving me enough time to take in the fullness of his girth.

Once I felt comfortable, I quickened my pace. Quillian as usual refused to relinquish his hold, he lifted the top half of his body and pulled me into his chest, with me still straddled on him. My legs wrapped around his waist, his hands stretched cupping each of my ass cheeks.

"Fuck, you will be my undoing," he grunted as our lips locked, and he lifted me up and down his dick relentlessly.

I moved my hair from my sweaty head and wiped the sweat from my forehead. Quillian pressed me harder against his chest, quickening the movements of his thrust and pace.

"Q.... oh fuck. Oh my god," I rested my head against his neck and scratched at his skin.

"Say it!"

He pinched my clit, and lowered his head to my breast, as his movements grew more desperate urgent, and fluid. He slapped my pussy, and I gasped out loud. "Tell me no one else can have this with you. No one else can fuck you like this," he growled against my chest.

"Oh my god, I'm coming," I screamed out loud, as he pounded me so hard, I was convinced I had died and gone to heaven. He erupted inside me, the warmth of his release making me gasp out aloud. My own followed behind his, as my body shook, and breathing became hard.

Quillian rested his head against my neck, inhaling for what felt like an eternity. I followed suit, wrapping my hands around his neck, needing to savor this for a little longer before the reality of the outside world sipped through.

the scent of our sex, sweat, and the steady beat of his chest against mine helped to cool down my jitters.

"Something is wrong," he finally breathed, after some time had passed. "Someone is coming up, get dressed," he instructed, rising from the bed with me still wrapped around his waist. "This...." he stated, as he stared down at me. My brows furrowed waiting for him to finish his sentence. "We will continue later," he stated, placing a kiss on my forehead. He placed me down on the floor and slapped my ass as he walked into his wardrobe.

I reached for my clothes on the bed, and hurriedly got dressed, unsure who was coming. A knock sounded on the door a few seconds later, and Quillian strolled out, the warmth he carried earlier gone, now in its wake was his usual skittish stoic expression.

He opened the door widely and Eugene almost tumbled inside. "I'm sorry, I tried to stop them, but Silas and Brielle were not here." she rushed through her words.

"Quillian," Loki spoke, moving from behind Eugene's shadow. I stepped forward, uncertainty coursing through me.

"You may go," Quillian said to Eugene. She hurried out of their presence with haste.

"What is the meaning of this Loki?" Quillian belted, as a loud blaring sound began to ring out in the house.

"You might want to fix that, the response is slow," Loki stated. I moved to stand beside Quillian, wanting to get a better view of what was happening. Loki outside of the door with three of his men in tow. Their eyes all turned toward me, then the bed. Their nostrils flared, and something transpired between them.

Sol and Blaze appeared within seconds, circling Loki, and his mean. "Enzo is on his way," Blaze stated as if reading Quillian's response. "The alarm has been deactivated.

"Why are you here?" I asked feeling the tightness in Quillian's body. Loki and his men turned to face me.

"I was following word that this marriage was a farce and I

needed to investigate," the words rolled from his tongue with hesitancy.

"You broke into my house to see what exactly, my king?" Quillian's words came across course and brittle. I opened the door wider, knowing if I didn't intervene the shit was bound to end up with bloodshed.

"Well, here you are your highness," I motioned to the room, looking from his men to him. "Or unless you want to see us having sex?" Quillian's snarled out loud, and Loki's men retracted.

Loki seemed unphased by this instead his eyes roved over my body, soaking me in as if seeing me for the first time. "Look at her like that again, and I'll burn down the whole of Oloh with every single one of your people in it., Quillian warned, using his body to cover my exposed thighs and breast.

"Now Quillian," Loki smiled, and before he could finish his sentence Quillian lunged for him. They moved across the passageway in a blur, making it hard to distinguish who was who and what was happening.

Sol, blaze, and Loki's men intervened, creating a divide between them. "The law is law, Quillian." Loki smirked, wiping remnants of blood from his mouth. "But I enjoyed that, it's been a while since you and I sparred, I was Beginning to think you had gone soft." Loki turned his focus to me, as I leaned against the hinges of the doorway. "My job here is done. You did an amazing job by the way Meraki. You surpassed everyone's expectations... even mine. And I'm not usually one left surprised."

"It's best, to save the pleasantries for tonight" Enzo's voice pierced through the crowd. "This could be perceived as a threat against Kinavari." he stepped beside Quillian, while Sol and Blaze crowded around them. With Loki and his men to one side, and I stood in the middle they stared at one another.

Quillian stepped forward, towering over Loki, as every muscle in his body pulsed with rage. "Coming into another leader's territory...their home without announcement is a threat," He gritted the words, his hand clenched into fists. "The law states we have every right to kill you on Kinavari soil."

"And we all know how particular you are about the law?" Enzo commented.

Loki laughed, his eyes still locked on me. "I guess my job here is done. We are not looking to start anything between our people now, are we?" he furrowed his brow. "Meraki, I'm looking forward to seeing you at tonight's event?"

"My husband and I can't wait," I turned to Quillian, covering my chest with my when Loki's gaze lingered for too long.

"Sol, Blaze, and I will escort you," Enzo motioned, creating a passageway for him to pass through. A tight exchange transpired between Quillian and Enzo, and Loki and his men passed and headed down behind Sol and Blaze.

"What the hell was that?" I asked, my eyes still fixed on the stairway once they had left.

"A warning and a threat," he stepped into the room.

"A warning?"

"Loki hates being outsmarted."

"Sounds familiar," I mouthed stepping into the room. Quillian shook his head, and stepped into his closet, picking out his attire.

"You winning was clearly not part of his contingency plan. He was here to scent and get a reading on you"

"You knew?" I accused. His hold on his hand tightened and the muscles on his back flexed.

"Yes," he answered slowly, as he arched his body to face me. "What else do you think that was?" he pointed to the bed, the same one we had just fucked a few minutes prior.

I stepped back back as bile rose in my throat. I swallowed hard to quench it down. Pushing down the whirlwind of emotions raging inside me.

"You needed to create the scent, and the atmosphere because you got word he was coming," noted, allowing the words to take root in my heart. he nodded, reaching into the center drawer space to pull out cufflinks.

"Now, no one will question the legitimacy of this," he motioned, a smile tugging at his lips.

"of course," I nodded, needing time to process the fact I had allowed myself to feel for this asshole, forgetting that this was all an act, a performance. I couldn't even be mad at him, he had stated from the get-go his intentions and had made his repulsion of my kind obvious.

"I'm going to the north to visit Ferguson," I stated taking a few more steps back and masking my face with indifference.

"Oh?"

"I want to see the gallery he was raving about, and I will stop at the library there." he walked toward me, and I began to make my way out of the room.

"Stay with Sol and Blaze." he placed the clothes on the bed, my eyes darting and lingering there for a few seconds too long.

"Little Hellion-"

"I'll see you before the event tonight" I interrupted making my way to the door, rebuilding the guards around myself I had stupidly lowered. Quillian Kingsley was no longer gaining access to any part of that.

"I might be late, I'm going to visit Amma" he pointed, and my hand halted on the door, recounting what she had shared that night. I closed the door without giving it any response. This was my problem not his, and I wasn't going to give him the satisfaction of seeing how his words affected me.

"GENTLEMEN" I SPOKE, WHEN I DESCENDED THE STAIRS and headed for the garage Sola and Blaze trailing behind me.

"What's the plan today, Meraki?" Sol asked, stretching his arm with eagerness.

"We are off to see Ferguson. Before that take me to the library near his?" I said, reaching for the key for the Cosmic Starship motorcycle. "Lead the way," I instructed as I placed my helmet on, turned on the bike, and swerved forward. The garage door opened, and I sped forward with Sola ahead, and Blaze behind.

The bike roared as we passed through the busy streets of Kinavari and then through a wide greenspace for a long time.

After some time, Sol and Blaze flew on adjourning sides of the bike veering at turns and straightening at junctions. The green-space disappeared followed by dome-sized buildings like that of the others scattered through the region. These buildings, however, did not carry their length. They were smaller in stature and ranged from the clearest shade of white to the darkest shade of umber.

The motorcycle was smooth, sleek, and made it easy to navigate into tight spaces and the crooks and corners of the alleyways Blaze and Sol followed. They finally stopped on the steps of the only brightly colored building we had seen on our commute.

I parked the bike, removed my helmet, and admired the blend of golds and blues that illuminated under the sunlight. Blaze and Sol covered me on both sides as we stepped up the empty staircase.

"This is Ogbun, the hub of wisdom in Kinavari," Blaze stated with pride in his voice. The first word he had uttered to me directly since we had met.

"He speaks?" I feigned shock, climbing further up the stairs.

"He's reached his daily word count. It ranges to about thirty a day," Sol snickered, and Blaze shot him a heated glance.

Blaze opened the door of the library, and light flooded the interior of the doubled-floor building with wooden structures and a large central space that oversaw the whole building.

A total of eight figures could be seen at various spots in the library but apart from that, the space was relatively empty. "You're not planning to follow me around, are you?" I arched my brow, as Blaze stepped beside me.

"Quillian's instructions were-"

"Quillian can go fuck himself," I whisper shouted, feeling a sense of relief at getting those words out. The room stilled and heads in the room turned to face me, their faces indignant.

"We will stay at a steady distance," Sol offered, pushing Blaze further back from me. Blaze watched shock marring his face from my abrupt words. "He isn't used to anyone...speaking to or about Quillian around him like that," Sol stated as he moved to my side. "He doesn't allow anyone to speak to him like that.... except you"

"It's part of the job criteria of a wife," I answered turning my focus to the navigation panel to the far center. "Or maybe he knows I'll kick his ass."

"The evening at the bar..." he trailed when my movements came to a halt. "You were good...really good. Some of the other guys would love to train with you."

"Just guys?" She smiled.

"Both guys and girls."

"I find it hard vampires don't know how to fight?"

"The problem is many of the younger ones rely on their bite or speed to fight. Blaze and I have been training them on combat."

"Why now?"

"In the time the Kingsley wasn't here, the other regions attacked our territory relentlessly and we lost many times." I arched my head watching the sway and movement of his body detecting no lie.

"You want to be able to protect yourselves just in case," I offered.

"Yes," he replied swiftly.

"Which region," I asked, keeping my focus on him.

"The east."

"Amma's territory?" He nodded and I groaned aloud, wanting to steer far away from that drama, especially after what transpired this morning. But then again, I was never one to back away from something because it made me uncomfortable, those things propelled me forward, and made me work, and fight harder.

I bit my lip contemplating the idea. "And how would she feel about this training?" I replied, my hands reaching for the screen before me, and typing out rings in the search criteria.

"She won't know," he answered, and my interest piqued. A series of results began to load on the screen.

"And how would Quillian feel about this?" I continued, needing the cards laid out before me.

"He won't need to know?" his voice heightened, and that note alone told me there was some revolt against her leadership.

"How often?"

"Once a week. We will arrange it," he stated.

"Okay," I answered, turning my full focus on the screen before me. What was the worst that could happen?

"We will give you space," he said, the excitement in his voice palpable. The screen before me loaded with five books on the topics, all situated near one another. I followed the markings around the walls headed for the top floor and pulled out each book. I moved to the seating area adjoining the row where the books were.

The books spoke about how rings were part of Esneoh society. Rings were seen as a showcase of each region's power and prestige. A series of rings with a similar structure to Alessia's killer was displayed across the pages of the various books.

These rings were noted as only being worn by leaders and passed on to their descendent. The books stated each region had its own emblem, distinct to its history and people. However, the practice wasn't prevalent now as it used to be eons ago

My heart stuttered as I read the words, thinking back to the fact after I had passed on the image of the ring to Quillian, and he had said nothing. Knowing full well, what it potentially could have meant, and even now he hasn't uttered a word. After having had enough time to trace where it could be from? Has he even been searching? Has he even tried to?

Anger burned through me, coupled with the raging emotions from this morning I found myself reeling at the fact, that he was intentionally not fulfilling his end of the bargain when I was risking my life at the trial to fulfill my end of the bargain.

"They are a leader" I muttered aloud when the weight of the books dawned on me.

My sister's killer was a leader in Esneoh.

Someone I had walked past, shook hands with, or even said hello to at one of these events. And Quillian had known all this time and said nothing. I opened each page searching through the images of each ring trying to locate the house that bore the symbol of the lion.

Oloh consisted of a horned skull. The Fleelens an animal with several head's representative of the various shifter types within the region. Aldrata comprised of an upside-down tree its root deep underground. Kinavari contained a sword upheld by two large, outstretched wings.

I continued to browse through the pages, unable to find the lion or any explanation of what it could be. A small voice in the back of my head whispered that perhaps my assessment had been wrong, and it was just a regular ring. But my gut told me that wasn't the case. There was something I was missing that wasn't adding up.

After some time had passed and I had exhausted all my options, I placed the book back on the shelf and headed downstairs to meet Sol and Blaze.

I followed behind them, disappointed that I had reached another dead end. I veered the motorcycle forward at full speed, hoping that perhaps my visit with Ferguson might fix my dampening mood.

PART III

"You only live once, but in his case, you can live a thousand lives in a thousand beds."

30

AN ENCOUNTER TO REMEMBER

M*eraki*

"MERAKI," FERGUSON WALKED TOWARD US AND hugged me. A current of electricity shot between us, and he stared at me with bewilderment as if he had felt it too.

"I had been expecting you when word of your visit to the library got back to me." He motioned for me to follow him. Two men and a woman stood at a distance, watching guard.

"Gossip travels fast in Esneoh," I noted.

"At the speed of light," he laughed, shaking his head at the thought. Sol and Blaze followed behind us, keeping a steady distance. But I was sure they were listening in and would report my movements back to Quillian.

No buildings could be seen from miles away since concrete walls surrounded the large landscape. "You live here?" I asked, trying to sound intrigued but failing miserably.

Ferguson laughed, shook his head, and pointed to the opening a few feet ahead us. In the middle of the ground was a piazza made of traditional tiles bending upwards, revealing space below.

He motioned for Sol and Blaze to remain behind, they hesitantly obeyed, but from Blaze's stern expression, I could tell he wasn't exactly too pleased about it.

Light penetrated the curve of the Piazza, and Ferguson took me around until we reached its entryway. We walked into a large modern build house divided into subsections. At its heart was a large art space taking up most of the room.

"You weren't kidding," I said, unable to keep my excitement. We descended a series of stairs until we landed on the main floors. Colors, images, and sculptures covered every corner of the room, and for a moment, I felt myself leave my body as I peered down what could only be described as heaven.

"You did this?" My voice hitched with emotion, unable to place the sentiment the pieces drew from me. "Me and my children, yes," he answered stiffly.

"Children?" he nodded, taking me around to the canvas and explaining the brushes, strokes, and colors, used for each theme.

"A son, you just missed him before you came," he said, pointing above at an abstract canvas of various shades of reds and browns in multiple shapes and forms.

"You said children, but you only mentioned your son?" I noted cautiously, knowing that perhaps the others were possibly dead.

"A daughter..."

"Ahhh," I muttered, his eyes filled with such vitality losing their spark. "I'm sorry for your loss."

"Don't be. She lived a rich life," he beamed. "Come, there's more," he excitedly continued ahead, taking me through a series of rooms and explaining their historical significance. Most of the pieces were not just familial, a majority consisted of architecture from the earlier time of Esneoh, and each piece spoke of a time of war or peace, and Esneoh, it seemed, had gone through a series of them.

"What about you? Any family?" he asked when he had left the final showroom and had settled on a large dining area at the far end of the house.

"A sister." I surprised myself at how freely the words flowed. There was something about Ferguson that put me at ease. He was different from the others I had encountered; I was attracted to his homeliness and authenticity.

"Oh?" he replied, his voice lowered.

"She died...no, was murdered when I was young."

"Tell me about her," he stated instead of asking, and I smiled as he watched me with genuine interest. "She was older than me. She was fairer and had freckles and light brown hair. No one believed we were related at the orphanage because we didn't have similar looks. While I was the polar opposite." I laughed, recounting some memories of how she had beaten the kids who had threatened or even looked at me wrongly.

"Your parents?"

"I don't remember; I was too young when they died in an accident. Alessia was in the car but suffered from memory loss after. Whatever occurred in the automobile was so traumatic that her mind would not allow her to think about it..." Ferguson's hand reached for mine, and that familiar cord of electricity passed through us again.

"Quillian, is he treating you well?" he asked, the lines on his forehead scrunched. "Though something tells me after seeing you fight that I should be more worried for him than you," he laughed.

"Don't worry. I can hold my own. I'm not as delicate as I look." I lightly tapped his hand. Servers walked into the room carrying an assortment of food, and I had never been more excited.

Ferguson and I ate as he recounted some of his experiences in the human realm and life in Esneoh over the years. I decided then and there that he wasn't going to be someone I reported back on.

"Can I offer advice?"

"Of course," I nodded, biting into my final piece of cheesecake.

"Be on your guard until the trial is over. Power corrupts, and many leaders here are led by nefarious means and have no regard for life to get what they want."

"Especially because I'm human," I chorused what was left unsaid.

"Yes, and after seeing you during the tournament...many will see you as a threat. And will not hesitate to attack." I nodded, wiping the remnants of the food with a napkin.

"However, I want you to know Esneoh can be a beautiful place when the right people surround you," he noted, taking a sip of the water before him. "I've known Quillian and his siblings for a long time and have always held them dear to my heart. Since they've accepted you as family, so to have I. Here is also your home, and you're welcome here anytime."

I felt a lump in my throat at his kindness. "Thank you," I replied, allowing the silence to linger between us.

"Is there a way to contact you?"

"Ahhh..." I stammered, realizing I hadn't even thought of looking or asking for a communications device. My stint here was supposed to be short, so owning one seemed inconsequential. "Not yet?" I lied.

"Wait here," Ferguson rose to his feet and returned with a small device in hand. The circular object looked like a pager with the added benefits of a camera and the ability to make and receive calls. "Something tells me you may need this"

"This is?"

"If you need help, I won't share anything we've discussed beyond these walls. I, of all people, know how important it is to protect the secrets of others," he said, continuing to hover over me. Something in his expression told me that Ferguson had lived a thousand lifetimes, and like me, he was versed in that art of reading people.

"Thank you," I clasped the device tightly in my arms and rose to my feet. "I have to leave and prepare for tonight."

He nodded and escorted me through the path we had taken. Sol and Blaze met us at the top of the stairs mid-conversation with the three guards stationed around the perimeter.

"Do visit again, maybe next time with something of yours," Ferguson beamed, and I nodded in agreement, knowing for the first time in my life that the idea of showing someone else my art wasn't so daunting.

THE CELEBRATORY EVENT OF THE FIRST EVENT TOOK place in Loki's estate, where a large outdoor tent covering the full extent of the space was placed.

Unlike the first event, this event was more informal and consisted of not just leaders but some of the citizens from the different regions.

"You can never say the demons don't know how to have fun!" Silas stated, his eyes widening at the tent's scantily clad incubus and succubus demons. Hanging tree lights and rounded cushions were placed strategically, creating a relaxed atmosphere.

My attention turned to the device Ferguson had given me, and my fingers itched with anticipation. After I arrived back in the house, I contacted the security detail number the bartender had provided. I was hoping that the video would be sent to me sometime tomorrow so that I could finally get a close-up of whoever wore it right that night.

"Where's Brielle?" I asked, noting that I hadn't seen her since the trial. "She's with someone. She said she wasn't sure she would make it tonight," he answered, intentionally leaving out who this someone was.

Sol and Blaze moved around the space, looking equally enthralled as Silas. I searched the area, hoping to spot Hera, someone in all the madness.

Her thick curly hair caught my attention before I even saw her. She raised her hand and headed for me. "Welcome to Oloh, where your wildest fantasies can be fulfilled," she motioned to the space around us.

"where's the husband?" She scrunched her face searching for Quillian but saw Silas instead.

"He will be joining us later," Silas clapped his hand and disappeared amid a group of naked succubi.

"He lives up to his reputation, doesn't he?" she snickered when the demons dragged him in their midst until his frame was hidden from us.

"You only live once, but in his case, you can live a thousand lives in a thousand beds." I clung to her hand and motioned for her to lead us through the room of people who were too busy having sex or making out to pay us any heed.

Hera moved us to a distant corner surrounded by cushions, shisha, and a plethora of drinks. "Are we expecting more people?" She shook her head, raised her hand, and chanted under her breath.

"It's to create the allusion that there's a lot of people here. I've placed a cloaking spell around our space so we can relax without being on edge." she reached for the shisha, inhaling and exhaling.

She passed it on to me, and we shifted back and forth, smoking it, drinking, and enjoying one another's company.

"Have you been yet?" she asked, implying my sister.

"Soon," I answered, turning to the stage where Loki and his wife stood peering down at the crowd.

"Welcome contestants, and those of you here looking for a good time, he winked." The room erupted into laughter. Hera raised her hand, chanting the exact words as earlier. She motioned to my ears, letting me know the guard had been lowered.

The room lights lowered, and soft stage lights filtered around, stopping directly atop of Hera, Althea and I, and the others who had attended.

I scanned the space, searching for Amma, who, like Quillian, was nowhere to be seen. "It seems everyone is here, and their partners are here." she beamed, scanning through the space, her eyes falling on me. "Amma seems to be missing, though, and overlord Quillian along with her," she announced, the implication behind her words not hard to miss.

Whispers echoed around the space, and I stared ahead, refusing to show that it affected me in any way. Hera choked on her drink, taken aback.

"Oh dear, I guess we will have to continue without them, and they may catch up with us later," she continued, relishing the moment. Every eye in the room turned to face me, and I lightly shrugged, finding it laughable that she thought this act would somehow be my undoing.

"To everyone having fun tonight, your highness," I raised my glass in the air and rose to my feet.

"Of course," she answered, taken aback. Everyone in the room raised their glasses and toasted. I sat back down, tilting my glass up to her, with a smirk on my face.

"To having uninterrupted rendezvous," Loki chimed his eyes, lingering in my direction for a little too long. The room erupted into shouts and cheers as people continued doing whatever they had done before.

Hera raised the guard she had erected before and stared at me with shock in her features. "You're made of stronger stuff than me. I would have caved. Teach me?" she laughed, inhaling the shisha, but the strain behind her words told me she wasn't joking

"People can only do to you what you allow. They'll continue to pick at you if you take their beatings lying down. You set the boundaries, and you determine what you are willing to tolerate," I echoed the exact words Alessia had repeated to me when I ran to her in tears on several occasions.

"Meraki," Loki hovered over us, his bare chest out. Hera raised her hand again, motioning to the fact the cloaking spell had been lowered

"Your Highness," I replied with added sarcasm.

"I want to introduce you to some people. Will you not accompany me?" he stretched out his hand as a demand rather than a query. Eyes trained on me in the room, and I knew declining now would come across as disrespect, especially as I was in his territory.

Silas and Blaze's eyes locked on mine from a distance and nodded for me to accept. "Of course," I replied sweetly, even though I wanted to cut off his repulsive hand, followed by his tongue before everyone.

I felt his hands lightly brush against the hollows of my back, and I cursed Quillian under my breath for placing me in this situation. "Where's your wife?" I shifted to my right and kept a steady distance between us.

"She's predisposed," he pointed to the darkened corner on the far right, where she lay naked with her breast and body exposed. Three demons surrounded her, two caressing her breast while another lay spread between her legs, making himself at home. She seemed bored in the midst of it, stuffing herself with grapes as if this was a regular everyday occurrence.

"Shouldn't you be predisposed?" I asked, motioning for him to lead the way.

"Something else has caught my attention tonight," he answered, staring directly at me.

"You did great." The words of strangers filtered through the crowd as Loki led me, and I responded by thanking them.

"Beautiful, humble, and the heart and body of a warrior. I'm intrigued."

We stopped at the head of the room, a few feet from the stage. The section consisted of more pillows, throws, and silk wrappings. Thale and Althea covered one section, their tongues and bodies intermingled.

"Meraki," Thale raised his head from his wife's breast. "It's good to see you still alive?"

"Same can be said. Good to see you're alive, Althea." I ignored his comment turning my focus on his wife.

"Nothing to worry about, honey; she won't make the next one alive." Althea arched her head to stare briefly.

"Maybe we should bet on that? I heard the Fleelens lost a lot of money yesterday by underestimating me," I smirked.

"Now, tell us. How does a human learn to move like that?" Thale asked, straddling his naked wife on his hips while she rode him.

Althea moaned and writhed as he moved his hips while his other hand caressed her breast. "I hope this isn't too much for you. I know how reserved your kind can be." he laughed as Althea pushed his chest and rode him reverse cowgirl.

"Focus on me, honey. You're not here to entertain her because her husband ditched her," Althea spoke, bending on all fours, as Thale rose and began to pound into her.

"Pay it no heed," Loki's hands moved to my thighs, his hold lingering. I removed his hand, making it clear nothing was going to happen between us tonight and ever.

"Tell me what your deepest desires are," Loki whispered into my ears. "Don't tell me, I can guess," his hands rested on my shoulders, and a faint thrill ran through my body. "You're an exhibitionist; you get a thrill from having sex in public places. Interesting..." he murmured as I jerked from his hold.

"There's more," he stated, wrapping his hand around mine as I attempted to do so. "You get off the thrill of killing, blood, and carnage." He laughed, and I rose to my feet, wondering how he was able to ascertain all that information even with the wolfsbane still in my system

Loki stood and reached for me, drawing my chin to his. "This is better than I anticipated," he smiled, his eyes clouding with lust, beckoning for me to submit to his request.

"I think that's enough for tonight." Quillian placed his hand on Loki's chest and yanked his hold from my chin.

"We leave now," he commanded, his gaze landing on me. The atmosphere in the room grew rigid, and as I turned, staring into the distance, I felt the full extent of Loki's power. Everyone in the room moaned and screamed aloud, caught in one compromising position or the other. Even Sol and Blaze were lost in the sea of bodies.

"My eyes fell on Amma behind Quillian. She smiled, shuffled her dress, and moved to the side, watching the whole interaction with amusement.

"Quillian, you finally showed up, with Amma for that matter," Loki's eyes fell on me. "I had assumed you had an open relationship. Since everyone here knew you were with your former lover tonight?"

Quillian snarled, straining his attention on Loki, I walked off and headed in the direction Silas and I had come through. The motorcycle keys were in the pocket of the pouch I carried.

When I found the motorcycle, I climbed on and drove out of the premises without turning back. I had paid attention when Silas and I drove down, marking key signposts and buildings in case I ever found myself in predicaments like these.

I veered ahead at full speed, needing to clear my mind from distractions and recall my original mission.

"For Alessia," I muttered, picking up speed. As I did so, I heard a car horn behind me, its lights blinding. I ignored the call assuming it was Quillian trying to gauge my attention.

I continued to speed ahead, paying it no heed, until a heavy force knocked me from the back of the motorcycle, making me tumble over the road through the surrounding forest space.

"Fuck," I muttered when the back of my head tingled with discomfort. I ran my hands through it, finding my fingers soaked with blood. My vision wavered as I struggled to get to my feet.

"Mon Cherie," Ryder said as he lowered himself to face me, a dagger and rope in hand. "Let's have some fun?" he laughed, tugging at the back of my head.

"Ryder, some could call this an obsession," I snickered, strategizing how best to salvage the situation. If I attacked too prematurely, I would exert the reminder of my strength, and he could easily overpower and kill me.

"I need to prove to Quillian that you are not who you claim to be, Red" he said, his tone curt and cold. My eyes widened, and I stared up at him. "Oh, you didn't think I would work it out?" He placed the dagger on my neck, and I swallowed, deciding then that I needed to kill him before he jeopardized everything I had worked tirelessly for the last couple of years.

"Do you want to know what's fascinating? The fascinating information I found out about the Alokari. Who knew there was an assassin guild right under our nose all this time, and you had gone under the cover?"

"I have no idea what you're talking about," I lied, watching as he raised the blade and cut deep wounds across my chest.

"That," he stared deep into my eyes, darkness dancing in his pupils; "is how I know I'm not mistaken. Not a scent of fear or pain. I've mutilated and jerked off the death of many of your kind. Want to know what they all had in common? I desire to live," he spat with vitriol. "They cried, begged, pleaded, and were willing to do deplorable things to live. But you?" He snickered, leaving no room for me to argue.

"What are you planning to do with me?" I asked when he kicked the back of my knees and steered me forward in the opposite direction of the main road.

"Taking you to my lair, I need a few days to have my way with you. I need to see you bleed and watch you respond as I cut off your flesh and stitch it back on again. Perhaps in all that, I might truly get a response from you?"

"You're sick," I replied without haste. I immediately regretted the words when his elbows made contact with my head.

"Keep talking, and that tongue will be the first thing I cut off Mon Cherie," he continued pushing me ahead, my hands above my head.

I scanned my environment, noting we were heading deeper

into the forest each minute, a chance I couldn't take, especially knowing what was at stake.

"You're not going to plead for your life?" he asked, as my eyes fell on a series of rocks overhead.

"Why would I do that?" I answered, anticipating his attack. I lowered myself and stepped back when he pounced on me.

His bloodshot eyes darkened, and whatever semblance of sanity he had left in there disappeared with that final push.

"You'll regret that, Red," he spat, circling me like a predator cornering its prey. I reached into my pockets and released the lipstick case that stretched into an angular dagger.

Ryder pounced on me, marking my skin with each swipe, and missed hit. "A worthy opponent," I tilted my neck, drawing upon the adrenaline inside me to guide my every movement because if it were my body alone, I would have lost the fight long ago.

"What if I told you I knew things about your sister, how she died, who killed her?" he stepped back and continued to circle me.

"You know nothing about her." I veered forward, the dagger leaving a dent across his chest.

"That's where you're wrong. Her name was Alessia, wasn't it?" he whispered her name, and the sound from his mouth made my skin itch. My skin buzzed with electricity, and I surged forward with the remainder of my stretch, plowing the dagger into his chest before he could move. He fell to the floor, blood spewed from his mouth, and he stared up, mocking and taunting me.

"Who?" I lowered myself until he and I were at face level. I pulled at the stake from his chest and trailed it on the engorged scar on his face, digging deeper into it. "Who?" I pressed down intending to inflict as much pain as possible.

"Fuck you," he spat as his saliva landed on my face. I raised the dagger, and punctured his chest, not for one moment halting or stopping in my pursuit. I moved from his chest to the lower half of his body, screaming, laughing, and crying at the release.

"Enough!" Quillian yelled, his hand reaching for the weapon in my hand; I jerked back, pointing the dagger at him, my vision nothing but crimson. He removed his blazer and flung it at me.

"What are you doing?" I shrugged from the material, finding he had taken the weapon and was now using his clothes to wipe the blood that coated my face.

"Don't" I stepped back, finally peering down and taking note of my scarred and bloodied body. Quillian reached for me, a low, strained, and pained growl emitting from his chest.

"Don't touch me," I jerked from his hold and staggered as I dragged my bloody body toward the main road. Flashbacks from the information I found in the library to being made an utter fool of before the leaders of Esneoh, flashed in my vision, and that rage propelled me forward, refusing to ever give into more of the games.

With each second, my vision became blurry, and my legs threatened to give way.

"Can I help?" Sol and Blaze's frames came into focus, and I nodded, leaning my body against his. A series of chatter and sounds moved around me.

"Give her to me," Quillian's voice echoed as his hands wrapped around me, laying my head against his chest.

"Get my siblings and tell Enzo to get the witch and clean this up," he instructed.

"Is she..." Sol's voice trailed.

"No, there's poison in her body," Quillian replied, his voice filled with rage, and his hold around me, suffocating

"Don't," I warned, struggling to open my eyes. His hands branded my skin, spreading warmth all through my body. I struggled to fight his hold as the cold breeze whipped against my heated skin.

"I need a potion from Hera," I stopped fighting, knowing I no longer had the strength in me, and doing so midair would prove useless. "I need to go home"

"I'm taking you home." He replied, his voice the most tender than I had ever heard.

"Did I kill him?" I asked, as Quillian draw me deeper into his chest, as if any space between us served as an obstacle.

"Hmm," he flinched as he murmured.

"Good," I replied, allowing the darkness to take over.

31

EVERYTHING COMES AT A COST

Meraki

When I arrived in Jersey Hill, I sent a quick message on the Alokari comms system, updating Darya on the fact I was back. It didn't take long for her to respond.

I'll see you at 7 pm for updates. Black-tie dress in your finest attire.

I stared down at the device, unsure what to make of the message. I had never completed a *Sneps* or *Sners* and had to report back face to face. Then again, this wasn't a regular target; we were dealing with the biggest asshole in Esneoh.

The black-tie aspect also surprised me, but I could only focus on one issue at a time. Right now, my focus was tracking down Hera's sister and seeing what she could do about this bond. I needed a clear escape plan out of it when shit hit the roof.

It had taken a few hours of tracking and countless search engine results, but the store finally showed up.

I passed through Third Street, headed through a series of

dingy alleyways, and ended up at the storefront of a simple-looking building with Tiara's Fortunes inscribed in a brightly covered sign outside the door.

Subtlety was evident, not strength.

"Hello?" I called as I opened the door. The room was a moderately furnished space, with white walls and overabundant plants and trees. Any other day, I would have spent hours admiring the array of peace lilies, monsteras, aloe vera, and an endless supply of herbs.

I ran my hands through them, admiring how well kept they were. "Meraki?" a soft-spoken female voice called from the back of the room, and I turned around, surprised that she knew my name and was looking forward to my visit.

Hera had explicitly stated she and her sister had not seen or spoken for decades.

"Tiara?" I replied, my hand resting on the concealed gun inside my blazer.

"I'm in the back," she called again, and I pulled the weapon out, convinced this was a setup.

"No need for the weapon. I need your help more than you needed mine," she admonished. I keep a hold of the gun regardless as I walk a small passageway where more plants are placed.

"Beautiful, aren't they?" the form of a petite and moderately tall woman with waist-length blonde braids came into focus. I lowered my gun slightly, taking in the space and unable to feel any immediate danger.

"Tiara," she introduced herself, attempting to stretch out her hand but realizing her gloves were covered in soil.

"I saw that you like plants. I guess you and I have that in common," she noted and turned to the plant before her. There was a subtlety behind her words that I couldn't fully comprehend.

"You saw me?" I stepped towards her, the gun still lowered.

"I'm a seer," she corked her head towards me briefly. "You don't think I chose this profession here for fun, did you?" she ran her hands through the soil as she watered the plant. "Give me a few minutes; this is the last one." She continued to sprinkle water on two more plants.

"You saved my sister," she said, stepping back from her handiwork. She turned, looking from the gun to me, as she removed her gloves.

"Occupational hazard." I shrugged, reading the questions on her face. "I didn't save her; we helped each other," I answered as she led me back through the passageway into a small discreet office to the right.

"Not from what I saw." She pushed the door open and motioned for me to enter. Unlike the rest of her space, the room only contained two peace lilies on the opposite ends. A midsized desk sat to the far back of the room, and on its side lay two green lounge chairs, directly facing one another, separated by a simple glass table. She stepped ahead of me, taking the wall-facing chair.

"What did my sister promise you?" She asked, pouring water into the two cups on the table. She pushed one toward me and took a sip of the other.

"You're a seer; I'm sure you've seen it?" I took the water from the table, eyeing it wearily. I took a quick sniff, unable to scent anything out of the ordinary.

"The water is clean," I announced, leaning back in my seat.

"You're intense," she stated without any condescension in her voice. I lifted the cup taking a sip. "Then again, I would expect nothing else from an assassin," she commented, and my hand froze as I lowered the cup.

She shrugged. "Occupational hazard," she said before I could respond.

"You want to break the oath you've promised to the vampire overlord," she said after a moment of silence. "That's a hard potion to create," she bit her lip.

"Why would the witches exile you with the sort of gift you have?" I asked, guessing that Valeria would have utilized her gift to get ahead of her enemies and opponents.

"You can see my conundrum."

"They exiled you because of it?" I sat forward, lightly shaking my head.

"Among many other things," she answered, her eyes distant.

"You found out something you shouldn't have," I relayed, reading the tension on her face and body.

"You're good," she nodded. "And Valeria didn't like it. You've seen her; she's not used to not getting her way." she laughed

"Why didn't you just tell the others what you saw?"

"She spelled me to never be able to utter it..." she trailed, her hands running through the hem of her floral summer dress.

"There's more." I arched a brow.

"I can never speak it even if I try; the words never leave my mouth.

"Now I'm intrigued by this secret," I noted, running my hands lightly against the arm of the chair. "Does Hera know?"

"No. She only knows my character and that whatever I am accused of is false."

"What were you accused of?"

"Killing another witch," she answered boldly.

"And that's bad?" She laughed mockingly.

"It's the worst type of crime, especially if it was proven unprovoked," she added, shaking her head. "I know my sister won't stop her quest until I return. Hera is hard-headed and goes into things headfirst sometimes without thinking-"

"I've noticed," I laughed as brief images of Alessia flashed in my vision. "Mine was the same," I recalled, assuming she had already seen it, so there was no point pretending otherwise.

I laughed inwardly, realizing in some inexplicable way, we were alike; family drove our motives. Mine is to avenge my sister's death, Hera's to reinstate her sister's position, and Quillian's to create a legacy that long outlived his brother. We were all a fucking mess.

"She is right to keep fighting for you," I broke the silence and crossed my leg. I stare at her, picking up on their physical similarities: the widow's peak, the fullness of her lips, and the thick halo of hair.

"And that's what I'm afraid of," she whispered the response, so low I may have missed it if I wasn't paying attention. It was evident Hera's alliance with the Kingsley was strategic, like her marriage to Valeria. If the Kingsleys won, they would be indebted to helping her. Yet I wasn't sure what that helped entailed or how she would go about it with Valeria as the leader.

"The spell you require needs time," she spoke, drawing me from my thoughts.

"How long?"

"Twenty-four hours," she answered. She rose to her feet and walked to the storage unit beside her office table.

"And what do you require in exchange?" I corked my head back, keeping track of her subtle movements. She pulled out a large black plastic container and retook her seat.

"Every transaction with a witch comes at a price," she replied, stating it as if it was a well-documented fact. "It the hazard of the trade," she added with a half-smile.

"And?"

"Blood. I will need your blood," she replied, the plastic container on her lap, her elbows resting against its lid.

"My blood?"

"Yes, 13 oz," she replied, her expression guarded. "once a month for three months," she added, her gaze locked with mine.

"Why my blood, and what do you plan to do with it?"

"The life of a man is in their blood. The blood of someone of your caliber and being is hard to come by," she replied, but everything within me told me there was more to the story that she wasn't letting on.

"You're lying," I replied tersely. She pressed her lips together, letting me know whatever it was had something to do with the secret she couldn't share.

"One month," I responded hesitantly, knowing my choices were limited.

"Two," she shook her head, refusing to concede.

"You need this as much as I do. Two months, and 15 oz." I offered, needing the debt not to be something that was prolonged

Her lips thinned as she ran her hands through the braid over her face. "You have yourself a deal," she finally responded, her eyes gleaming with unspoken relief.

"You will need to make a pact with that," I added, the smile on her face wavering. I grinned in response, noting my initial suspicions were correct.

"I know the ways of witches and how they can stray from their initial word. A pact ensures that the words you speak, and we agree upon is what you will use my blood for."

"Of course," she replied, sounding more optimistic than I anticipated. Had she seen this? And I had fallen into her plan?

She opened the lid of the container and removed a 15 oz container, placing it on the table between us. She pulled another series of dried plants, leaves, and a small blade.

"Give me a few minutes to prepare." I nodded; my gaze darted across the room, eventually settling on the outline of sketches on the wall beside her table. I rose to my feet, facing a large mural of similar images embedded in the Throne Room.

"You miss Esneoh," I noted, my head turned back to her. She stared at me, a confused and questioning manner in her glare. My head followed the trails of the sketches, and her expression softened. She smiled meekly in response, then turned her attention back to the container, this time her movements slower than before.

I stared at the mural, then back at her, and began formulating a backup plan in my head.

"The blood will help you and your sister reunite?" I asked, and she hesitantly nodded, trying to get a feel of my intentions.

She began to mutter a series of chants under her breath. "Let's begin," she motioned to my seat, the razor in her hand.

"The pact should be this, if you want to use my blood for

nefarious reasons, you will first need my permission," I said, sitting back down.

"Are you offering to help me...us?" she stepped towards me with the razor.

"Nothing is for free."

"Thank you," she cut me off before I could respond.

She reached for my right hand. "A blood pact. This is usually done between siblings, but something tells me our lives are more intertwined in more ways than one," she noted, pricking my thumb with the blade's sharp edge. Blood lightly trickled from my thumb as she repeated the same move with her thumb.

"Repeat after me," she motioned, bringing our thumbs together. "gẹ́gẹ́ bí okùn ìgbà." As I repeated the words, her eyes rolled back into white balls, and a current of electricity ran up my spine.

"It's done," she said, her eyes returning to that warm brown.

"You never asked what it is needed in return?"

"I already saw it," she answered, stepping back, and handing me a paper towel.

"You're looking for your sister's killer." She replied, her expression softening.

She rose and stood beside me again, citing another series of foreign words. A tourniquet appeared on my right hand. The prickle of a needle followed. "This should take about an hour."

After some time had passed, and she had collected the blood, she instructed me to come back tomorrow, and I gave her my number to update me when it was ready.

As I stepped outside the building, I took out my phone and dialed Skye's number as I made my way to my motorbike. I also reached for my other device from Esneoh, scanning its screen to see if the company had yet to send the video.

"Hey hoe," Skye singsong as she picked up the phone. "I got your message. Are you back? Everything went well?" she asked, and I hesitated with my response, knowing there was only so much I could divulge.

"Yes, and no, but I've come across more details about Alessia's killer," I replied, changing the conversation's trajectory. "I need your help," I exhaled, connecting my phone to my Bluetooth device.

"I think that's the first time you've ever asked." she grew silent on the phone. "This must be pretty serious?" Her voice hitched at the question.

"Yes." I breathed into the phone. "This stays between us," I warned.

"Of course. Shoot, I'm listening. What can I do?" she asked, and the familiar sound of her keyboard echoed in the background.

"I need you to access the CCTV video on the day Alessia was killed." Skye whistled loudly.

"Are you sure you want to see that?" She asked cautiously.

"Yes," I replied, clutching the phone, and placing the other device in my blazer pockets.

"That means hacking into the Alokari, Raki"

"I know." I reached for my keys, and my hold on them tightened as I questioned whether this was a good idea.

"Okay," she replied after some tapping on her keyword.

"Okay?" I asked, reaching for my motorcycle. I unlocked the helmet, placed it over my head, and turned it on.

"You know, I find it hard to say no when it comes to hacking systems. And I find it equally hard to say no to you or Iris," she laughed. "Besides, this isn't the first time I've done it."

"Wait! What?" I screamed into my helmet, the motorcycle lurching forward.

"Not all of us are sticklers for following the rules," she scolded. "And don't you already have the recording?"

"Yes, but the view is restricted. I want a view from all angles that day." I replied, filling her in with what I had discovered without going into the specifics of Esneoh.

"You want to know if there was someone else with them? To explain the woman?" I nodded even though she couldn't see me.

"I've hacked into the encrypted file," she said, the clicking sound growing in intensity. "The warehouse in midtown?"

"Yes"

"3 am?"

"Yes? What's wrong?"

"I'm looking at the video, and I see nothing for that period." she drew her breath. "Nor…" she trailed. "Give me a few seconds," she continued, the clicking sound halting altogether. I continued driving ahead, making my way towards the Upper West side for the late lunch Iris and I had planned.

"Nothing. Let me try something," she added, and I leaned my weight to my right as I reached the curve of the upcoming road.

"I checked the same for Ava" she noted, and I sensed the discomfort in her voice. Unlike me, Skye was able to get justice for her sister, that was killed during one of her jobs.

"The same issue with her video…" she drew a long breath. "I checked her timestamp, and there's also nothing for the time we were told. It could be some sort of decoy for nosy hackers like me," she commented and exhaled a frustrated breath. "Getting through further system checks will take time; I need at least 6 hours. It will give me time to check her phone records too."

"You're the best."

"That's what they all say," she laughed as we exchanged goodbyes, and she promised to update me in a few hours.

I sent Iris a quick message once I found a parking space for my motorcycle, letting her know I would be with her in a few minutes. I made my way through a series of boutiques and a large open green space covering the restaurant's back end.

"Hey, girl!" Iris rose, waving to me from the restaurant's outside seating area. "Well, look who the cat dragged in." she reached forward, wrapping me in a tight hug. "I've already ordered for us; I'm waaaaay past hungry, I'm close to hangry, I've barely eaten anything all day." she smiled as we sat down.

"Hi, Ms. Brown," I put on my teacher's voice, taking in her all-black attire.

"Piss off," she playfully glared while tapping my hands on the table. "Don't remind me," she rolled her eyes, reaching for her mojito cocktail.

The waiter arrived at that moment, placing a plate of salmon on the table on top of mixed vegetables and quinoa.

"You know me so well," I squealed, realizing I had barely had time to eat or think of anything since I had come to Jersey Hill. Iris ordered her steak and usual bed of mashed potatoes.

My gaze turned to scan the perimeter, taking in the local surrounding quickly. I had to ensure I covered my scent and went on a tailspin route to confuse anyone following me from Esneoh. Instinct still had me on edge, watching my back and anticipating the worst.

"Can I have the house red?" I turned my attention to the waiter before she left.

"When does your promotion officially start?" Iris took a sip of her drink. I raised my fork, ready to bite into my meal. "Bitch, you better not. I'm waiting for our drinks so I can post on social media."

"Seriously? Iris?"

"I've amassed 650k, and the fans need to know I have food with my BFF. Don't worry; I'm still maintaining anonymity. They only see the food and location, nothing else." I laughed, thinking back on when Iris started the account, more from boredom than interest a few years back.

"Alright heffa, hands off the table. The waiter is here," she motioned to the woman headed toward us.

As she placed the drink on the table, Iris rearranged everything, taking several pics from the top view, then turned to stand where the waiter had to get a better view of the green backdrop. I leaned back, waiting for her to finish her antics.

In every friendship, you had Iris, the food photographer, Skye, the group photographer, and me, the one who cared about nothing and just wanted to eat.

"Iris!"

"Okay, okay, I'm done. Let's eat." She sat down and placed her phone in her bag. We sat in companionable silence for the first few minutes, enjoying the food.

"You didn't answer my question," she pressed, cutting into a piece of stake.

"After this job is done, I might discuss it with Darya later today."

Her face grew somber after a few seconds. "I worry about you," she confessed, tightening her grip on her knife.

"Worry about me?" I rolled my eyes, knowing which direction this was going.

"Since...you know who, you've retracted into your bubble." She shook the top part of her body.

You know who James was, a gaslighting, egotistical asshole I had entertained for over two years. I stayed because everyone knew toxic dick was the best kind of a dick.

"These jobs we do can sometimes eat at pieces of you. It's good to sometimes go home to a warm body..." she stated cautiously.

"I don't have any time or place in my life to entertain men right now," I confessed, running my hands through my naked ring finger. Quillian was a handful, and after last night's attack by Ryder, I needed far away from the mess of emotions that came with that.

"It doesn't have to be a man, Raki. I want you to get back to painting-"

"I paint," I answered, cutting her off with a mouth full of food.

Iris's placed her fork down, raised her, and pouted. "Portraits Raki."

"I did some recently," I placed my cutlery down, excited to share the small piece of victory.

"Oh?" she beamed, and I raised my hand to dismiss her before she made a scene.

"I'm getting back to it. Alessia would want that," I confessed, and Iris' face lit up like a lantern inside a lighthouse.

"I can't wait to see some of them in the future...when you're ready...obviously," she added, reaching for her drink.

"How long are you going to be at this teacher job?" she smiled, leaning back in her seat.

"A while," she answered briefly. I didn't press further, reading from her face alone; the role involved more than just governing the school.

"Don't turn back but..." I instinctively turned back, scanning the other seats and pathway to the restaurant. "Oh my god, Raki. I said don't turn back!" she whispered shouted.

"What is it?" I chuckled light. "Never tell someone not to turn around; they will always turn around."

"There's a guy at three o'clock who's been checking you out since you came. He came in with a helmet, so I assumed he also drives a death trap?"

"Don't call my baby a death trap," I scolded, turning my gaze to the bar inside the restaurant, where the outline of a tall blonde-haired male over six feet sat, his hand clasped over a drink, and his attention trained on me.

"The death trap's name is Ivy; she's been a ride or dies for a long time," I replied as Iris scrunched her face.

"Skye is right; we need to seriously have an intervention about your need to name inanimate objects." she shook her head. "He's *fiiiiiiinnnne*" she stressed the words. I kept my eyes focused on her, but I could almost make out how fine he was through my peripheral vision.

"Hi ma'am, the gentleman over there asked me to give you this" the waiter stood over our table with refills of the drinks we had ordered.

"Oh, a gentleman too?" Skye mouthed.

"Tell him we can't accept it," I turned to face the waiter, who seemed genuinely baffled.

"Wait, what? We are not?" Iris looked from the waiter back to me.

"Accepting means he will come over, and we must entertain him. I want it to be us today. No men, no interactions." I stated, as the waiter hesitantly walked back with the drinks.

"Don't turn down dick on my behalf."

"I'll turn down a lot on your behalf."

"I knew there was a soft, squishy part inside all this hard exterior," she teased, raising her glass for a toast.

"To friendship"

"And family," Iris chimed in.

We spent another hour catching up before we agreed to go our separate ways.

"Promise to call me when you come back?" Iris asked as she headed to her car, a few feet from my motorcycle.

I waited to ensure she had driven away before turning to face the man who had followed me from the restaurant.

"Yes?" I turned around, my voice coming across harsher than I intended.

"Matheo," he stretched out his tanned hands, the veins bulging from his all-denim attire. "I'm not going to get a name?" he sauntered before me, one hand resting against the bike's body. This guy had balls that I could give him. I sat atop the bike, turned it neutral, then fired the engine.

"Meraki," I answered, unsure why I was entertaining this conversation.

You have a thing for possessive alpha males.

"Meraki," he rolled the name in his tongue, a smile creeping on the corner of his lips. "It's beautiful, like you."

"Is that your usual pick-up line? I'm sure you can do better" I smiled, unable to contain the laughter bubbling inside me.

"See, it worked," he pouted as my eyes fell on his lips. He sure was fine.

"I wanted to see that smile," he pointed to my face, his eyes devouring my body.

"Soo sexy," he mumbled

"What?"

"The bike," he ran his hands through Ivy, stepping back to admire her.

"Oh, you have jokes."

"My friends won't agree," he answered, stepping to my right. "H2R?"

"You know your bikes," my eyes fell on the helmet in his hand. He pointed at the Leggera motorcycle that had caught my attention when I had first parked here.

"How can a guy get you to agree to a date?"

"A date?" I asked, playing oblivious, as I placed my helmet on.

"Yes, the awkward social thing where two strangers meet at a public location and interview each other to check compatibility?" he offered, his smile not wavering. I lifted the darkened lens of my helmet.

"Simple," I answered.

"Yes?"

"Chase me," I laughed, placing the lens back down, pressed down on the lever, and drove off. After a few minutes, I caught sight of his bike in my mirror. I smiled, excitement bubbling inside me.

32

THE CHASE

Quillian

Meraki Irinhera was her name. And no, the intel she had requested was not of a close friend but her sister. And she worked for a secret assassin guild that had been operating a few years before my imprisonment. In Jersey Hill, right under our fucking noses. And even with all this intel, I still wanted her.

What the fuck did that say about me as a person?

My siblings were right, I was enamored, bordering on obsessed, and if life had taught me anything, it was that I always get what I want. And right now, I wanted her.

Meeting at the club that evening may have been coincidentally, but what happened now was fate, and nothing was going to stop me from owning the little hellion.

"Lucas has been trying to hack into their systems, but from the little he could get, there was a hit on you and your siblings."

"Fuck!" I muttered as my grip on the steering wheel swerved to the right, almost colliding with another car on the left.

"How much?"

"On you alone, half a million to collect data around you and another half for assassination?" Enzo methodologically relayed the information, his voice devoid of emotion.

"And you think that's the intel Ryder obtained before she killed him?" without a doubt, we found it on his server, near an abandoned building a few miles from where he was killed."

"Someone placed a hit on us, and the most important thing was to find out who and why," I replied, my hands clutching against the steering wheel.

"I feel this may have something to do with your imprisonment. The records in the Alokari began a few days after Hera and I had gotten to you. Long before anyone knew or rumors of you had gotten to Esneoh."

"Fuck!"

"Fuck indeed," Enzo replied, the evident frustration in his voice. "You need to be careful, Q. We still don't know everything about her," he warned.

"Hmm," I replied, not wanting to get into the semantics. No amount of persuasion could sway me away from her, as I had already made up my mind regarding the matter.

She had stated that she would become a target if I focused too much attention on her. As a result, I maintained her at a steady distance, trying to keep her face. So, we had created a ruse, allowing Loki and his wife to play into it.

The threats we had been warned about had been somewhat neutralized thanks to their public declaration, but after seeing her expression as I walked in with Amma, I realized I had completely screwed things up. But when Ryder had made such a public move against her, we were finally able to weed out the threat and traitor within Kinavari.

"It was too big of a job for it to be done alone," I offered, pressing down on the steering wheel to ensure I didn't lose sight of the little hellion on the motorcycle ahead of me.

"Records show that Ryder met with each leader before your

imprisonment. He is undoubtedly the main player," Enzo noted, followed by a flurry of movements in the background.

"What did you find?"

"Money, and unlimited access to poor unsuspecting humans. The trails go back decades," he breathed.

"What are you saying?"

"I'm saying he was heavily involved in human trafficking operations," he said, and the line between us grew silent. I was involved in some despicable behavior, but the trafficking of any beings was far worse and against the principles upon which Esneoh was built.

Hating humans was one qualm, but this was unjustifiable. "This has been happening under Loki's nose?" I gritted the words through clenched teeth.

"Either he is as stupid as he looks, or he was unaware, and either case is bad."

"I need men on this..."

"We are stretched, Quillian-"

"On what?"

"The trail on Meraki, the trials, pursuing any leads on Vera's life before Esneoh... There are only a few people we can trust within our circle..." he trailed, the weight of the responsibility clear in his voice.

"Stop trailing Vera's case," I breathed, unable to believe it was falling from my mouth. "For now," I added, not sure whether I was able to let go of it completely.

"Okay." Enzo hesitantly replied, but I could hear what only sounded like relief in his voice.

"I said for now," I pressed, needing him to know we would come back to it later but right now, Meraki was my priority and everything else that surrounded her.

"Of course," he answered, and I could feel his smile through the phone.

"What about the others that worked with him?" I blew my horn at the pedestrian who had crossed the road when the pedestrian lights were still red. Now I remembered why my patience for humans was so low.

"They covered their trails well. His interactions were never with our kind though, always with the other regions."

"That at least narrows down the scope of who the culprits could be."

"Just you and me at the moment."

"Let's keep it that way. We will update Silas and Brielle later," I noted, not particularly pleased at even keeping this secret from them for a single day. But the circumstance warranted it, and I just hoped they would still embrace her in our fold when the truth came out.

"Interesting," I mumbled, watching her enter a fortunate telling store. I scanned the surrounding area and noted this was entirely out of her usual schedule and routine. But humans were strange and fickle creatures, and I had given up on trying to understand them long ago except for her.

I parked at a steady distance from the premise, ensuring I didn't draw any unwarranted attention to myself. It went without saying that Meraki was smart, intuitive, and always on guard. She had the instinct of a predator, and I knew if I didn't thread carefully, she would sniff me from a mile away.

After a while, she exited the building, seemingly screaming a slew of instructions to a female voice on the other end.

Today she dressed in a two-piece red suit, accentuated with a red lace undergarment, that made my dick immediately stand to attention.

She mounted the motorcycle, and I followed her through Jersey Hill, my eyes locked on that rounded ass the whole time.

She stopped thirty minutes later, parked her bike at an underground parking facility, and sashayed to an outdoor restaurant overlooking a large lake.

She met with who I could only assume was a close friend. A freckled face covered by her short hair.

I took a series of images and forwarded it to Lucas, asking for intel on her.

"Who is she?" I asked when he called a few minutes later.

"Iris Brown, a member of staff at a local orphanage. The same one they were both noted to have grown up in since their childhood," he answered.

"Keep an eye on the orphanage and find out what you can," I instructed as I ended the call.

I hid behind a series of trees, watched, and listened to their interaction and how at ease they were with one another, and I was more than convinced that they were close—family closeness.

I moved closer as the waiter placed a drink on their table. "From the gentleman over there." They pointed at an average-looking man inside the bar. Meraki turned back and smiled, and I clenched my finger, stopping myself from strolling inside and cutting his head clean off."

Was this what she liked? Human men with basic manners?

Yeah, he needed to die.

I held back, watching from a distance as she departed from Iris.

The man from the bar followed her steadily to the parking area where she had left her motorcycle. He boldly introduced himself, running his hands through its body, and it took everything within me not to step forward and bring an end to the whole fucking flirting and charade between them.

"I'm Matheo," he introduced himself, and I concluded his death needed to be imminent.

His intents were explicit because he could barely take his eyes off her chest. I expected her to shrug off his advances, but she didn't. Instead, she did the one thing that all men loved more than life itself - she lured him into a chase.

I sped through traffic lights and maneuvered through hidden pathways, chasing after them as they both embarked on a wild goose chase across the city.

She finally stopped at a deserted field, and Matheo followed suit. She removed her helmet, and the hair flowed through the wind as I caught a glimpse of her scent.

"Down, boy," I murmured to my dick, that refused to take a nap. They walked, talking, as they moved deeper into the space. The ring I had given her was no longer in her hand, and my body was coiled with rage.

They stopped after some distance and sat on a bench, the space between them non-existent.

"So, tell me, Meraki, what did you want to be when you were younger?" His hands brushed against her thighs.

"Promise not to laugh?" She flirted, the move subtle, alluring, and downright fascinating.

"I promise." The asshole replied with a smug grin.

'A florist," she giggled. She fucking giggled. "I was obsessed with plants... I still am."

Each minute, each second, his hands grew more comfortable, and she shared more of herself, and I was entranced, berating myself that this stranger got more from her in twenty minutes than I have in the time I had grown to know her.

I snarled aloud as her hands moved through his chest without restraint. He lowered his head; she leaned into him, allowing him to kiss her.

Time to end this game.

She climbed onto him, ran her hands through his hair, and tipped her head up to stare at me. A smug grin spread through her features, and she moaned aloud as his mouth moved to her chest.

I stepped out of the shadows of the trees behind them, ready to put an end to his life, but I stopped midtrack when she lifted her head and stared directly at me with a smug grin on her face.

She knew. She fucking knew.

She arched her head back, and he suck on her breast. My dick strained in my pants, and her gaze followed it. She snickered, challenging, questioning, and goading me.

"Are you sure you want to do it here?" Matheo mumbled against her chest.

What a fucking moron.

"Here, this spot is always empty at six," she replied, never once removing her eyes from me.

Why the fuck was I so turned on by this when a few minutes ago I was willing to rip his head off and choke her until she remembered who she belonged to?

Her eyes fell, and she slowly unbuckled his pants as he fumbled with her blazer. She pushed the lace fabric aside, exposing her other breast, for my viewing pleasure.

Fuck.

"Take your dick out," she instructed, and I knew it wasn't aimed at him but me specifically.

She moved from his lap and lowered herself to him on the floor. I switched angles, moving to a tree to their left to get a better view. If she was going to go ahead with this, she needed to finish it to the end, and then I'll kill him.

His dick sprang out, and I watched as she licked her lips teasingly. My dick was bigger.

He leaned back, running his hands through her wild lustrous hair, and she moaned. She moved her hair from her face, ensuring I got a full glimpse of the show.

I was never letting her go now.

I chastised myself as I released my dick, my hands running up and down at the sight of it. Matheo moaned as she swallowed his dick whole, slurping and licking it like she hadn't eaten all day.

This woman was going to be the death of me.

He gripped the back of her head and pumped into her mouth with ferocity as he roared aloud from his release. She turned to face me as she swallowed his cum. Every single fucking drop.

"That was..."

"Your wildest fantasy, she quipped, my hands still strained on my pulsing dick. I was fucking screwed.

"I need my release, too," she stated, making no effort to face him. Instead, she lowered her pants, showcasing her red lace thong.

"Fuck! you're so hot," he mumbled. The only thing he had said all day that I agreed with.

With the blink of an eye, she was atop of him, her back pressed against him, as she rode him. In fucking public, without once batting her eye at the possibility of being caught.

Her eyes locked on mine, that seductive smile forming across her lips. Trying to find release with my hands was useless; my dick had become bloodied and bruised.

She moved her waist in a slow rhythmic motion and moaned loudly, as his hands cupped her chest.

"Fuck! so big," she spoke, her eyes never leaving mine. I had seen his dick; it was average at best. But a human man's ego was in direct proportion to their size. So, I couldn't fault her for the lie.

I should be mad, pissed, enraged even, but everything about this moment was hot. She was a raging inferno, an all-encompassing and consuming fire that couldn't be tamed. Her siren called an irresistible tune, and I was heading first to my destruction without heed to the warning signs.

Her moves quickened, and she bit her lip as she moved and played with her erect nipples, each pull, and stroke made me moan aloud and pump myself even harder. I moved closer.

"Fuck," I mumbled as I came, and she followed behind. She rose from his lap, reached for her blazer, released her gun, and pointed it at me as I walked toward them.

"What the fuck..." Matheo scrambled to his feet and feebly struggled to zip his pants. Meraki fired a warning shot before I blurred in front of her.

"I don't know what the fuck you two have going on, but I want no part of it," he jumped over the chair, tilting it back, and another gun fell from her blazer pocket.

He ran off in the opposite direction they came, and I shook my head.

An average-sized dick and a coward. It must be hard being a man in this day and era.

With her gun still pointed at me and her gaze fixed on my chest, I quickly reached for the gun on the floor and shot him in his groin and the back of his head.

He fell, and before I could turn back to face her, the sound of another gun went off. I stared down my abdomen, feeling that she had shot me.

She fucking shot me.

A total of four shots pierced through my body by the time I was able to turn and face her.

"You shot me, Little Hellion," I stated, attempting to move forward, and finding that I could not do so.

"That should keep you paralyzed for a while" she disregarded my previous statement as she reached for her blazer.

"Little Hellion-"

"What, Quillian? Another threat? Take your threats to Amma," she laughed bitterly, and I could scent the disdain behind those words alone.

"That was a spectacular performance."

"Go fuck yourself!" she spat; our eyes were falling to my still erect dick. She swallowed and tilted her head back to face me.

"You belong to me."

"No, you belong to the streets. Keep following me, and you might not have a dick left," she stated as she loaded her gun again and fired three more shots inches from my cock. The bastard still refused to go down.

"Take care of that husband," she pointed at my groin as she walked away. "And did you have to kill him?" She sighed, her steps echoing from a distance. "Make sure you clean this shit up before anyone else notices." Her footsteps continued ahead until they hit the pavement, and the engine of her motorcycle roared to life.

"Meraki!" I called, replaying what just happened. Slowly, the bullets began to fall from my body, and movement returned. Laughter bubbled inside of me; I picked up the bullet and scented silver, wolfsbane, and yesire, a poisonous plant found in the gardens of our estate.

Laughter bubbled inside me as I rose to my feet.

There was no way I was ever going to let her go now. She matched my crazy, and she would be mine wholly, whether she liked it or not.

33

THE BIG REVEAL

M*eraki*

It was no secret that Quillian was trailing me and bumping into him a few hours ago wasn't a coincidence. I had spotted him when Iris had taken her initial photo for social media, and as I stared at it, I couldn't help but notice a shadow I had become all too familiar with.

So, I intentionally turned down Matheo's drinks, hoping he would follow me when Iris and I left the restaurant, and he did. Men, no matter the species, were all predictable.

So, I lured him into the spiderwebs and left him a gentle reminder that he could fuck me senseless and make me lose my mind in the sheets. Out here in the real world, he had no sway over me. Somehow that got lost along the way with the sex and his erect dick, and now I wasn't sure if I was out to hurt him or myself.

I placed a black trench coat over myself, dousing it with the familiar scent of my perfume, and closed the curtain of my apartment. I was a hundred percent sure the possessive asshole was stalking me from the adjourning building, and since I couldn't prove it, I came up with another trap.

The doorbell rang, and I moved to open the door.

"Here for Ms. Irinhera?" A college student with similar height, hair, and build stood awkwardly at my door. I pulled open the door and motioned for her to step in.

"Here is 300. I need you to be a distraction for my ex," I lied, opening the gold crystal-encrusted purse in my hand.

"Wow, ummm, okay. I didn't believe this gig was real," she shuffled awkwardly.

"It's very real, and you gain free clothes with it too," I smiled. "Change into this." I handed her an identical outfit to the one I had worn and directed her to the bathroom to change.

"Are you sure?"

"Very sure, sell it with the bag, and you'll make a couple of grand from it," I spoke, motioning her to enter the bathroom.

When she returned, I motioned for her to spin around, admiring the brown silk off-shoulder dress with its streamlined silhouette. I handed her a hat and instructed her to open the blinds and pretend she was checking on the plants by the balcony area. She then closed the balcony door and the blinds.

I ordered a taxi for her ensuring it was headed for the suburbs, far enough to keep Quillian on a wild goose chase without arousing his suspicion. She left a few minutes later, sending me intermittent messages through her journey.

I moved the moving boxes that covered the room and shot Iris a message about picking the boxes up once I had left on Monday morning. When I return, another property will be waiting for me in the suburbs.

I walked to the room, then back out, my attention falling on the wedding ring on my bedside table. I reached for it, running my hands through its outline. I reached for my travel bag of weapons under the bed and took out the tracking detector. Placing the ring on my palm, I moved the sensor over it, and it beeped.

I headed to the kitchen, fetched a small knife, and lifted the diamond from its base.

"I'm impressed, vampire," I muttered when my eyes fell on a small locator device pressed against the interiors of the diamond.

I reassembled the ring, placing it back on my finger, not wanting to draw any suspicions from Darya. I placed the tracker inside my drawer space, opting to leave it there after I returned to Esneoh

My comms device rang, alerting me that Darya had arrived. Putting on my heels, I reached for my bag and headed downstairs, anticipating what came next.

Darya's blacked-out limousine sat amid the entryway of my apartment complex, drawing more attention than was needed.

The driver stepped out of the limousine, opened the door, and motioned for me to step in.

"Red," Darya smiled, the familiar scent of her flowery perfume, thick as musk. I slid into the seat beside her, and her hands rested on my thighs, drawing my attention. "I'm sure you have questions?" she asked, eyeing me with unspoken ease in her demeanor.

She wore a long-sleeved asymmetrical gown that accentuated her frail body.

"I'm sure you have even more," I commented, and her eyes sparkled.

"I know whatever you have gathered will be of great benefit," she smiled, her eyes falling on the ring.

"Where are we going?" I leaned back in my seat as the car drove off.

"We are meeting the client. They've insisted on a face-to-face conversation with the type of money they are investing in."

"Oh?" This was news to me.

"I know, it's outside our remit, but this job is pretty big and outside your commission. The check is big, and we want to keep our partnership with them," She answered curtly, slowly removing her hand from my thighs. "The dress is perfect for the event," she noted as she reached for a hidden compartment between us.

"Here," she handed me a Champagne glass. "Have a glass, it's going to be a long and intense night, and we both might need it," she added, popping the champagne's corks and filling our glasses.

"It is also a masked event for the newer recruits to give them time to get acquainted. It's a perfect distraction for the meeting, without drawing any unwarranted attention," she commented as I took a sip of my drink and preceded to update her about the trials.

"How did the first tournament go?" she asked, leaning back in her seat.

"I almost died, but you know me. I'm a cat with many lives." I shrugged.

"Be on your guard and remember your purpose there. Now, what about the oath? Have you found a way to sever it?"

"No," I lied, not wanting to divulge information about Tiara's connection. Doing that would cause her collateral damage later. "I'm working different channels to see what I can do. I'll find a way; no matter, always find a way. I'm not worried," I replied confidently, my eyes landing on the passing landscape outside.

"Midtown," she stated as if reading my mind.

We spent the rest of the journey in silence as Darya navigated through coded phone calls and messages.

After twenty minutes had passed, the car came to a halt, and the driver, appeared by the door again.

"Welcome to the Strand Hotels," he spoke, his hand outstretched. Darya and I exited the car one after the other.

"The Alokari knows how to do it big," I muttered, passing through the long passageway of the building. We headed to the elevator, pressed the 10th floor, where two of Darya's guards waited, and handed us two silver face-concealing masks.

Darya immediately placed hers on, and I followed, not needing any explanations. The sound of house music filtered the walls as the guards led us through the celebration hall and then the private rooms a few doors down.

We stopped at one of the smaller doors, and the doors opened. The guards walked ahead first, and I trailed behind Darya.

"Darya, we were beginning to think you weren't going to show," a raspy female voice spoke. The voice was between two men, whose attention immediately turned on me.

"You must be Red," the male closest to the door said, his face cloaked, and voice masked.

"Your reputation exceeds you," the other on the far end of the female commented.

"We didn't think this job was possible, but you proved us all wrong here," the woman stretched out her hand and motioned to the other two. There was something regal, yet familiar about her raspy voice, and twitchy movements.

"I'm sure there were no issues getting here," Darya said, stepping forward and taking the seat at the head of the room. She motioned me to stand at the center of the table, and all eyes turned on me. The two security guards exited the room.

"Now, why don't you start with telling us everything you know about the vampire overlord?" the woman led the discussion, letting me know she was in charge.

I reached into my bag and pulled out my comms device, detailing the trials, my suspicion about what led to Alaric's death, and Quillian's disdain for humans, without going into detail about the specifics of our relationship.

"Does he have a lover?" The man closest with bleach blonde hair asked. "He's infamous-"

"Yes, he had a long-standing tumultuous relationship with the leader of the eastern region of Kinavari," I shared, knowing where the conversation was headed.

"The house, did you find anything out of the ordinary?" The woman questioned, her eyes observed me as if she could see through the walls I had around me.

"No," I lied again, recalling the key I had found in Quillian's room, the one I had suspected Alaric had left behind.

"What about his siblings?" she pressed, and my brows furrowed.

"I was assigned on the job for Quillian Kingsley. If I'm not mistaken, information for his siblings is another job and requires a different payment?" I searched the room looking from them to Darya.

"She's right. Unless it is explicitly tied to their brother, then that's a different case," Darya offered, lighting her cigar. "What else, tell me more about Quillian," the woman motioned for me to continue.

"He is an impenetrable safe," I stated, ensuring my voice remained stable and my movements never wavered. "He is shrouded in secrets and distrusts everyone except his family. They are his weakness," I confessed, my chest constrained, and guilt prickled my skin.

"Did you sleep with him?" the brown-haired man asked, his head corked to the side.

"Excuse me?" My skin heated, and my stomach coiled with irritation.

"You are trained to attain information at any means. Did you try sleeping with him to ensure you found as much as possible?" He continued.

"If the world were simple, divorce rates and cheating scandals would be nonexistent. Don't you agree?" I placed my hand on the table, to signal I was done with the direction the conversation was going.

"Is there something, in particular, you wanted to know or needed from me?" I asked, sensing that this interrogation had a purpose, otherwise, the answers to these questions could have been sent through our system. It did not require a face-to-face conversation.

"No, it seems we have all we need from you," the woman rose from her seat, and the men followed her. I watched as they left the room, unable to shake the unease about that interaction. Something was up, and I couldn't place my hands on it.

"Wait here; I'll speak with them and see what the hell is going on" Darya rose to her feet and headed for the door.

I sat on the chair where my hand rested, and before she exited the door, Darya turned to me and smiled brightly. "You've done well, Red," she said, and the door closed behind her.

My hands instinctively reached for the gun in my purse as I lightly napped my feet on the floor. I opened my purse reaching for my other phone to see if there had been any updates. The device was under the table, and I lowered myself to reach for it.

The door opened, and before I could rise. Unfamiliar voices made me still my movements.

"She was supposed to be here. Where did she go?" a masculine voice said.

"How the fuck am I supposed to know? The job was to take her out," another voice chimed in, and the unease in my chest disseminated as my hold on the device tightened.

This was an ambush, and Darya knew?

"Check every fucking corner of this room," the first voice instructed. I strapped my bag around myself, pointed my gun, and waited for them to draw nearer.

"Not any of the..." I released two shots as the first body moved beside me. I jumped to my feet and fired another two shots at the other guard headed toward me. He fell to the floor, and the alarm system in the hotel rang out. The building shook, and the smell of smoke filtered through.

I jumped forward and picked up the weapons of the two men. Gunshots awaited as I opened the door to the room, and I released my own sets. I rolled onto the floor, spotting three bodies angled a few feet from me.

I moved forward, releasing a series of shots in each direction as bodies fell around me. More movement caught my attention, and instead of rising to my feet, I crawled on the floor, following the fire exit sign to the far right.

I removed my heels when I reached the door to the exit.

Running down a flight of stairs while being pursued by Alokari agents with heels on isn't a smart move.

I ripped my dress into a slit to allow more breathing space, and kicked the door open, as I released another series of shots ahead of me.

I rose to my feet, finding three pairs of bodies aligning the stairway, confirming my suspicion that this had been planned and instructions had gone out weeks before.

I slowly tiptoed down the stairs with a gun in my hands. Using the stairs' railing, I rested my back against it and propelled my body downward, shooting each target before reaching the first floor.

Chaos awaited me on the main floor as smoke and debris covered every corner making it impossible to see what awaited me outside if I went through the main exit. I opted for the back of the building, anticipating further attacks. Debris fell over me, and I covered my nose, ensuring not to inhale the smoke that was growing in intensity.

Light permeated the room's far end, and I lunged forward, raising my gun with one hand in case of unexpected attacks. I swung the door open, finding over a dozen dead bodies sprawled outside. "Get in," Quillian's voice called amid the chaos, the door to a range rover opened.

"Get in, Red," he commanded as my eyes filtered through the space for another means of escape. No one could be trusted, not even him.

I made no effort to argue about the name, if he had come this far, he already knew everything. Yet he was here...

"How did you find me?" I asked, my gun aimed at him, and my chest heaving with emotions I thought I had buried deep down.

"Get in the car; we don't have time." Quillian shouted, the vein on his forehead prominent.

"You expect me to trust you and get in there after this?" I

arched the gun and motioned to the building behind us.

"Yes, because even with all I know, you're still alive!" He blurred before me. "The Alokari has a hit on you."

"That makes no sense," I pressed the gun in his chest, my attention straightening to the sound of incoming footsteps. "Who and why?"

"Alessia Irinhera, your sister," he stated, and I shook my head and took several steps back. "You're lying." I released a warning shot, motioning for him to stay back. He blurred before me, maneuvered the gun from my hand, and pulled me into his car, while I kicked and fussed.

The exit door of the hotel opened, and gunshots followed, aimed at the car. Aimed at me.

Quillian veered forward, through streets and alleyways, as my body began to shake from the shock of it all.

I was ambushed.

"What is going on!" I asked, my voice louder than I anticipated. My phone chimed, and I raised my hand motioning for him to wait.

With shaky hands I reached into my bag and opened the device from Esneoh. A video immediately popped up on the open screen, showcasing the CCTV image of The Den.

There sat amongst a group of people was Alessia. Her hands moved through her hair, and the ring glimmered in her hand. I stilled the image and zoomed in.

It was her; it was the ring.

My sister wasn't dead.

ALSO BY MAYA MORRISON

SHE WOLF SERIES

She Wolf

Marked wolf

Wolf Queen

THE FALLEN SERIES

Queen of the Heavens

The Fallen Queen (tbc)

THE DARK CROWN TRIALS

Blood and Potions

Stakes and Poison

Flames and Chaos

Wolf Moon

Wolf Moon

ABOUT MAYA MORRISON

Maya Morrison is a self-diagnosed bibliophile and logophile. She was raised in London but currently resides in Seoul, South Korea. Because of a lacuna in her previous life, she spends her days writing - hoping to one day account for the missing parts.

When she is not painting, reading, or obsessing over food, she spends most of her time with her husband, Coffee.

ALSO BY S.L. KINGSGATE

THE DARK CROWN TRIALS

Blood and Potions

Stakes and Poison

Flames and Chaos

THE UMBRA GUILD: THE HIGH PRIESTESS

Witch, Please!

Burn Me!

Stick It!

THE DEMON DATING AGENCY

Dating the Gargoyle (tbc)

ABOUT S.L. KINGSGATE

S.L. Kingsgate is a new author with a passion for change. She seeks to create diverse kick-ass heroines within the PNR/UF sphere.

Printed in Great Britain
by Amazon

25325667R00276